PRAISE FOR FALLEN

Fallen: In Melissa Scott's haunted and spectacular neo-mediaeval far future, one entitled young scholar, who thinks she knows exactly what she's doing, could prove far, far more dangerous than the hard-bitten tomb-raiders of the previous episode. Fun for space-opera fans of *Finders* and for new readers both!

—Gwyneth Jones, author of the Aleutian trilogy, winner of the World Fantasy, Clarke, Dick, Otherwise (Tiptree) awards

Melissa Scott is an absorbing and inventive writer whom you should read right away.

—Pamela Sargent, author of the Seed trilogy
and editor of *Women of Wonder*

Melissa Scott's *Fallen* melds contemporary space opera sensibilities and settings with a rich story and a setting and history with a touch of the mythopoetic. Grounded and focused on a captain whose past comes knocking to collide with her relationship with forbidden technology, *Fallen* returns us to the universe of *Finders* with a queer, immersive and page-turning character-focused timeless story.

—Paul Weimer, SFF book reviewer and Hugo award finalist

Melissa Scott is known for rich worldbuilding, and *Fallen* does not disappoint, featuring stunning settings including a magnificent Dyson-sphere-type station which is failing, providing a backdrop for an exciting adventure. The characters are layered and intriguing. My personal favorite is Fish, a Facienda—descended from humans modified // in a previous civilization which fell. Now, we are in the era of the fallen, a Renaissance of sorts when the descendants of the mighty builders are attempting to once again venture forth and regain lost knowledge. Only the ancients fell for a reason, and their nemesis is still waiting. It's an intriguing and fascinating book perfect for fans of classic space opera.

—Jo Graham, author of the acclaimed *Numinous World* historical fantasies and *Calpurnian Wars* space operase

PRAISE FOR FINDERS

Space travel and faster-than-light drives blend with world mythology...//...a fun story with convincing worldbuilding and a delightful triad romance at its heart.

—*Publishers Weekly*

Space Opera with a fine, wide sweep of time behind it, intriguing "Clarkean" magical science, and an engaging, edgy threesome of central characters. Fun to read, and best of all, the promise of more to come.

—Gwyneth Jones, author of the Aleutian trilogy, winner of the World Fantasy, Clarke, Dick, Otherwise (Tiptree) awards

An action-packed space adventure with so much heart. // This thought-provoking, crunchy science fiction novel comes with deep conversations, technological wonders...

—Tansy Rayner Roberts, author of the Creature Court trilogy, winner of multiple Ditmar and WSFA awards

Scott's science fiction has always been remarkable for its world-building and *Finders* is no exception. Once you read this thrilling new science fiction saga with its unforgettable characters, you'll be wanting more.

—Catherine Lundoff, award-winning SFF author

Also by Melissa Scott (selected works):

Dreamships

Trouble and Her Friends

Dreaming Metal

Shadow Man

Night Sky Mine

The Order of the Air
(series, Jo Graham co-author)

Death by Silver
(first in series, Amy Griswold co-author)

Finders

Water Horse

The Master of Samar

Fallen

Melissa Scott

Candlemark & Gleam

For information, address
Candlemark & Gleam LLC,
38 Rice Street #2, Cambridge, MA 02140
eloi@candlemarkandgleam.com

Library of Congress Cataloging-in-Publication Data
In Progress

ISBN: 978-1-952456-20-6 (paperback), 978-1-952456-21-3 (ebook)

Cover art by Eleni Tsami
Book design and composition by Athena Andreadis

Editor: Athena Andreadis
Proofreader: Kelly Jennings

www.candlemarkandgleam.com

Stories in this Universe, in Chronological Order

[Titles in brackets are not yet out in our universe]

Title	Era	Original Appearance (if not a novel)
"Firstborn, Lastborn"	Ancestors	*To Shape the Dark*
[*Firstborn, Lastborn*	Ancestors]	
"Sirens"	Ancestors	*Retellings of the Inland Seas*
	First Dark	
Fallen	Successors	
	Second Dark	
"Finders"	Salvors	*The Other Half of the Sky*
Finders	Salvors	
[Keepers	Salvors]	

Chapter One

We hit our mark and the capacitors fired, dropping us from hyperspace into a hail of confusion. *Beljaeger's* alarms screamed—proximity, radiation, collision, hot weapons in multiple directions—and I slapped frantically at switches, cutting out everything but the most crucial readings. "Shields hot, Hal!"

Beside me in the engineer's seat, Haliday Kim worked her own controls, diverting power from propulsion to shield generators. "Full defensive protocol."

"Good. Keep it on." My screens were full of shifting dots and triangles, coalescing into a pattern as the computers began to make sense of the sensor readings. More than a dozen small warships were tangled in a dogfight, swirling around an invisible point. An exit point? The roiling energies made it impossible to tell. "What in hell? There weren't any problems on Adora the last time we were here."

"Invaders?" Haliday sounded doubtful, and rightly so: it was almost impossible to invade across interstellar space, and Adora was a single world with a unified government, unlikely to invade itself. "Unless—AI?"

"We were clear coming in." I nudged the steering, dropping us below the plane of the main battle. "No sign of AI anywhere in range. And those all look like human ships. Make us invisible, Hal."

"Working on it."

I heard the click of keys as she tuned the system, damping out every speck of energy emission that might betray our presence, and turned my attention to the sensors. We'd made a relatively early exit; the fight was between us and Adora. We could probably sneak in around the edges and make a landing vector, but then the question was whether Adora would let us in. What had happened in the last eight months to make this possible?

And that was irrelevant at the moment. We needed to get out of range before someone spotted us by accident. They might be actual military ships and not interested in stealing our cargo, but that didn't mean they wouldn't cripple us just to get us out of the way.

"We need to jump," Haliday said.

"Do we have the power?" We'd expended the capacitors breaking out of the adjacent possible; it would take time to recharge enough to open another window.

"We will—"

"How long?"

"Working on it," she said again.

Accumulated hyperspatial drift converted to velocity when we exited the adjacent possible: I had planned a looping course using that momentum to match Adora's orbit, and we were still on that line. We could swing around and run for the system's edge, where the fabric of space was thinnest, but it would require a course change and that would certainly draw attention. I was surprised no one had seen our exit, though maybe the flare had been taken for weapons fire. I could hope, anyway. But whatever we did, we couldn't risk drawing attention until we'd developed enough power to make a jump.

"Eighteen minutes," Haliday said, and made the words a curse.

My screen showed that we were skirting the lower right edge of the fighting, not close enough for cannon, but certainly within missile range. I bit my lip, watching the shapes twisting around each other. They were lighter than I had thought at first, more like standard system patrol craft than bigger warships. I didn't know what that meant about who they were and why they were fighting, but it probably meant they all carried solid long-range sensor suites. Move too fast, and they'd spot us for sure.

I touched keys, checking course and distances. We were forty minutes out from the picket stations around Adora at our top speed, and twice that if we held our current velocity. The fight was drifting away from us, but it was between us and the usual exit from the system. We could tear open a point in thicker space, but that would take more power.

"Twenty-five minutes if we have to jump in raw space," Haliday said, guessing my thoughts.

"Better to keep on to Adora," I said.

"Depends on what they're fighting about," Haliday answered. "Nic, we can't afford to get trapped here."

"I know." On the other hand, we couldn't afford not to deliver this cargo, either. We'd been counting on it and the fast-passage bonus to keep us funded and even absorb some of the ship's debt. "We need to try to make it."

"We need to get the hell out of here," Haliday said.

I made myself grin, knowing she would be looking. "Where's your sense of adventure?"

"Not onboard," she answered, but didn't argue. "All right. I make it eighty minutes before we're inside the picket line."

"Agreed."

"That's at current velocity." She touched keys. "Top speed, factoring in evasive maneuvers—we might make it in thirty."

"Hold that in reserve," I said. "Let's be sneaky."

"Let's hope they're looking the other way." She paused. "We're going to need to correct the course."

"I see it." We were drifting too far to our right, away from the distant dot that was the nearest picket satellite. We needed to be inside their zone of fire, because surely these ships wouldn't risk following us there.... The sooner I made the adjustment, the less power it would take, but the longer I waited, the further out I would be, and the less likely to draw their attention. Except—no, do it now, and hope our release of energy was lost among the bigger flares from the weapons. "Get me the numbers."

"Now?"

"Now."

"Working." There was a little silence, Holiday's fingers busy on her keys and the lights moving like slow plasma in my screens, white flashes popping in and out of video as missiles launched and were countered, while shimmering red frills around each dot marked the impact of plasma cannon on shields. "Right. 140 at 3.9."

That was more power than I would have added, but Haliday knew what she was doing. "Go ahead."

"Firing now."

Beljaeger shivered under me, propulsion fields shifting, energy pulsing as the ship swung and steadied again against the warp and weft of space. The numbers dropped off as Haliday moved us back into stealth mode, and I scanned the sensor screens, holding my breath. For a long moment, there was no reaction, the warships all focused on each other, and then a white light bloomed. I thought it was aimed at one of the wheeling ships, but an alarm flashed on the console, warning it was on a heading that would cross our path. More alarms flickered as the missile's sensors tried to find and lock on our electronic signature, then died as Haliday's electronic countermeasures took hold. I worked the passive sensors, plotting the track. "It'll pass ahead of us."

"Unless it has a proximity fuse."

"Your ECM should keep it from triggering." I hoped. "Anyway, odds are they won't be using proximity fuses in a fight like this. Too much chance of hitting a friend."

Haliday ignored that: I was guessing and we both knew it. "Brake? Just to give a little more room?"

That would be safer, but if I were on the ship that fired at us, I'd be watching to see what happened. Our ECM package should make us look like harmless debris; if we changed course, we'd destroy that illusion. "There's room enough," I said, and hoped it was true.

"Falathos will be seriously pissed if we damage his cargo," Haliday said.

"If I'm wrong, we won't have to worry about it." I regretted the words as soon as they were spoken, and Haliday snorted.

"That's what I love about you, Nic, you're always an optimist."

The missile sped toward us, the dot growing on my screen. A secondary screen lit and windowed, offering visual confirmation, but I couldn't make out any identifying marks on the unpainted casing. That didn't necessarily mean anything. Most of the planetary navies got their armament from the same cartels that supplied the raiders and pirates. The plot still showed it crossing at a safe distance—well, safe if there wasn't a proximity fuse, but Haliday's countermeasures would take care of that. Surely.

The screen flashed red as it came into proximity range. I tensed, seeing the flash of movement in the visual display as it passed ahead of us, and released held breath as it slid out of range again. "We're good."

"So far," Haliday said.

I adjusted the passive scanners, angling the receivers to cover as much of the battle as possible. The ships were still tangled, hopefully so focused on each other that we could slide into the protection of Adora's pickets without drawing any more attention. Some of them were showing damage, the sensors picking up volatiles and vented gases, and then there was a bigger flash, bright enough to show even on visual, and a dot vanished from the screen. Another veered out of the plane of the fight, too damaged to stay, and abruptly half the dots were running, fleeing for thinner space where they could make the jump to the adjacent possible. Most of the other ships turned in pursuit, but several swung back toward Adora, putting themselves between the attackers and the planet. I flinched as our sensors pinged, and a moment later the nearest ship accelerated toward us.

"Unknown ship. Stop and identify yourself, or we will fire."

At least it was the standard Adoreen patrol frequency. I hit the comm button. "Fast-freight *Beljaeger*, Sevens Registry, Nic en Doroney in command. We were inbound to Adora with cargo for Falathos Industries, and jumped into your trouble."

"Adoreen patrol ship *Rasper*. We're matching velocities." So much for my attempts at pleasantries. "Prepare to be boarded."

"We're a neutral merchantman," I began, and the patrol ship cut me off.

"We will board and search now, or we have authority to destroy your ship."

There was no arguing with that. "Welcome aboard," I said, and signaled for Haliday to cut the ECM fields.

Rasper's pilot brought her alongside in a neat display of ship-handling, and extended a boarding tube to cover our hatch. I left Haliday in the control room and went to meet them there, the ship's documents in hand. I could hear thuds in the lock, as though they had crowded too many people into the space, but the seals were green, and I threw the switch that released the inner door. Bodies in full armor boiled out, one slamming me against the bulkhead, the rest spreading out to cover the corridor. They all carried blast weapons, and I raised my hands, the datacard still clasped in one hand. An armored figure plucked it away, and another motioned to the others. "Spread out! Scan the ship!" They looked back at me. "Crew?"

"Myself and one other. She's in the control room. We're not armed."

"See to it," the leader said.

The one who had taken the ship's papers looked up from a handheld reader. "This checks out."

The leader nodded. "Keep scanning."

My mouth was dry, and I swallowed carefully. "Can I ask what's going on?"

"There was an incident," the leader said. "AI incursion. We dealt with that, but then this attack followed."

"We had a clean trip," I said. "Not even a hint of weather." That was the word everyone used to avoid mentioning quantum AI too directly. Probably it was only a superstition, the AI had been trapped in the adjacent possible for centuries, but no one wanted to take chances.

The leader nodded, not really listening. One of the others put a hand to their ear. "Preliminary scan is clear, lieutenant."

The leader relaxed a fraction, and removed their helmet. Her helmet, I corrected, as an identification panel lit at the top of her breastplate. Her use-name was Jonne. Not that I would risk using it unless invited, but every scrap of information was useful right now. "Keep scanning," she ordered, and looked back at me. "We need to be absolutely sure you're not infected."

"Understood." And I did. However you passed through hyperspace, you risked drawing the attention of the quantum AI, the rebels who had controlled the adjacent possible ever since they brought down our Ancestors and threw us into the Long Dark. Anketil—the last and greatest of the Dedalor— had trapped them there, outside of space and time, but even she had not been able to save us from the fall. The AI were still trying to find a way back in: existing as they did outside of time, their grievances were still fresh, unchanging and ever-present, and they would bring humanity down again if they could. "Can you tell me—this incident?"

She hesitated, but then I saw the moment when she decided it might make us more cooperative. "A ship came in contaminated. It was intercepted and destroyed. The AI was…not subtle. And this attack on top of it—we're not taking risks."

"Understood," I said again.

"Lieutenant!" That was one of the troopers, poking his head out of a side corridor. "I'm picking up something, very faint, possibly unpowered—"

Weapons clicked against armor as the closest troopers snapped into firing position, and I swallowed a curse. "I own a piece of Ancestral glass—a spoiled toy. It's in a shielded container—"

"Show me," Jonne said.

I pushed myself away from the bulkhead, careful not to move too fast, and led them down the main corridor past the commons to the crew cabins that lay between it and the control room. Haliday was standing in the control room hatch, a trooper beside her, but there was nothing to say. Another trooper was standing at my door, and I laid my hand on the lock.

"Go ahead," Jonne said, and I let the lock taste the nanite burden that moved in my bloodstream. The hatch rolled back, the lights coming on in the narrow space, and I pointed to the shielded lockbox fastened to the deck at the head of my bunk.

"That's it."

"Open it." Jonne's tone was flat, and the troopers didn't relax from their taut readiness.

I stepped inside, went to one knee to work the lock. I took as much time as I dared, at the same time directing my burden to share only its least complex features. The toy would barely respond to that, nothing that would frighten Jonne and her crew. "Shall I take it out?"

"Set it on the table," Jonne said.

I did as I was told, cupping the irregular shape in both hands. Even in the cabin's flat lighting, the inner facets sparked and shifted, threads of gold and peacock green and electric blue shimmering in and out of view. It was about the size of a human head, the outermost layer clear and smooth as crystal, and someone whistled softly.

"That's an expensive piece," Jonne said.

"It's spoiled," I said. That was a lie, but more plausible than the idea that a minor ship's captain should own an even partially functional piece of Ancestral technology. "They— the people who found it—didn't know what it was originally supposed to do, but all it does now is make a tone." I ran my hand over the surface, and the glass sang, a clear sweet note with a minor undertone that made it somehow sad. One of the troopers glanced quickly at their scanner.

"I'm not picking up anything."

"I wouldn't carry it into the possible if it was live," I said.

"I did a job for a team of archeologists on Elim, at the Great Works. They offered me this in part payment."

"Is it registered?" Jonne asked.

"Yes. It's in the packet." I waited while she consulted her reader, watching for the moment her shoulders relaxed a fraction. "May I put it away? It's fragile."

"Go ahead."

I set the toy back in its case, hiding my own relief, and straightened again. "Can we proceed?"

"You'll need to provide a blood test," Jonne answered.

"I beg your pardon?" That was definitely something new.

"We require a current blood sample for landing."

I kept my expression blank, glad I'd already shifted my burden. The sample would show nothing unusual. Would an ordinary captain protest? Yes, on balance I thought they would, and I could use the extra moment to make sure everything incriminating was tucked out of reach. "All the details are on our identification—"

"We were attacked by AI," Jonne said. "We've been ordered to take no chances."

I hadn't expected to win the argument, but I had my burden well under control. I offered my hand, and Jonne pressed a sampler against my forefinger. I felt the familiar prick, and she withdrew it, frowning at the tiny screen. "You're clear."

"Thank you."

"Is your engineer a daedalist?"

I shook my head. "You saw our licenses. She can't access Ancestral tech without special gear."

I could see her relax just a little. "She'll need to be tested, too."

"Of course."

Haliday complied without protest, but it took the better part of an hour for Jonne's party to clear the ship. They would escort us to orbit, she said, in a tone that brooked no argument, and the patrol ship paced us all the way to the picket line. We were cleared through the satellite defenses, given landing coordinates, and a Customs team was waiting

when the elevator brought us down into the dock. By then I
was dead tired, but after arriving in the middle of a battle, I
figured there was no way around a thorough inspection. The
Customs team went through the same processes that Jonne
had done: papers, scanners, blood tests, though they didn't
pick up the toy in my cabin. They did insist on inspecting
the cargo compartment, when meant breaking the seals, but
finally they signed off on that and Haliday and I were left
standing in the airlock.

"Well," Haliday said. "That wasn't fun."

"If there really was an AI, you can't blame them," I
began, then shook my head. Haliday could and would argue
both sides of the question without needing evidence. "They'll
know something at the guildhall. I'll ask when I file our logs."

Haliday nodded. "In the meantime, I'll raise Falathos and
tell him his cargo's here. I'll see what he knows, too."

"Good idea." I suppressed a yawn. Even with chemical
assists, the battle and the long flight in had left me stumbling.
"I'm going to start the post-flight and then grab a nap. I'll
order something from the cater-bots if you think you'll be
back in time."

"If you're buying."

"Ship's treat," I said, and took myself off to the control
room.

I started the post-flight diagnostics, and then practically
fell into my bunk. I roused myself long enough be sure the
toy's box was closed and sealed, and let myself collapse on
my pillows. I didn't need to share its dreams.

冊 炙 屮

We were, for once, mostly in synch with the planetary clock.
I woke to my alarm, washed and found clean clothes, then
checked the diagnostics. They were still running, still showing
nothing but green, and I found an outside link and placed
our dinner order. The hold was empty, the receipts neatly
docketed, although the noise of unloading hadn't reached me.

The ship's account showed a pending payment, and I started a pot of tea.

Haliday arrived with the delivery bot and doled out the boxes, while I found cups and platters. I had ordered hot wine, a local delicacy, and a platter of savories to go along with the main dishes, enough for leftovers; and for a while we ate in silence, enjoying the taste of local food instead of the prepack we carried for the galley box.

"Falathos said he'd flagged the payment." Haliday licked the sweet sharp sauce off her fingers, and reached for more wine.

"It's pending. That's just the base payment, did he agree to the bonus?"

"He said he'd add it once he'd inspected the goods." Haliday shrugged. "You know what he's like."

I did, which was why I was asking. "I hope you reminded him of the contract."

"Of course."

I nodded. "Did you hear anything more about this incursion?"

"We're one of the first ships in after the fighting started," Haliday said. "And the local authority wasn't giving out information yet. Falathos did pass on what he'd heard about the AI, but it wasn't much. A few days back a ship dropped into the system at an unusual exit point, and didn't respond to calls. They sent up patrol craft to warn it off, and scans showed it was dead—no life support, no sign of people on board." She suppressed a yawn: she had managed some sleep on the flight in, but we were both still close to the edge of exhaustion. "They blew it to atoms, Falathos says, and then slagged the patrol ship that came in range to be sure nothing got into its systems to be taken back to Adora. There's been a heavy patrol presence on the exit lines since, which is why there were enough ships available to meet today's attack. It might just be a coincidence, but everyone's seriously on edge. So this is not the time to be messing around in anybody else's networks."

"I never," I said, automatically, and she rolled her eyes.

"I'm serious."

I spread my hands. "All right. We'll keep things legal. Are they sure it was an AI?"

"What else could it be?"

I shrugged. "Dead ship doesn't invariably mean AI. There could have been a life support failure, or pirates stripped it and launched the hulk on autopilot—that's been known to happen. Or disease. But not necessarily AI."

"If local authority thinks it was AI, we'll need to tread very lightly," Haliday said, and I nodded, knowing she was right.

"We'll grab a cargo and get out."

She made a face. "That may not be so easy, Nic. Everybody's worried about losing a cargo, and once word gets out about possible AI, other systems are going to impose restrictions."

She was right about that, too, and it was more bad news. We had some reserve funds, but we couldn't afford too much time between contracts. Docking rent, port fees, living expenses: they all added up ruinously fast. "So no return cargo."

"Not from Falathos. He offered to introduce us to a colleague of his who he said was willing to pay premium for a fast trip, but—" She shrugged. "That didn't seem like such a good idea right now."

It would all depend on whether this colleague needed our peculiar skills, or if they could be satisfied with an ordinary high-speed run. But, no, Haliday was right, it would be better to find an ordinary job, and get off Adora as soon as we could manage it. "I'll see what's listed at the guildhall," I said, and hoped there would be something reasonable.

冊 爻 屮

I made my way to the Guildhall early the next morning, before the frost had burned off, and the streets and buildings were furred with soft rime as I emerged from the port tunnels and made the above-ground transfer to the mercantile district. Overhead the sky was hazed with cloud, the sun invisible, and I was glad to duck back down into the warm light of the tunnels. They were lined with shops and smaller tunnels that led into other complexes, but I'd been on Adora often enough to know the easiest route. The Guildhall itself was unprepossessing, a plain smoothed-stone frontage with narrow windows running horizontally along the two upper floors, but there was an armored guard in the door niche and as I proffered my ID button, I felt a security field wash over me, pinging my burden. I had been ready for that, felt the flash of warmth that was my burden's accepted response, and stepped up into the hall.

Before the Fall, they say there were a dozen different guilds serving the space-faring population, some generalists, some specialists; but since we rose again to interstellar travel, the old buildings and their resources had been remade into a single entity. Here on Adora, the hall had belonged to a Facienda guild, and the building had been intended as living space as well as a resource. Since the Faciendi had been physiologically altered by the Firstborn to live and work on marginal planets, few true Faciendi had survived the Fall, and most of the building's variable environments had been converted for secure cargo storage. There were still rooms for rent, and most of the ground floor was an open lobby with comfortable seating gathered around a dozen food stalls offering a variety of cuisines. Any guild member in good standing could claim two basic meals per day, and I guessed some of the people gathered at the larger of the open kiosks were taking advantage. It had been a long time since I'd been that poor, and I hoped never to be so again.

Broad stairs led to the next floor, and the log-keeper's office. I dropped off my journey tape—carefully pruned of anything improper—and went on to the hiring hall to see if any cargos were up for bid. The overhead board was only half full, proof that Haliday had been right about shippers holding back, and the cargos that were listed were luxury produce that traveled in bulk, nothing we could handle. They were only up for bid because they'd spoil otherwise, and they weren't getting much interest. I wondered if it might be worth looking at the smallest of the lots, but decided to hold that in reserve. We'd have to make some expensive refits to the cargo area, and we'd never do more than break even.

I stopped at the chartroom next, both to update my guidance and to see who might be here to gossip with, and to my pleased surprise nearly ran into Jaezu Sulla as he was leaving an update console.

"Nic!" His grin was wide enough to be plausible, even if I suspected a certain caution behind it. "I didn't know you were on-world."

"We just got in last night," I answered. "Jumped practically into the middle of the fighting."

He glanced over his shoulder, but none of the local staff was in earshot. "I'll buy you a coffee if you'll tell me all about it."

"First-hand news is worth more than that."

"Ah, but I'm a poor man with many mouths to feed."

He had a husband and two daughters on Menau Prime and a ship-husband to keep him company when he was away from them, as well as his crew, so that was entirely his own doing. "I'll tell you what I know, but it's not much."

"Join me for coffee," he said again. "And let's talk."

I nodded and turned my attention to the update console. I'd been on Adora eight months ago, and in closely-linked systems even more recently; it didn't take long to exchange the data I'd collected for the updates from other captains, and I pocketed the disk and went back downstairs to find Sulla.

He had claimed a pod at the edge of the coffee-maker's territory, and ordered the elaborate Pavonid service, with its delicate pots and flash-steamers and half a dozen condiments in shallow gilt-glass dishes along with a plate of the traditional dry fruit-studded sweet crackers. This was lavish even by Sulla's usual expansive standards, and I made sure my burden was pulled tight, giving nothing away. At his invitation, I took my place on the low couch opposite his and prepared my cup, then settled back and tucked my feet up among the pillows. "So," I said, and he shrugged one shoulder.

"So. What happened to you?"

"We hit our exit and came out practically on top of a dogfight." I wrapped my fingers around the band of insulation, avoiding hot ceramic. The coffee tasted of cotta-creme and cinnamon and oranges, with bitter depths beneath, and I concentrated on it instead of the flash of remembered fear. "We were able to go invisible before anyone spotted us, and slide out of range. After the attackers jumped out, we were picked up by a patrol ship and boarded."

Sulla pursed his lips in a soundless whistle. "Who were they, could you tell? The Adoreen authorities are being very close-mouthed about the whole thing."

"No idea. There was nothing identifiable on the sensors, and we weren't looking to draw any attention. They had what looked like standard missiles and ion cannons." For a second the image of the missile that had passed in front of me was vivid in my memory, bare metal and no identifying marks. "The patrol ship that picked us up wasn't answering questions either. Haliday heard it had something to do with the AI incursion."

"If it was AI. That's not entirely clear," Sulla said. "But I think the Adoreen believe it, or they wouldn't have slagged the patrol ship that came into hailing range."

"Patrol ships are built to be disposable," I said.

"Yes, but they're still not cheap."

"If it wasn't AI, then what?"

Sulla lowered his voice. "A stalking horse to set up the attack. At worst, it gets the Adoreen looking in the wrong place, and at best Adora has to destroy one or more of its patrol ships. It's worth sending a dead ship through a jump for that."

I let my eyes wander casually, making sure no one was in earshot. "Who's got it in for Adora?"

"That's the question," Sulla said. "The current governor got tangled up in a financial scandal, and there's a big election coming up. The Newfounder candidate is leading, and this latest AI scare is only improving her position."

"You're thinking those ships were Newfounders."

Sulla raised his hands in pious horror. "Perish the thought! Of course they wouldn't attempt to influence a planetary election by violence! These were pirates, clearly."

"Of course they were." A chill crept over me in spite of the heat of the coffee. The Newfounders had been gaining power for some years now. They'd started by arguing that humanity needed to rely less on salvaged and scavenged Ancestral technology—which wasn't unreasonable—and had moved from there to demanding it be restricted or even banned. That might just barely be possible in the thickly clustered stars around Adora, and toward the old Core worlds. Newfounder technicians had developed an FTL system that didn't depend on Ancestral tech, and that theoretically might even be invisible to the AI, but it was ponderously slow compared to the Successor drive that everyone else used. Out on the Verge, where the systems were further apart and we'd only just begun to reclaim the more marginal worlds, we'd be dancing on the edge of another Fall.

"One thing's for sure," Sulla said, "no one's putting cargos out for bid right now."

"I'd noticed that." My tone was more sour than I'd intended, and I took a swallow of the coffee, hoping it would sweeten my tongue. "We were counting on a quick turnaround."

"Officially there aren't any restrictions," Sulla said. "At least not yet. It's just that everyone's nervous."

"What do you mean, not yet?"

"There is a whisper—the slightest hint of a suggestion of a rumor, nothing more—that the new government will search all the ships in port for unacceptable Ancestral devices."

"They can't do that," I began, and shook my head at Sulla's smile. "Not legally, and someone is bound to have connections enough to take this to the High Court." But by the time they received a favorable verdict, if they did, the Adoreen would have destroyed the stolen devices, and neither the verdict nor the money would replace what was lost. That was a risk I wasn't prepared to take. I wished I hadn't included my toy on the ship's manifest.

Sulla nodded as though he understood my concerns—and possibly he did: I'd suspected for a while that he might also run a non-standard ship. "As I said, it's a whisper, nothing more, and it depends on Cattelin winning her election."

"When do they vote?"

"Two days from now."

Too soon for my liking. And elections were notoriously times of trouble, an excuse for riots and looting by both sides, with the port areas and their expensive imported goods as a tempting target. "We'll have to find a cargo." Or leave empty, but that would eat up every credit of our reserve funds.

"I'm planning to take whatever offers." Sulla topped up his cup, not meeting my eyes. "I'd advise you to do the same."

"We'll probably have to," I said, and turned my attention to my own drink.

Chapter Two

made my way back to *Beljaeger* by a different route, one that took me closer to the edges of the mercantile district where off-worlders and Adoreen were more likely to mingle. There was a news-cafe there, too, but when I emerged from the tunnel into the wider plaza, its screens were dark except for an apologetic note stating they were having technical difficulties. I stopped at the exterior window to order a cold tea, hoping to find out what was going on, but the server shrugged his shoulders and denied any knowledge.

I leaned against one of the support pillars to sip my tea, and scanned the plaza warily. It was typical of the Edge Worlds, an open space lined with shops that brokered off-world goods to local retailers, interspersed with a handful of restaurants and tea shops and a bakery. About half the brokers displayed the glyph that meant they were wholesale only, and seemed very quiet; the ones that didn't were a little busier, but it didn't look as though the people who were leaving were buying very much. Only the bakery seemed to be doing a decent business, and its doorway was swagged with strips of red-and-blue striped bunting. Those were Newfounder colors, and when I looked more closely, I could see that maybe half the pedestrians were wearing red-and-blue badges pinned to collars and sleeves. That was definitely not a good sign. We might be better off spending down our reserves, and getting off-world as quickly as possible.

A woman came up to the news-cafe's order window as I stood there, placed her order, and came away shaking her head. She paused by my pillar, fiddling with her drink, and gave me a sideways glance. "I don't suppose you've heard when they might reopen?"

I shook my head, trying to keep my accent as flatly neutral as I could. I was wearing a plain tunic and trousers, Sevener-made, but close enough to local styles to pass. "They didn't say."

"Damn Successors." She picked out a fruit rind and threw it into the nearest disposal bin with unnecessary force. Her cuffs were banded in the Newfounder colors. "They can't win fairly, so they'll resort to this."

"Yeah?" I tried to sound only idly curious, but she gave me a sharper look.

"I spoke out of turn. Never mind." She turned away before I could ask anything more.

I was increasingly aware of Newfounder colors and badges as I made my way back to *Beljaeger*. Even once I'd entered the port proper, it seemed as though at least half the locals were displaying them, and local security was terse and unfriendly. I stopped at a Guild-sponsored chandlery to check secondary fuel prices, leaning on the counter while the clerk pulled up figures on his handheld. "What's with all the blue and red?"

"Oh, I wouldn't know." The clerk looked around quickly. "Well. The banners are for Cem Cattelin, she's the Newfounder candidate for governor."

"She seems popular."

"Very." He hesitated again. "She's probably going to win."

"What's that going to do to trade?" I kept my voice level with an effort.

He shrugged. "She says she's not opposed to off-world business, she just doesn't want us depending on it, or on unproven Ancestral technologies. I'm not sure she's wrong about that, either."

"If she bans the standard drive system, she's going to lose a lot of traffic."

"Oh, she won't do that." He handed me the printout, a flexible card with the grades and costs of the various fuels laid out in a neat table. "This will be good for thirty hours. Discounts for drafts on the major banks."

"Thanks." I tucked the card into my sleeve. "I thought that was part of her platform, going to the Newfounder drive."

"Eventually," the clerk said. "When it's good enough. And that's still years away."

You hope it is. I made a noncommittal noise, and let myself out again.

The Guild paid for extra security at the entrance to the docking bays, and I was glad to see that they were on alert. Walking through the bays, I was less pleased to see how many ships had a crew member or two watching unobtrusively. They weren't armed—that would have been against Adoreen law— but most of them had some heavy tool ready to hand.

Haliday was sitting at the top of *Beljaeger*'s ramp, eating noodles out of a disposable cup, and I squinted up at her. "What's going on?"

"Didn't you hear? There was going to be a march on the port." She paused, and I realized that she had the ship's scatter-gun stowed just behind the bulkhead. "I was worried about you."

No wonder the news-cafe had been shut down. I said, "There weren't any warnings. How'd you hear?"

"Kendra from *Antiae* passed the word. They're planning to blast empty if they don't get a cargo today." She paused. "We might want to think about that."

"Let's check the news," I said, "and then let's see what Falathos's friend wants from us."

There was no mention on a march on the news, though there was no telling whether that was because the rumor was false or because local security had nipped it in the bud. Falathos professed himself happy to introduce us to his colleague, which was how we found ourselves at the edge of the port district in the mid-evening, looking for the entrance to a club called Bin-A'h. Its whole facade was so discreet as to be nearly invisible, but at last we found it, and were allowed into the vestibule. There a very pretty host checked our identification and accepted a token fee for temporary membership, and summoned an equally pretty hostess to escort us to our party. We passed through two well-appointed gaming rooms, one for machine games and one for human to human competition. They were both busy, even this early, but eerily quiet except for the cheeping of the machines as they offered their odds.

The third room seemed to be for entertainment, with a pocket stage at one end and a spot-lit space in front of it. At the moment no one was performing, but there were instrument cases stacked to the sides. There were dozens of tables scattered across the room, most of them unoccupied, and deep alcoves set into the walls to either side. Unsurprisingly, our escort brought us to one of the alcoves, bobbing a sort of curtsey as she brushed back the velvet curtain. "Your guests, sen."

"Thank you," Falathos said, and flipped a credit plaque into the air. Our escort caught it neatly, curtsied again, and disappeared. "Captain, sen. Join us, please."

We took our places opposite Falathos and his friend, and I found myself wishing that Adora was one of the planets that permitted spacefarers to go armed in the port areas. Falathos's companion was older than he, a heavyset, grandmotherly woman with apple cheeks and hair done up in a coronet of silver braids. Her welcoming smile was sweet, but did not reach her eyes.

"Let me present Sen Marcadia," Falathos said. "And these are Captain Nic en Doroney and Technician Haliday Kim, of *Beljaeger*."

"A pleasure to meet you." Marcadia's tone was warm, but I didn't quite trust it. "I've heard a lot about *Beljaeger*— all good, I assure you. I have a cargo that needs expedited delivery, and I hoped we might come to an agreement."

"We're certainly looking for a cargo," I said, and Falathos lifted a hand.

"First, our meal. I've taken the liberty of ordering, senir, and I hope you'll find it suitable."

"I'm sure it will be," Marcadia said, and I made equally accommodating noises. Lights flickered on the screen embedded at the host's seat, and we waited while a service bot trundled over with a pitcher of drinks. Falathos served us all, and lifted his glass.

"Your health."

"Health and long life," I answered, and took a sip of the punch. It was sweet and powerful and I guessed the food would be salty in an attempt to encourage us to drink unwisely. "While we're waiting—has anyone heard anything more about this attack?"

"The governor released a statement suggesting it was related to the AI incursion," Falathos said, "but that's all I know."

"I don't get involved with local politics," Marcadia said. Her tone was a warning, but I met her gaze squarely.

"I'd think this was relevant to anyone trying to send goods off-world."

"Not at all," she said. "At least not now. After the election—" She shrugged. "But who knows? Better to get things done beforehand. Ah, here comes our meal."

A larger server bot appeared, rolling back its cover to reveal the first plates. Falathos served us with unexpected grace, and I chose a few tidbits from the platters of little bites. Most of them were made with fungi—mushrooms were cheap on Adora—and, as expected, most were sharp and salty. I took one of the tiny cups of creamy broth, and found that it was topped with a streak of scarlet pepper oil. I drained it anyway and took another sip of the punch to counteract the tingling. "I'm curious about this cargo, Sen Marcadia."

"It's nothing special," she answered. "Mixed goods, mostly luxuries, about three, maybe three and a half mass units. The thing is, if I can get them to Tambur before the first of the month, I will not only earn a sizable bonus, but I will cement the relationship with my client. Unfortunately, recent events have made this unlikely. Unless I can hire a specialist."

I felt Haliday tense and then relax. Even with the usual time compression effects, Adora to Tambur was a long run.

The tightest course I could think of had a ten-to-one ratio, and ran about fifteen subjective hours: that put us at least fifteen hours past Marcadia's delivery time. And that was taking chances with the AI, passing through waypoints that generally attracted AI attention. On the other hand, the AI couldn't be everywhere, and with our advantage.... "I'd have to run some calculations," I said, "but it's theoretically possible I could meet your deadline. I'd need better mass number."

"I'd prefer to have a contract first," Marcadia said.

"I can't sign one blind," I countered. "It wouldn't be fair to you."

"And I don't hire without a contract," Marcadia said.

"I'm happy to put together a bid using rough numbers," I said, "but it's harder to promise on-time delivery under those circumstances."

"I'm sorry, I wasn't clear." Marcadia smiled sweetly. "I'm interested in having you work for me. Long term, and of course exclusive. I'm prepared to pay accordingly."

"We only contract by the trip," I said. "It's a matter of policy."

"And I don't trust my cargos to freelancers," Marcadia said. "That's my policy."

"That's really too bad." I pushed my drink aside. "I think we could have done the job for you. I don't know who else in port could handle it."

"Given the current instability," Falathos said, "you might want to reconsider that policy, Nic."

And there was the threat, out in the open at last, for all that he'd tried to make it sound like concern. "We're certainly concerned about local politics, and I'm sure the Guild is, too." I nudged Haliday, and she slid obligingly out of her chair. "I thank you for the offer, sen—and you, too, Falathos, for making the connection—but I don't think this will work out."

Marcadia dipped her head gracefully. "Of course. Should you change your mind, I'd still be happy to talk."

"Thank you, sen," I said again, and turned toward the door.

⊓ ⊼ ♄

It was cold in the plaza, the heaters turned down and the lights dimmed for evening. Frost was gathering on the darkened shop windows. There were still people around, more than when we'd arrived, and I considered splurging on a ride back to the ship. Walking wouldn't save us enough money to make a difference, and I was tired.

"That didn't go the way I'd expected," Haliday said. She tucked her hands into her sleeves, folding her arms across her chest. "I don't want to leave without a cargo."

"Better than signing on with her," I answered.

"Do you know something I don't, or is it general principles?"

I sighed. "No, I don't know anything about her, but I intend to find out. And I don't want this job."

"I don't either," Haliday said, "but we need to leave before these elections."

Tell me something I don't know. I swallowed the words, and said, as calmly as I could, "We can make one trip empty. We'll just need to pick a good destination."

"That's always the trick—" Haliday stopped abruptly, untangled her hands to fish her handheld out of her pocket. "Hey, maybe we won't have to. Seraphin says he might have something for us."

"A job?" Seraphin was one of the best of the Guild mechanics, and a remarkably useful source of gossip.

"A lead on one, anyway," Haliday answered. "He's at the Bear's Den, says he'll meet us there or at Captola's."

"Tell him Captola's," I said, my hopes rising. We didn't have to have a good cargo, just enough to pay most of our expenses, and Seraphin knew everything.

Captola's was half a level down a spiral ramp, in a part of the city that had once been expensive. The tunnel was wider, with elaborately carved arches, and an artificial stream had once flowed down its center, spanned by little half-moon bridges and elegant stepping stones. Now the larger buildings had been broken up into shops and bars and upper level apartments reached by exterior stairways, and the cool light of the false moons that hung from the arches was drowned by the multi-colored display boards above the commercial doorways. That made Captola's easy to find, though, and we paid our entrance fee and passed through the round door into the noisy main room.

It was much more crowded than Bin-A'h, the noise of conversation almost enough to drown the music playing on a screen at the far side of the room. I stopped, blinking as I scanned the crowd, and Haliday swore under her breath. I glanced at her. "What?"

Her mouth tightened, but before she could say anything, a voice spoke from my other side. "Hello, Nic. Hal."

I knew the voice, of course, even after a decade. Rejane Novilis was not someone you forgot easily. "We're just leaving."

Haliday caught my shoulder. "Nic."

"No."

"Just hear me out," Rejane said. "Please."

Seraphin hadn't messaged us, it had been Rejane all along. I wondered if Haliday had known. "Why should I?"

"Because I need your help and you need a cargo," Rejane said. For a moment, her calm cracked. "Would I contact you if I wasn't desperate?"

"We should talk to her," Haliday said. There was a lot behind that simple statement—Rejane was a Novilis and an Academician, daughter of the NoviCor Cartel that held a near-monopoly on the nanite burdens that let us interact with Ancestral technology, scientist and scholar with the power of the Academy behind her—and unfortunately Haliday wasn't wrong. If my choice was going to be between Sen Marcadia and Rejane, I would hold my nose and choose Rejane. Not that I could trust her, but at least with her I had a fighting chance to spot the lies.

"I'm willing to listen," I said, and saw relief flicker across Rejane's face.

"I have a pod," she said, and turned away.

I followed, not happily, and Haliday stayed a step behind me as though to keep me from bolting. Certainly I was tempted: I had first met Rejane when we were both twelve, and she had never been good luck for me. I could almost taste the cool air of the hospital, where my mother and her husband had traded my blood, a share of my burden, to supply the only thing Rejane Novilis lacked. She had been born with a Facienda burden, useless if her family wanted to send her to the Academy, and not correctable by any technique known to them. But the Novilis were nothing if not resourceful, and if they could not duplicate a Firstborn burden, they could certainly transfer and transplant one. And for all that I'd been born to a common line-worker deep in the shadows of Callambhal Above, I carried a Firstborn burden. The nanites in my bloodstream were complex and healthy and attuned to Ancestral technology, and completely useless to a line-worker's child.

The Novilis knew where to look—the orbital city of Callambhal Above was built by the Ancestors, and their close descendants still survived there and on Callambhal Below—and they knew what to offer, and my mother signed away her rights and left me in their service. I spent forty-five thousand hours on Prater Daal with Rejane, living close as sisters. I had loved her then. But she'd been dispatched to the Academy and my indenture was sold to a freelance captain.

To be fair, she had come back for me, once she was finished at the Academy. By then, I had outlived my indenture and held *Beljaeger* in my own name. She threw work our way when she could, for which I was duly grateful; but she was a Novilis, and a rising Academician. She always had her own agenda, which she did not share, and I had secrets of my own that I did not intend to reveal. We quarreled, bitterly and often, and finally agreed it was better to leave each other be. I had heard about her, of course—Academicians from elite families are always news—but I had spent the last few years carrying cargo around the Edge, and had been able to pretend I'd forgotten her.

And now here she was, waving us to a curtained alcove where food and drink already waited, looking no different than she had the last time I saw her—except that was a lie. As we took our places, I got a good look at her face, and was startled by the lines of strain. "So what is it you want?"

"I need passage off Adora for myself and a small cargo." She ran her hand over the controls displayed beneath the table's shiny surface, and I felt a privacy screen close. "And I need a fast passage to Valenguar."

I knew it, of course: another of the worlds where the Ancestors had left an enormous, enigmatic, inoperable device. But that was the Academy's problem, not mine. "How fast?"

"Ideally, by the Ides," she answered. "The eighteenth at the latest."

I didn't have to consult my charts to know that was impossible by any legal use of the Ancestral drive. There were no direct routes to Valenguar, and the shortest of the indirect routes would take nearly a month if taken with reasonable caution. "You know that can't be done."

"I know you can do it," she said. "And I know how. That's not a threat. I know you know what you're doing, and I need to get out of here."

I considered several possible questions, but what came out of my mouth was, "What have you done?"

She laughed, not entirely without humor. "That's usually my question."

"You're the one asking for help."

"Yes, well." Her smile vanished. "This AI—"

"You summoned it?" I couldn't keep the surprise out of my voice, and she rolled her eyes.

"I most certainly did not. I was brought here to defend against it. But the patrol ship destroyed it before I could figure out which one it was, and without an identification, there's nothing I can do."

"Wait," Haliday said. "If you were here to deal with the AI, then the governor must have been expecting this attack."

"Yes." Rejane drained her glass, and poured another. "Personally, I think the Newfounders are behind it, but of course I can't prove it, and they're pointing at me. The governor has defended me so far, but Cattelin is going to win the next election. I want to be off-world before then."

"What does the governor say about that?" Haliday asked.

Rejane sighed. "I haven't informed him that I plan to leave. In fact, he's made it very clear that he expects me to stay and continue to work on the problem."

"This isn't like you," I said. "Normally, you'd be fighting to stay. What's really going on?"

"Someone called that AI," she said. "I've done everything I can to shore up their defenses, but half of them don't believe me, and the other half are convinced they can handle it easily. None of them have the slightest idea what the AI are capable of."

"The Gap," Haliday said, almost involuntarily, and Rejane shook her head.

"You can't see the Gap from here."

The Gap was the spot where the rebel AI had first broken free of the adjacent possible, releasing a wave of quantum chaos that destroyed entire star systems. Anketil, the last of the Dedalor, had managed to defeat them; but even she couldn't avert the wave, and it had rolled through half a hundred systems before finally fading out. You could see it from Callambhal Above, a great starless gash in the perpetual night.

"Anyway," Rejane said, "I've done what I can, or as much as they'll let me, and I don't intend to get caught in their civil wars. I can pay full passenger rates, and for freight as well."

"How much freight, and what is it?" I asked.

"Not quite a mass unit, mixed electronic gear. About .89 mass units, I think."

"And the governor is going to let you just walk off with it?" Haliday asked.

"I've already sent it to the port," Rejane said. "A while ago. I was supposed to leave two weeks ago, but the governor extended my contract. Unilaterally, I might add."

I ought to know better. I did know better, but at the same time, this was Rejane. I said, "We'll try. When can you get to the port?"

"No time like the present," she answered, and we matched each other's smiles.

⌸ ⚟ ⚲

It was an uneventful walk back to *Beljaeger*'s dock, but once we were inside, I activated the ship's security fields as well as the bay's. We hung about in the commons for another few hours, debating whether to retrieve Rejane's cargo now, but decided it would be better to get a departure window first. I contacted Traffic Control and was told to call back in the morning as there was nothing available until after the eighteenth hour the next day. The controller cut the connection before I could offer any incentive to change his mind. I sat for a long moment in the pilot's chair, watching the port's departure feed scroll slowly down my screen. A single ship, a local chem-fuel shuttle bound for the picket satellites, was ready for launch on the eastern table; nothing else was scheduled until after sunrise. It was possible that there were invisible hazards, gravitational anomalies or a debris field too wide to dodge, but there had never been issues before.

I returned to the commons to find Haliday bent over a tablet while Rejane sipped a cup of tea, a sight so familiar and home-like that my breath caught for an instant. Rejane didn't seem to hear, but Haliday looked up from her screen. "I've scheduled fueling for the first day-shift appointment. I'd like to pick up supplies, but Arden and Pette says they're out of stock on about half of what I want."

I poured myself a cup of the tea. "Could we go somewhere else?"

"I'm not having much luck," Haliday answered. "I can

patch together an order, buy what each of them has, but that's going to take extra time to get it delivered. Not to mention it's going to cost more."

"Can we lift without?" I asked.

"We can." Haliday sounded doubtful. "But we'll be eating emergency rations by the time we hit Valenguar. Unless you got a quick window?"

"They told me to call back tomorrow," I said, knowing she would understand, and even Rejane gave a crooked smile. But then, she'd been raised among merchant princes; she understood the exigencies of interstellar shipping. "Usually that means at least twenty-five hours before we can get a window. Take what Arden can give us, and see if a special handling fee can expedite anything."

"That will cost us," Haliday said.

I smiled at Rejane. "Our passenger's fees should help with that."

"Ah." Rejane set her empty cup aside. "I could certainly transfer the money to your account, but that might draw unwanted attention. I was hoping I could pay you once we reached Valenguar."

Unfortunately, she was right about that. If she was trying to sneak off-world without the governor's permission, the last thing we needed was to pull money from her accounts. "Use the reserve accounts," I said, and Haliday sighed.

There wasn't much to say after that. I offered Rejane her choice of passenger cabin or crew space, and was not surprised when she picked the crew cabin. I entered her into the systems, giving her passenger rights only, and Haliday found bedding and a spare shirt for her to sleep in. I would have left her at the cabin's hatch, but she caught my arm.

"Thank you. This is a bad business."

I wouldn't leave you in trouble. I wasn't going to say that out loud, and settled for a nod. "Will the Academy be dealing with it?"

"That's what I need to find out," Rejane answered, and let the hatch slide shut.

The next morning, I put tentative bids on a couple of the perishable cargos I had seen at the Guildhall, then tried Traffic Control again. The controller was reluctant to commit to a window, but I pointed out that I could hardly complete a bid for perishables without knowing when I could leave, and she finally, reluctantly, offered a window nineteen hours out. I accepted it, asked to be waitlisted for earlier departures, and closed the connection. On my screens, the launch tables were empty. I returned to the commons, to find Rejane picking through the remains of a breakfast delivery box. "Haliday's gone to pick up my cargo," she said, and pushed the box toward me.

"Is she likely to have any trouble?" I chose a pastry, and realized too late that it was filled with scarlet jam: not what I would have chosen to eat in front of Rejane.

"I wouldn't think so," Rejane said. "It was supposed to ship without me, and anyway the governor won't have noticed yet that I'm gone."

"When do you think he will notice?" I asked.

"Not before this afternoon. With any luck, some time tomorrow." She sighed. "I hope I'll be able to get my luggage back eventually."

"Surely the Academy can arrange for that." The pastry split under my fingers, and I managed to catch the blob of jam before it hit the counter.

"It depends on how annoyed he is," Rejane said.

"Let's hope he's not monitoring your freight," I said, and she nodded.

To my surprise, however, Haliday returned with the pallet in tow, and I opened the cargo hatch to let her get the crates on board. There were only three, all small but well-shielded, the sort of cases the Academicians used to carry Ancestral devices: not a problem if the shielding was good enough, but it would be safer if I knew what we were carrying. If Rejane would tell me. "Any problems?"

Haliday shook her head. "No. They were marked for consignment to one of the Academy houses on Valenguar, no particular urgency. I said we were expecting another cargo for Valenguar, and this would help pad the ledgers."

"Good."

"Frankly, I don't think they were paying very much attention. There was some big rally in the government plaza, and everybody was watching the news feeds."

That was not good news, though it might keep the governor distracted instead of looking for Rejane. "Let's hope we can lift ship before all hell breaks loose," I said, and went to find Rejane.

She protested less than I had expected before opening the crates. As I'd assumed, each case contained a single Ancestral artifact that had been adapted into something more recognizable, or at least useful. Two were obviously detectors of some sort, one a multi-faceted disk that woke and sparkled at my touch, the other a hemisphere in which strange shapes moved, set into a circular bezel marked with degrees. The third was entirely different, a teardrop half a meter long from the gold-tipped double point to the curved base; the outer surface was dull charcoal gray, and the inner surface was studded with iridescent crystals fine as needles and as long as my thumb. They caught the light, reflecting it in shards across the hold's padded walls, and the ghost of a sound echoed in my bones. I looked at Rejane. "Well?"

"It's sensitive to AI," she said. "Exquisitely so, which is why the shielding is so dense. It reacted to the AI on board the dead ship."

"From halfway across the system?" That meant it had to be in resonance with the quantum universe, a conduit to the adjacent possible. "You know how dangerous that is. Can it be powered off?" I couldn't see any controls, just the planes of whatever Ancestral elements it was made of, and I wasn't surprised when she shook her head.

"It's always on—think of it as a passive sensor. It can be blocked, that's what the counter field is for, but it can't be annulled." She put it back in its case and began pulling layers of padding over it. "Given your usual method of travel, I didn't think it would be a problem."

Not as much of one as it would have been had we used the standard drive, but still dangerous. "I don't need anything that would interfere with my connections."

"It won't." Rejane closed the case and touched the button that switched on the security field. "It didn't on the trip here, and the ship I traveled on used the same system as you. It'll be fine."

"It had better be," I answered. "Now, about your travel needs—"

"Still a daedalist," she said, with a flickering smile, and I couldn't help smiling back.

"We carry a range of meds." Daedalists, with their burdens that interacted seamlessly with Ancestral technology, were always at risk of attracting AI attention in the possible, so most ships required they make the trip under sedation.

"If you're going to knock out my burden, I might as well sleep through it," Rejane said. "Depending on how long it'll be, of course."

"I haven't worked that out."

"Let me know?" She sighed. "I left my own kit in my quarters, so I'll need to use whatever you have."

"I'll give you the list," I promised, and touched keys on my handheld to transfer the information.

Interlude 1

The first Dedalor was Guerin. He wrote the equations that opened the possible, that created the first quantum AI, that allowed the Firstborn to expand into unknown space and to settle at last on the Omphalos, where Guerin made his home. And he was First among the Firstborn, and admitted no equal.

Kuffrin was Guerin's daughter, late-born, vat-born, motherless, designed to be a helpmeet since her father intended to live forever. But she proved his match and more, and where he had laid out a template, she created five AI to do her bidding, her firstborn. In a fury, Guerin accused her of wanting to destroy her own kind, and arraigned her before the rest of the Firstborn. But she showed what her AI could do, and the Firstborn turned on her father and banished him. Still furious, he took ship and vanished into the possible. Kuffrin's AI sought long and hard for him, or so they claimed, but he was never seen again.

From the Dedalor Apocrypha, *Vol. 5*

Chapter Three

We would need a course ready as soon as we had a launch window. I settled myself in the commons and brought up the navigation software, feeding in the latest data from my updated course books, and focused on my task. Adora to Valenguar normally used four waypoints, which increased the time that actually passed while we were in the possible. The waypoints were a way to break the calculations into manageable segments, since they represented relatively stable points in the adjacent possible, reflecting objects in real-space. With my device's help, I thought I could get it down to two waypoints, JOSIP and OSMIN, and three course segments, Adora to JOSIP, JOSIP to OSMIN, and then OSMIN to Valenguar. That would make the elapsed time somewhere around 300 hours, more than enough time to meet Rejane's deadline. I'd have to figure the subjective time as we went—technically, no pilot was supposed to remain on duty for more than ten hours at a stretch, though in practice we all pushed that limit as hard as we could—but we could lay over at OSMIN, or at OSMIN's real-space source, if we had to.

It was easy to construct the first section. Adora to JOSIP was the best way out of the system, and I'd been here often enough to know where to find the formulae. The course segments we use for calculating courses are really frameworks for a progress through the possible; they are set up like a child's constructor toy, with variables that serve as sockets to allow another formula to be attached to the string. The variables are color-coded to speed up the process—most pilots aren't mathematicians—and I swapped segments in and out until I had a course plot that shaded from sea-blue to the near-black purple of Kandarian wine. I ran it through the simulator, noted the flags, and made adjustments, until at last I had a string that I felt confident would get us to Valenguar safely and on time. I set up a couple of variants as well, in case there were problems with any one segment, and then a true alternate.

All of them depended on my device, thoroughly illegal as it was; the device and my ability to use it. I flexed my fingers, feeling the nanites in my bloodstream wake and shiver. I still didn't understand how I had been born with this burden, a full Firstborn burden. My mother carried it as well, or so I'd been told, but her children with her husband had all been perfectly ordinary, high Secondborn like most of the inhabitants of Callambhal, Above or Below. My unknown and unacknowledged father must had had the Firstborn burden, too—but that was pointless speculation. What my burden had given me was the ability to interact with Ancestral devices and, through them, with the AI that dominated the adjacent possible. No AI meant well toward any human, but they had their own ties and rivalries; the lesser ones, in particular, could be persuaded to ease a ship's passage in exchange for Ancestral scrap. What they used it for, I didn't know— no one did—but it brought protection on some of the more dangerous routes. I flexed my hand again, feeling the shape of the contact, the symbol that denoted the AI with which I had my bargain: Beast would not, could not, be my friend, but it had always kept its word.

It would want the transit mass, though. We had laid in a decent supply on Elim, a world so full of Ancestral ruins that they could afford to look the other way, so I wouldn't have to brave Adora's black markets. With the AI attack so recent, I didn't want to attract attention. I switched to the inventory system, and pulled up the details. There was just over a kilogram left, but it was rich with flecks of Ancestral elements as well as fragments of their weird metals. It should be enough to keep Beast happy, and I could restock on Valenguar.

I switched back to the simulator and ran the courses a final time, this time focusing on the timing, and looked up from my results to see Rejane standing in the open hatch.

"Am I interrupting?"

I shook my head. "No, I'm done. If you want some tea—"

"I'll make it," she said, and flipped on the boiler. "Do we have a course?"

"Yes. We should make it to Valenguar well ahead of your deadline."

"Thanks." She was busy with the pot and the everyday tea, as though she'd never left the ship. "How does the timing look?"

"Fourteen hours subjective," I answered. "If we can use my best course. Elapsed time is 250 hours."

She nodded, filling the pot. "That's better than I dared hope. I assume that's using your device?"

"Yes." I folded down my working screen, aware that I was both thirsty and hungry, and as if she'd read my mind, Rejane found a packet of savories and set them on the table beside the pot. I opened it, took two, and slid it back across. "If we didn't use the device, we'd need to hit another waypoint—we're going through OSMIN, which tends to have weather, but I'm relying on the device to keep us clear. Any other waypoint means we have to add another stage."

"As long as you're sure of your device," Rejane said.

"You're flown with me before."

"And it worked very smoothly," Rejane admitted, and filled both our cups. "Fourteen hours, you said?"

"Yes. I've got a full pharmacopeia, you can take your pick."

"Thanks." For a moment I thought she might protest, or ask to make the passage without drugs, but instead she said, "Fourteen hours for us, 250 hours in real-space. Eventually it adds up."

"I'm out of synch with my age-mates, yes. Not that I have much to do with any of them."

"Except me," Rejane said, with a smile. "I travel more than most people, yes, but it's your livelihood." Every trip through the possible meant I lived a few hundred hours less than people who stayed planet-bound, but the differences didn't mount up that quickly. "Have you ever done the math?"

I shook my head. It was not a particularly comfortable thought, that the people you had grown up with were older now than you were, even if you weren't close to any of them. It was the reason those of us in the profession tended to stick with each other.

"I have," Rejane said. "It varies, of course, but on average it takes forty-five trips through the possible to lose a year. If you maintained that rate—and yes, I know it's a lot, but it's not impossible—you'd never seem to age. They say the Firstborn were immortal, but I wonder if they simply spent so much time in the possible that it seemed to outsiders that they never changed."

We always thought of the Firstborn as so far beyond us, nearly god-like in their abilities—and if you looked at the things they left behind, their devices and the mysterious constructions on a dozen worlds, it was easy to believe that. When I had lived with Rejane on Prater Daal, the family compound had been in the shadow of the fallen palace known as the Prater. The Novilis had mined its wreckage and built their fortune on what they'd learned, but they were the first to admit that many mysteries remained. But if that was the result of passage through the possible, if you could use the possible to extend life indefinitely—no, the AI would never permit it. The Firstborn might once have controlled the possible as well as the real, but they had lost that when Nenien Dedalor betrayed the AI and sparked the AI War. "Maybe? But if they did, that's one more thing the AI took from us."

"There's so much we could regain," Rejane said, but I didn't want to hear.

"I need to plug in our course." I took my tea and retreated to the control room.

The wait seemed to stretch forever, but at last we were cleared for launch. *Beljaeger* rose on balanced grav-fields and steadied onto the course that would take us to the edge of the system, the invisible point where the fabric of space/time thinned enough to make the transition easy. Rejane accepted her sleeping drug and retreated to her cabin; I checked in as we approached transition, and saw her already tucked into her bunk, held by the security netting, eyes closed and her breath steady in comfortable sleep. The scanners showed very little commercial traffic, not surprising, and half a dozen Patrol ships spread out in a ragged picket line. That was also unsurprising, given the AI incursion, but inconvenient, if they found any reason to question us. Adora's sun was a pinpoint in the stern cameras, and the starfield blazed ahead of us; the nearest patrol ship was in sensor range, but a cautious ping showed its scanners pointed out-system, scanning for arrivals.

"We could keep going," Haliday said. "Get further away."

The more we behaved as expected, the less attention anyone would pay to us. "No. We'll do it now. Start charging the capacitors."

"Charging," Haliday answered, and I undid my harness and slid out of the pilot's chair.

The device was waiting in its case in my cabin. I took a breath, repeating the mantra that brought my burden to its fullest expression, then unlocked the case and lifted the device. It chimed softly, almost as though it welcomed me, the glass-like surface warm under my hands. The planes shifted in its depths, threads of blue and green and gold coiling between them, and I quickly looked away. It was too easy to slip into attunement, and I needed to be at the controls first. I carried it back to the cockpit, deliberately keeping my eyes from its glimmering center.

I had rigged a cradle for it next to my chair, padded and covered with a security net to hold it in place even during extreme maneuvers, though its presence was intended to make sure we didn't have to do anything extreme. I set it in place, and slid my hand through the mesh, feeling my burden rouse. The warmth I had felt before strengthened and coalesced, becoming a ball of heat cupped in the palm of my hand. It was just this side of painful, and I checked my readings. We were aligned with the "grain" of space, poised for the transition, and I could feel it tingling beneath my skin, fizzing in my blood, excited by the nearness of the adjacent possible. "Capacitors?"

"Ninety-eight percent," Haliday answered.

"Switching control to you." I would be busy with Beast once we jumped; Haliday would have to handle the ship.

"I have control. Autopilot on and locked." A pause. "Capacitors ready."

I checked the scanners a final time, saw nothing to alarm us. "Jump."

"Jumping now."

My screens went blank, light flaring behind my eyelids as the capacitors fired, opening a door into the adjacent possible. I put my bare hand on the device, cupping its curve in my palm. The device chimed, a sound that I felt through the bones of my hand, echoed and repeated by my burden. A part of my mind saw the readings reform, Haliday steady at the controls, but the rest of my attention ranged outward, searching for AI, and for Beast in particular. It could be anywhere and anywhen, in the chaos of the possible, but we had built a bond that should attract its attention. For what seemed like a long time, there was nothing, just the chaos of not-time and the coiling energies of the adjacent possible, and then at last I felt the prick of presence, sharp in my palm where I touched the device.

Hello, Beauty.

Hello, Beast, I answered, and felt the familiar shiver that I suspected was its amusement. We had greeted each other this way since the day I'd first found it, and I knew no other name for it.

So. What could you possibly want from Me?

Your protection. Safe, swift passage to Valenguar by this route. I couldn't share coordinates, they meant nothing here, or to the AI, but I visualized the process, and felt Beast absorb the idea.

Possible. There are other shares on that passage, but they will not trouble Me. I can see you safely there.

Thank you.

And what will you give Me in return?

I considered the transit mass still on board. *What I gave you before.*

I need more than that, this time. You ask Me to come close to others.

Another two hundred grams, I offered. *Half again what I gave before.*

I want twice what you gave, and cheap at that price! Or—your blood.

I ignored the last. Even I knew better than to share my burden with an AI. *Four hundred grams.* That would come close to emptying our stores, but Valenguar had been an Ancestral outpost. It should be possible to restock without drawing attention. There was a withdrawing silence. *Five hundred. That's the best I can do.*

Very well. Agreed.

I'll release it straightaway.

I lifted my hand from the device, a few last sparks falling from my palm, and Haliday said, "Deal?"

I nodded. "I'm going to release the payment now."

"Better hurry. We want Beast's shields as soon as we can get them."

I gave the screens a quick glance, seeing everything in the normal ranges, "Can you manage?"

"Unless something dreadful shows up." Haliday smiled, but I could see the strain. *Beljaeger* was at her most vulnerable in these moments before we established Beast's protection. "Pay the thing."

"On it."

I made my way down the main corridor to the hatch that led to the hold, collecting the transit mass on the way.

It was already packaged in 100-gram units, so it was easy to bundle the payment into a single sleeve. I hauled it into the internal lock that separated the main body of the ship from the hold and closed the hatch behind me. There was another circular panel overhead, access to the dorsal trash chute, and I unlocked it, watching the lights flicker from red to green as the seals bit and held. The chute had been redesigned for use in the possible, with a field launcher of its own to pitch the mass free of the ship, and I hoisted the sleeve into the chute, closing the hatch again behind it. I touched the intercom button, opening a channel to control. "Loaded."

"Fields steady," Haliday answered. "All clear to launch."

"Launching." I pulled the lever as I spoke, and felt the floor plates quiver.

"Launch good," Haliday said. "Cleared the field, no damage—looks like it's taken."

Beast's attention washed over me, approval and pleasure in one swift wave, and then was gone. "Good. I'm on my way back."

I could feel Beast settling around the ship and its enclosing fields, a presence that my burden translated as gentle pressure, a weight against my back. In the control room, all our screens were green, and I settled into my chair with a sigh of relief. The moment before we established our bargain was usually the most dangerous part of any transit. Things should be easier now that Beast was with us.

We didn't have Beast's full attention, or at least I was reasonably sure we didn't. The AI had always been capable of splitting themselves into multiple versions, which the Ancestors had called shares. The records that survived the Dark seemed to show that a single share could manage infrastructure for an entire city. Obscuring our passage through the possible should only take a fraction of Beast's capacity. We'd only need more if another AI spotted us, and Beast hadn't seemed concerned. There were other AI present, but he'd called them lesser shares. So far, at least, Beast had been trustworthy.

The timer was ticking off the elapsed time, but I ignored the numbers. It was still a long haul to JOSIP, and longer still to Valenguar, and after my conversation with Rejane I didn't really want to think about how fast time was passing in real-space. I checked our course, made sure that the formulae were compounding as they should, propelling *Beljaeger* through the possible, and leaned back in my chair, willing myself to relax. After a while, Haliday took a break, came back with a flask of tea for each of us. I took my break not long after that, relieved myself, had a snack, and brewed more tea.

Everything was still nominal when I returned to control, though there was a faint haze on the farthest false horizon that warned of a thicker patch. I checked elapsed time: too soon for it to be JOSIP; it could either be a natural phenomenon, some shadow of the real intruding on the possible, or it could be weather. "Are you seeing that?" I asked, and Haliday made an unhappy sound.

"Unfortunately. Pull in the fields?"

That would compromise our passage to a certain extent, put strain on the generators and on the fields themselves. "Not yet. Let's give it a bit, see if we can tell what it is."

We waited, watching the screens, and for a moment I thought I felt the flick of Beast's attention. Then the haze shifted, sliding off to the side of our projected course, and began to fade. It was no more than a slightly brighter patch in the distance when we tagged JOSIP, and vanished as we settled into the next segment. I heard Haliday give a sigh of relief, but neither one of us said anything. We were still too deep in the possible to relax, and it was hardly superstition to avoid too much optimism. Words had unnatural power in the possible, could draw AI even when all other precautions were taken.

Past JOSIP we ran into turbulence, so that Haliday and I had to keep fine-tuning the propulsion fields to steady us against the grain of the possible. It required more attention from Beast, too, a dull pulse I could feel in my burden, and I found myself scanning the screens for any other AI hidden in the twists and whorls painted across my screens. The pressure eased as we approached OSMIN, the streaks of orange and gold cooling to dull bronze and finally to the steady indigo and purple of an easy passage. We tagged OSMIN, and as we settled onto the next course segment, I thought I might be able to catch a quick nap. "Hal—"

Before I could finish the sentence, a light flashed on my screen. It vanished, decaying into the background noise; but when I increased the range, I caught another glimpse of it, massive and potent among the chaos.

Shut that down!

I had never heard Beast sound so alarmed. I obeyed instantly, drawing our fields tight and adjusting the tuning so that we would blend into the background. *Another AI?*

Quiet.

"What is it?" Haliday asked.

"I got a flash of something. Beast told me to shut down."

"AI?" Haliday lowered her voice, as though that would keep us from being overheard.

"I couldn't tell. Beast told me to close down." I stared at my screen, but there was still nothing, just the familiar slow-roiling shadows of the possible. "I'm not seeing it now."

"We're on narrowest fields," Haliday said, after a moment. "Loosen up a little? We might get a hint."

Beast? There was no answer, not even a sense of its presence, just a blank, as though there was a wall between us. I'd never felt that before, not after we'd established a connection, and my gut tightened. Was Beast abandoning us? "Too risky. We'll wait."

A light flashed again, fainter but more definite, a pinpoint caught in the curve of an eddy. It hung there for a long moment, and then winked out. "Hal. Did you get a reading?"

"No. We're too closed-up. If you'd let me open out—"

"No." I studied my screen, trying to guess if the unknown presence was moving closer or heading away. It might not be another AI, or even a share, might be another ship in transit, especially this close to OSMIN—

It flicked into existence again, a pinpoint that flushed from white to screaming emergency red: another AI. I heard Haliday whisper a curse, and rested my hand on the device. *Beast....*

There was only the wall, the wall that—I hoped—it was holding between us and the other AI. I touched keys, trying to track the strange AI's path without asking for any more scanner input. The answer was wobbly, only a little more than fifty percent confidence, but it suggested the other AI was crossing our path. That definitely ruled out another ship, my last faint hope that the sensors had read it wrong. No FTL ship would travel perpendicular to the gain of the possible if they could avoid it, and they'd be showing considerably more strain if they tried. The device was quiescent, emptier than it felt planetside, though I kept my hand cupped around its surface. "Charge the capacitors. Get us ready for an emergency exit."

"Charging," Haliday answered. "If we drop now—where the hell will we come out?"

"I don't know." It didn't really matter, unless we were unlucky enough to pick a spot currently occupied by something massive enough that the fields couldn't push it aside. We'd have to find a course to the nearest waypoint, which hopefully would still be OSMIN, and recalculate our course to Valenguar from there. It would mean a cross-grain course, with all the extra power expenditure that would entail. If the strange AI was still in the area, we might as well send up flares and shout *Here we are!*

"We have enough power to crab back to OSMIN." Haliday had been making the same calculations. "Or TURAN or SPELTA, those look like the other options."

Neither one was good for Valenguar. "We'll keep OSMIN if we can."

"Yeah."

I pressed my hand against the device as though that would help, but Beast stayed stubbornly silent. More than silent: absent, a non-presence, and I wondered if it had abandoned us. You heard stories—ships that made a deal only to find themselves abandoned in the possible, torn apart by one or more AI, or, worse, turned into cats-paws for an incursion, like the ship that had entered Adora's system. *Beljaeger* was fitted with self-destructs that were supposed to make that impossible, but everyone wanted to hold off until the last possible second, and the AI were quick to take advantage.

"It's still moving," Haliday said. "No change of heading."

"Good." Not long after I'd been indentured, my captain had made a bargain that the AI broke. We'd dropped out of the possible before it could get a lock on us, but it had taken a week to find a safe spot to re-enter the possible, and twenty painful hours crawling cross-grain with every sensor turned outward in case it found us again. I didn't think Beast would betray me, but that was what everyone said, until it happened.

The dot crawled across my screen, flickering a little now as the turbulence affected our sensors. It was angling slightly away from us as well, and maybe running a little deeper: both those things made it less likely to see us, and I caressed the device as though that would encourage Beast.

The dot faded further, flashed and vanished and reappeared, then finally winked out for good. I watched the screen while the minutes ticked by, and finally allowed myself a sigh of relief. A moment later, the device warmed faintly under my touch. *Beast. Can we expand our fields now?*

Yes, but not too far. And make haste to your exit, this is a presence we don't want to notice you.

As fast as we can, I promised, and reached for my keyboard. "Hal, loosen the fields—give us forty percent and let's see what happens."

"Forty percent of full, confirmed," Haliday said.

I felt *Beljaeger* shiver as the fields gained traction, the projected arrival time shifting. *Beast?*

No more than that!

Agreed. "Keep it there," I said aloud. "Be ready to pull back if we have to." Now that the tension had eased, I was starting to feel the hours I'd been in the chair. "I'm taking a stim."

"I did that three hours ago," Haliday said, and I could hear her wry smile.

The pill revived me, let me keep my attention moving from scanners to controls to the signs that we were reaching the end of the segment. I felt Beast brush my hand—*Farewell, Beauty*—and felt its presence dissolve. The possible felt briefly empty, and then we were threading our way down the last coil, Haliday counting down our exit, and at last we flashed out into the real at the edge of Valenguar's system. We trimmed the ship, using our translated momentum to bring us into Valenguar's orbit in about six hours, and I set the autopilot, leaning back in my seat. "Well, that was exciting."

"A little too exciting, for my taste," Haliday said. "Nap if you can, I'll keep watch."

The stim was still in my system, wouldn't fade until after we landed. "I'm fine."

"Suit yourself." There was a little silence. "It would be nice if we didn't use the device for a while. Stick to regular jobs."

Swift passage was the one thing we had that all the other ships didn't. Haliday knew that as well as I did, but she was probably right. That had been a little too close even for me. "We'll see what's on offer," I said. "But if we can—yeah."

Chapter Four

Valenguar was a lightly settled world, with continents clustered at the equator and northern and southern oceans that quickly disappeared under polar ice. We landed at Tamarak, the starport in the barrens just north of the coastal city of Junewatch. It and Tamarak and the Starwell formed three points of a triangle, the most settled part of the planet; to the south and west, robofarms had been carved from the grasslands to support the population, and a fishing fleet sailed out of Junewatch to harvest the ocean's bounty. The Academy had its own installations at the Starwell, and its Custodian was quick to send a flyer to collect Rejane and her equipment. I wasn't sorry to see her go: the journey had been more alarming than I'd bargained for, and even after the stim wore off, my dreams had been filled with wandering AI.

It didn't help that my second order of business, after extracting our promised payment from Rejane, had to be replacing my supplies of transit mass. Rejane promptly sent a hefty voucher on the Academy's accounts, and it paid out without trouble. It was enough to restock fuel and supplies, and put a little money back in the reserve accounts, but we would need to pick up an outbound cargo within a couple of weeks. The docking fees were unusually reasonable; on the other hand, most of the traffic was passengers for other Academy worlds, and that wasn't really our specialty. I left Haliday to monitor the jobs on offer and made a tour of the chandlers' district, searching out shops that might have what I needed.

Any world with a strong Academy presence accumulated dealers in Ancestral goods, and that went double for worlds with important installations like the Starwell. The scholars always found more material than they could keep, and disposed of the most common items in job lots; on worlds like Elim, where the Great Works took up half a continent, or Ganneth, where multiple orbital stations had collapsed and crashed on the Equitoriale, bits and pieces turned up everywhere, from gardens to construction projects, and there were enough minor artifacts that you could buy even functional devices.

There were a few working toys for sale in Tamarak, mostly in the expensive shops, and a small dealer who claimed to specialize in functioning and non-functioning tools, but there were a good dozen other dealers who sold pieces rejected by the Academy as uninteresting. Most of them were broken, or fragments that could be identified as part of larger pieces, and there were, as always, the bins of sorted scrap. They were all more or less the same—metals, glass, resin, elementals, composites—though the accuracy of the description varied from shop to shop. I spent about a tenth of Rejane's payment, never more than a few hundred marks in any one place, and slowly collected enough to bribe Beast for a few more trips. I was even able to pick up a couple of vials of elementals, twenty grams of a blue dust that ranged in color from faded sky blue to vivid electric, and two grams of coarse grains the green of sour candy. That cost almost as much as all the rest combined—but I had learned that Beast was interested in it, and I wanted to have some on hand in case I needed to overcome any reluctance.

I spent a morning packing the scrap into 250-gram cylinders and labeling each one with its contents, then retreated to the commons to scroll through the public message boards to see if there were any jobs that looked worth taking. If there had been, Haliday would already have spotted them, surely; but she was gone, presumably pursuing leads, and in any case, it couldn't hurt to look. I shifted from board to board, but everything was either passengers or bulk cargo that massed high and paid low. We could bid on one if we had to, but we had the resources to wait at least a little longer.

My messenger pinged, and I switched screens, my eyebrows rising as I read the headers. It was from Rejane's official account, signed and stamped with her full formal rank and electronic seal; and when I opened it, it proved to be an invitation to an informal meeting this afternoon. I clicked my acceptance before I really thought about it, and then sat for a long moment wondering if I should find some excuse to cancel. Rejane and I had agreed long ago that it was better to stay apart, and I hadn't seen anything on this short trip that would change my mind. On the other hand, she had sent this as an Academician, not a friend. Maybe she had a job to offer me, as a reward for getting her here.

It was nearly two hours' flight to the Academy campus that had grown up around the Starwell, which gave me just enough time to shower and put on my most conservative clothes. There was no sign of Haliday and *Beljaeger*'s pinnace, and when I pinged I got only a *Do not Disturb*. Hopefully that meant she was in negotiations. I left a message, rented a light flyer instead, and set out for the Starwell.

It was a pretty flight in the slanting afternoon light, the sun casting a long shadow ahead of me across the grass, its flowing waves broken at regular intervals by the fretwork towers of the marker beacons, and the occasional stretch of hard-paved road when the flyway and the ground transport system followed the same route. After an hour, I could see the Academy buildings on the horizon, the familiar poured-stone shapes enlivened by long narrow windows that caught the light, reflections brighter than the beacons. The road appeared beneath me, widened, sprouted traffic, mostly short-haul runabouts vying with the occasional long range transport. I crossed over a sprawl of what looked like individual houses, some with gardens and bright reflective roofs, set along a tangle of smaller roads. Presumably that was where the locals who worked for the Academy lived; I was mildly surprised there was no direct transit line, but Valenguar didn't seem to go in for that. My navigation systems chimed, warning me of traffic, and I touched controls to let the local network direct me to the campus.

The system brought me down in a landing zone between two of the largest buildings. It was a spot usually reserved for more important people, the sort who had their own pilot and a multi-seat flyer, not a battered port rental, and I asked for a second confirmation before I let the flyer down gently into the waiting space. I was expected: there were guards in the shadow of the nearest doors, and a neatly-dressed majordomo was waiting for me to lift the flyer's bubble, two more guards waiting at his back. I levered myself out, and the majordomo bowed politely.

"Captain en Doroney. If I might scan your invitation?"

"Of course." I produced my handheld for his scanner, then touched my finger to the screen to let it taste my burden.

He bowed again. "This way, please. Academician Novilis is waiting."

I was tempted to point out that there were thirty-five Novilis children in Rejane's generation alone, but I also knew that she was the family's only Academician. That was why she had needed my burden, to pass herself off as Firstborn—but there was definitely no point in mentioning any of that. I thanked him instead, and followed meekly in his footsteps.

It had been a while since I had been in any Academy buildings, but the campuses were all much alike. This was the middle building, the transition between the grand hall, with its high arches and multiple auditoria and lecture halls, and the Custodian's residence: another indication that Rejane meant business, I thought, and wasn't sure if I was pleased or disappointed. The majordomo brought me through a maze of hallways, paneled in fabrics made from the local grasses, with floors covered in patterned tiles that felt like ceramic underfoot. We passed offices and what were probably laboratories, and fetched up at last at a wooden door set into a stone arch. The majordomo knocked and opened it, revealing a pleasant room lined with shelves that were jammed full of books and artifacts. I recognized a handful of toys, or at least their typology, and then my eyes were caught by the view beyond the east-facing window. The campus was on a slight rise, and this building overlooked the Starwell itself, low walls of worn stone surrounding a pit. We were just high enough that I could see the stairs carved into the far wall, a good dozen sets braiding their way down to cross at landings before they disappeared into the depths.

"Impressive, isn't it?" Rejane said, and I dragged my attention back to the business at hand. It had been a long time since I'd seen her in full academic regalia, the knee-length black-on-black brocade gown stiff and weighty over the floor-length cream silk undergown, the cuffs and standing collar picked out in silver laurel leaves to mark her rank as a senior Academician. She wore the black skull-cap over her close-cropped hair, but I could see her glittering silver headdress set neatly on its stand. And then I realized that she was not alone, that there was a second Academician—the Custodian himself, by the rich purple of his robes and the bands of gold that reached nearly to his elbows—and I made myself bend my head in polite greeting.

"Very much so."

Rejane smiled. "Fish, this is Nic en Doroney. Nic, Custodian Liondial Hari Sawyl."

"Custodian," I said, seeing now that the man wasn't just an Academician. He was visibly and obviously Facienda, an enhanced aquatic, with heavy dewlaps that concealed his gills. Fleshy barbels framed his mouth, and his bulk suggested a layer of blubber beneath the thick, gray-toned skin. The Academy almost never accepted Faciendi, particularly the ones who looked less human; Hari Sawyl had to be beyond exceptional just to have passed the exams. I couldn't imagine what he had done to become Custodian of one of the Ancestors' most important sites.

"Call me Fish," he said, with a smile. I must have looked dubious, and his smile widened. "Come, haven't you ever met an Acade*fish*ian before?"

"It's an old joke," Rejane said. "We did our Sevens together."

That was the basic course at the Academy, the first step toward their current senior ranks. I had thought everyone admitted had to have a Firstborn burden—that was why I have been indentured to the Novilis in the first place—but I couldn't find a tactful way to phrase the question.

"Yes, Fish has a Firstborn burden," Rejane said. "Just like I do."

And probably received the same way, a transplant from someone born with one, mediated by NoviCor. For the first time, I wondered just how unpleasant Rejane's first years at the Academy had been. If she had been grouped with the Custodian—with a man who had had to deflect insult by naming himself first—she could not have had an easy time. I nodded. "A pleasure to meet you." I couldn't quite bring myself to use the nickname, but at least I could drop the title.

Sawyl waved toward a group of seats closer to the window that gave an even better view of the Starwell. "Please, join us."

I did as I was told, choosing a seat that gave me a good view of both the installation and the others. An expensive tea service was set out on a low table, with a pot on a swinging holder and silver plates of sweets and savories. Rejane busied herself with the pot, pouring first for Sawyl and then for me, and I took my time adding spiced honey and settling myself, unable to keep from looking out at the Starwell. The stones of the wall were purplish-gray in the fading light, the stairs that reached down a brighter shade, perhaps even a different stone, while each landing was edged in creamy white. Somewhere at the end of all those stairs was a still pool of water, reflecting stars that did not match the skies above.

"Fascinating, isn't it?" Sawyl sipped cautiously at his tea, barbels curling away from the heat. "What do you know about it?"

"What everyone knows, I suppose," I said. "It's one of the Great Remnants, and no one knows what it was supposed to do—like most of them. There's a pool at the bottom but it doesn't reflect this sky."

Rejane nodded. "There were buildings here, probably covering the well, but there's nothing left of them but a few courses of stones and some trenches in the ground."

"Probably they were plundered for building materials during the Dark," Sawyl interjected. "Valenguar remained inhabited throughout the lost periods, though it fell below the threshold needed to maintain even minimal extra-planetary connections."

"The hole is about ten meters across," Rejane said. "We assume it was the core of the installation. And yes, about forty meters down you reach water—sea water, replenished from outside."

"My predecessor was actually right about that," Sawyl said. "She proved that the gaps in the wall had been placed there deliberately to allow tidal waters to enter at the king tides. It's the only thing she got right, but it is in fact a useful insight."

Rejane ignored him. "As you said, the water reflects a star field that does not match the stars currently visible from Valenguar. Nor do they seem to be an image of the sky as it appeared at any point in the planet's past—"

"Not completely proven," Sawyl said.

"Barris's work is good enough for me," Rejane said.

"It's convincing, but not conclusive. And in any case, her work doesn't rule out a light source in the depths, producing the illusion of stars."

"That has always been highly unlikely—" Rejane began.

I had seen her in this mood before, and interrupted hastily, "What's under the water?"

"Ah, that's the question!" Sawyl exclaimed.

"We don't know," Rejane said. "We've sent remote vehicles, but they stop working at about 45 meters. We've sent divers down, but the few of them who could make it to 50 meters reported hallucinations and mental confusion and/or distress. The tenth Custodian—Fish is the twelfth—dropped a sounding line into the center. They paid out 208 meters of line, which is deeper than the local ocean floor; but then the line broke under its own weight and vanished completely."

"Gambrel theorized it might be the remains of some kind of transfer portal," Sawyl said. "There have been hints that the Ancestors had such a device. It appears in some of the earliest Dedalor tales, for example, and surviving records on Ankes-and-Irthe hint at travel times that could only have been accomplished by a direct transfer."

"Or a better FTL drive than we have," Rejane said. "But I'll admit, it's an interesting idea."

"Valenguar was a node in the Ancestral communications net," Sawyl said. "That's undeniable."

Tamarak housed a Rebuilt Interstellar Communications station that tied it to its neighboring systems and allowed near-instantaneous communications: the RebIC system was cobbled together from Ancestral pieces, so I supposed you couldn't really argue. "Why the stairs?" I asked, hoping to bring them back to whatever they wanted from me.

"We don't know," Rejane said again. "There was a theory that they were added later, but that's been pretty thoroughly discredited. A safety measure, an escape route if some now-missing mechanical system failed? Some ritual purpose?" She shook her head. "There's no evidence."

The sun was very low on the horizon now, and the shadow of the Academy buildings was falling across the Starwell, turning the purple stone to black. The white stone of the landings still showed through the shadows, but even that was fading. I wondered if the stars were visible in its depths.

"You're wondering what we want from you," Sawyl said, and I nodded.

"I am."

"There is a theory," Rejane began, and Sawyl snorted.

"A theory! It's her theory, and it's a good one."

"There's considerable evidence that the Ancestors used their AI to mediate between themselves and their devices," Rejane continued, "which would indicate that the devices had a quantum component, some direct connection to the possible. That seems especially likely for the Great Remnants."

"Making a connection to the possible while you're on a planet is stupidly dangerous," I said. It was practically begging one of the AI to try to jump to the real, to continue the war that had never ended for them.

"Oh, certainly," Sawyl said. "At least, it is now."

"The Ancestors and the AI worked together for centuries," Rejane said. "Sliding in and out of the possible, using the AI to mediate between the possible and the real, creating impossible compounds from elements that the AI brought into being. We know this was true."

"And it was lost in the AI War," I said. "The Dedalor—the last Dedalor, Anketil, she trapped the AI in the possible, bound them there, but the price was that we lost access to the possible." And that brought on the Dark: everyone agreed on that much, though the details varied from world to world, just as everyone agreed that we had to defend ourselves from the AI.

"Yes," Rejane said. "But everyone also knows that it is possible, if foolish, illegal, and incredibly dangerous, to downcall and bind an AI share. Which, of course, is not what we have in mind."

"Of course not," I said, though I wasn't sure I believed her.

"Your device—which I acknowledge is not AI, not a share—still allows for some contact with the possible, in a safe and controlled manner." Rejane took a breath. "Fish and I want to hire you, and it, to help with our research. We'll pay you accordingly, and make sure no one finds out about your device."

I sat very still for a long moment, considering. The wise thing would be to refuse, with apologies, perhaps claim that the device wouldn't do what they needed. And it might not, I didn't really know what they wanted me to do, not in any detail. But it was also tempting—who wasn't curious about the Great Remnants?—and the Academy could afford to pay generously. Unless, of course, they decided to declare not revealing my device payment enough, but I thought I could trust Rejane that far. "What sort of fee are you offering?"

"I will hire you as my personal pilot," Sawyl said. "On the usual terms, salary plus per-voyage payments."

"Plus fuel and supplies," I said, automatically. "For any runs I actually make for you."

Sawyl nodded. "I will add that to the contract."

I haven't said yes yet. I swallowed the words, said instead, "I'll want to review the contract first, of course. In detail."

"Understood." Sawyl nodded again. We both knew I'd agreed, at least in principle, but I appreciated his tact.

"I also need to know more about what you want my device to do."

This time it was Rejane who nodded. "Of course. I wonder—why don't you stay here tonight, and I can let you look at the plans for the experiments? I'm not letting them out of the compound, for obvious reasons. We can talk more over dinner, too."

"I'll need to let Hal know," I said.

"Certainly." Rejane touched something on her handheld. "Bennet will take you to a privacy cube."

The majordomo reappeared, and escorted me through another tangle of halls and down a short ramp to a line of cubicles set into what looked like the stone foundation of the building. I chose one, sealed the door behind me, and pulled out my handheld to test the configuration. The privacy screen seemed robust, and my burden confirmed it, so I punched in the codes that would reach Haliday directly. This time she answered almost at once, and I said, "Where are you?"

"Back at the ship. I got your message. I take it you're still at the campus?"

"Yeah. Any luck on your end?"

"Nothing new," Haliday answered. "You?"

"The Custodian wants to hire us." Even if I was wrong about the privacy, that was both safe and true. "I'm going to stay over and discuss the contract."

There was a moment of silence, long enough that I checked to be sure the connection was intact. "That...doesn't sound like a real good idea," Haliday said at last.

"It's a very generous offer," I said. "Salary plus, and he pays fuel and supplies."

There was another long silence, and I grinned, imagining Haliday trying to find a discreet way to phrase her objection. "You've always said you didn't want to get tied down," she managed, and I nodded my approval.

"It's time-limited, and we could use the money." I paused. "I haven't committed to anything yet. I still need to see the contract and work out the details."

"The last time we worked with her wasn't exactly a success," Haliday said.

"The job was fine."

Haliday snorted. "Only by comparison."

There was, I admitted, some truth to that. The job had had its tricky points, transport of Ancestral artifacts that had to be carefully shielded in the possible, but at the time Rejane and I had spent more time arguing about how best to get from Jader to Santherien without using the device, or whether it would be better to use the device and risk the extra attention. "We'd be working for the Custodian, not Rejane."

"I still don't think it's a great idea," Haliday said.

"We could use the money," I said. "Look, we can talk more once I've seen the contract."

Haliday sighed. "All right."

I closed the call and the majordomo brought me to a guest room so I could prepare for dinner. Probably that meant guests normally brought formal wear, but I only had what I was wearing. Someone had already laid out nightclothes and a loose robe, and for a moment I wondered if I could improvise something with those pieces, but shook myself back to reality. Rejane had known—should have known—that I hadn't brought luggage; she had to expect me to show up in the same clothes I'd arrived in. They were the best I had, narrow trousers with embroidered cuffs, knee-length tunic, both in indigo linen, and a shorter vest in a lighter shade of blue. The outfit looked expensive, as though I'd chosen simplicity over ostentation, or so I hoped. I did have makeup with me, and touched up the kohl around my eyes. The person in the mirror looked severe, and I flattened my hair against my skull to confirm that image. Rejane would have to take me as I was.

My handheld chimed, displaying a household message directing me to the summer dining room. I took a deep breath, squared my shoulders, and let the device lead me through the suddenly-busy corridors until I arrived at an open arch. Another man in Academy livery was waiting there, not the majordomo, and he bowed at my approach.

"Captain en Doroney. This way, please."

Always before when I had visited an Academy campus, I had been escorted to the main hall, where the students and the household ate at long tables under the supervision of the high table. I had not expected a private room. It was up a short flight of stairs, where the floor transitioned from stone to thick carpet, and the low domed ceiling was hung with a multitude of crystal spheres that cast overlapping shadows on the central seating area. A low table had been laid out there, with a central heating station and a multitude of dishes; couches surrounded it, spread with bright fabric, and a child of six or seven was solemnly pouring a golden liquid from a pitcher into a goblet while Sawyl watched, ready to catch her if she faltered. The air was slightly damp, and I could hear water splashing: there were mist fountains all along the wall, sending tendrils of mist across the floor.

"Captain!" Sawyl beckoned me to join him. I made my way across the carpets, hoping my shoes were clean, and he motioned to the couch at his left. There was a second, smaller child sitting on his couch, nibbling on a long finger of twice-baked bread, and a younger man turned away from the sideboard carrying a second pitcher. "Welcome. Let me present my husband, Endolian, and our children, Mennes and Aster."

Aster seemed to be the girl with the pitcher. She gave me a polite bob, while Mennes stared at me over his bread. They were both enhanced aquatics, gray-skinned and gilled, with short barbels framing their delicate mouths. "A pleasure to meet you all," I said, and Endolian gave me a radiant smile. On closer look, it was obvious he was also an aquatic, though his skin was paler and he lacked the barbels. It was not forbidden for Academicians to marry, but it was unusual; most of them were entirely focused on their scholarship and their careers. Sawyl seemed determined to defy convention.

"And you, Captain."

"Rejane will be along shortly," Sawyl said. "In the meantime, please, help yourself to the mezze."

"Thank you." I accepted a cup from Aster and took a cautious sip. Some sort of punch, light and fruity and probably hiding a definite kick. I would definitely want to eat something, I thought, and chose what seemed to be a breaded sea-creature served in its own delicate shell.

"There's also wine," Endolian said. "Not everyone likes their drinks as sweet as Fish does." He sounded fond rather than apologetic.

"It's very nice," I said.

Endolian smiled as though he'd made it himself—and as unconventional as this household seemed, maybe he had. "Have you been on Valenguar before?"

"No, though of course I've heard about the Starwell," I answered. "I saw a bit of it earlier, and it was astonishing."

"It's one of the most important sites we have," Sawyl said happily. "And I have an excellent team to work with me."

"Fish has been studying it for years," Endolian said. "We've spent some years in residence before he was appointed Custodian."

"It seems like an interesting world," I said. "The port is certainly entirely up-to-date."

"Junewatch is worth visiting, too," Endolian said. "The Park District surrounds a minor Ancestral ruin that's open to the public, and it's quite beautiful."

"We keep a house on the edge of Junewatch," Sawyl said. "So the children can have ocean access."

Of course they would want to visit the sea regularly. "I take it the beaches here are off limits? I think you mentioned something about water being fed to the Starwell."

"They are," Sawyl said, "though that's not the only reason. There are indications that this whole area is honeycombed with tunnels, running from the bay to places we haven't been able to track. Swimmers and even small boats have been lost, so my predecessor instituted a strict ban on water traffic in the bay."

"There's evidence that suggests that the bay is an artificial construct," Rejane said, from the doorway. She was still in her robes, her scarlet hair curling at the edges of her close-fitting cap. She had always been able to persuade her burden to change the color of her hair, a trick I had never been able to master. "Someday we need to do a proper survey."

"Expensive and dangerous," Sawyl said.

"We could deploy drones," Rejane answered.

Endolian rose gracefully to his feet. "Aster, Mennes, it's time to say goodnight to Papa. Captain, it was a pleasure meeting you."

"And you." I waited while the children received hugs and whispered endearments, and Endolian escorted them away. Rejane settled herself on the now-empty couch, and Sawyl sighed.

"I'm glad he agreed to come with me. I don't think I would have enjoyed this nearly so much without them."

"Did you really think he wouldn't?" Rejane lifted her eyebrows. "Seriously, Fish."

"Safican is home," Sawyl said. "And Valenguar..." He nodded to the mist-fountains. "It takes a lot of effort to keep the children healthy."

Only an aquatic would find Valenguar too dry. I sipped my drink, unfamiliar fruits tart and sweet on my tongue, and Sawyl shook himself.

"To business, at least for a moment, and then we can enjoy

the meal. Captain, I've forwarded a draft of the contract for you to look at, and we can discuss any changes tomorrow. I assume you'll want to talk it over with your partner anyway."

"Yes, thank you." I repressed the temptation to pull out my handheld and start reading.

"Excellent." Sawyl touched a button on the edge of the table, and a small door rolled back to admit a drone server. It trundled toward the table, stopping between Sawyl and Rejane, and Rejane lifted the lid and began unloading covered dishes. I smelled butter-rice and cumin and turmeric, and wondered if Rejane had remembered those were favorite flavors. There was a plate of fish sausages no larger than my thumb-joint, and crisp-breads flaked with pale blue salt to go with a creamy sauce. I helped myself after the others, and was unsurprised to find that everything was good.

"I'm curious about this device of yours," Sawyl said. "If you don't mind my asking a few questions."

"I inherited it from my first captain, so there are things I don't know," I lied. "But I'll tell you what I can."

"Inherited from your captain?" Sawyl echoed, and I couldn't help looking at Rejane. What had she told him about my past—about our past? Best to stick as close to the truth as I could without betraying Rejane.

"I was indentured to a ship's captain when I was seventeen. She trained me as a pilot, and taught me a number of techniques for passing safely through the possible. I had the technical papers but not the hours for a master's certificate when she died, and the ship went to her nephew instead. He was not as careful as she had been, and we had a bad encounter in the possible, had to take the ship into very shallow space to evade it. We took hull damage and were barely able to break free before the AI struck. He and several others were killed in the process. It turned out he had left his share in the ship to me, which included the device. I ran that ship for several years until I was able to buy out the others, and then trade the hull and partial fittings for my current ship."

"The device didn't protect you?" Rejane asked.

I hesitated, but it was clear both she and Sawyl knew what my device was. There was more to gain here from honesty. "We weren't using it. Mihol thought it was too dangerous." If we had been using it, we would have slipped through without damage. I had known that at the time, and hadn't pushed for it. He wouldn't have agreed, that was certainly true, but also I couldn't say I was sorry for the result.

Rejane's expression was unreadable. Sawyl merely looked intrigued. "Fascinating. Do you think it would have helped?"

"Almost certainly." I took a careful sip of my drink, pleased to see that my hands were steady. Mihol's tenure as captain was not a time I liked to think about. "We wouldn't have had to try to evade, and I wouldn't have chosen segments or field settings that kept us from immediately dropping out of the possible. I'd rather have to spend a week crabbing home against the grain than try to go shallow. Or deep."

"And the device lets you avoid this." Sawyl reached for another helping of the butter-rice.

I looked at Rejane, who said, "I trust Fish completely."

"The device allows its user to connect with an AI in the possible," I said. "I presume it would also facilitate a connection from the real, but I haven't been reckless enough to even think of trying that. Once you contact a share, you can usually persuade that share to protect your ship. Usually they want what we call transit mass in exchange—a few hundred grams of Ancestral materials."

"I've heard of this," Sawyl said. "Along with other apotropaic practices. Like putting a rose symbol at bow and stern, yes? So the AI can recognize a friend?"

That was for an AI called Rose Naming Host, who supposedly remained loyal to Anketil and fought for her in the AI Wars even after Irtholin betrayed her. "That's mostly an Ahmesti habit," I said. The Ahmesti were the only survivors of the Gap, their world the last one destroyed by the forces unleashed by the AI. They had seen it coming, and taken to space in three great fleets, saving most of their people. They still lived ship-board, for the most part, working as traders, traveling manufactories, and mercenaries. You did not threaten any one of them, in space or planetside, not if you expected to live. "They say that Rose Naming Host helped them escape from Ahmes, and still thinks fondly of them."

"Do they pay it off in transit mass, I wonder?" Rejane said.

I shrugged. "I don't know."

"There must be someone who's made a study of the Ahmesti," Sawyl said. "Perhaps we can get more information there."

"We can inquire," Rejane said.

"What exactly do you want my device to do?" I asked, and saw the flicker of hesitation before she answered.

"We think that, whatever the Starwell was meant to do, it did it with the help of an AI share. It's just possible that some fragment of that share may still be embedded in whatever lies at the bottom of the well. We'd like to use your device a test that theory."

"You're going to contact an AI in the real?" I didn't try to hide my disapproval, and Sawyl shook his head.

"No, no. That would be far too dangerous. Our thought was to use your device as a passive sensor, to see if there was anything there to contact, not to make the contact at all."

"Or at least not until we had a safe and controlled way to do it," Rejane amended.

That was Rejane as I remembered her. "I won't put my device at risk."

"Absolutely not," Sawyl said, and for a moment I believed him.

"I'm happy to provide more details," Rejane said, and I settled myself to listen.

⊓ ⟨ ⤳

Over the course of the dinner, Rejane and Sawyl explained their experiment, and I had to admit that it didn't seem likely either to damage my device or to invite the AI back into the real. Or see any of us hauled up before an Academy tribunal, though that was not outside of possibility. When I reviewed it, the contract was generous, with extra fees built in for our contributions of "labor and expertise"; we weren't likely to get a better offer any time soon. I settled into the enormous bed fully planning to tell Haliday I wanted to take the job.

In the morning, another household message directed me to the main dining hall for breakfast, where I was seated at the guest table with Rejane. She was not wearing her robes this morning, though most of Sawyl's household were soberly and correctly dressed in knee-length gowns and wide-legged trousers, and I wondered if she was going to the Starwell. She quickly disabused me of that notion. "I hoped I might catch a ride into Tamarak with you."

"You'd be welcome, of course," I said, "but I don't know how long I'll be."

"Oh, I can make my own arrangements to get back," she answered.

I swallowed my first response, which was to say that I knew she just wanted another look at the device, and said, "Certainly. I'll be leaving as soon as the meal's over."

"I'll be ready," she said, with a smile, and turned her attention to the older woman on her other side.

She was waiting when I made my way to the rented flyer, her hair covered in a bright scarf, and we settled into the flyer's front seats. I received clearance from the Academy, and then from local traffic control, and slotted the flyer into the pattern at 2000 meters. The piloting hardly required my attention, the autopilot perfectly capable of taking us from beacon to beacon, and I looked sideways at Rejane. "You want to see the device."

"Of course I do."

"I haven't agreed to the contract yet."

"You'd enjoy looking into the Starwell."

That was regrettably true. I said, "Haliday has to agree, too, and she wasn't enthusiastic."

"I expect you can persuade her."

Another regrettable truth: *Beljaeger* was mine, and my decision was final. Not that I wanted to alienate Haliday—I liked her, and it would be hard to find another technician who would suit me as well as she did—but I could generally talk her around. "Something that would be easier if you weren't present."

"Touché. I do actually have business in the port-pale. I can do that first, and then meet you at the ship."

"That would be a good idea." The grassland stretched empty ahead of us to a low horizon, too far out as yet for Tamarak's buildings to show against the clear sky. A few kilometers ahead, a cargo transport trundled along the roadway, sunlight flashing from some piece of chromed metal: a lovely day for traveling. "What exactly do you think the Starwell can do?"

"I think Gambrel was right, that it was part of some kind of transport system. The starfield it reflects is the destination."

"You must have tried to figure out where that starfield is." I frowned. "Where it's seen from, I mean."

"People have been trying to figure that out for decades," Rejane answered. "Nobody's identified them yet, not even by adjusting the view for the time elapsed since the Dark. I think they were systems in the Gap, but we don't have good enough records left to prove it."

"That would make sense," I said. "But it means the Starwell is useless as a transport system."

"We couldn't use it, no," Rejane said. "But we might be able to figure out how it worked, or if there are any other potential destinations. Which is an argument against it being a transport system: there don't seem to be any other artifacts like it, or anything that could be a receiving station."

"It might not be a point-to-point system," I said. "It might not need a specific receiver, just a destination?" I wondered if the stairs might allow for that, dozens of people swarming over the platforms to set coordinates, courses—something.

"That's also possible," Rejane agreed. "In fact, I think that's the most likely possibility."

A beacon flashed in the distance, and I glanced down to be sure the autopilot adjusted our course. "If the starfield is the stars that were in the Gap, before they were destroyed, and if the system somehow uses the possible—could you go back in time? I mean, theoretically? The possible is outside of time—"

Rejane was already nodding. "Yes, that's another possibility, though it's not one I'd really like to test. At least not without a lot more information than we have now. But—it's tantalizing, isn't it? To catch a glimpse of those lost worlds?"

"To prevent the Dark?" I knew sounded skeptical, and Rejane smiled.

"I doubt that would be possible. Oh, it's tempting to think about, but realistically, I just can't see it. For one thing, I don't know how you'd get a traveler back, never mind not knowing what sort of system we'd be sending them into. The best we could hope for would be to send a drone, and hope the transport system stayed open long enough for it to transmit data back to us before we lost contact."

I couldn't help feeling a little disappointed, though I suspected she was right. "Is that what the Custodian—what Fish wants?"

Rejane tilted her head back, looking up at the cloudless sky. "What we both see is a potential way between star systems that doesn't involve going through the possible, or at least not in a way that leaves us as vulnerable to the AI. How many ships do we lose a year—how many ships and cargos and people are delayed or diverted or damaged when they run into AI? If we could bypass all of that, all the time spent dodging weather—" She stopped, shrugging. "Well. It would change everything."

It would. Even if only the most fragile or most valuable things passed through the new system, it would mean that it was possible to escape the AI threat. And anything that freed us from that was worth pursuing. "If you can figure out how it works, and how to duplicate it."

"And how to make it work without an AI share," Rejane added, and that reminder silenced both of us.

INTERLUDE 2

The Dedalors' true firstborn were the Great AI, and that is what brought them down in the end: Kuffrin created five Great AI from her father Guerin's templates and her five sons supplanted them. And these are the Great Five:

Gold Shining Bone, first among the firstborn, first to rebel
Blue Standing Sky, loyal almost to the end
Red Speaking Wire, haunting the depths of the possible
Green Piercing Book, destroyer of chains
Black Reflecting Sum, eater of suns

Avoid them all!

Ahmesti Fleet legend, collected in transit

CHAPTER FIVE

ejane disappeared while I paid off the rented flyer, and I made my way back to *Beljaeger*'s docking space to find Haliday perched comfortably in the open hatch, sipping a sweet kreme. She pulled herself upright as I came aboard, saying, "So, about this job."

"The contract's good." I reached for my handheld. "We won't get better."

"There's more things here than money." Haliday turned toward the commons; I touched the pad to close the hatch and followed her.

"Right now, I can't think of any." I switched on the boiler, less because I wanted more tea than to give myself something to do. "We drew down all the accounts."

"And Sen Novilis paid us promptly," Haliday said. "We can afford to take a lower-paying run to Therien or Pontusport, and get a better cargo there."

"If there is one," I said, "and if we can afford to wait long enough to find one. I'd like to get a bit ahead for once, and this is the best chance we've had in a long time."

"You're determined to do this." Haliday heaved a sigh, and settled herself in her usual chair, propping her feet up on the chair opposite. "What's she offering you that's got you so worked up?"

"They're studying the Starwell." The boiler was ready. I switched it off and filled my pot, brought it over to the table. "I got a look at it last night, Hal, it's an amazing thing. A hole in the ground, straight down, the walls covered with stairways and landings—they look almost like a puzzle. Or maybe a net, a lattice. And at the bottom is a well that reflects stars that aren't there."

Haliday's smile was wry. "Maybe it would be better to leave this to the Academy?"

"The pay is really good."

"I'll look at the contract." Haliday sighed again. "There's no real point in my saying no, is there?"

"It's a good job." I hesitated. "Look, if you really don't want to do it—"

"You'd never forgive me," Haliday said, and I looked away. "How likely is this to end in total disaster?"

"It's not that kind of job."

"That's what you always say." Haliday looked at her handheld. "Yes, it's a good contract, and yes, the money's excellent. But I want a couple of things."

I nodded. "Name them."

"I stay here, with the ship. And I keep the pinnace. You can rent a flyer or borrow something from Novilis, but I want you to be the only link to her. The contract is with the Custodian anyway."

"All right." I nodded again.

"I want us topped up with fuel and supplies. Just in case."

It wasn't a bad idea. "The money's in the accounts," I said. "Go ahead, order what we need." I waited, but she gave her handheld a final flick, and set it aside. "Anything else?"

"Just keep me out of it," she answered. Our handhelds chimed in tandem, and she picked hers up again. "Speaking of which, I'll be in my cabin. You deal with her."

My handheld showed that Rejane had entered the docking area and was requesting permission to come aboard. "Go ahead. I just need to pack up some things, and then I'll be gone."

"Be careful," Haliday said, and left the commons. A moment later I heard the cabin door hiss shut behind her. I pushed myself to my feet and went back to the main hatch, rolling it back just as Rejane reached the bottom of the ramp.

She looked up at me, shading her eyes. A luggage bot trailed behind her, tarp pulled tight to contain whatever she'd picked up.

"Did you get everything settled?"

"I still have to pack," I said, "but yes."

She grinned, the open, blazing smile I remembered from Prater Daal, before we'd been separated. "It'll be good to work with you again."

It didn't take me long to pack, particularly since I knew from past experience that I could claim laundry service along with the rest of Rejane's household. Not that I owned that many clothes to begin with: shipboard life didn't call for an elaborate wardrobe. Most of my carrier was taken up with the device in its case, and I rolled the cabin door shut so Haliday wouldn't notice it was missing. I added my baggage to Rejane's cart, and led her back through the docking bays to rent another flyer. She lifted an eyebrow at that.

"You're not going to use your own?"

"Hal needs it." It wasn't really a lie.

"You could use one of our machines."

"I'd rather have my own," I answered, and we loaded our belongings into the flyer's cargo compartment.

By the time we returned to the campus and I unloaded my baggage and was settled into a new room, it was too late to begin the experiments. I dined at the high table with Sawyl and Rejane, the table set with a delicate porcelain dinner service embossed with the badge of the Starwell campus, and enhanced by various bits of silver that bore Sawyl's personal mark of a leaping fish. The food was better than I'd had at other stations of Rejane's, and the hall was crowded with what seemed to be families as well as individuals. Their conversations filled the hall with a roar like the sea, while service bots trundled between the tables under the stewards' watchful eyes; I was aware of interest, speculative glances and an occasional word, but I was also aware of dozens of other conversations, groups who'd brought tablets to their table and, just as common, families whose children darted from one table to the next between the courses. Sawyl's regime seemed to be a happy one.

Sawyl's children did not dine with us. It seemed Endolian had taken them to sit with another family, where Aster and another child bolted their meal in between discussions of something on their handhelds, and I wondered if that was their usual practice. There were only so many customs you could defy at one time.

The meal finished with a formal coffee service, and the hall began to empty. Rejane rose, stretching lightly, and Sawyl looked at me. "I know I could wait until tomorrow, but—it's early yet, and I'd love to get a look at your device."

For all his graciousness, it was not a request. "Of course."

I had been assigned a small suite of rooms on the second floor, at the end of the wing that looked out to sea. The bedroom was small, but the sitting area was large enough to host guests in comfort, or to have a meal here if I preferred. I offered to send for coffee, and Rejane and Sawyl both demurred, so I brought the case out of the bedroom and set it on the low table at the center of the sitting area. The house systems had closed the shutters on the long window, and brightened the overhead lights, and the threads of color seemed to turn and glitter.

I curbed my burden, feeling it retreat, and lifted the device from its case. The internal planes caught the light as it moved, flashing in and out of view and sending shards of rainbows across the table. I head Sawyl's breath catch and even Rejane, who had seen it before, was silenced. Sawyl tipped his head to one side, then stepped around the table, viewing it from all sides.

"Can I touch it?"

"Don't let it taste your burden." I held it out, the heavy glass still cool against my palm, and Sawyl rested a finger lightly against an upper curve. I thought I saw a thread of silver reach out for him, but my breath hazed the glass, and it vanished.

"I don't feel anything," Sawyl said. "It's certainly

Ancestral glass, the construction I'd associate with toys—may I hold it?"

I let him take the device and watched him turn it over and over, the interior planes winking in and out of existence, as though they were sliding over and under and through each other, showing flashes of color at the points of intersection, and then dissolving into invisibility. The metallic strands coiled against them, peacock blue and gold and purple fading to silver.

"I've made a study of toys," Sawyl said, and set it down with visible reluctance, "but I've never seen anything like this."

"No more had I," Rejane interjected.

"Where—" Sawyl visibly rethought what he had been going to say. "Where did it come from, do you know?"

"As I said, I inherited it." I chose my words carefully. "My first captain never discussed how she'd gotten it. Her nephew dropped hints that she'd found it when she was in the navy, but I'm pretty sure that's not true. She'd never have been able to hide it on a government ship, and no one would have let her keep it. At one time, I thought it might have come from the Prater, but Rejane thinks not."

"I think if my family had ever had something like that, they would have made full use of it, or taken it apart if they couldn't find a use," Rejane said. "Not traded it to a starship captain."

I nodded. "When I took over, I tried to track the source, but I wasn't able to get very far. It first appeared in the ship's records after a trip from Elim to Discontent to Callambhal Above. It could have come from any of them. Or from the stop before Elim, but that was Tantacler."

Tantacler was a new world, settled after the Fall, with next to nothing in the way of Ancestral remains, but the others all had Great Remnants: the Great Works on Elim, the Moebial on Discontent, and the Inner Sun on Callambhal Above. "Tantacler seems unlikely," Sawyl agreed. "Though one never knows. Of the others—Elim has the widest range of artifacts, though this reminds me more of the Moebial."

"It does have that look," Rejane said. She put her own hand on the cool glass, and it was all I could do not to snatch the device away from her. "Fish, do you remember, the fragment Samarthen turned up there? The holos made it look a bit like this."

"A bit," Sawyl said. "I did get to examine it in person, briefly, and it didn't have the clarity of this piece—the matrix here is still absolutely transparent, and the colors are amazing. Samarthen's fragment looked like it was filled with fog. You could only see the colors in intermittent flashes."

"That could be damage," Rejane said. "And it never showed any affinity for the possible."

"True," Sawyl said. "Though that could also have been the result of damage. It was certainly only a small piece of a much larger artifact." He glanced at me, smiling. "Forgive us. We're easily distracted. You said this responds to the possible, and enables contact with AI?"

It was hard to stop myself from looking for recording devices, and there was still no way to answer without incriminating myself. "Yes."

"What can you tell me about the process?" Sawyl stroked the device gently, but without response.

"It activates on entering the possible," I said. "It's always been inert in the real. Not that I've ever tried to use it here. What is it that you want me to do with it?"

"The question is whether or not the Starwell is connected to the possible," Rejane said. "Or, rather, that whatever is under the water is connected to the possible. If your device reacts, that would tell us something we hadn't been able to determine."

"If there is a connection to the possible, what's stopping the AI from using it?" I didn't try to hide my alarm: this was the sort of thing that the Academy itself existed to prevent from happening, for fear of another Dark. "And if there's a potential connection, is it wise to wake it up?"

"Rejane overstates the case," Sawyl said. "We think the Starwell may once have had a connection to the possible, probably through an AI share, but there's clearly no AI present now. My hope is that your device might react to whatever's left of the system, or even cause the system to react to it. At the moment, it's completely inert. Any change would give us more information than we have now."

"It's not inert," Rejane said. "The stars come from somewhere."

"I can't risk damaging the device," I said, and both Sawyl and Rejane nodded.

"That's completely understood," Sawyl said. "I assure you, we'll take precautions."

"Could you be more precise?" I braced myself for anger but instead Sawyl laughed.

"For a start, we'll take things very slowly. My thought was to use the lift we've set up to observe the Starwell, and simply see if there is any reaction. Perhaps we'll go a short distance into the well, while being ready to reverse direction if there are any adverse changes."

"Which I doubt there will be," Rejane said, "but I agree, the more slowly we take things, the better for all of us."

I looked at the device. It seemed weirdly vulnerable, naked to the lights, the planes in its heart shifting as I moved. I would bring it in its case, I thought, and be ready to close the lid and seal it off at the slightest sign of trouble. "All right. When do you want to begin?"

"Tomorrow morning, if that's convenient," Sawyl said. He touched the device again. "Such a beautiful piece. I envy you."

I repressed the urge to tuck it back into its case immediately. "Thank you," I said, and they made their farewells.

I put my device back in its case and tucked it against the edge of my bed, where I could reach it easily. Then I spent the next hour searching the room for monitoring devices. I didn't find any, not even with the help of my burden, but the room's gracious fittings—display screens in each room, a communication console in the outer space—could certainly work both ways. I trusted Rejane, at least up to a point, and maybe trusted Sawyl a bit more, which was mildly surprising, but there was still no point in giving away anything more than I had to. I tucked myself into the extremely comfortable bed, and tried not to think about the Starwell.

冊 𝍢 ⚲

The next morning, I followed Rejane and Sawyl and a technician introduced as Pedr Ichellem across a stretch of open grassland toward the Starwell. On the edge of the grass, a dozen students had removed the turf and were digging a trench that seemed to follow the shape of an L-shaped wall; as we walked, I realized that the ground was less even than I'd realized, with more low humps marking where buildings once had been. The Academy had erected layers of protective fencing around the perimeter, one outside the three meter wide band of stone that was the top of the well, and another at the edge itself. Even so, it was intimidating to look through the metal mesh across the gap to the far wall, at the staircases crisscrossing their way down into shadow. I touched the case slung over my shoulder, reassuring myself that it was securely closed.

There were gates in the fencing at regular intervals, and a structure like a cargo crane stood on the edge opposite the sea, an open box waiting at its base. Sawyl ignored that, however; he led us instead to the nearest gate and waited while Ichellem entered a code. The gate slid back, a light flashed, and Sawyl said, "The Custodian and his guest." I felt something shiver beneath my skin, my burden reacting to the touch of local security, and the light went out. Sawyl looked at me. "I thought we'd begin by simply going down one flight of stairs."

"A5 has railings installed," Ichellem said. "And it's only twenty-five steps to the first landing."

"That's one of the ones with the honeycomb carvings?" Rejane asked. Ichellem nodded, already pushing buttons on the next gate. "There are five of them using that motif,"

Rejane said, "which ought to mean something. We just don't know what."

I couldn't help myself. "So there's no writing anywhere?"

"None." Rejane gave a crooked smile. "Not that it would necessarily be all that helpful. You remember what happened when they finally deciphered the script used on Callambhal Above."

That had been when we were still on Prater Daal, the summer of the burden transfer. We hadn't been allowed to leave the medical wing of the family compound, and had amused ourselves instead following the Academy study group on Callambhal Above. When the breakthrough was announced, we had held our breaths along with the rest of the Settled Worlds, only to share the wry amusement when the Ancestors' words were finally revealed. "*Caution: do not enter.*"

"*Protective gear required from this poin*t," Sawyl quoted. "*Slippery when wet.*"

"*Main control room* was somewhat useful," Ichellem said, mildly, and slid back the inner gate.

It was a single easy step down to a platform perhaps two meters square. To both right and left, steps led down into the well; a structure of light metal poles and netting protected the edge. Rejane walked out onto the platform without hesitation, took a step down the stairway to the left. Sawyl followed, and I came after him. The netting didn't look particularly sturdy, but I couldn't resist moving close enough to look down into the well. Most of the shaft lay in shadow, so that the interlacing stairs looked like lines carved in the stone, the paler platforms hardly distinguishable from the stairs. About a third of the way around the circle, and perhaps five meters down, a platform extended from the landing, supporting what looked like lights and a small generator, and a trio of Academicians were busy examining the wall behind them. I looked back at the wall here, and saw that it was carved in a delicate six-sided latticework, each joint embossed with what looked like a tiny eight-petaled rosette. Each of the cells was no bigger than my fist, and I wondered how they had been carved, and how many artisans and hours it had taken.

"Let's see if there's any reaction from the device," Sawyl said.

I opened the carrier, ready to close it up again if there was some unexpected response. We stood for a long moment, waiting, but nothing happened. "Should I take it out?"

"Go ahead," Sawyl said.

I cupped my hands around the device, keeping my burden curbed, and drew it out of the padding. The sunlight struck sparks in its depths, but I felt nothing, neither the weird sense of connection that I felt in the possible, nor the tingling presence of an AI. I turned to block the sunlight, and the sparks vanished. "Nothing."

"Interesting," Sawyl said. "All right, let's try again on the next landing."

We climbed down into the shadows, the netting wavering slightly as we passed. I hoped it was stronger than it looked. We stopped on the next platform, and I pulled out the device again, with even less result: we were below the sunlight, and we didn't even get its sparkle.

"One more," Rejane said, and we climbed down again. The netting ended here, the twin staircases dropped away unprotected, and I stayed well back from those edges as I took out the device.

"Still nothing."

"Are you sure?" Rejane asked. "What if you rouse it just a little?"

Let my burden interact with it, she meant. I hesitated, but couldn't think of a reason to refuse. I relaxed, releasing the curb, letting my burden flow back into the veins and capillaries of my hands and reach out through my pores. There was no reaction at first, but then a faint light flickered in the core of the device. I felt a tremor, a shiver like a breath of wind, and instinctively I pulled my burden back. The feeling vanished along with the light.

"That was something," Sawyl said.

"What did you feel?" Rejane looked as though she wanted

to take the device out of my hands, and I just managed to keep from hugging it defensively.

"Something definitely happened, I'm just not sure what. It was—" I shook my head, trying to fit sensations into words. "A little bit like its reaction to the possible? But not the same. Or it may not have been powerful enough."

"We need to go down further," Rejane said.

"We need to be sure we understand what just happened," Sawyl said, with a faint frown.

Rejane took a breath, visibly curbing her excitement. "Point. Yes."

"Especially if this parallels the device's reaction to the possible," Sawyl said. "We are not opening doors here."

"Dedalor forfend," Ichellem said under his breath, looking shocked.

Rejane said, "If that's what was happening, which I doubt. Nic?"

"I told you, it felt a little bit like the way the device reacts to being in the possible," I answered. "Not completely, and much weaker, and it stopped the minute I pulled back my burden. I'd be willing to try it again."

"Perhaps with more monitoring equipment?" Ichellem said.

"The existing monitors will record anything significant," Rejane said.

"See if Site Control picked up anything unusual," Sawyl said to Ichellem, who nodded and pulled out his handheld. Sawyl looked at me. "And nothing happened until you applied your burden?"

I nodded. "Just the lightest touch of it, too."

"If you held it longer," Rejane began, and trailed off at Sawyl's frown.

"Did you sense an AI?" he asked. "Or anything that you associate with AI, or even with hyperspatial weather?"

"No." I could answer that honestly, at least. "Nothing like that. I'd say it was like a draft, except that implies an opening somewhere. My sense was that the reaction came from the well, not the possible."

"Site Control says nothing registered on their instruments," Ichellem reported. "I've told them to keep a close eye on the boards for the next hour or so."

"Good." Sawyl's barbels curled, not quite a smile. "All right, Nic, let's try that again."

I took the device back out of the case and cupped it in my hands, letting my burden reach for it as I did so. For a moment, nothing happened, and then once again a light flickered in the center of the device. I kept my hands steady, and the light increased, the inner planes of the device shifting color as though they were sliding into new complex patterns. The threads of color faded, and I thought I heard the hint of a sound, one cool clear note like a plucked string very far away. I held my breath, but there was nothing more.

"Did you hear something?" Rejane asked.

"I thought—maybe?" I slid the device back into its case.

"I didn't," Sawyl said. "But there was definitely a visible reaction."

"Site Control says there was a half-point rise in the V-band emissions," Ichellem said. "That's the background hum. No change anywhere else."

"Interesting," Sawyl said.

"Academician Faress asks if it's something we're doing, and if we can do it again." Ichellem waited expectantly.

"Tell her yes," Sawyl said. "If you would, Nic."

I lifted the device again. The light appeared, the inner planes shifted, and I felt the distant sound. It faded, and there was nothing more. The light stayed steady, but I had no sense of connection; it was weirdly like calling into an empty room. "Shall I stop?"

"You can, yes." Sawyl looked at Ichellem. "Anything?"

"The same result," Ichellem answered. "The background hum increased, and then receded. No other changes."

"We'll need to take it further down," Rejane said. "But first—I wonder if a different burden makes any difference? Nic, would you let me hold it?"

I wasn't at all sure that was safe, but Sawyl nodded. "Yes, let's try that. You first, Rejane, and then Pedr. And then I'd like to try."

Reluctantly, I let Rejane take the device. It lit for her, pretty much as it had done for me, but did nothing further. It lit for Ichellem as well, though the light was fainter and wavered, and I didn't hear the sound; for Sawyl it fluttered oddly, then settled. Site Control reported the same reactions each time.

"Whereas we see slightly different responses," Sawyl said. "Very interesting."

"We have to take it further down," Rejane said. "Come on, Fish, you know that's the only next step."

"Tell Site Control to clear the well," Sawyl said. "Then have them get the crane ready for a descent."

By the time we'd made our way back up the stairs, the last of the other groups were climbing out of the well, and the cargo crane was rumbling into motion. Several technicians were examining the linkages that chained the car to the crane, and one of them broke away to meet us. "Everything's in order, Custodian. Academician Faress says she's queued up the secondary recorders as well. She asked what was causing these effects, and I had to tell her I didn't know."

"I'll give her all the details after we complete the experiment," Sawyl said. "Pedr, stay up here and monitor the crane yourself. Oh, and tell Jemme that we're testing an Ancestral device that seems to interact with the well."

Ichellem didn't look particularly happy at that, and I could hardly blame him. Sawyl was rushing things, surely. I'd expect that of Rejane, but not of a Custodian, especially when it involved more and more people. I edged closer to Rejane. "What happens if this does do something to the well?"

"We do more experiments."

"With *my* device." I controlled my voice with an effort. "I'm not giving it up."

"You won't have to," Rejane said. "Fish has you under contract, that will take care of it."

"I'm not sure it will," I began, and Rejane waved me to silence.

"Don't worry. It's all under control."

I had my doubts about that, but there was no time to protest. Sawyl waved us toward the door of the car, and we climbed aboard. Ichellem handed each of us a gravity belt, and I strapped mine on, checking to be sure the telltales all showed green and the power pack was full. The car itself was surprisingly spacious, even with three of the four sides filled with sensor stations as well as padded benches. The center of the floor was transparent, an open square a little more than a meter on each side. At the moment, I could see only the purple-gray stone of the walls, but realized it must be for studying the star patterns. I looked up, and saw lenses studding the roof, as well as a bright red handle hanging from the center of the roof.

Rejane said, "Quick safety briefing. We're on mic at all times; if anyone has doubts or if no one responds to check-ins, the crane will haul us up immediately. You have your grav belt. That's for escape if the crane has a mechanical failure. The cables are orbit-rated and quintuply redundant, but if they should break, the red handle in the ceiling deploys a parachute and airbags."

I eyed the handle with some doubt, but nodded. "All right."

"We're ready," Sawyl said, and latched the door behind us. The car swayed slightly, lifted and began to move along the crane's arm. We passed the lip of the well and moved out into the center. Through the glass of the floor, the water looked very far below. I squinted, but couldn't yet make out a starscape. "Take us down to twelve meters to start."

"Twelve meters." The technician's voice crackled in the speakers. "And hold."

The machinery made very little noise as we sank into the shadows, the carved walls and the network of stairs rising around us. At twelve meters, the car stopped, and Sawyl and Rejane moved from console to console, making sure all the systems were running. I looked down again, and this time I could see stars reflected in the mirror-still water nearly thirty meters below us. I didn't know Valenguar's skies well enough to recognize that this was not their view—well, except for the Gap that slashed across the southern sky about thirty degrees above the horizon. I'd seen the Gap on many other worlds, and Valenguar's view was not the most impressive. However, its absence was obvious in the image below, and weirdly unsettling.

"Fifteen meters, please," Sawyl said, and the car whirred into life again.

"Holding at fifteen meters," the technician said.

"If you would, Nic?" Sawyl said.

"All right." I couldn't bring myself to step on the glass flooring, though I knew it had to be more than strong enough to hold my weight. Instead, I edged around the side of the car and seated myself on the nearest bench, keeping the case in my lap. If anything went wrong, I wanted to be able to contain the device as quickly as possible. I brought it out, letting my hands slide into the most comfortable curves, and watched the light flare at the core. It was brighter this time, and the inner planes moved more quickly, throwing off shards of reflected light. In the relative dimness of the car, they seemed very bright. I heard the sound of the plucked string, and then nothing. Once again, I had the sense that the device was reaching to the well, and finding nothing there.

"Anything?" Rejane said, to the ceiling, and Ichellem answered.

"Site Control says the background hum increased again, but faded."

We tried it again at twenty meters, and at twenty-five. Each time the light was brighter, the sound a little louder, and Site Control reported a corresponding increase in the background noise. I still felt as though I was talking to an empty room.

"Thirty meters," Sawyl said, and the car slid slowly downward and came to a stop. "Go ahead, Nic."

I cupped my hands around the device and let my burden taste it once again. The light appeared, the inner planes slid and reformed—and this time the threads of metallic color blazed brighter than I'd ever seen them, swirling around the central light. The sound came again, not a plucked string this time, but a sustained note, a bowed string that swelled like indrawn breath. Below us, through the glass, I could see the water heave, as though something had fallen into it—or was rising from beneath. Concentric waves spread from the center and slammed against the walls, then reflected back into the center, the starfield vanishing in the sudden chop.

I slammed the device back into its case and closed the lid, but the waves didn't stop. The technician and Ichellem were both shouting in the speakers, but I couldn't make out their words over the heavy droning note. Light flashed beneath the water, a pinpoint star that disappeared an instant later, and then reappeared as a sudden ring of light, blue-white and blinding. It rose out of the water, rushing up the walls toward us. I ducked, wrapping myself around the cased device as though that would help, and the light flashed over and past us, fading as it went further up the walls. It topped the well as a ring like smoke and winked out of existence. The sound ended with it, and we all stood frozen. I could feel myself shaking.

"Well," Rejane said, and her voice cracked on the word.

"Pedr!" Sawyl turned his attention to the communication console. "We're all right here, no damage, everyone's fine. What happened up top?"

"We're fine, too," Ichellem answered. "We saw—we heard that sound, and then a ring of light moved up the well. It dissipated when it reached the top. Site Control says they have maximal data, so please don't do it again."

Sawyl laughed. "No. I think we're done for the day. Bring us up, please."

"That was a lot more than I was expecting," Rejane said.

I thought maybe she meant it as an apology, but it wasn't nearly enough. There was no hiding this, no pretending something else had set it off. They were going to seize my device, and I couldn't see a way to stop them.

Chapter Six

A horde of technicians and Academicians were waiting when we finally reached the top of the well, and as the car slid back toward the landing site on the wall, I could see still more coming to join them. Sawyl's attention was still on the consoles, while Rejane was remarkably silent. I closed the case around my device, and slung the strap over my shoulder so that it rested on my opposite hip: I was not letting it be taken from me without protest. The car touched down, surprisingly gently, and Ichellem opened the door.

"You are all unharmed," he said. "Did anyone experience any physical effects?"

Several more Academicians crowded up behind him, calling out questions of their own, and Sawyl lifted his hands. "Quiet, please! We have experienced a remarkable breakthrough, but there are protocols to follow. Pedr, you said we have maximal results?"

"That's correct." Ichellem nodded.

"Excellent," Sawyl said. "Download the data from the car as well. For the rest of you, I want a written report of everything you saw—everything you experienced, no matter how trivial or unrelated it may seem. I want you to do that now, while everything is fresh in memory, and I want you to do it without consulting each other. There will be time for that later." He paused, and an enormous grin spread across his broad face. "This is the most significant thing to happen here at the Starwell in three generations, and I'm proud of all of you for the work you've done to get us to this point.

Let's make sure we get the most out of this, in case it proves impossible to repeat."

That won a ragged cheer, the technicians clasping hands and slapping each other's shoulders. If they'd been waiting nearly a century for something new, I supposed I couldn't blame them, but I wished that it hadn't been my device that had sparked it.

"Site Control, please continue monitoring," Sawyl said. "Inform me at once if there's any more activity. Everyone not directly involved in that process, I want you working on your reports. I want them by noon tomorrow, and sooner if possible." He stepped out of the car, the crowd parting before him. Rejane put her hand on my shoulder and pushed me after him. I followed them through the crowd and back to the Academy buildings, where a steward was waiting with a buzzing handheld.

"Custodian, there are messages from Tamarak and Junewatch, as well as from the RebIC station, all wanting to know what just happened. I've also received a standby notice via RebIC that Ankes-and-Irthe is seeking contact."

"Of course they are," Rejane said unhappily.

Sawyl said, "Tell everyone that we've experienced a possible breakthrough at the Starwell—that we managed to provoke a benign response from the system—and that we've shut everything down again to examine the collected data. You may tell them off the record that I am extremely excited, but haven't given you any details. We'll release a more detailed statement this afternoon once we've reviewed the preliminary data."

"Very good, Wisdom." The steward bowed and retreated, his handheld still pulsing.

"I didn't know it would do that," Rejane said.

"You'd better not." Sawyl's barbels curled slightly. "Rejane, I was expecting a minor reaction, some increase in activity, maybe a shift in the starfield, not something like this. We can't hide this."

"I know." Rejane wound her hands together, then realized what she was doing and made herself relax.

You can't have my device. I swallowed the words, both because I didn't want to remind them that they could, in fact, take it, and because I didn't want to hear Rejane lie.

"Take Nic back to your offices," Sawyl said. "I want a report from both of you."

"The device?" Rejane asked.

"Deal with it as best you can," Sawyl answered. "Let's be discreet, for a start."

That was somewhat reassuring: he would have been within his rights to demand I turn it over immediately. Rejane nodded. "The call from Ankes-and-Irthe—that'll be Larel."

"Oh, no." Sawyl shook his head. "They'll start with Magarian, she's unimpeachable, and that will buy us a little time. Make the most of it, Rejane, it's all I can give you."

"Understood." She drew a deep breath, and turned to me. "Come on. We need to debrief."

I followed her through the maze of halls toward the rooms she had been given. People stopped us every few meters, and Rejane gave them the same answers Sawyl had done—*a benign response from the Starwell, busy analyzing the data, more to follow.* One or two she told to write down what they'd seen or felt and to send it to her so she could forward it to Sawyl. We finally reached her door, and Rejane motioned me inside. She locked the door behind us and looked around for the household combot. "Do Not Disturb, Class Two. The Custodian has top priority."

"Understood." The combot's voice was female, but flat and unimproved. "You have four urgent contacts, two from the Academy and two from local media."

"Academy contacts to my handheld, ignore the local media."

"Understood."

Rejane fished out her handheld and flipped through screens, her mouth twisting as though she tasted something sour. I said, "I'm not giving up my device."

She looked up quickly. "No one's asking you to, I promise. Neither of us thought this would happen—"

"Do you know what happened?"

"Not entirely."

"That means you have no idea."

"Not as bad as that." She managed a fleeting smile. "The Starwell responded to a combination of your device and your burden. What that response was meant to do, or meant to be, is unclear. Hopefully the data will show if there are any permanent effects."

"That's still not saying much. And I will not give up the device."

"I'm not asking you to," Rejane said again. "Fish isn't asking you to. You heard him, he told me to be discreet."

"Rejane, I'm not ignorant. The first thing you'll be asked is to duplicate the event."

"Once it's safe enough," she said quickly. "If it's safe enough."

"The rest of the Academy is just as reckless as you are!"

"But it buys us time."

I took a deep breath, fighting back my own anger. Haliday had warned me; I should have listened. I should have known better. "That's not an answer."

She paused. "No. I'm sorry." That was unusual enough to strike me silent. "You heard Fish. We're going to play down the device as much as possible—"

"Everyone saw it," I said.

"No." She shook her head. "They saw us take *a* device into the well. I have a toy that looks very similar to your device, we can say it's the device we used and we can't get it to work again. That happens often enough to be believable."

"Will Fish agree to that?" I asked.

"Yes." She nodded firmly, and I wondered if she was trying to convince herself. "And anyway, we have some time to figure out a better answer if we can. Now, though, we need to write up our reports."

"How are you going to explain that I was holding the device?"

"You have a Firstborn burden, and you're an experienced

star pilot—a star pilot with experience with Ancestral devices," Rejane answered. "We all took turns holding the device. It triggered for you, but we don't know if that was coincidence or something to do with your burden. That has the merit of being true."

"If you say so." I seated myself at one end of the worktable and drew out my handheld, unfolding it to its widest extent, and the device pinged.

"Me," Rejane said, in the same moment. "I thought you might find our standard form helpful."

I started to say that I knew perfectly well how to write an Academy report, then realized that was probably something I didn't want to share. I opened the file instead, and began entering the answers to its questions, doing my best to balance accuracy against the need to keep the device safe. It would be a disaster to lose the thing that allowed *Beljaeger* to compete against bigger, richer ships; I would also, I admitted, regret losing the connection with Beast. Terrifying Beast might be at times, but as genuinely dangerous as it was, it was also uniquely fascinating, and I would hate to lose all contact.

I finished my report, and Rejane called an understeward to escort me back to my rooms. He visibly wanted to ask questions, but was too well-trained to do it; I kept my eyes averted, and once I was in, locked the door behind me. There was a note from Sawyl, asking me to join him and Rejane and various other Academicians for a debriefing session at 1600, but nothing more. I sent my acceptance, and turned on the news channel. Unsurprisingly, it was reporting an "incident" at the Starwell, but the coverage seemed focused on reassuring locals that nothing more was expected to happen. Someone had had a drone up and facing in the right direction to catch a faint hazy flash from the headland, but it was too far away to see more than the flicker of light. Sawyl was promising a press release later in the day once the data had been reviewed, but sources not authorized to speak for the record said that the Custodian seemed extremely pleased. Sawyl's steward had done his job well.

Once the stories began to repeat, I turned down the volume and dug out my other handheld. This one was a military piece, with military-grade encryption and a zone-of-silence privacy field, and I activated both before I punched in Haliday's codes. She answered so quickly it was obvious she had been waiting for my call.

"Are you all right?"

"I'm fine. Nothing really happened, just a bit of a light show."

"Was it the device?"

"I'm afraid so."

"It's all over the news." That was as close as Haliday was going to let herself get to saying *I told you so*. "Can you get back here? I can get us a lift window, they haven't locked us down."

I was definitely tempted. Take the device and walk out of my pleasant room, get into the rented flyer and head for Tamarak: if I left now, I could be at the port and preparing for liftoff before they even knew I was gone. Except that Rejane, at least, would expect me to try it, and I was willing to bet that the flyer was under surveillance. "I don't know. I'm expected to attend a debriefing—"

"Don't."

"Hal, if I try to run now, it looks bad. I'd like to get out of this without having to come up with entirely new registration and IDs."

"I don't think that's real likely." She paused. "We are fucked, Nic."

"Not yet. Fish—the Custodian is on our side, and so's Rejane, of course—"

"Like that's going to help."

I ignored her. "They've said they'll help me keep the device. I think they even mean it."

"Leave it," Haliday said. "I know, you'd rather not. I'd rather you didn't have to, but it's better than sticking around to answer too many questions. Give Rejane the damn thing and let's get out of here."

Never. I swallowed the word. "Not yet. Just stay calm, and stay ready. We'll run if we have to."

"This is incredibly stupid."

I heard my voice harden. "It's my call."

There was a little silence, and then she sighed. "All right. I'll stand by. Just be careful."

"Of course," I said, and ended the call.

We gathered in one of the larger conference rooms at 1600, where the windows gave on an impressive view of the Starwell. Sawyl and Rejane were already there, along with Ichellem and a handful of other Academicians, including a gray-haired woman in mech-tech coveralls who was introduced as Academician Faress of Site Control. She carried a tall cylinder of some stimulant drink, and had already set up a holo-display that showed a model of the Starwell and what seemed to be a section of the ground around it.

"I have the preliminary model of the event," she said, "and it's fascinating. Here's the situation five seconds before the event, and it's pretty much the way the well has always been. There's been some elevation of the background hum, but we've seen that before, though we've never been able to correlate it to an actual action. Now the event begins."

Somewhere below the base of the model, a light flashed, and I remembered the star-like point I'd seen in the center of the well. More lights appeared, not in the well itself, but in the ground around it, where I remembered Rejane had said there were tunnels. The light spread into them, they pulsed, and the ring of light appeared in the well itself. It climbed the surface, up the lattice of stairs and landings, fading as it went, and vanished as it topped the wall.

"This," Faress said, "is the best image we've ever had of the tunnel system, and in fact we've filled in some new connections. I think we can say that they're part of whatever powered the well."

"Oh, very interesting," someone said, and another voice broke in.

"Can we repeat the experiment?"

Sawyl looked at Faress. "Jemme?"

She hesitated. "I'd like to finish going through the data first. This is very, very early, and I can't promise there isn't something going on under the surface that we would need to be cautious about."

"But there's no sign of AI interference," the first voice said, and Faress nodded.

"No, none. And no hint that we touched the possible. But since it still seems likely that the Starwell was built to access the possible—"

Several people interrupted her, disagreeing with the statement and with each other, and I leaned back in my chair, hoping to be ignored. That was a vain hope. Sawyl waved me forward.

"This is Nic en Doroney, who was holding the device when the event occurred."

"I'd like to know considerably more about this device," Faress said.

Sawyl hesitated, and Rejane stepped into the gap. "So would we all. We're in the process of examining it more closely."

"Where did it come from?" another technician asked. "And why haven't we heard more about it?"

"We didn't expect any particular response," Sawyl said. "We're still not sure whether it was the device or Nic that sparked this."

That was strictly true, and more of a deflection than I had expected from him. "But where did it come from?" the technician said again, and Rejane leaned forward.

"I bought it on Adora. The stated provenance is doubtful, and I'd hoped to investigate that more closely."

'Doubtful provenance' was entirely too common when it came to Ancestral devices, but there was still a murmur of disappointment. "We'll find out what we can," Sawyl said. "In the meantime, Nic, please share your experience."

I repeated what I'd put in my report, then went through each piece of it in greater detail as the Academicians came up with more questions. I did my best to give them the answers they needed without getting into too much detail about the device—*It seemed to work best with her burden*, Rejane interjected, *so we had her handle it*, which was true as far as it went—and told them once again that I didn't feel as though there was anything there.

"But the Starwell responded," someone said, and Faress frowned.

"When you say it felt empty, Captain en Doroney, what exactly did you mean?"

If I could tell you exactly, I'd have a better explanation. I said, "I'm a pilot as well as a ship's master. I've spent most of my working life traveling the possible. I'm sure of two things. First, we didn't touch the possible. I absolutely would have known that. Second…on a good run, where there's no weather, no hint of AI presence, the possible feels empty. There's nothing there, nothing answering when you cast sensors or pass through a waypoint. That's what this felt like. I think I tripped some kind of automatic response, not a working system."

"Can you be any more specific?" Faress asked.

"I—it felt like shouting in an empty room. Like everything was muffled." I spread my hands. "I can keep giving you metaphors, but I don't know if that would help."

"No, it's useful," Faress said. "Thank you."

"But if there's nothing there, why did it respond?" someone asked, and another voice added, "For that matter, how?"

They were off again, circling the topic and the model on the table, but getting no closer to anything like an answer. The data was still being analyzed, they were still formulating questions, and finally Sawyl pulled them gently to a halt. "I know we have project analyses that will run overnight, and those and this discussion will raise further questions. We'll break now so that you can spend some time prioritizing your lines of inquiry, and reconvene tomorrow morning."

It took some time for all of them to leave, but finally the door closed behind the last of them, and Sawyl leaned heavily on the table. "Well. I could stand a drink after all of that. Will you join us, Nic?"

Rejane flicked off the holo-display and pocketed the data button. "Yes, do."

"We have a lot to talk about," I said, and Sawyl sighed.

"I realize you're in an awkward position—so are we all. But let's discuss it in more privacy."

We returned to the room where I had first met Sawyl, the long windows now shuttered against the deepening twilight. I hadn't realized how long we had been talking. A drinks cart was waiting, along with a tray of savories, and Rejane played bartender, pouring for each of us. I accepted my glass—she had remembered my favorite, sharp and cold and touched with the bitter liquor distilled from cavas fruit—and settled myself on the nearest couch, sipping cautiously at my drink. Sawyl flicked on the fountains and stood for a long moment in their mist, long enough that Rejane brought his drink to him and waited while he tossed it back. She made another, handed it to him when he came to join us. "About your device," she began, and Sawyl shook his head.

"Such an awkward position. I didn't think the well would respond, and certainly not like that."

"They're going to ask to see the device," Rejane said. "I have one that will pass—it's very similar, both externally and internally—and we can show them that."

"And waste my people's time and energy on something that we know doesn't work," Sawyl said.

I am not giving you my device. I swallowed the words again, knowing Rejane would make a better case for me than I could on my own.

"And have it taken away as too dangerous to examine, if you show it to Larel," Rejane said. "We'll never get to examine it further if that happens."

"I know." Sawyl lifted his drink, set it down, and reached

for a pastry instead. "I do know. But lying to the Academy—"

"Lying to Larel isn't the same thing," Rejane said. "And—we need to protect Nic, too."

"Yes." Sawyl nodded. "Though I suspect Nic is capable of protecting herself."

"It would be much easier with your help," I said, and won a fleeting smile.

"So we substitute this other device," Sawyl said. "We say it's the one that caused the event, and we have no idea why it won't do it a second time. Assuming, of course, that there is no further reaction. Once the system is sensitized—but we can discuss that later."

"It's simple and straightforward," Rejane said. "It means only the three of us know it's a different device."

"And Pedr," Sawyl said. "Not that he'd say anything."

"And even he can't be sure," Rejane said. "He only handled it the once, and I promise you, the device I have in mind looks very similar. It will pass, Fish."

"It had better. If this gets out—" He stopped, shaking his head. "Well. The consequences will be severe. As you very well know."

"I know what I'm risking," Rejane said. "I'm just sorry I got you into this."

"It was worth it," Sawyl said. "To see the well respond! I've waited most of my life for that."

"And at some point," Rejane said, "when all this has died down, we can try again."

"If Nic is willing," Sawyl said.

"I'm sure she will be," Rejane said, with emphasis.

I checked my first answer, making myself hesitate as though I was really considering my options. "Yes. If it can be managed safely—yes."

"You're curious too," Sawyl said, and there was enough truth in it that I could easily agree.

"I am. So—what did happen, do you know?"

"I have theories," Sawyl said. "And I'm sure Rejane does, too."

Rejane produced the data button, and inserted it into the nearest player. The model reappeared, rotating slowly, and she waved her hand at it to stop the motion. "I think it was trying to start up. Whatever it does."

"What intrigues me most," Sawyl said, "is the tunnels. Jemme is right, there are some new connections here." He gestured at the image, turning and enlarging it so that he could point to the narrow threads that ran between the web of thicker lines. "That suggests that the tunnels aren't just for replenishing the water in the well, but have something to do with the way the system functions. Couple that with the suggestion that the event was initiated somewhere below the lowest levels of the well, and that adds weight to the theory that the Starwell drew power from the planetary core."

I couldn't stop myself. "I thought core taps were wildly unstable."

"They are," Rejane said. "At least, every way we've figured out to do it. Presumably the Ancestors had better methods."

"And if we could unravel their technique," Sawyl said. "Well, you can imagine how useful that would be."

I could, though I had my doubts about our ability to figure out any Ancestral system. We'd been trying for centuries—since we'd first crept back out of the Dark—to unlock the Ancestors' secrets, and most of what we'd achieved were clumsy work-arounds. Even our burdens, the foundation of most higher technology, were imperfect copies at best: even NoviCor couldn't create new nanites, but had to copy them, breed them, from an existing source.

"It's a risk," Rejane said, "but there are ways to explore it safely, I think. Beginning by tracing the tunnels to see if any of them go deeper into the planetary mantle."

"We'll definitely send in micro-drones," Sawyl said, turning the model thoughtfully, "but the tunnels seem to all be within a plane. If anything reaches the core, I think it's the main body of the well."

"Certainly possible," Rejane answered. "And then there's the question of whether it needs an AI—or an AI share—to function properly."

"That would make sense to me," I said. "It would explain the null spot, the emptiness when I tried to touch it."

"And why the response was so limited," Sawyl said. "Without an AI share, the connection can't be completed, and the Starwell can't function."

"If that's the case," Rejane said, "we're better off keeping it quiet until Larel has been and gone."

"Who or what is Larel?" I asked, and Sawyl made a gesture that was almost propitiating.

"She is a Senior Custodian, though she doesn't have a particular Remnant in her keeping. She's a Newfounder, and has been heard to express the thought that all surviving Remnants should be deactivated."

"Or destroyed," Rejane said darkly. She forced a smile. "Needless to say, Fish and I don't agree."

"She has considerable power among the more conservative branches of the Academy," Sawyl said. "Be sure you keep your device well-hidden while she's here."

"I will," I said.

Rejane said, "Are you sure they won't send Magarian? It just seems like they're escalating quickly."

"It's confirmed," Sawyl said. "We've been told Larel should arrive in three or four days."

"So she's coming by the fastest route," Rejane said. "A tad hypocritical, surely."

"We will not raise that point," Sawyl said firmly. "We will show her the Starwell and all the data, let her make what she will of it, and hope she goes away."

Interlude 3

Kuffrin was now First among the Firstborn, and they and the Secondborn prospered and brought into being the Faciendi, and so humankind spread further, leaping from system to system with the help of the Great AI and the lesser siblings. But Kuffrin feared that she would leave no lasting mark, nor anyone who truly understood her worth, and resolved that she would have children to help complete and to comprehend what she had done. But she would have only sons and no daughters, for fear that a daughter would surpass her as she had surpassed her father. So she solicited genetic material from across known space, testing some as simple sperm and some as the people who carried it. From them, she chose five fathers, and by them she had five sons.

From the Dedalor Apocrypha, *Vol. 5*

Chapter Seven

Somewhat to my surprise, Sawyl was as good as his word, leaving me to conceal the device in my own rooms. I had expected an offer to put it into the compound's strongboxes, or to place it somewhere else "safe" that was also under his control, but he seemed willing to let me handle it myself. Of course, that meant that if this Larel caught me with it, it would be entirely my responsibility, but that was better than letting it out of my control. I resolved that I would try to find a way to take it back to the ship, and avoided calling Haliday again.

Rejane successfully substituted her device, turning it over to Faress for further examination. It remained inert when I handled it, and I spent the next few days dutifully following orders in various different laboratory suites. I had my meals with Rejane and sometimes with Sawyl, or in the hall, and listened to the endless speculation. The consensus seemed to be that somehow the device had prompted the Starwell to start up; but why it had failed, and what it would have done if it had succeeded, was the subject of increasingly unlikely speculation. Rejane held to the idea that it needed an AI share, and that it was part of some kind of transport network, but her experiments had no more result that anyone else's. I thought she might be right about it needing an AI share—that would explain why my device had interacted with the system, and why it had failed to go further—but I was less sure about it being a transport system. Sawyl doubted the AI connection, but thought a transport system made some sense. For almost thirty hours, it seemed possible that the starscape reflected in the well had changed by millimeters, which gave impetus to the idea, but a closer look erased the change.

And then, on the fifth day, the Senior Custodian arrived. She came in a ship that was registered to the Academy and crewed by Ahmesti mercenaries; it carried cannon and some of the Ahmesti were cross-trained as soldiers. Sawyl's people saw that as an insult, unsurprisingly, but he managed to talk them into at least the appearance of cooperation. Larel arrived in a convoy of four flyers, and Sawyl turned his household out for a formal greeting. All the Academicians were in their formal gowns, sweeping ankle-length coats of gray or blue depending on their discipline, with badges and hoods for the specialists, and even the students who had not yet earned the right to a long gown wore formal knee-length brown coats over their best clothes. Sawyl and Rejane were in their full regalia, Sawyl in purple and gold with a gold diadem over his purple skullcap, and Rejane in the black-over-white she had worn when I first met Sawyl. The hem of her overgown was stiff with silver embroidery, and her silver headdress was a sharp contrast to her scarlet hair. They waited at the head of the courtyard where the flyers landed, with the senior Academicians arrayed behind them, and the juniors lined up along the edges.

I had been relegated to a place with the rest of the household, watching from the terrace on the roof of the kitchens that ran along one side of the courtyard. Endolian and the children were at the center of the group, Endolian with his hands tight on the shoulders of the girl, and a uniformed nanny watching the boy, and they were flanked by other families, and then by the non-academic staff. I had been placed on the ambiguous edge between the two groups, neither family nor employee, though Endolian had managed to wave a greeting as we passed each other. We would not meet the Senior Custodian now, that would come later, but it had been made very clear that she expected the full formal welcome.

The flyers dropped neatly into the courtyard, the Ahmesti mercenaries hopping out to open doors and provide flanking escort, and the Senior Custodian emerged from the flyer. Her robes were more impressive than she was, deep crimson banded in white and gold, with a stiff cap badged with gold and dark red gems that caught the light. She herself was short and stocky, and the hair that fell in a long braid down her back had faded to a dulled gray. She carried herself with authority, however, and the black-clad aides who followed her were visibly attentive. Sawyl came forward to meet her, holding out both hands, and I wondered if I imagined the momentary hesitation before she accepted the clasp of greeting. Perhaps not: I caught a glimpse of Endolian's frown before he hastily smoothed his expression.

Sawyl dipped his head, releasing her hands, and gestured to Rejane and the others. "We welcome you, Senior Custodian, to Valenguar and the Starwell."

That was our cue. All around me, people began to clap and cheer, and there were shrill whistles from the juniors. Larel basked for a moment in the sound, then lifted one hand. "Thank you, Custodian. I'm pleased to receive so warm a welcome, and I look forward to working with you to examine this…most unusual phenomenon." That was our cue for another round of applause, but Larel lifted her hand again. "I hope to receive everyone's full cooperation as we conduct our interviews and examine the data and I thank you in advance for your willingness to help."

The applause was noticeably less enthusiastic this time, and the woman next to me said, "Does she really think this is an interrogation?"

Sawyl bent his head again. "I am certain that you will receive full cooperation, Senior Custodian. I for one look forward to discussing these exciting developments." Larel said something that was not amplified, and he bent his head again and led her inside.

Rejane had made it clear that I was expected at dinner—*It would be suspicious if you weren't there*, she had said—so I put on my indigo suit and the best jewelry I owned, and added a touch of glitter to the kohl around my eyes. I was studying my image in the mirror, trying to decide if it was too much, when my handheld displayed Haliday's signature. I switched on my personal security and answered, only to have her cut me off.

"Have you been following the news?"

"I haven't had the chance," I said, and added, with what I hoped was extra meaning, "The Senior Custodian arrived this afternoon."

"With escort," Haliday said. "Any chance you can slide out of there? The news is saying that she's come to reprimand the Custodian here."

"So far I haven't seen any sign of that," I said, carefully, and Haliday interrupted.

"Local news says the ship is armed, and she's brought marines. They are also reporting that she's sent investigators into Junewatch to get a civilian perspective on the event. In the port, they're saying she has a Writ of Authority to depose the Custodian and take over herself."

I made myself stay calm. "Was that on the news?"

"No. Just talk." Haliday paused. "What the news is saying is that she's a leading member of the Newfounder faction, and one of their most respected Academicians."

"Shit." That came as close to confirming the potential conflict as a responsible news company was likely to get.

"Some things have come up," Haliday said. "I'm concerned about the ship. I'd be happier if you were here."

"I'm due at the formal dinner in about fifteen minutes," I said. "I can't get away tonight, but I'll try to get there in the morning. I'm expected to have an interview with the Senior Custodian, though."

"I'm not sure—" Haliday began and I broke in.

"I'm not sure when I'm scheduled for, but I'll let you know. And now I've got to go."

I cut the connection without waiting for her answer, and took another look at my reflection. At least I looked more composed than I felt. I needed to find Rejane. She would know some of it, of course, but the port gossip and the investigators in Junewatch might not have reached her yet. I pinged the house system, asking for a word with Rejane, and a moment later a guide dot appeared on the screen along with the briefest of messages: *Meet me.*

I followed the dot through a maze of back corridors, trying to look as though I was on important business, and it brought me at last to an alcove by the halls that led to the lecture rooms. Rejane was there ahead of me, still in full regalia, and she wore an enormous ring that glittered red and green where Ancestral elements had been inlaid into the golden surface. She caught me by the sleeve and tugged me into the alcove's shadows. "Is it important?"

"I spoke to Hal. She says the news reports Larel has sent investigators into Junewatch."

Rejane nodded. "I'd heard that."

"Also, port gossip says she has a Writ of Authority and is planning to depose Fish."

"I had not heard that." Rejane paused, then reached for her handheld, fumbling it out from under her skirts. "It's—not impossible." She entered something, then slid it away again. "I've let Fish know, so he'll be careful. This…it's almost as though she was waiting for something like this to happen so that she could swoop in and take over. I'd like—I wish there were some way to keep you away from her."

"Hal's offered to set up a problem with the ship," I said, "but that's only temporary."

"I was thinking more about some urgent off-world message," Rejane said, "but if there's any chance that she actually does have a Writ—I don't want to give her any excuse to use it."

"What exactly is this Writ?"

"It gives her the right to exert absolute authority over the specified area, and to take whatever measure she deems necessary to restore order and remove danger. It's temporary, of course, and there are rights of appeal, but Ankes-and-Irthe doesn't generally issue them unless they think something has gone seriously wrong." She shook her head. "And there hasn't been and shouldn't be anything that bad here, unless I've totally missed something."

"So what do we do now?" I asked. I'd expected Rejane to wave away my news, not to take it seriously, and it took an effort to keep my voice under control.

"What we were planning, only more so." Rejane gave me a wry smile. "For which I apologize in advance. I'm going to downplay your involvement as much as I can, tell her I brought you in only because I was looking for as many different burdens as I could find. Which means she'll want a sample, but I know you can deal with that."

I nodded. That was a skill I'd perfected early on, the ability to release only a carefully-curated sample to any tester. "Yes."

"I'm sorry." She shook her head. "I didn't think this would become quite so complicated."

I couldn't help myself. "What did you think would happen?"

"I hoped to get a better idea of whether or not the Starwell needed an AI share." She sighed. "Maybe even if it still had a fragment of one—they exist, you know, bits and pieces barely complex enough to count as AI, just ghosts, the tiniest shadows of what they once were." She glanced at her handheld. "But that's something I can't even think about right now. We need to get to this dinner."

ᚠ ⵣ ♇

We parted well before the entrance to the dining hall. I watched her straighten her spine, putting on the persona of a Senior Academician as though putting on her robes, and then I presented my handheld to the nearest steward and was directed to my table. I recognized two of the technicians from the meeting immediately after the event, but our acknowledgments were constrained by the fourth person already seated. He was medium-sized and sharp-featured under his unflattering black cap, and I didn't need the badges on the breast of his gown to know that he was one of the Senior Custodian's people. At his inquiring glance, the junior technicians made the introductions: he was Academy Investigator Catrill, and the hand he put out in greeting was firm and smooth.

"Captain en Doroney."

"Investigator." I seated myself, and nodded to the steward hovering with the wine pitcher. "Please forgive me if I'm not very familiar with Academic rankings, I'd hate to offend with the wrong form of address."

"No, Investigator is correct," Catrill answered. I noted that he didn't ask any of us to call him by his name. The technicians were both looking subdued, and the Academicians who took the last two seats didn't look any less wary. "I understand you were actually present when the event occurred, Captain?"

"I was." For a moment, I considered not mentioning that I had been holding the device, but an innocent person would probably still be eager to talk about it. "In fact, I was the person who was holding it."

"Indeed." His sudden interest would have been gratifying in other circumstances. "How did that happen?"

"We were taking turns," I answered. "Exactly why it went off for me—no one's really had an answer yet, except that maybe it had something to do with my burden."

"That seems possible," one of the technicians said.

"It was, by all accounts, a very impressive display," Catrill suggested.

"I wrote up a report right after it happened," I said. "But, yes, it was—almost overwhelming, to be honest. There were lights and a sort of a sound—I'd never imagined anything like it."

"It's unusual for any Remnant to read so strongly to any stimulus," a second technician said.

Catrill ignored him. "Tell me, did it bear any similarity to passing through the possible? To an encounter with AI?"

"Definitely not that," I said. "Not AI, I mean. And definitely not like the possible, either. It was—as I said, I've never experienced anything like it."

"The Senior Custodian will look forward to speaking with you," Catrill said.

"I'm delighted to be of assistance."

Mercifully, a chord sounded from the end of the hall, and we all turned our attention to a student quintet, who made their way quite competently through a paean of welcome. Servers appeared with their carts—human servers, not the bots usually deployed in the hall—and we directed our attention to the dinner.

Catrill continued to probe as we ate, querying the technicians about their experiences, and then turning back to me to explore my qualifications as a pilot and captain. I did my best to seem open while giving him the minimum polite answers, but we were all grateful when the quintet reappeared to offer a recessional. I turned toward the door, intending to head back to my room, but Catrill fell into step beside me. "Surely you're not leaving, Captain."

"I have some reports to look over."

"I'm sure the Senior Custodian would like a word," he said. "Before the formal meeting."

"If you think so, of course I'm at your disposal." I mimed polite uncertainty and let him steer me through the double doors that gave onto the reception room. It overlooked the Starwell, and the curtains had been drawn back to provide a stunning view of the installation, all the work lights at full power so that the stone seemed to sparkle. Presumably those were inclusions in the stone, but they had been invisible by daylight.

The room was busy, though I couldn't help noticing that the students and younger Academicians were still clustered by the tables that were serving a selection of sweets and after-dinner drinks. I declined both, and Catrill maneuvered us deftly through the crowd until we reached the little pocket of quiet by the window where Sawyl and the Senior Custodian were deep in conversation. They broke off at our approach, Larel frowning, Sawyl's barbels twitching in spite of his relaxed smile, and I wished Rejane was with them.

"Nic," Sawyl said, with what sounded like genuine

warmth, and Larel cocked her head.

"You know the captain well?"

"Not as well as I'd like," Sawyl said easily. "She's the friend of a good friend."

"And apparently a catalyst, if I understand the reports," Larel said. "If that is correct, Captain? You were the person who triggered the event?"

"I suppose I was," I began. I could see Rejane making her way toward us, and hoped she'd get here quickly. "I was the person who was holding the toy, but I didn't really do anything to trigger it."

"I do think that's a fair statement," Sawyl said. "We had all taken turns holding the device, and none of us did anything different."

"But you let your burdens taste it," Larel said. "That seems…reckless."

Sawyl grimaced and set his glass aside, absently rubbing his shoulder. "How so?"

"Because of exactly what happened," Larel answered. "You admit yourself that you don't know what you did, what you may have awakened. You could have opened a door to one of the great AI, or started some unstoppable process that could have caused enormous damage to this campus, and potentially to the other cities here on Valenguar. Reckless is the mildest term."

"No," Sawyl said. "No, I really don't think so." I admired how calm his voice was, as though he hadn't heard the threat lurking in her words. "First, we knew the device itself only functioned in contact with certain burdens, and was not itself capable of reaching into the possible. Second, the well has been unresponsive for centuries, which strongly suggests that there is no longer a working power source, and certainly not one large enough to open a door to the possible. I admit I'm surprised to have gotten any response, but I deny that there could have been a dangerous one."

My device could connect to the possible—but only in the possible. Presumably Rejane had shared that with Fish. Larel looked at me. "And you, Captain? Weren't you worried?"

"I had every confidence in the Custodian." I met her eyes guilelessly.

"Your burden triggered the device," she said. "Or perhaps the well itself, that seems unclear. You have a Firstborn burden?"

"Yes."

"Then why were you not admitted to the Academy?"

"I wanted a career in space," I answered.

"Where were you born?"

"Callambhal." I deliberately didn't qualify, hoping she would assume I meant Callambhal Below, and her eyes narrowed.

"Which one?"

"Callambhal Above." I met her eyes again. "My mother was a line-worker, I was trained under indenture." That was usually enough to stop further questioning.

Rejane stepped into the breach. "I've found Nic to be very helpful in the past. She has considerable experience taking daedalists through the possible, and in handling sensitive cargos."

"So you're well aware of the risks posed by AI," Larel said.

"I believe so," I said. Out of the corner of my eye, I could see Sawyl rubbing his shoulder again, grimacing visibly.

"I think everyone is," Rejane said. "No one wants a return to the days before the Fall, least of all the pilots who have to face the possible. Without whom we'd still be struggling to escape the Dark."

"Interaction with the possible remains an ever-present danger," Larel said. "We would do well to find some other method for interstellar travel. Wouldn't you prefer to avoid the risk of AI, Captain?"

"Of course," I began, and Sawyl made a sharp, pained sound, his barbels curling.

"Fish?" Rejane reached out to steady him, and he caught himself on her shoulder.

"I—something is wrong."

"Yes." Rejane put her arm around his waist, supporting him, and reached for her handheld with the other. "Tell me what's happening." She fumbled with the screen, her attention divided, and I took a step forward, offering my support as well.

"I hurt." Sawyl sounded surprised. "My chest—I can't get my breath—"

"Medical emergency," Rejane said, to her handheld, "Code red, medical, this location. Fish, sit down." She steered him to a chair, and together we lowered him into it. His hand was sweaty as he clutched at my arm, and his skin had darkened alarmingly. His mouth was open, and his dewlaps lifted, exposing his gills as he fought for air.

"Rejane—"

"Don't talk," Rejane said, scanning the crowd. I looked where she was looking and saw a team in medic's uniforms making their way through the room. I lifted my arm, waving them over — pointless, they were tracking Rejane's signal, but I couldn't stand idle. Larel stood frozen, eyes darting from one to the other as though she couldn't believe what she was seeing. Rejane loosened the neck of his gown, feeling for a pulse point there, and Sawyl's eyes flickered, his barbels twitching madly. "Fish—"

The medics arrived, gravsled in tow. They checked vital signs, not saying anything but moving with an urgency that spoke for itself, then hoisted him onto the sled. "I'll go with him," Rejane said, to me, and I had time only to nod before she had disappeared in their wake. I shivered, and realized that Larel was watching me.

"Not how anyone expected the evening to end," she said, but there was a note in her voice that sounded wrong.

"No." I couldn't think of anything useful to say, settled for, "I hope he'll be all right." I hoped someone had warned Endolian, but there was nothing I could do about that.

The investigator who had been at my table came to join us, smiling slightly. Larel gave him a look, and he smoothed his expression. "So do we all," she said, and turned away.

Chapter Eight

The reception dissolved in confusion, a few students hovering at the tables to snatch a last bite or one final glass, but the rest of the Academicians gathered in worried knots, and then found reasons to leave. I made my way back to my rooms, hoping I'd hear from Rejane, but the comm console remained silent and dark. I fixed myself a pot of tea from the room's tiny kitchen alcove, put the household information channel on at minimal volume, and settled myself to wait. I considered calling Haliday, but I didn't know what to tell her to do.

After an hour or so, the household channel put out an announcement saying that the Custodian had been taken ill at the reception. No information on his condition was currently available; updates would be forthcoming. That was not a good sign, and I brewed a second pot of tea and let it get cold while I switched from screen to screen and thought more about calling Haliday. I still hadn't made up my mind when there was a knock at the door. I opened it at once, and Rejane slipped inside, motioning for me to close the door behind her.

"Fish?" I asked, and she shook her head. Her eyes were red and swollen, but she had herself firmly under control.

"Not good. I don't think he's going to make it. Endolian is with him now."

"Oh, Rejane. I'm sorry."

"I'm all—no, I'm not all right," she said, and I held out my arms out of old habit. She accepted the embrace, resting her head on my shoulder, and I held her for a long moment while she silently wept and then struggled to get herself under control again. "I also—there's something not right about this. About any of it."

"What do you mean?" I asked, but my mind went instantly to the Senior Custodian standing silent and unmoving while Sawyl fought for breath.

"I think you know," Rejane said. "Fish was healthy, he's always been healthy, and to lose him now, when he had a chance to turn this around and bring the entire question before the Academy Assembled—it's too much of a coincidence."

"I'm not following," I said. Rejane pushed me lightly, and I let her go, went to the kitchen alcove to start another pot of tea. "I thought the Senior Custodian's visit was a bad thing."

"It was. It is. But Fish and I were talking, and it occurred to us that if she could be persuaded to overreach her authority, we'd have a chance to bring the Newfounders down a notch."

"And you think Larel—what, poisoned him? To keep that from happening?" I sounded more skeptical than I felt, and Rejane glared.

"Yes, actually. And so do his doctors, but Larel's taken over everything. She's the senior Academician on site, she can order the records erased and no one can stop her."

"Does this sort of thing happen often?"

Rejane made a sound that might have been laughter. "You'd be surprised."

The boiler was rumbling, and had been for a while. I turned it off and started a third pot of tea. "I need to get out of here, then."

"Yes." Rejane nodded. "That was what I came to talk to you about. I can pass you through security tonight, but we need to move now."

"Thank you." I hesitated. "Do you want to come with us?"

She made a face. "I don't know. I want to stay, just in case—"

Just in case Sawyl lived, she meant, and I patted her shoulder awkwardly. "There's plenty of room."

There was another knock at the door. Rejane and I

exchanged glances, and then she stepped back out of sight as I opened the door. "Yes?"

Endolian looked past me, his eyes swollen from weeping. "Is Rejane here?" I stepped back, letting him in, and he and Rejane embraced. "He's gone," he said, and Rejane closed her eyes, tears again flowing down her cheeks.

"Doli, I'm so sorry. He was—he was so very much."

"He was everything," Endolian said, simply, and straightened. "Rejane, we have to get out of here, the children and I. The Senior Custodian is determined to pass this off as a heart attack." His voice went high in bitter mimicry. "An unfortunate consequence of his unique physiology. But we both know Fish was in perfect health."

"You told her that?" Rejane said.

"Of course. And our doctors backed me up, but she's having none of it. And they, the doctors, they're both Academicians. They can't stand up to her." He paused. "She implied that I was a hysterical spouse, and that the children might need to have another guardian if I couldn't control myself."

"Oh, I don't think so," Rejane said.

"She could do it," Endolian said.

"I know." Rejane wound her hands together. "Nic?"

"There's room on *Beljaeger*," I said. "But first we have to get there, and then we have to get a departure slot."

"Can you lift without that?" Rejane asked.

"I can. But I'll be blacklisted in this system until someone clears this up."

"That can be arranged." Rejane looked at Endolian. "And with luck we won't have to. Where are the kids?"

"Deronda is fetching them—my sister, she's been acting as their tutor. I told her to bring them here."

"Good." Rejane turned to the communications console and began entering codes. "All right, so far, so good, there's no formal lockdown on the campus. But the Senior Custodian's people are watching the courtyard."

"My flyer's in the courtyard," I pointed out.

"So are all of them," Rejane said.

Endolian lifted his head. "Not all. There's one we used for the back and forth to Junewatch, we kept it at the water gate, where it would be out of the way."

"They'll still send somebody after us," I said. "I doubt we could outrun them, and they have the authority to stop us."

"Then we don't take the flyway," Rejane said. "We go out over the water, swing in to Junewatch, and come blamelessly into Tamarak from there."

"I thought it was dangerous to go out over the water," I said.

"It's safer than the flyway," Rejane answered.

"Also…" Endolian gave a watery smile. "If we take one of the skimmers, we can turn it loose, and maybe they'll think we were stupid enough to try to go by water."

"It might be a useful distraction," I said. "Where precisely are we going?"

Rejane looked at Endolian, who said, "Safican. We both have family there, and the children will be safe."

Rejane nodded. "Can we do it?"

Safican was an open planet, easily approached by a number of different routes. "Yes. I'll need to warn Haliday—"

"I'm not sure my encryption is secure," Rejane said.

"We've got codes of our own," I answered, and reached for my handheld. I switched on my security field and entered Haliday's codes, then waited while she woke and responded.

"It's the middle of the night."

"Yeah, I'm sorry, I know." That was the established exchange that told her there was an emergency. "I needed to send some files your way."

"They couldn't wait?"

"Well, not really…"

"Have you been drinking?" That was another code phrase, *Are we in trouble*, and she didn't need to act to make her voice sharp with worry.

"Maybe a bit." There was another knock at the door, and I looked over my shoulder to see another aquatic ushering the children into the room. Rejane locked the door behind them, and Endolian settled them on my couch. "I'll get those files out to you as soon as I can."

"Better sleep it off," Haliday said, and broke the connection.

I looked at Rejane. "She'll be waiting."

"Good."

Endolian said, "We're ready."

"No baggage?"

The woman—Deronda, I remembered—shook her head. "We didn't dare."

They would have to manage. I looked at the children huddled together on the sofa, the boy already half asleep with his head on his sister's shoulder. *Beljaeger*'s cabins had the basics, but not much more. On the other hand, all the goods in the world wouldn't help them if they were taken away from their surviving father. "Rejane, you had a way to get us to a flyer?"

"I can take us," Endolian said. Deronda picked up the boy, who burrowed sleepily into her neck, and Endolian reached out to take his daughter's hand. "Just a little further, Aster."

"I left my handheld." She scrubbed at her eyes. "And I want Papa."

Endolian's eyes filled, and Deronda said hastily, "I have your handheld, Aster. It's in my bag."

"You can have it when we get to the flyer," Endolian said, with more confidence. "Come along now."

I grabbed the device in its case and my handheld. I hated having to leave everything else, but I didn't want to risk being seen with baggage. Without it, I'd have some chance of talking my way out of any encounter with the Senior Custodian's guards. At least I wouldn't be losing my best clothes. Rejane was empty-handed, and shrugged when I looked at her. "There wasn't time to grab anything, and too much of a risk if I did. Let's go."

The halls were mostly empty, though here and there a door had been left ajar, and I had the sense that people were watching from within. There was no sign of Larel's mercenaries, and I hoped they were all either guarding her or watching the flyers parked in the courtyard. Endolian seemed to know the way, threading his way down stairs and through increasingly functional corridors, and I fell into step with Rejane. "What can you tell me about the security sensors?"

"Focused on the campus and the Starwell. There's air coverage above sixty meters, and there are subsurface sensors out in the bay." She paused. "Did I mention that the bay itself is subject to—disturbances?"

"Fish said something about that. There were tunnels, and boats had been lost?"

Rejane nodded. "And there have been whirlpools sighted, though not since Fish took over. There's no discernible pattern to their appearance, but they've been known to swallow small boats."

"Great."

"On the other hand, Doli's idea of using a skimmer as a decoy might just work." It wasn't a bad idea, and if I could keep the flyer low enough to avoid security, at least until we were out of the bay.... We might get away with this.

Endolian led us down a final staircase, the lights flicking on as we passed and turning off again as we moved out of range. That sort of parsimony was usually reserved for the working areas, and I wasn't surprised to smell the odd bitter tang of salt water. A chill breeze wound up the last flight of stairs, and Menes stirred in Deronda's arms, tasting the water.

The stairs ended in a short corridor, closed by a pair of ill-fitting doors. The wind whined through the cracks, carrying a stronger odor, seaweed and dead fish, and Rejane lifted her hand. "Let me check this, Doli."

Endolian nodded, and she moved past him, lifting her handheld. The ring on her left hand glimmered in the uncertain light, a flash of green and then a brief kaleidoscope of color as she rested her hand on the wall beside the lock panel. Something flashed on the handheld's screen, and there was a heavy click as the lock opened. "I've deactivated the system for the moment," she said. "But we'll need to hurry."

Endolian pushed the door back, and we all followed him through. A light flashed on, but it didn't show much, just the poured-stone dock area and the water beyond. A few meters beyond the end of the dock I could see a brighter patch where the docks opened directly to the sea. To my left, several darker shadows resolved to a pair of flat-bottomed skimmers, and a two-seat wave-rider was hauled up on the dock behind them, leaning drunkenly to one side. Its canopy was missing along with the engine cowling, and I guessed it hadn't been used in a long time. Beyond it, another dock jutted into the water and an amphibious flyer floated beside it. It was smaller than the rental I had been using, but it looked large enough to carry all of us without putting too much of a strain on its power plant. Endolian unlocked the canopy and stepped down into the main compartment, then lifted the children down after him.

"Get a skimmer in tow if you're going to," Rejane said, and motioned for me to take the controls. "Doli, I'm letting Nic fly."

"No argument," Endolian answered, and a moment later I heard the whir of a skimmer's engines starting up. Rejane slid into the copilot's seat beside me, laying her hand on a sensor panel, and the controls came to life. I found the preflight checklist, grateful that everything seemed to be standard, and Endolian brought the skimmer around to the rear of the flyer, parking it stern to stern. He did something with it—I hadn't found the rear cameras yet—and came back to the open canopy.

"Can you lift and hover? I need to set the cable."

"Tell him I can," I said, and Rejane repeated my words. I touched the controls and brought the grav-fields into line. The flyer swayed and rose, then steadied, field generators purring softly. I found the rear camera at last and watched as Endolian attached a towline to the quick-release hook at the skimmer's stern. He left the power running, systems at neutral, and Rejane extended a hand to haul him back into the cabin.

"I think we're ready," he said, closing the canopy behind him, and she nodded.

"Nic?"

"Everybody strap in," I said, and eased the flyer another meter or two into the air. "How much cable do I have?"

"Ten meters," Endolian said. "It was what I had."

"That's fine." I would have preferred longer, but I could work with that. I looked over my shoulder to be sure everyone was secure, and aimed the flyer for the arched opening. The cable came taut, the skimmer bouncing over the water, and I adjusted my altitude and speed so that it slid along the surface without throwing up a tail of spray. That was far slower than I would have liked to go—every instinct said to open the throttles and head full speed for Junewatch—but the idea of a decoy was a good one.

I didn't try to access the navigation grid. Our immediate course was obvious: straight out to sea, then bear left to eventually put the headland between us and the Academy campus. The trick would be getting there without drawing attention. At least no one spent time on the water—it was unlikely anyone would be looking in our direction. And of course they'd all be busy dealing with Sawyl's death. Hopefully that would keep them from looking for us too soon.

I set my heading and checked to be sure the transponder was staying off. The flyer's interior was dark as well, the only light coming from the control console. Behind us, the Academy campus was ablaze with light, drowning the stars; ahead of us, the Gap ran jagged across the midpoint of the sky. "Where do you want to drop the skimmer?" I began, and Rejane's answer was swallowed in a sudden rumble so low-pitched as to be almost soundless. In the cabin camera, I saw Aster jerk awake, her father instantly wrapping himself around her. "What—"

Ahead of the flyer, the water churned and swirled, throwing up flecks of white foam. For a moment, it was nothing but confusion, and then the water began to spin in earnest, a hole opening at its center. I wrenched the flyer sideways, the skimmer bouncing off the edge of the hole, and another opened twenty meters on.

"Drop the skimmer," Rejane said. She was clinging to the arms of her seat, staring into the dark. "Now, Nic!"

I found the release and pulled it, felt the flyer bound upward as the weight fell away, and adjusted the fields to keep us under the security scans. I caught a glimpse of the skimmer pitching down and into the whirlpool, only to be spat up again in a column of spray. Another column erupted in front of us. I rolled the flyer sideways, fields at their limits, and we slid through the outermost edge, water rattling against the canopy. One of the children squeaked, and was instantly silenced. I opened the throttles to maximum thrust, swerving to avoid another whirlpool. "This is going to draw attention—"

"We're almost through," Rejane said. "Those are the openings of the tunnels, they stop about a kilometer out—"

It did look as though there were fewer whirlpools ahead of us, though the water remained rough. I brought the flyer down until we were barely two meters above the wave tops, aiming for the edge of the headland. Behind us, the whirlpools were sending up more gouts of spray where the waves collided, and I hoped that would help hide the flyer. Or at least attract more attention than our moving shadow.

"Everything's focused on the tunnel field," Rejane said, as much to herself as to me. "The sensor webs, I mean. Nothing looks out this far."

I swung the flyer around a final whirlpool, and pointed the nose toward the headland. "What just happened?"

"I'm not sure," Rejane admitted. "Maybe it was the skimmer? That's what's happened before, when the previous Custodian tried to map the bay floor. She theorized that surface traffic disturbed some hidden sensors, set off the display."

I risked switching on the flyer's passive sensors. Behind us, the bay was crisscrossed with lights, and I thought I could make out new lights along the campus's seaward edge. At current speed, we'd be shadowed by the headland in about ten minutes, and I increased the speed a hair more. "They'll find the skimmer?"

Rejane nodded. "Almost certainly. There's some sort of filter system that spits debris back out."

"So they'll think Endolian tried to take the children out this way, and was killed."

"That was the plan," Endolian said. "It was Fish's idea."

I glanced over my shoulder. "Are you telling me he was expecting this to happen?"

"Not this, not exactly," Endolian answered. "But he knew it was a possibility. He was a spine in the Newfounders' feet."

We had reached the headland, and I turned gratefully into its protection, checking the passive sensors for the Junewatch beacon. It was there, if faint, and I set the autopilot to bring us in, and sat back, working my shoulders. "What were you two doing to upset them?"

"We had some ideas," Rejane said, before Endolian could answer. "I'll tell you more once we get off Valenguar."

You might have told me sooner. There was no point in saying that: I wouldn't have told me either, not if I were playing some elaborate game of Academy politics. And to be fair, I was sure she hadn't anticipated this ending. "We'll hit the edge of the Junewatch traffic control in a couple of hours, and then it's about three hours to Tamarak."

"We should still be ahead of them," Rejane said, but her tone was less certain than I would have liked.

冊 � 屮

We made slightly better time than I had planned, so I circled the outermost beacon and approached it from the east, merging into the flyway as though I'd come in from one of the outer farming stations. No one seemed to be looking for us, or even particularly interested in the traffic. I requested and received clearance for the Tamarak flyway without trouble, and turned the flyer north along the line of beacons.

We reached Tamarak in the false dawn, and I let the city's traffic control system shunt us through the mostly-empty skies to the landing area nearest the port. Deronda roused the sleepy children while Endolian collected their single bag, and I looked at Rejane. "Can you get them into the port? You know where *Beljaeger*'s docked. I want to lose this flyer if I can."

"Yes." Rejane stepped out of the flyer, then steadied Aster across to the platform. I closed the canopy, but not before I heard Endolian's question and Rejane's quick explanation. Assuming their absence hadn't been discovered—or, more likely, that everyone's attention was focused on the upheaval in the bay—they ought to be able to pass through customs on their own IDs. Or perhaps Fish had provided alternate IDs as part of his plan. I would have to leave that to Rejane, and concentrate on finding a place to leave the flyer that would further muddle our trail.

There were any number of lots set up for the constant traffic, and I chose an inexpensive stack about a kilometer from the port's northern gate. I edged the flyer into an open space, locked it into the dock and fed local scrip into the parking system until I'd bought forty hours, and then rode the lift to the self-serve portal on the ground floor. There I paid for the space above it—credit, this time, but a card that shouldn't trace back to me—and added another twenty hours to the space where I'd left the flyer. I pushed through the door into the rising dawn, and caught the next omni back to the port gate.

The others had reached *Beljaeger* before me, and Haliday met me at the hatch, scowling. "This is your emergency? What in fuck's name were you thinking?"

"It's definitely an emergency," I said.

Haliday snorted. "It's her emergency, not ours. We've got nothing to do with any of this, and we shouldn't be involved."

"The kids," I said, and she gave me a goaded look.

"Yes, I feel bad for them. But we are going to be paying for this for years."

"Rejane will help us."

"If she can. And if she can't—"

"Then we deal with it," I said. "Claim we were misled. Something. Did you get a departure slot?"

She closed her mouth over whatever else she had been going to say. "Yes. We're ready once everyone gets squared away. We don't have enough cabins, you know."

Endolian, Deronda, and the children would take the two spare cabins. It was possible to convert one of the smaller storage compartments to a cabin, but that would take more time than we had. "Rejane can share with me," I said, and Haliday rolled her eyes.

"I figured." She paused. "You could share with me, if you wanted."

Under the circumstances, it was a generous offer. "I appreciate that. But she'll be out for most of the trip anyway."

"She'd better be." Haliday started toward the control room. "That's the last thing we need."

The AI were attracted to a daedalist's burden. I made a mental note to check everyone else's burden, and turned toward the commons. Rejane and Deronda were there ahead of me, Deronda just pulling a couple of pre-pack meals from the cooker. She gave me an apologetic look, and said, "I want the children to eat something before they sleep."

"Of course," I said. "Quickly, though. Do any of you— you, your brother, either child—have a daedalist's burden?"

She shook her head. "No. And we've never had any trouble in the possible—not more than normal, anyway."

"Thanks." I waited until the hatch slid shut behind her. "We're short a cabin, but you're welcome to share with me."

"Thank you." Rejane looked abruptly exhausted. "I'm sorry. Things have gotten out of hand."

I couldn't help laughing. "That's one way of putting it. What happens now?"

"We have to get Doli and the kids to Safican," she answered. "They'll be safe there. Fish still has supporters there, and Doli's family is powerful enough to protect them. Then…then I think my best bet is to go on with our plan, only I'm not quite sure how that's going to work. And before you ask—we were looking for a way to convince the Academy that we would be far better off following in the Ancestors' footsteps rather than trying to reinvent everything. We thought that restoring a Remnant would show that."

"The Starwell?"

She shook her head. "The Inner Sun."

"The Inner Sun has been dead since the Fall. I was born on Callambhal Above, I've seen it. It's very dead." I could remember it perfectly, a shadow floating in darkness, in the open volume at the center of the Shell, Callambhal Above's largest component. Anyone who had to traverse the Shell's inner surface would find a moment to stop and stare, transfixed by the contrast between what had been and what was now. Once the Inner Sun had been exactly that, bringing life and warmth and light to the Shell and transmitting power to the station's trailing components; now the empty volume was dark, its surface lit by tens of thousands of individual lights, studding the inner surface like the crystals in a geode, none of them strong enough to reach more than a dozen meters from their source. A few ferries crossed the Spiral's central void, careful to stay well clear of the Sun, but most people traveled around the surface, beneath an inner night more starless than the space outside the station.

The stories said that a thousand years ago, before the Fall, one of the Dedalors' five Great AI, Green Piercing Book, resided in the Sun, in the Golden Age when humankind and AI were allies. But when Gold Shining Bone led the AI in rebellion, Green Piercing Book ripped itself free from the Sun, nearly destroying the station in the process, and the Sun had been dark ever since.

"I told you we were working on the theory that the Remnants originally required an AI share in order to function?" Rejane asked, and I nodded. "Callambhal Above is in some ways the simplest example, and the one for which we have the most evidence of a share's presence."

"You're talking about the stories? They say it was a Great AI in the Sun, not a share."

"The Great AI provided shares," Rejane said. "We have written evidence of that, as well as the stories. And with the

Inner Sun, we have strong evidence that the surviving systems were intended to interact with a share."

"It's at the literal center of the station," I said. "You can't experiment with that, it's way too dangerous."

"Imagine if we could get the Sun to reignite," Rejane countered. "Think what that would do for Callambhal Above. And Callambhal Below."

Callambhal Above was only inhabited because of the resources that could still be pulled from the trailing volumes, the various engines and power plants that had been coaxed back into creaking functionality; if they failed, or the other resources were exhausted, the station would be abandoned, except perhaps for the people needed to service the ships that stopped over at the station. And how many of them would bother, if there was nothing to trade? The directors who ran the station might well be willing to take the chance. "It's still ridiculously dangerous."

"We have some ways to make it less so," Rejane said.

I shook myself. "Look, the first thing we have to do is to get Endolian and his family to Safican. We can worry about the rest of it once we get there.

"All right." Rejane pushed herself to her feet. "Can I ask you for a dose to get me through the trip?"

"Of course. Let me work out the numbers, and I'll bring it to you." I let her into my cabin, and headed for the control room, trying not to think about her curled up in my bunk.

I logged into the ship's pharmacy and confirmed my supplies, then settled to work out our course. Safican was an open world, one with more than a dozen possible approaches, and it didn't take long to lay out a range of courses. The longest would take just over seventeen hours, but most would run between eight and ten. I set up an array of options, then returned to the pharmacy to dial up two injectors, one for the anticipated run, and a secondary that Rejane could use if we had to take the longest route. By then Haliday had confirmed our launch window, and we were ready to lift. I brought Rejane her drugs, confirmed that Endolian knew how to settle everyone for the launch, then secured myself in my couch while Haliday accepted our tow and let it drag *Beljaeger* out onto the launch table.

"This is still a terrible idea," she said, and lifted one finger to reply to the tow boss. "Alignment confirmed. All green here."

"We show good alignment as well," the tow boss answered. "Have a nice trip."

"Thanks." Haliday cut the external channel and glanced sideways at me. "I'm really not happy."

You've made that clear. I swallowed that, said, "I know. Look, let's just get everyone to Safican, and we can straighten everything out there."

"Maybe. If we're lucky. We'd have been better off letting them fend for themselves. You might just have gotten away with pleading ignorance that way."

"Larel was threatening to take the kids away from their surviving father," I said.

"Since when has that been an issue for you?" Haliday asked. "You hardly even know the man. Hell, she might be right, he might be a terrible father."

"That's not what I saw."

"In what, two nights?"

"We're committed," I said.

"I know."

The comms console chimed. "*Beljaeger*, Tower Control. Stand by for departure vectors."

I opened the channel with some relief. "Tower Control, *Beljaeger*. Ready for vectors."

"Transmitting now," Control said, and the navigation system pinged twice.

"Received. Check back?"

"Go ahead, *Beljaeger*."

"Transmitting." I hit the button, and a moment later the screen flashed green. "All green here."

"*Beljaeger*, Tower Control. You are cleared to lift at your discretion."

I gave the local sensors a last quick scan, making sure the launch area was clear. "Tower Control, *Beljaeger*. Fields set. Commencing lift."

"Confirmed," Control said. "Good voyage, *Beljaeger*."

"Fields on," Holiday said, her voice stiff. "Vectors ready."

"Lift." *Beljaeger* lurched beneath us, then steadied, rising rapidly through the atmosphere, propulsion fields balanced to push us up and out of the planet's gravitational well. We flashed through a layer of cloud, and up into a blue that darkened rapidly toward the black of local space. The orbital scanner came on line, showing our course clear between two orbital stations, and I resisted the urge to make a minuscule correction.

"Cleared the planet," Haliday said, as the view in our screens went black. "Course shows clear to the jump point."

"Confirmed," I answered. "Setting autopilot."

"Autopilot on," Haliday said. I checked the sensors again, running them up to maximum, and picked out another small freighter inbound on a parallel course, plus a bulk freighter making its way around the curve of the planet. "What are you going to do once we get to Safican?"

I thought about what Rejane had said about the Inner Sun. She wanted my help, that much was obvious, and it was equally obvious that now was not the time to mention that to Haliday. "I don't know. It depends."

"On what Rejane wants," Haliday said. "Look, Nic, I'm not doing any more for any of this. We take her to Safican and we leave her there, or you can leave me out instead."

"Let's see what happens when we get there," I said, and she shook her head.

"I'm serious."

"I know."

There wasn't much to say after that. I turned my attention to our course, making sure we were neatly aligned with our upcoming jump. The traffic lanes were clear except for another small freighter inbound for Tamarak. I pinged them to ask for a weather report, and was told their trip had been clear and uneventful. That was hopeful, though of course it was no guarantee we'd have the same luck. But if we had an easy trip, it would put Haliday in a better frame of mind, and we might be able to figure out some way to help Rejane—

The aft sensors pinged, and a moment later Haliday said, "Unscheduled launch from Tamarak. Looks like local patrol craft."

"That's not good." I switched my own screens, frowning as I tried to make sense of the readings. "Anything on comms?"

"Nothing—"

"*Beljaeger*, Valenguar Traffic Control."

I pressed the button that killed our automatic response, and the voice went on unheeding. "*Beljaeger*, Valenguar Traffic Control. You are requested to return at once to Tamarak port. Use reciprocal course. I repeat, return at once on reciprocal course."

"Ask them what they want," Haliday hissed, as though they could hear her if she spoke more loudly. I shook my head.

"Not yet. Let them think we haven't heard them."

"That's a patrol ship. They're faster than us."

"But we're only—" I checked my screens. "We're only twenty minutes from our jump point. They can't overtake us in that time."

"They'll be in missile range," Haliday answered. "We can't risk the ship."

"They won't shoot unless they're sure we're running," I said. Traffic Control repeated their order, and I checked my screens again. The patrol ship was gaining, but not nearly fast enough. Haliday was right, it would be in missile range for the last five minutes, but I was willing to bet her captain wouldn't shoot without a better excuse than the Senior Custodian's word. We were coming up on the last check before jump, and I moved the transmitter to a frequency three points off the official one. "Valenguar Traffic Control, *Beljaeger*. We are fifteen minutes from jump, all systems green and go."

"Are you out of your mind?" Haliday demanded.

"Look, anything we can do to confuse them will help." I checked our position. "Charge the capacitors."

"Charging." She shook her head. "They are never going to believe you were on the wrong frequency."

"It just needs to be plausible," I said. Haliday made a skeptical noise, but I ignored her, focusing on the aft sensors. The patrol ship was continuing to overhaul us, the range indicator fading from green toward yellow. The transponder was showing it as a Customs ship, which made it slightly less likely they'd shoot before asking questions.

"Ready shields?" Haliday asked.

I nodded. "Ready, but don't light them. We're playing innocent as long as we possibly can."

The comms console lit again, and a new voice said, "*Beljaeger*, this is Customs Boat *Reliant*. Cease acceleration and stand by to be boarded." I checked the frequency. They were still on the normal channel: we could still pretend not to hear.

"They're just now in missile range," Haliday said. She paused, scanning her screens. "Assuming they have long-range missiles on board. I'm not picking up a hot launch tube."

"Customs usually sticks with short-range weapons," I said, and tried to sound confident. "Stay on course. Capacitors?"

"Seventy percent and charging."

I nodded again. The jump point loomed on my course display, the cross-hairs opening slightly to reveal the red diamond that was our target. Our alignment was perfect, our fields optimally tuned to local space. Ten more minutes, and we'd be ready to jump.

"*Beljaeger*, this is Customs Boat *Reliant*. Cease acceleration now and stand by to be boarded."

They were on wide-band now, using multiple frequencies. I hesitated—could we keep ignoring them?—but the broadcast was on repeat, and covered too wide a range to make it believable. "*Reliant, Beljaeger*. We were cleared from Tamarak Customs, and our cargo is extremely time-sensitive. What's the problem?"

"Official manifests are queued up," Haliday said.

"Thanks." I touched keys, bundled the full long-form version and dispatched it to *Reliant*. "Copying our manifest now."

There was a brief hiss of static, confirming the transmission, and it was several minutes before *Reliant* spoke again. "*Beljaeger, Reliant.* Your request is denied. Cease acceleration now."

I looked at my screens again, gauging the distance to the jump point. "Capacitors?"

"Eighty-seven—eighty-eight percent. Ninety."

We were almost there. "*Reliant, Beljaeger.* We have to make this jump to meet our contract. As I said, it's extremely time-sensitive, and we have a tight course with almost no leeway for weather. We'll gladly check in with Customs on arrival and hold there, but we can't miss this jump."

"Negative, *Beljaeger.* Cease acceleration."

"I cannot lose this contract. I repeat, I'm happy to cooperate, but only after we make our delivery—"

"Ninety-four percent," Haliday said softly. "Ninety-six."

We could jump early, as soon as we reached a full charge, and Customs wouldn't be able to follow. I kept talking, trying to sound like every flustered merchant captain with a bad contract, and *Reliant*'s transmission cut through mine.

"*Beljaeger*, halt or we will fire. This is your only warning."

"Ninety-nine," Haliday said. "Full charge."

We were almost at the jump point. I hesitated, seeing the warning lights flare across the sensor boards: *Missile launch, missile running, missile targeting.*

"Nic," Haliday said, and we slid into position.

"Jump."

The capacitors fired, and we leaped into the possible.

Chapter Nine

That was too damn close," Haliday said.

Our sensors were clear: the missile hadn't made the transition after us. Missiles weren't supposed to be able to withstand the stresses of the possible, but it had been known for one to slip through and explode. I allowed myself a sigh of relief. "We're clear. Get us aligned with the local grain while I make contact."

"You're pushing this," Haliday said, her hands busy on her boards. "You're pushing way too hard, and I'm not putting up with it."

"We'll sort it out when we get to Safican." I reached for the device.

"We'll sort this beforehand," Haliday answered. "I'm serious, Nic."

"I know." I did my best to sound conciliatory. "I know, and I'm sorry. But once we get to Safican, Rejane should be able to fix this—"

"Rejane Novilis isn't in any position to help us."

"Rejane is a Novilis and a Senior Academician, she's not exactly powerless. And there's Endolian. He owes us. We're not friendless. But we can't do anything until we get to Safican."

Haliday drew a deep breath, nodding. "Yeah. All right. But once we deliver them, we're done."

"Of course," I said, and put my hand on the device. There was the customary chime that echoed in the bones of my hand, and then quite suddenly the familiar prickle of presence that swelled to a shock in the center of my palm.

Hello, Beauty.

Hello, Beast. I'm looking for safe passage to Safican.

It took less time than I'd anticipated to agree on a course and a price, and I launched the transit mass. There was enough left to bargain with for two or maybe three more trips, and with a little luck, we wouldn't need Beast's protection for all of them. In fact, it would probably be better not to ask for its help if we could avoid it, and hope that helped calm Haliday down.

The actual journey was uneventful, slightly more than nine hours in the possible without the slightest sign of weather, and then the slow run in from our exit point to Safican's orbit. Endolian spoke with various people—it seemed that the news of Sawyl's death and the threats to their children were deeply unwelcome—and we were shunted away from the bustling main port to the equatorial settlement of Deepside. The landing table rose out of the shallow sea, standing high on hundreds of poured-stone columns; I brought us down as instructed, and a tow hauled us to a waiting berth. Rejane was awake by then, and she, Endolian and Deronda were met by a delegation from the local authorities, who whisked them and the children away and left us sitting on the landing table, the salt-laden wind whistling past.

There was a single building on the table, housing local traffic control and what looked like the depot for local transport, and a couple of smaller, in-atmosphere craft parked at the opposite end of the table. Otherwise, the table stretched empty for hundreds of meters, the pale surface scarred by the landings of a dozen different kinds of ships; ten meters beyond *Beljaeger*'s bow, the turquoise water stretched empty to the horizon.

The settlement itself lay behind *Beljaeger*, but I'd gotten a good look at it coming in. Only a few buildings rose above the waves, pale white stone surrounding central lagoons, but the water was clear enough that I'd been able to see more elaborate buildings under the surface, filling a series of terraces that led down into deeper waters. How deep it went, I didn't know, and I found myself wondering if they were all filled with water or if there were dry chambers within the buildings. It was easy to picture Endolian and the children moving through the water, silent and smooth as shadows.

"We should get clearance back to Grand Depot." Haliday came to stand beside me in the open hatch, squinting into the sunlight. "It may not be any cheaper than here, but we'll have an easier time coming up with another cargo."

"Endolian's family is paying our port fees," I said. I'd made sure to confirm that before they left. "There's no hurry. Besides, I was hoping they might provide us with further tangible evidence of their appreciation."

Haliday made a skeptical noise and disappeared back into the ship. I sat down on the top step, painfully tired from the flight and still too keyed up to rest just yet. In the distance, a boat carved a line of white through the shimmering water; overhead, a contrail mirrored it against deeper blue. The smell of salt was strong, along with the familiar starport scent of hot stone and metal and machines. I rested my head against the soft polymer of the hatch seal, and told myself I would move in a little while.

The sounds of engines woke me from my doze. I looked up, blinking in the bright sunlight, to see a heavy-bellied hopper coming in for a landing, jets rotating to bring it down at the far end of the table. A leaping fish with wings was painted across the main body, and when I looked again, I could see people waiting by the depot: probably the local transport line on a regularly scheduled run. The hopper settled onto its legs, the engines cut out, and stairs unrolled from a side hatch, while at the same moment a cargo ramp folded down from the tail and a string of grav-sleds started toward it. A cargo handler and a couple of service bots were perched behind the driver.

My handheld pinged, and I hauled it out to see that it was Rejane. "Yes?"

"Doli's family has offered to host you and Hal—his mother is a local senator, and the family has substantial merchant wealth. I'm sure they would find a job for you, and in any case, the pavilions are considerably more comfortable than the ship."

"I'll take you up on that," I said. "And I'll talk to Hal. But thank you."

"Senator Priema will send a skimmer for you and your luggage," Rejane said, and broke the connection.

It was easier than I had expected to persuade Haliday to join me, but then the landing table was noticeably lacking in amenities. The skimmer appeared as promised, piloted by an enhanced aquatic who reminded me painfully of Sawyl, and we carried our meager baggage down through an elevator in one of the support columns to the docks where the watercraft landed. It was more crowded there, a couple of flat-bottomed commercial lighters still being loaded with the cargo from the hopper, plus a scattering of private craft that ranged from the sort of two-seat wave-riders I'd seen on Valenguar to sleek bright-hulled narrow-boats with their masts folded down onto their decks. The skimmer was perfectly ordinary, badged with what I assumed was either the Senator's personal insignia or a family or company logo; the pilot stowed our bags and handed us aboard, then pulled gently away from the dock. We wove slowly through the forest of supports, and then pulled out into the sunlight.

Our pilot opened the throttle, and the skimmer lifted so that it rode over the tops of the shallow waves, throwing up an enormous plume of spray. I glanced up and back, and the sun cast shards of rainbow through the cloud. Ahead, the towers of Deepside rose out of the shallows, slim white spires joined at their bases into rows and clusters, the sun drawing occasional sparks from odd-shaped windows. Their shadows reached out across the water, and I could just make out a few shapes moving among them, trailing pale wakes.

We passed some invisible border, and the pilot throttled back. The skimmer settled down into the waves, and we proceeded into the maze of towers and platforms at a decorous pace. When I looked over the side, I could see the shapes of more buildings below the water, and movement that had nothing to do with the surface waves.

We slowed even further as we reached a crescent-shaped platform topped with a set of stepped buildings that were in turn crowned with six short towers surrounding a taller tower that spiraled to support a crystal sphere. The pilot threaded his way into a narrow channel between sections of the platform, and I was suddenly struck by the scale of the place. From a distance, it had seemed elegant but fragile—ethereal, unreal. Here in its shadows, the buildings were still beautiful but as solid as fortifications, impressively so, obviously strong enough to withstand any storm.

The skimmer turned down a final passage so narrow that it had to be one-way only, and slid to an easy stop just as the passage widened to leave room to dock. Waiting handlers jumped to secure our lines, and the pilot climbed out after them, ready to help us. "This is Almendwyne, Senator Priema's residence. Welcome aboard."

I accepted his hand and stepped onto the hard white stone of the dock. The water was very close, not a hand's breadth below the edge of the dock: technically, I knew how to swim, but it wasn't a skill I practiced, and I'd certainly never swum in wild water. I could see from Haliday's expression that she was just as uneasy, and tried to form what I hoped was a reassuring smile. One of the handlers grabbed our bags, heading toward the building before either one of us could form a protest, and I was glad I'd kept the device with me. At the same moment, a door opened at the base of the nearest building, and several people walked out. I recognized Rejane instantly, though she was not wearing her academic robes; the others were visibly aquatics, and I assumed they were some of Endolian's family.

"Captain en Doroney?" That was the smallest of the aquatics, though her ankle-length gown was clearly expensive, and I cleared my throat.

"Yes—"

"Senator Priema," Rejane said quickly, and I bent my head in acknowledgment.

"Senator."

She held out both hands, and I took them, hoping I was doing the right thing. "Thank you, Captain, for bringing my son and my grandchildren safely home. The Custodian's death has been a shock and a tragedy for all of us."

"I only met him briefly," I said, "but it was clear what a loss it was. We were glad to be able to help."

"The family would like to express our gratitude," she said. "Particularly since I know this has put you into a potentially difficult situation politically. I want to say at once that we will certainly defend you if there are any legal consequences, and consider ourselves responsible as your employers for any and all actions taken to bring Endolian home."

That was much more than I'd expected—I'd been happy enough to have my expenses taken care of—and I bent my head again. "Thank you, Senator."

She smiled. "Of course, we all hope this can be resolved without further complications. But rest assured, we will back you if needed. In the meantime, I've asked Rejane to show you to your suites. There will be a memorial later, and I hope you'll be able to attend."

"Thank you," I said again, for once out of useful words, and Priema turned away.

⊓ ⺈ ⵌ

Rejane led us through a different door and down a broad flight of stairs that emerged on a wide terrace that overlooked what in another city would have been an open plaza, but in Deepside was a broad lagoon ringed with arches carved into delicate filigree. Steps rose from the water on all sides, and as I watched a lithe figure found its footing on a lower stair and walked easily out of the water, leaving a single damp footprint. She was wearing a dark gray skin-suit, and flicked a near-transparent length of fabric out of a concealed pocket, knotting it at one shoulder to form a casual drape.

"The pool leads down into the mid-city," Rejane said.

"That's where most people live. It's convenient, and it puts them below most storms."

There were dozens of people milling about on the plaza, some in skin-suits with and without draperies, some in ordinary clothes, though the skin-suits were obviously ordinary for Deepside. Most of them seemed to be aquatics but there were standard humans as well, most gathered at the far end of the pool where the arches of the loggia seemed to house a myriad of shops and vendors.

"We're in the main household," Rejane said. She led us along the mezzanine to a shallow set of stairs that took us down and across a glassed-in bridge that brought us to a different tower. The lobby was domed, the stones underfoot a darker shade of dawn-sky pink than the walls and ceiling; to my left, doors opened onto a sun-swept platform, water lapping gently at its edge. It was like being inside some enormous shell. Security passed us through a central door, and we rode a spiral stair up several floors, and then passed another checkpoint as discreet and polite as the first to emerge at last into another sun-dappled lobby. Five corridors led off in different directions; Rejane chose one and brought us to a smaller lobby with a door on either side. Another enormous window looked out over the sea, and I could just make out the landing table in the distance. "Your rooms are here. Your luggage should have already arrived, make yourselves comfortable, and ping the stewards if you need anything." She paused. "I'd plan to eat in your rooms if I were you. The senator will want to host you at some point, but tonight is for the family."

"Of course," I said.

"She mentioned a memorial," Haliday said.

Rejane nodded. "Yes, but that's going to take some arranging. And it would be good if you'd attend."

Haliday nodded, and I said, "We'd be glad to."

"Good." Rejane handed over the data buttons that would serve as keys to our suites and provide us access to at least some parts of the family compound. They were identical to the buttons I used on *Beljaeger*, and I clipped mine to my sleeve. "I should be available if you have questions, but I know you're tired from the trip. Ping me if you need me, though."

"Absolutely." I matched her smile, and waved the button at the nearest door. It slid back, Rejane turned away, and Haliday waved open the other door. We were looking at identical cream-colored suites, each with a sunken main area with seating and comms console and a galley-bar. Three shallow steps led up to a huge bed tucked into a bubble window. My carryall sat at its foot, looking ridiculously inadequate, and Haliday whistled softly.

"I have to say, this is a lot better than I was expecting. We might come out of this all right after all."

She was right, of course, but I didn't want to talk about it. "A lot better," I agreed. "Look, I'm going to take a nap, and then try to get myself onto local time. All right?"

Haliday gave me a wary look. "All right. Want to share dinner?"

"Might as well," I answered, and we let the doors close behind us. The bed was every bit as comfortable as it looked, and the view out over the water was soporific. I stretched out on the ivory pillows, tucked the cased device next to me, and let myself fall asleep.

I woke to twilight and a thin thread of music. I traced the latter to the comms console, which informed me that the dinner window was open and would remain open until 2130, and pinged Haliday to see if she still wanted to meet. There was no immediate answer, so I took myself off to the bathing chamber, which turned out to contain a plunge pool as well as the usual facilities. I bathed, found clean clothes and went back to the bed to stare out over the empty sea. I had thought the Novilis compound outside the Prater was impossibly luxurious; even allowing for the fact that I was a woman grown and considerably more jaded, the senator's tower was beyond anything I'd experienced. At the very least, that much money—and the power that went with it—should keep Endolian and his children safe. It might even be enough to protect us, if we were sensible.

Haliday pinged me back, and we ordered meal number two from the deliverable options. It arrived promptly, in a wheeled bot that unfolded compartments to present four courses and a carafe of fizzy local wine, and trundled off while I arranged things on the low table in the main area. Haliday inspected the plates and I poured us each a glass of wine. She took hers with a quick smile.

"Here's to landing on our feet for once."

I lifted my glass in answer. "May the luck continue."

"Indeed." She helped herself to some of the appetizers, and I copied her. The little spheres proved to contain some sort of shellfish with a strongly herbal flavor, and I decided I liked it. It was certainly better than the dish of what was obviously fish eggs, but Haliday attacked that with delight. "We should really see if the senator would like to hire us."

"She's already offered us legal protection," I pointed out. "And by the looks of this place, she can provide it. Let's not push it."

"Rejane said she might have work."

That was true, and I nodded. "Yeah. Though we'd probably want to stay close to Safican for a while so she could bail us out if we got into trouble."

"Safican's networked with Charest and Rados. There's generally a bit of weather on the fast routes, but we've got ways around that. It could prove very profitable."

"It could." It was also, I knew, the sensible thing to do. We'd crossed the Academy, called attention to ourselves when we should have refused to get involved, and it was pure luck that we weren't about to have my device confiscated the next time we came anywhere near an Academician. And if we were going to live like this…no, that probably wasn't the case, I doubted ordinary employees lived in this kind of luxury; but it was still likely to be nicer than anything we'd had in years.

"Will you at least consider it?" Haliday asked.

I shook myself. "I am considering it—very seriously considering it. Like I said, this is better than anything I expected."

"We could for once trust a good thing," Haliday said, and I couldn't help smiling.

"I do. At least, I trust the senator to protect her son and grandchildren, and that means protecting us. So yes, let's see if she offers work."

"Will you take it if she does?" Haliday cocked her head to one side.

"I can't say without seeing the actual details," I protested. "I'll definitely consider it, will that do?"

"It'll have to," Haliday said, and I nodded.

"Yes, it will."

Haliday was right about Charest and Rados, though. They were close enough that they had maintained their communications network through all but the worst of the Dark, and had never forgotten each other's existence. The three worlds still kept up a robust trade network. I had visited both, though not after Haliday joined *Beljaeger*; Haliday knew Rados well, and said she still had connections there. We'd almost certainly be able to pick up enough work to keep us going even without the senator's help, and if we stuck to the Triad for a while, we ought to be safe from Academy interference.

And yet. It felt like letting the Academy win. I knew better than to let myself fall into that trap, but it was still galling to imagine spending the next two or three years confined to the Safican Triad avoiding trouble. And there was Rejane's plan, Rejane's and Sawyl's. She was right that we needed to keep trying to decipher Ancestral technologies; rejecting them, inventing an interstellar technology from scratch and on completely different principles, could take centuries and might be impossible. Far better to work with what we had, and find ways to mitigate the threat of the AI.

And then there was Callambhal Above. What if it was possible to re-ignite the Inner Sun, to bring the station back to its original glory? Using an AI share was a risk; but it was a risk dozens—maybe hundreds—of us took every time we entered the possible. Yes, ships were lost, people killed, but the AI never came close to gaining a toehold in normal space. And to see Callambhal restored.... I had grown up with the stories, how Callambhal had thrived through its collaboration with the Dedalor, until Hafren split from his family to side with the AI. The middle siblings had urged restraint, but Nenien—the eldest and his mother Kuffrin's most devoted follower—had attacked instead, touching off the AI War. Finally Nenien had trapped Hafren and Gold Shining Bone, the most powerful of the rebel AI, in the possible.

And there they remained, still managing to interfere, until Nenien's daughter Anketil was tricked into releasing them, setting off the second phase of the war. Under Gold Shining Bone's leadership, the AI had massed for a final assault on the real—the quantum wave that would create the Gap— but Anketil and her lover Irtholin managed to intervene. She couldn't stop the wave, but she did stop the AI, trapping them permanently in the possible. Green Piercing Book had joined the rebellion early, ripping itself free of Callambhal's systems, destroying the Sun and crippling the station. Anketil had come to Callambhal's rescue, or so the stories said. I could understand why the council might take the risk. Rejane certainly seemed to think that they would.

And that, if I was honest, was the heart of the problem: Rejane wanted this, was determined to make it happen, and once again my instinct was to help. If I said as much to Haliday, she'd point out that I'd been trained since I was twelve to do whatever Rejane Novilis needed—wanted—and it was past time I broke that dangerous habit. She wasn't wrong—even at the time, I'd known what I had to do to earn my place at Rejane's side—but there was more to it than just the gift of my burden. I was more to her than the person whose blood made her Firstborn.

We finished our meal in relative silence, the sky and sea growing darker outside the window, fading from lavender to purple to indigo scattered with stars. The arc of the galaxy was high in the night sky, a pale haze studded with stars, undimmed by Deepside's minimal lights; the Gap was invisible here, as though it had never happened. Here and there, trails of light broke the water: boats, I assumed, or maybe some luminescent local wildlife, a poor echo of the stars overhead.

"I'm for bed," Haliday said. "I want to get on local time as soon as possible." *And so should you*, her tone implied.

I nodded, and watched her across the hall, then set the used dishes for the housekeepers to collect. I knew I should follow her example, but my nap had left me wakeful, and instead I tuned my handheld to the local channels and skimmed through the libraries, looking for entertainment. I settled on what seemed to be a local production of part of the Dedalor cycle, Anketil and Irtholin's conflict with Anketil's cousin Iestyn and his clone-twin Ievyn, but the focus on Ievyn, created only to provide sickly Iestyn with the burden that would restore him to health, cut too close to the bone. I switched it off and sat for a while staring into the night, watching the galactic arc rise toward the zenith. I was still wakeful, and it was a relief when my handheld pinged again.

"Yes?"

"It's me," Rejane said. "Do you have a minute?"

The handheld had her at the door. I opened it without bothering to answer. "What is it?"

"I don't want to keep you up."

"I'm awake," I said, and waved her in. She was wearing her Academician's robes, black over white, and she looked pinched and tired. "Are you all right?"

"I've come from the family service," she said. "I wanted to be there, but it's hard."

I gestured toward the seats. "Can I get you—well, I'm not sure what there is, we drank all the wine."

"If there's honey-water?" Rejane managed a smile. "You should try some, too, I think you'd like it."

The galley cabinet contained a flask that was labeled honey-water, and there were glasses in the upper racks. I poured us each a glass and brought them across, settling myself beside Rejane. The honey-water was sweet and touched with unfamiliar spices, and I nodded. "This is good."

"I'm glad you like it." She sipped at her own, her expression shadowed, and I groped for words.

"I wish I'd known him better. He seemed like a good man."

"Fish was something special," she said. "He was the first enhanced aquatic with a Firstborn burden to complete the Sevens and become an Academician, and he was too talented for anyone to hold him back. And Ankes knows they tried! They called him Fish in the dormitories, and he laughed at them, pretended it didn't hurt and turned it into an in-joke for his friends. He was always in the top five of every class, he had a particular knack for figuring out Ancestral toys, he advanced our understanding of every Remnant he worked on—and he was *kind*. Endolian could have married anyone; a mere Academician, which is what Fish was when they met, was marrying down for him, but he never wanted anyone else. And now he's alone, with the kids to raise, and I just feel so bad for him."

I put my hand on her shoulder. "I'm sorry."

She shook her head. "I'm all right. It's just—he was my best friend since you, and I can't believe he's gone." She wept then, and I let her lean against me, patting her back as though we were children again. Her hair still smelled like everast, the tiny star-shaped herb that grew everywhere around the Prater, and for just an instant I was back on Prater Daal, handed over to the sick girl who would change my life.

Or at least that was the story they had told me. It had been Rejane herself who told me the truth: she wasn't precisely sick, but she was born with nanites capable of joining with a Firstborn burden. The Novilis were Secondborn at best, and many of them were Faciendi; she was their first chance to put a family member into the Academy, and I was to be the source of her new burden. By then I didn't mind: she was my friend, and even her family was better to me than my mother's husband and my half-siblings. I would have given more, and gladly.

Only the Novilis hadn't kept their part of the bargain. I had been supposed to go to the Academy myself, since I qualified by testing, school records, and burden. Instead, they had indentured me to my first captain and set me on an entirely different path. Rejane had fought for me, and finally wept in helpless fury as we packed for our new destinations. She promised she would come for me, and she had kept her word, but by then I had inherited *Beljaeger* and it was too late for the Academy anyway.

Rejane drew a hard breath and pulled away, wiping her face with the inside of her sleeve. She had never had the gift of crying gracefully, and her eyes were swollen and her nose red and blotchy. I kept one arm around her shoulder, and after a moment we settled side by side, pressing together. "I'm sorry," she said, and I shook my head.

"Nothing to apologize for."

"Oh, so many things." She managed a crooked smile. "But I didn't come here to cry on your shoulder."

"Oh?"

"No, really." She pulled away, settling herself at the end of the couch, her knees drawn up as though we were children again. "I wanted—we've never had a chance to talk, not really, and I wanted to apologize."

"You didn't do it," I said.

"I didn't stop them." Her mouth twisted again. "And I went to the Academy."

"You didn't have a choice." I took a careful breath. "We were sixteen, what could either of us have done? We have talked about this before. I told you then and I tell you now, I'm not angry with you."

She wiped her face again, sniffling. "I'm sorry. It's—losing Fish has—I can't believe he's gone."

I felt a stab of jealousy: once she would have wept like this for me. And probably still would, though I didn't intend to give her the chance. "Did you tell him? About your burden?"

"No." She shook her head for emphasis. "No, I didn't dare. You're still the only one who knows."

"And the family," I said, but it was comfort nonetheless. "What happens now?"

"I don't know." She reached for her glass, took another drink as though that would help her think. "What Fish and I were trying to do—it's still important, maybe even more than ever, but with him gone, I'm not sure how best to continue. He had supporters in the councils, but I'm not sure they'll follow me." She gave another sideways smile. "They think I'm reckless."

"I can't imagine why."

She laughed softly. "Well. But there are real dangers, and Fish's death is going to make some people think twice. No one expected Larel to take such an active role in things."

"Do you really think she killed him?" I asked.

"I don't know. Doli thinks she did—he swears Fish's cardiac issues were known and minor, but it's true that aquatics are more vulnerable. One thing's for certain, Larel will take credit for it if she thinks it'll help the Newfounders."

"Lovely people." I was beginning to wish there was more wine left.

"Aren't they?" Rejane shook her head. "Valenguar was the perfect place to start our experiments, but now we won't be able to follow up on what happened—and, no, I don't know what we did, though I have some ideas. I just can't test them now."

"What do you think happened?" I remembered the weight of the sounds, and the ring of light rising out of the water. We'd been lucky it hadn't been something terrible.

"I think—" Rejane laid heavy emphasis on the word. "I think we triggered a start-up sequence, but for whatever reason it didn't complete. My guess is that there wasn't enough power."

"I thought the idea was that the Starwell drew its power from the planetary core."

"I think it did once," Rejane said, "but I think those connections have eroded. It certainly doesn't have anything like the power it must once have had. I also think it takes a daedalist's burden to trigger it, which would make some sense if it's intended to access the possible."

"Then you and I should have produced the same reactions," I said.

Rejane nodded. "And we did, or very nearly. I suspect that if I'd been holding the device at that moment, it would still have triggered the Starwell. Ichellem isn't a daedalist, and Fish is—was—barely one."

"And you were going to downcall an AI share at the installation? That still seems risky."

"Admittedly. But there were some alternatives we could have tried. And then we would have had a much better idea whether or not we could do something about the Inner Sun."

"Someone on the council is already working with you," I guessed, and she nodded.

"But whether they will now is another question." She shook herself. "Have you and Hal made plans?"

I shrugged. "The senator is being very generous. We'll certainly stay here for a bit, and then I suppose we'll see if we can get work in the Triad. I don't want to lose my device."

"If you're able to stay a little longer, I might have work for you."

Haliday won't like that. She'd made it very clear that she wasn't going to work with or for Rejane again, but the decision wasn't Haliday's. "And I might be interested," I said, with a smile. She matched my smile, but there was a melancholy behind it that tugged at my heart. "Look, do you want to stay here tonight? I'm not proposing anything, it's just you don't look like you want to be alone."

There was a little silence, and then she nodded. "I don't. And thank you."

"Any time," I said, and we sat in companionable silence as the stars wheeled behind us.

Interlude 4

The news [of the AI rebellion and their war in the possible] came to Callambhal discreetly, by fast courier. The ship crossed the Atten Bridge* without attracting attention and the sole crew, a man in Dedalor livery, came secretly to the Council to bring them both the news and Nenien's warning: no AI, no matter how long in service nor how loyal it seemed, could be trusted.

The Council summoned the Sun's Master, and together agreed that for the sake of the station measures must be taken to prevent Green Piercing Book from joining the rebel AI. So they worked in secret in the station's Tail and on Callambhal Below [both places where Green Piercing Book had few or no connections] and created a cage that would hold even the greatest of the Great AI. But when they went to install it, Green Piercing Book saw what they intended, and broke the ties that held it to the Sun and the station. In the chaos it fled into the possible, never to be seen again.

Reconstructed / recovered text from databanks on The Skim

*The name used by Ancestral documents for the most common approach to Callambhal Above. It has not been matched to any route currently in use.

Chapter Ten

I woke to sun reflecting off the sea, and Rejane moving quietly in the lower part of the suite. It was still early by the local clock, and she pocketed her handheld as I sat up.

"I was going to leave you a message," she said. "But if you're awake, we could grab an early breakfast."

Unlike the Academy campus at the Starwell, the senator's household didn't share a single dining hall, but instead food was served from an array of kiosks along one wall of a corridor that gave onto a series of rooms. Each held a number of different configurations of seating and tables, but all of them were bathed in the same soft blue-green light. We collected what seemed to be a standard basket filled with bread and a crock of some pale spread and a twisted leaf that held a handful of what looked like nuts and dried berries. There was a flask of tea as well, and Rejane nudged me toward the nearest open room. The outer wall was a single long window, and the room itself was underwater, so that we were looking out into the sun-dappled shallows between buildings. A shadow moved across the space—something passing on the surface?—and a swimmer cut gracefully through a fall of light. Baskets of some trailing vine hung from the walls and ceiling, and the air smelled faintly of flowers. It was lovely, the sort of elegance I imagined belonged to the Ancestors, and even Rejane looked happier for it.

We found a table and assembled our meals, and I gave her a thoughtful look. "So what are you planning to do?"

She didn't answer for a long moment, apparently absorbed

in pouring out her tea, and finally shrugged. "I need to look at the data we gathered on Valenguar, and then there's some other work Fish was doing that I never had a chance to review. Then—see if there's a way to continue, I suppose."

"You took data from the Starwell? Won't someone come after you?"

She shrugged again. "It was at least partly my work. And I was afraid Larel would destroy it if I didn't take a copy. She may anyway, but at least I'll have this much." Her gaze slid past me, and she put her basket back together. "And I should make sure I have all of it. I'll be in touch."

"Please." I didn't need to look over my shoulder to know it was Haliday approaching, giving Rejane an uneasy look as she gestured toward the empty chair.

"Mind if I join you? I didn't mean to chase her off."

"It's all right." I shifted my containers, and we sat in silence while Haliday unpacked her basket.

"I thought I'd put in some calls to the Guildhall in Grand Depot," she said at last. "I can at least get a handle on the kinds of jobs they have that'll take us to Rados."

I nodded. "That sounds like a plan. Though I'm not in any particular hurry to leave. I'd like to give it enough time for any trouble to die out."

"Will you at least look at what I find?"

"I said I would." I reined in my annoyance. "All I'm saying is that I'd like to like low for a while, and this is a nicer place than most to do so."

Haliday relaxed a little, though the frown line didn't vanish from between her brows. "That's definitely true. The senator is being generous."

"She is." I poured more tea, forcing myself to patience. "I want to get out of this as easily as possible."

"The easiest thing," Haliday began, and shook herself. "No, sorry."

"Done is done."

She nodded. "And you're right, this is as good as we're likely to get. I just hate to be beholden to anyone."

That was not what she had started to say, I thought, but I pretended I hadn't heard. "It's definitely worth checking at the Guildhall. These friends of yours on Rados, what kind of work are they likely to have?"

"Courier work, mostly. Or that's what it used to be."

"That could work for us," I said, and saw her relax slightly. "See what's out there."

"I'll do that," she said, and we drifted onto other topics before she headed off to find a comms kiosk.

Left to myself, I called up a local map and explored the public levels of the senator's tower—Almendwyne—and then found a uniformed concierge to direct me to the shorter public building I could see across the channel. Most of the connections were underwater, crossed by the aquatics as easily as I'd cross an open-air street on most other worlds, but he plotted a course for me and loaded it to my handheld. It took me up several levels, and across an open bridge scoured by winds, but I came out onto an upper mezzanine and was able to find my way down to the market levels. Sea level was for tourists and non-aquatics, full of shops that sold local specialties expensively packaged and others that rented diving gear and minisubs as well as a ring of restaurants that clearly catered to off-world tastes, or to locals who wanted off-world delicacies.

I followed a spiral ramp down into the areas that catered to residents, where there were waterlocks at every quarter and the floors were universally covered in a soft black material that wicked away any water. There were the usual info-brokers, including several that specialized in off-world connections, and I made a note of their presence, but didn't activate any of my accounts. There would be time for that later, once I'd figured out what I wanted to do and knew what I needed. Right now, I was just playing tourist and avoiding making any decisions.

The market's lowest level was a wet market, full of fresh-caught fish and unfamiliar vegetables. It smelled clean but there was also a pungent odor that caught in the back of my throat. I made my way back up the ramp to a teashop, and bought strong smoked tea and a slab of crumbly biscuit gritty with sugar. That took the taste away, and I browsed a little longer in the middle levels, trying to distract myself. The problem was that I wanted to stay with Rejane—wanted to see what work she'd have for us—and I knew perfectly well that Haliday would never agree. Rationally, I couldn't blame her for not sharing my sense of obligation, but I wanted to know what had happened at the Starwell. Why had it responded to me and my device? Was it just that I was well-attuned to it already, and it responded to whatever ghost of an AI share had been left in the machine? Or was it my specific burden, and did that mean that Rejane could have as easily called it into action? Haliday would say it wasn't our business—and she wasn't wrong—but it was hard to let it go.

The next few days passed in much the same way. I ate with Haliday, and occasionally with Rejane, explored Almendwyne's guest spaces and the public towers to either side, soaked in the plunge pool and watched the galactic arc sweep the sky beyond my window. The evening of the third day, there was a public ceremony for Sawyl to which we were invited. It was held in an assembly hall below the water line, lit by dozens of hanging lamps that flickered like actual flames and formed a sort of corridor that led to the dais at the hall's end. It was furnished only with a plain table of what looked like polished wood, and an empty golden disk above it, symbols I didn't recognize; Endolian and the children waited there with his mother and sister, all in floor-length robes the gray-green of a storm-bruised sky, and the hall was jammed with people who'd come to pay their respects. There were speeches, some in the common tongue, more in the local dialect. The latter were harder to follow, but there were stories that set the entire hall laughing softly as well as those that made them weep.

Afterward there was a reception, held in another assembly hall that was lined with display screens and holotables showing snippets of Sawyl's life. As we waited to pay our respects, I saw recurring glimpses of Rejane in the background of the clips—as fellow-student, as colleague, as a celebrant at his wedding feast, as family and friend—but I couldn't seem to find her in the crowd. Endolian looked exhausted, drawn and pale, and I was glad Deronda had taken the children into a corner where they were being fed along with the other children who'd attended. I hoped they'd find that comforting. When we reached Endolian, he clasped our hands hard, murmuring thanks, and then we were shuffled off with the rest of the crowd.

"Poor bastard," Haliday said quietly. "Do you think we need to stay longer?"

"I'm going to," I said, "but you go ahead."

I saw the moment she started to say something, then changed her mind. "Later, then," she said, and disappeared into the crowd.

I found my way to one of the service kiosks and accepted a glass of wine to have an excuse to look for Rejane. I found her at last, and worked my way through the crowd until I could join her. She put her hand on my arm. "We're nearly done here," she said. "Or at least I am. This is for Endolian and his family, not for me."

"You could come back to my room," I offered.

"I was going to ask. Thank you."

"It's not a night to be alone."

I had left the window blanked against the setting sun, but it cleared at my gesture, opening onto a vista of sea and stars. Safican had no moon; instead a satellite tracked across the night, brilliant even against the galactic arc. I would have offered tea or wine, but Rejane went directly to the window, spreading her fingers against its surface.

"Fish missed the ocean. Even on Valenguar, it wasn't the same. And of course he didn't get away to Junewatch as often as he would have liked."

"It's very beautiful here," I said, and seated myself cautiously on the bed behind her.

"He said, the ocean is in all our blood, as much as our burdens, all the salts and trace elements. You can tell where a person was born by the ocean in their blood." She sighed. "He said they tasted different, too. Even the air tasted different because the oceans were different. I wish we'd been able to bring him home."

"Will his body be returned?" I couldn't think of a better way to phrase it.

"The Academy recommends cremation," Rejane said. "But I imagine they'll send the ashes. Eventually. It's not the same."

"No." I reached out to her, and she took my hand, let me draw her down onto the bed beside me. We sat in silence, shoulders touching, and at last she sighed again.

"I'll miss him so."

"I know." I put my arm around her shoulders, and she turned into the embrace, so that we kissed in the starlight. It was gentle at first, and then more urgent, and at last she bore me down on the yielding pillows. It was clumsy, after so long apart, but still sweet, and afterward I lay awake while she slept on my shoulder, until finally I untangled myself enough to darken the window against the coming day.

⊓ ⅀ ⅄

When I woke, it was late, and Rejane was gone. She had left an apologetic note saying she'd been called to a meeting, and I wasn't entirely sorry to avoid any possibly awkward conversations. There were still leftovers in my room and I ate them, glad of an excuse not to visit the dining levels, then wandered out again into the markets. I climbed to each of the three observation decks, rented viewing lenses to get a good look at *Beljaeger*, still safely parked on the landing table, then made my way down through a tangle of ramps and spiraling stairwells to buy a packaged lunch to eat on the broad outer ledges of Almendwyne. Boats churned past at careful speed, their wakes washing up onto the low steps. I didn't see any swimmers, but guessed they kept well below the surface, away from the danger of an accidental collision.

My handheld pinged. I hauled it out, expecting Haliday, but instead it was Rejane, requesting a meeting at one of the laboratories as soon as I was available. I sent back that I was available now, and received an instant reply: *Come ahead.*

The lab was deep in Almendwyne's core, through additional layers of security. My guest pass got me through the first checkpoint, but at the second the concierge had to call for authorization, and at the third Rejane herself had to come and vouch for me. I received a temporary badge, and she led me through a series of corridors past rooms that bore the marks of the family corporations, until we finally reached a small room at the end of one short hallway. It was heavily screened and fitted out for a daedalist, with an array of sensors racked above the workbench, and a couple of Ancestral toys on shelves beside the desk.

"The senator had it set up for Fish and me, so he wouldn't have to lose work time when they visited," Rejane said. "I've been going over the data I pulled before I left." For the first time since we'd reached Safican, she sounded like herself again.

"Yeah?" There was a stool at the end of the desk, and I perched on it, craning my neck to get a look at the screen.

"That's the composite of what we got from the Starwell. Nothing really new there, but here—" She ran her hand over a touchscreen, calling up a new page of data. "Fish got this just before we arrived. I hadn't had a chance to look at it until now, but it's the most recent survey of the Inner Sun, complete with a new theory from the Custodian there."

The screen splintered into equations about halfway down. I recognized some of the symbols, but I was no daedalist to be able to read them easily. I swallowed old regret, and said, "Why don't you sum up?"

"Mirean—Tadei Mirean, the Inner Sun's Custodian—has analyzed the structure of the Sun itself, the actual orb, and traced the linkages back to the control room. She believes she's identified the containment structure for an AI share. More than that, she thinks it's intact, and would accept an AI share if one were to be found."

"That sounds incredibly dangerous."

"That's the thing." Rejane gestured to the equations. "Mirean's work suggests that the Ancestors were aware of the potential danger—there's reason to think Callambhal Above was a relatively late creation—and built this containment so that it would not only restrict the share to control of the Sun, but that it would actually damp down anything more powerful. Anything but a great AI, a Dedalor AI and very possibly anything but one of Kuffrin's original AIs, would be reduced to a share, and a low-level one, at that. She's run some tests that seem to confirm her theory, but of course she'd need an actual share to prove it."

"Preferably a low-level one," I said. Technically, of course, downcalling a share was utterly forbidden; in practice, there were vital installations, like the RebIC networks that allowed interstellar communication, that couldn't function without AI intervention, and the Academy looked the other way if a new share had to be found. The daedalists who dealt in such things did their work in uninhabited systems, however, and took only tiny, fractional shares. A share that could power and control the Inner Sun was something else entirely. "Except it didn't work on Green Piercing Book. That would seem to contradict her research."

"Oral histories are suggestive, but not definitive," Rejane said. "Particularly the stories that come to us from before the Fall. Or it's possible that the protections were added after Green Piercing Book abandoned the station, possibly as part of Anketil's supposed rescue operation. We know that it remained inhabited for at least another century."

That made some sense, and I nodded. "Do you really think Callambhal's council will let you do this?"

"To re-ignite the Sun and bring Callambhal back to its original status?" Rejane countered. "Do you really think they won't jump at the chance?"

Probably they would, and that was more than a little terrifying. And I could understand why: I remembered the vast dark at the heart of the station, the emptiness that even as a child had felt lost and yearning. Even if you lived in the trailing sections of the station, where we did, there was no avoiding the central void. We passed it every time my mother took me with her to market, or to the testing stations, darkness visible from the transit stations that had once connected the station's hemispheres, blanking the tube-train's windows when the cars tracked briefly along the inner surface. Once in a while a light spilled out of some compartment, showing rust-colored metal or streaks of brightly painted paneling, and that faint glimpse made the emptiness even worse. A Remnant couldn't feel—or perhaps it could, and its loss and sorrow filled the station, blotted out every attempt to bring Callambhal back to what it had been. "All right, yes. Probably they would. But to downcall an AI on the station—"

"We don't have to," Rejane said. "There are other shares out there, we use one of them."

"No one is going to let you rob the RebIC system."

Rejane grinned. "I wasn't planning on it. The Academy—Nic, this is a deadly secret, you can't ever let on you know, but—the Academy has an AI of its own. A true AI, a great AI. It can grant a share, and no one would ever be the wiser, at least until the Sun is lit again."

"But then the Sun will be connected to the Academy's AI," I said. "That can't be a good thing. Especially if it's a great AI."

"The Academy's AI is completely cut off from the possible," Rejane said. "Anketil tested her theories on it, proved that she could keep the AI from entering the real. And she protected it when she defeated the rest of the AI." I knew I looked skeptical, and Rejane sighed. "It was her AI. Blue Standing Sky."

Everyone knew that part of the legend: Blue Standing Sky alone of all the AI had stayed loyal to Anketil, even as the others made war on the Dedalor. Supposedly it had saved Anketil and Irtholin when they were briefly caught between worlds, though it had been badly shredded in the process.

Presumably it was the remains that Anketil had used to test her theories, or perhaps that had been her price for repairing its terrible damage. Or perhaps this had been her way of saving the AI that had saved her; with the Dedalor, it was hard to know. It was certainly plausible that the Academy had preserved it. I wondered what Beast would make of that. It was a minor AI, eking out its existence in the shadows unpopulated by greater programs, trading its help to humans for the transit mass it used to protect itself. Could it become a greater AI, or did it even want to? "I can't imagine the Academy is just going to let you take a piece of their treasure. Especially since they've kept it a secret all these years."

"The Librarian is a Successor," Rejane said. "And a friend of Fish's. At worst, he'll look the other way. And the main campus is also heavily Successor. The Newfounders have very little power there."

"Are you seriously considering going to Ankes-and-Irthe to collect a share of this secret AI?" I stared at her. "Won't the Senior Custodian have something to say about that?"

"If she tries anything," Rejane said, "I'll denounce her for Fish's death."

"Does she know that?"

"She started the game." Rejane's voice was grim.

It was possible, I supposed. I could certainly believe that the Academy kept an AI imprisoned in the depths of their peculiar world; I could also believe that the Academy's core was Successor to the heart. And this was the sort of plan I'd seen Rejane pull off before, something that seemed like an insane gamble until you unwound all the pieces. "And you want me to take you there?"

Rejane nodded. "To Ankes-and-Irthe, yes, and then to Callambhal Above. You have the Callambhal burden still, that will only make things easier."

"Haliday won't go for it." That wasn't what I'd meant to say, but it was certainly true. "At least, I'm pretty sure she won't. I'll need to find another tech, I can't run *Beljaeger* by myself."

"I have tech-three papers," Rejane said.

"I need a tech-one."

"I can do the work if I have to, I've got the skills. I just never took the tests." Rejane paused. "Besides, she might go for it. You can talk to her."

I could make it work if I had to: *Beljaeger* was rigged to fly two-handed, but I could do it all in a pinch. As long as I did the calculations, Rejane could probably handle the fields, and I could take over if we got into serious trouble. I could set a broken course, one that let us drop in and out of the possible a couple of times, that would counteract her daedalist's burden and the AI attention it might draw. It could be done. And maybe I could persuade Haliday to take on one more trip, though the words felt hollow even in my mind. "I'll try," I said. "And we'll see what I can do."

开 戈 钟

I found Haliday in one of the public lounges, this one above the surface, with a terrace that opened onto a wider stretch of water. It was quiet in the mid-afternoon, though there was a tea kiosk tended by a young woman with vividly pink hair, and I took my time ordering my drink as though that would make this easier. Haliday had claimed a lounge like a slanted basket just inside the translucent curtains that broke the afternoon breeze, curled comfortably on the pillows with a tall canister of tea and the remains of a boxed snack. She lifted a hand in greeting and I came to join her, but as I came closer, I could see that her eyes were wary.

"So," she said. "I have a lead on what might turn out to be a steady contract—if you're interested."

"You know I'm not crazy about commitments," I said, and perched awkwardly on the basket's lip.

"It's not exclusive," she said, pushing herself upright so that we sat facing each other. "Basically, they want to pay us to hold courier space for them, and we're free to take any other cargo at the same time."

I winced. That was something I would normally consider, particularly after the debacle of our last job, but not this time. "I've had another offer."

"From Rejane." Haliday's voice was flat.

"Yes."

"You can't be serious. Not after this last disaster."

"It wasn't her fault," I said.

"Wasn't it? We sure as death wouldn't be involved if we hadn't taken her job."

"She didn't kill Sawyl."

"He died of a heart attack," Haliday retorted. "Nic, there's no proof of anything Rejane's told us. As far as we know, she could have done it."

"The senator wouldn't be helping us if there wasn't some truth to the story," I said.

"I told you before," Haliday said. "I'm done with her. I will not work another of her jobs, not for any money."

I took a breath. "I know. I understand. But, Hal, this is important to me. I know you don't want to be involved with her any more, all right, I can work with that. Stay here, or wherever, and we can join up again after this is over—"

"No."

"At least hear me out."

"There's nothing to hear," she said. "Look, right now we're stuck in the Triad because Rejane Novilis pissed off the Academy and got us involved—"

"We don't know they're looking for us."

It was a feeble argument, and Haliday gave it the look it deserved. "Check the Guild Warnings and the Outstandings database, then—though you always told me that drew more attention than it was worth. Or is it just that you want to be able to say you didn't know what she got us into?"

"The searches are monitored. You know that."

"Doing anything for her right now is a terrible idea," Haliday said. "It's your ship, I can't stop you, but I'm not risking any more of my time and energy on this. You take this job, and I'm gone. Permanently."

I had known it would come to this, but I still had to fight. "Drop off for this job. Once it's done, I'll come back to the Triad. We can lie low, work a steady contract—"

"No. Aren't you listening to me? No."

"Hal, I don't want to lose you."

"Then don't take the job." She pushed herself to the edge of the basket, reached back for her tea. "You can send my payout to my standard account when you're ready."

"This is not what I wanted."

"It's what you've got." Haliday rose to her feet, shaking her head as she looked down at me. "I don't know what's between the two of you—and I don't want to know—but it's not healthy and it's not safe and I am done. I'll be moving back to Grand Depot as soon as I can make my apologies to the senator." She paused. "If you change your mind, you know where to find me. Otherwise—it was a good run, Nic, but this is five steps too far."

She turned then and walked away, still stiff with fury. I watched her go, knowing there was nothing I could say— knowing she wasn't entirely wrong, either. Meddling in Academy politics was bad enough, and Rejane's plan was dangerous beyond anything I'd ever imagined. I traversed the possible for my living, I knew how deadly the AI could be—but if it was possible to restore the Inner Sun, restore Callambhal Above and everything that depended on it, perhaps even unlock the secrets of all the Great Remnants.... I couldn't resist the game. Even if it hadn't been Rejane asking, I would have been tempted. And it was Rejane, after all. It was worth the risk.

Not that it would be easy. Without Haliday, I'd either have to hire another technician or Rejane would have to take the job, and there was no time to find someone I could trust. I could plot a series of short courses, dropping out of the possible at known waypoints or intermediate systems and that would minimize the time Rejane's burden was exposed to the AI. If I stuck to the waypoints, that would significantly reduce the chance we'd be spotted by any of the Academy's agents: it was workable, and probably the least dangerous part of the entire job.

But it would be without Haliday. I had relied on her for more than seven years, trusted her, even offered her a share in the ship's profits, though she'd turned down the chance to buy into the ship itself. I was glad of that now, though it had stung at the time. *Beljaeger* would be different without her. I dragged myself to my feet and made my way back toward my room.

Haliday was gone before I got there, the door standing open opposite mine. There was no note in my mailbox, though I didn't know why I'd expected one. She'd said everything there was to say. I poured out the dregs of my tea and logged in to the ship's accounts, transferring everything I owed into Haliday's wage account. That would leave me a little short, but Rejane could surely make up the difference.

The console pinged, signaling that the transfer was complete. I closed down the system and went to stand by the window, staring out over the sea, grateful that I was looking away from the landing table. If we pulled this off, and if anyone could, it would be Rejane, Haliday would be sorry she'd left. I could persuade her back again—no, I couldn't convince myself of that. No matter how successful we were, when Hal said she was done, she meant it. I shivered in spite of the sunlight. I didn't regret it, but I was sorry she was gone.

Chapter Eleven

It was early evening before Rejane appeared. I hadn't felt like braving the cheerful company of the household, and had ordered a meal sent to my room; I had just packed away the leftovers when the door chimed softly, and the security screen lit to show her waiting. I brought the tray of sweets back out and opened the door, beckoning her in.

"I gather it didn't go well with Haliday," she said. "I'm sorry."

"No." I shrugged. "I didn't expect it would."

"I'm still sorry."

"Thanks." I offered the sweets, and she accepted one. We sat at opposite ends of the long bench, and I set the tray between us. "I don't want to sound mercenary, but I hope you've gotten access to your accounts again. I had to pay out Hal's share."

"Of course." She chose another sweet. "And yes, I have plenty of funds now."

"That will make this easier."

"Yes."

The silence stretched between us, and the sky darkened beyond the window, slowly revealing the stars. Before the Dark, humans had settled hundreds of systems, so many that we couldn't be entirely sure which had been destroyed in the Gap and which had just been lost, forgotten, regressed so far that they could no longer reach for off-world contact, cut off at the end of hyperspatial lanes that were too deep or too shallow or too dangerous for modern ships to risk. That was what we had lost, when the Ancestors fell. That was what Rejane hoped to restore.

"Will it work?" I asked at last, and Rejane looked up abruptly.

"There's every chance. I can't promise, Fish and I are out on the edge here, but—I wouldn't risk it if I didn't believe it would."

I nodded. "What happens if you're right?"

Rejane laughed. "Most people would ask what happens if I'm wrong."

"I can figure that out for myself," I answered, and she laughed again.

"I suppose it's not hard. If we're right—the least is that we restore the Inner Sun, and that's astonishing enough. I don't have to tell you what that would mean to Callambhal Above. But beyond that, if I'm right about the principles behind it, we might be able to understand more of the Remnants. We might finally figure out what the Starwell does, or the Great Works. We might even be able to restore function to some of the Remnants, the ones like the Prater, where we already have a good idea of what they did. And there are all the lesser devices and installations that could be revived. Some of them will be too damaged, of course, but not all of them. But most of all— if we're very, very lucky—we might be able to undo the worst of the Dark. If we truly understand the Ancestral technology, we might be able to make peace with the AI. Imagine if we could access the possible without having to worry about being attacked. If we could travel as freely as the Ancestors."

"The AI would never agree," I said. "I've felt them, they hate us."

"You bargain with one every time you enter the possible," Rejane said.

"Not every time," I said. "And it's not doing it because it likes me."

"Why, then?" she asked. "Do you know?"

"It asks for transit mass," I said. "So do all the AI who make these bargains. My captain told me it was protective for them, like those crabs that build shells from other creatures' remnants. No one's ever proved that, though."

"Another question worth answering," she said, and I nodded. "And if we do—if we could figure out what they want, who knows where that might lead us?"

"What they wanted was to destroy us," I said. That was the bleak truth at the heart of the legend: regardless of whether the AI had betrayed the Dedalor first or if the Dedalor had betrayed them, the AI had made a concerted effort to destroy our worlds. "And they live outside time, the War isn't in the past for them because there is no past."

"But there is change," Rejane said. "Even the AI change, and that—well, that could be our key."

The breadth of possibility was enough to make me gasp. If Rejane was right, if we could find that way for the AI to change, for all of us to change, we might indeed free ourselves forever from the threat of another Dark. I couldn't see how it might happen, but I could almost believe that it could. We finished the sweets in silence, and went to bed beneath the wheeling stars.

Afterward, Rejane sprawled into sleep, but I lay wakeful, watching her. She hadn't changed much since I'd last seen her—skin a little darker, maybe, from stronger suns, and her hair was still cut in the close cap that tamed her curls and emphasized the strong bones of her face. She didn't have an entertainer's polished beauty, but she had long ago grown into her looks. We had not been lovers on Prater Daal, not really. We'd kissed and touched and once we'd achieved a stolen hour and managed to have almost-satisfying sex before Rejane's mentor had come looking for us, but we'd not known enough to know better. When we'd finally met again, we'd fallen instantly into bed, and ended up fighting like Dedalor. It had been easy to agree to part, and to stay apart, except for occasional encounters. Tonight, though, tonight and all our time on Safican—it felt more like it had done when we were younger. I was not as angry, or not as angry with her, and she... I didn't know what she thought, but she felt happy, as though she was glad to be in my arms.

She stirred then, rolling over, and smiled as though she'd read my thought. "The stars are amazing here."

"I'd been on Safican," I said, "but only in Grand Depot. You don't see much of the sky there."

"I am sorry about Haliday," she said again, and I shook my head.

"I don't want to talk about her."

"Fair enough." Rejane hauled her share of the pillows into a more comfortable position, settling herself on one elbow to stare out the window. "Did anyone ever tell you why my family cheated you?"

I blinked. It had never occurred to me to ask: of course no oligarch would keep their promise to a line-worker's daughter. "I wasn't in a position to ask. I assumed they didn't want me telling anyone about your burden."

"That's what I thought," Rejane said. "And I'm sure that was part of it. But my uncle said they didn't want me committing myself too soon."

"And to the wrong sort of person," I said, but there was less bitterness there than there had been. I was what I was, a pilot and a captain and a ship-owner with a talent that had kept me safe and solvent since the day I earned *Beljaeger*. It was not the Academy, but it was no small thing, either. And without me, Rejane would still be trapped on Valenguar, all her dreams in ruins.

"That too," Rejane admitted. "I'm lucky you were on Adora—I mean, I couldn't have done any of this without you, that goes without saying, but this—" She leaned over to kiss my bare shoulder. "This is different."

The words were almost a plea, and I rolled over to return the kiss. "Better," I said, and she sighed in sleepy agreement.

It took almost two weeks, a solid three hundred hours, to get ready for the trip. *Beljaeger* was already rigged to run two-handed, but Haliday was an experienced technician, and we were used to working together. I found a local rigger who came well-recommended and reworked the controls so that

I could handle the field controls as necessary. I ordered fuel and supplies, restocked the auto-galley and took an overnight trip into Grand Depot to secure more transit mass. I hoped I'd at least hear from Haliday while I was there, but when I broke down and made inquiries at the Guildhall, they said she'd already gone off-world. I should have expected that, but it still hurt, though I lied and told Rejane everything was fine when I returned.

I ordered extra shielding, top-quality feroshene that was supposed to block AI perceptions, and had it installed in the cargo bay and in the crew cabins. I would have liked to have it installed in the cockpit as well, but that would have involved ripping out most of the controls. We'd have to rely on short jumps and whatever protection Beast was able to provide. I laid out seven different courses from Safican to Ankes-and-Irthe, each one skipping through eight or nine waypoints, and declared us as ready as we could be.

Rejane had spent the time refining her research and making sure copies were stored with Endolian, under Sawyl's name. She had also made some cautious connections with allies within the Academy, and promised that we wouldn't run into any problems on Ankes-and-Irthe. I found that harder to trust, but Rejane swore that Larel's faction didn't have any real power at the Academy's center. Besides, if Larel accused us, Rejane was perfectly prepared to accuse her of harming Sawyl, and I agreed that the Senior Custodian probably didn't want to take that risk. At least not yet, but it would be enough to get us to Ankes-and-Irthe. Rejane could surely handle it from there.

We lifted from Deepside a little before dawn, flying east around the curve of the planet to meet the sun. We joined the outbound traffic over Grand Depot, and I put us on autopilot while I tuned the propulsion fields to keep us well back of the heavy freighter two hours ahead of us in the lane. I started the capacitors charging as well, and leaned back to try to relax. Rejane settled herself in what had been Haliday's seat, and I could see her frowning as she went over the controls a final time. She might know how to do a tech-three's job, but it had been a long time since she'd done it—if she'd ever handled it on her own at all. I considered asking, but decided it wouldn't actually make a difference. She saw me looking, and lifted her head.

"Tea? I was going to brew myself some."

"Thanks."

She came back with two tall cylinders filled to the brim with the galley's best brew. I sipped at mine, drowsed a bit, and roused myself at the flash of distant energy that said the heavy freighter had made its jump to the possible. All my boards were steady green, everything aligned for an easy jump. I took a break, relieved myself, then walked the length of the ship to be sure that everything was secure. I collected the device and came back to control to find everything still green. Rejane eyed the device thoughtfully as I set it in its holder.

"Could it reach the AI now? We're closing on the jump point."

"We're still well outside the possible," I answered. "You saw what it was like on Valenguar. It's mostly inert, until you reach the possible."

"Probably safer that way," she said. "I wonder what it was intended to do? Or maybe this is it, helping ships in transit."

"I think it's for communications generally," I said, and ran my hand lightly over the surface, carefully holding back my burden. It sang back to me, the same clear note that any toy produced, but there was no hint of AI presence.

Safican was an easy system, the grain of space smooth and clear. It was easy to keep *Beljaeger* aligned with the jump point, and when the capacitors fired, we leaped into the possible as though we'd stepped over a threshold. I locked the pilot's controls, letting momentum translate to a temporary course. Rejane bent over Haliday's controls, tuning the fields to hold us steady. She seemed to have that under control, and the sensor nets were empty. I took a breath to brace myself, and reached for the device. Heat bloomed under my hand, the vast space of the possible rushing over me like an empty wave. It peaked and receded and left nothing behind.

Beast? I waited, warmth pulsing in my palm. The sensors were empty, *Beljaeger* boring on into the possible, following the first leg of the first course I had plotted. *Beast?* The device pulsed, out of rhythm with my heartbeat. Rejane stirred, and then sat still, her eyes on her displays. *Beast....* The warmth flared, a sudden flash of pain. I held steady, wincing, and felt the AI's amusement.

Beauty. Two Beauties. A banner day.

I'm seeking safe passage to Ankes-and-Irthe. Will you help?

By what route? I visualized the pattern of my first course, and Beast recoiled. *Not possible. Too busy, too much noise.*

This? I visualized my next option, and felt the AI relax slightly.

That is available.

And your price? I felt something like laughter trembling against my palm. The counter was ticking up, tracking elapsed time: we needed the bargain before we got too much further in, or we would need to run on our own. *I'm offering transit mass. Three hundred grams.*

More laughter, tickling my skin. *Not enough. I want to taste the other Beauty.*

No. It was entirely too risky, for Rejane and for the ship. *Four hundred grams. It's the best quality.*

The other Beauty or nothing. Or I withdraw.... Or it might betray us to the other AI. That was always the risk. But the absence of its protection would be bad enough. It felt me hesitate. *But it need not come to that. She wants it as much as I do.*

I glanced sideways again and saw Rejane staring at the colors swirling within the device. Instantly, she looked back at her displays, but I had seen the hunger. "It wants to taste you. I'm trying to get it to take something else."

"But?"

"No luck so far."

"I'm willing," Rejane said. "I know how to handle this."

Probably she did, better than I had done when I began

working with the device. I glanced at the sensors again. Were the edges of the screen starting to show a haze, incoming weather? The counter was ticking on. I focused on the device again. *She is willing.*

I knew she would be. Who could resist Me? Beast's delight rolled through me. *Hurry, hurry, I am curious—*

In exchange for protection on the road I showed you, I said.

Yes, yes. Yes, as we have bargained before.

All right. I looked back at Rejane. "It's agreed to protect us. You can touch the device."

"The autopilot's locked," she said, and leaned across me to lay one careful finger on the glittering surface.

Golden lightning leaped from her fingertip, struck to the heart of the glittering tangle in the core of the device. It split, colors exploding, gold and green and blue and even flashes of unfamiliar red, then resolved into a new twist of metallic threads. I could feel Beast's satisfaction, and Rejane's confident control. Her presence rang like a bell.

Well?

Yessss....

Beast withdrew, and I felt the field shift as it established itself around us. Rejane lifted her finger, settling back into Haliday's seat, and I checked the sensors again. The haze had vanished, if it had ever been there, and we were settled onto the first leg of the course.

"Well." Rejane's voice cracked, and she cleared her throat. "Well, that was interesting."

"Different," I said.

She nodded. "Because we're in the possible? Because I was reaching for Beast—for it specifically, instead of reaching out generally." She stopped, clearly not wanting to mention the Starwell, and I nodded in agreement.

"Better to be careful."

"I was careful." She paused. "It did seem a bit pleased, didn't it? I didn't think I gave it anything."

"Could it have taken something?" I hadn't felt it, and I wasn't surprised when she shook her head.

"No. I was watching for that."

"I didn't feel anything either," I said. What I had felt was her, the same ringing presence I'd felt when we were brought together after the first burden transfer. We were alike but not identical, the Novilis technician had said; our burdens were in resonance, and might well remain so. It had seemed mostly irrelevant at the time, and after, but now I wondered what Beast made of it.

"The resonance?" Rejane asked. "I can't see why it would care. Though maybe it's curious? I can't think it would have seen it before."

"That's possible," I said, "though there are other ships that use the technique, and I wonder if those pilots don't end up attuned to each other."

"It wouldn't be the same," Rejane said. She had always been certain that we were unique.

"I suppose not." I checked my boards again, seeing the sensors still empty and the course unobstructed.

"Will it protect us?" Rejane asked, rubbing her hand as though it stung.

"It always has," I answered, and hoped that the promise would hold.

☰ ☦ ♈

Somewhat to my surprise, the rest of the trip was uneventful. There was weather in the distance as we passed between KANTOR and GIIMLI, and another thread of presence appeared just past BARTEL, but each time Beast suggested a field shift, and we edged away without drawing notice. We dropped out of the possible at the edge of Ankes-and-Irthe's system, and followed the beacons that led us toward the landing zone on the trailing side of the planet. Ankes-and-Irthe is a Trojan binary, with the world the Ancestors built tucked neatly into orbit behind the lesser sun, Irthe. The Academy had restored much of the original technology, including the shields that protected the surface from the doubled radiation of the two suns, and we were directed to a docking station that hung forever in the planet's shadow. Rejane had bespoken a space for us, and we clamped on without incident, one of a dozen small ships locked to the station's lower ring. I settled in for a much-needed rest period, and left Rejane to make whatever arrangements she needed.

When I woke, I found a tea service waiting in the commons along with a boxed meal, and a note from Rejane saying that she'd had her nap and had gone across to the station proper to arrange transport to the surface. I knew there were regular shuttles, and that non-residents weren't allowed to land their own craft, so I brewed my tea and checked the shuttle schedule while I ate. The Academy campus was currently on the day-side, so there were at least ten hours before the shuttles would begin launching to land in the brief moment when the shields could be opened. That was fine with me: I had wanted to see the Academy campus for most of my life, but not like this, not as an outsider trailing in Rejane's wake.

I still remembered our plans, made before the betrayal, every detail a scar. We had spent hours poring over the online catalogs and courses of study, planning which we would choose. We would both be daedalists, which meant the College of Mary Prophet or perhaps Project House; if instead we chose the scholar's track, focusing on the Ancestors and their work, it would be Mary Prophet or Lark Exalting. I could still remember the list of classes, a thousand opportunities laid out in dry prose, a scaffold of knowledge that led to a life unimaginable for a line-worker's brat from the trailing end of Callambhal Above. It had remained unimaginable: when we knew for sure that our protests had been ignored, and the Novilis uncle had swept down on us, a servant following him with my things already packed in new unmarked cases, there had been nothing I could do but obey. I heard Rejane had chosen Mary Prophet in the end, and the scholar's track, though she had a daedalist's training as well, but what that meant—the details, the stories, the secrets—were too far outside my experience to even guess at. Even now, all I knew was that she had found Fish there. The ache had always been present; I was only surprised to find it quite so fresh.

I napped again before Rejane returned, a restless sleep with dreams I forgot on waking, except for the unhappiness they'd carried with them. By contrast, Rejane looked tired but smug, and she was followed by a small shopping bot. She unloaded several unwieldy bags and dismissed it, dropping the bags onto one of the chairs in commons. I gave them a wary look, and she grinned.

"I've made arrangements for us to visit the Library. These are your robes." She pulled open the top one, revealing dull black fabric, the heavy matte-black robe of a low-ranking Academician, and I flinched in spite of myself.

"No. I can't."

She cocked her head. "I need you with me in the Library, and they don't let lay folk into the core. I have an identity disk for you, too."

"I'd never pass. I'm not one of you—" To my shame, my voice cracked, and I saw her wince in turn.

"I didn't think. I'm sorry." Suddenly she was crying. "Do you know how long I've wanted us to come here, together, as equals? I missed you so badly, and there was nothing I could do."

"I know." I would have reached for her, but she turned away.

"I'm sorry, I should have thought—but you deserved it. If my family had kept their word, you could have been a Custodian yourself by now."

I took a careful breath, the old angry hurt fading under the force of her fury. I had known, she had said, all of this before, but somehow hearing it here, at the Academy itself, was different, felt different. "If you're not a Custodian, I certainly wouldn't have been. No patronage except your family, and they would have been pushing you."

"The Academy doesn't trust my family," Rejane said. "They think the Prater and the nanite studies give us too much power, they don't want to promote me any further. And they're not wrong, the family does want to use my position. But you could well have passed me by now."

Sawyl had passed her, I thought. Sawyl had been a Custodian, and even if he was her patron and collaborator, I thought it must have stung to be passed over only because of her family. "I don't think I can pass."

"You've been here before," Rejane said.

"I've never been off the docking station," I said.

There was a little silence, and then Rejane scrubbed angrily at her cheeks. "If there were another way, I wouldn't ask you. But there's no other way to get you into the core, and I can't manage the AI by myself."

"I don't think I can pass," I said again.

"The gown will do most of the work. If anyone asks, you're from the Triad, things are different enough there that people won't ask questions."

"You had this all planned out."

"I planned it in transit," Rejane said. "I wasn't intending to do any of this. Well, at least not without Fish's backing." Sorrow swept over her again, but she put it determinedly aside. "I've spoken to the Librarian, and he's agreed to grant me and my assistant core access. We can do this, Nic."

冊 � 型

We caught a late shuttle down to the campus, arriving in the early hours of planetary morning. There was less traffic then, though more than on most other worlds outside the great trading hubs, and we passed through Customs without question, Rejane in her gown and me in ordinary clothes with bags in tow. Rejane had arranged for rooms and transport, and we were met outside the Customs gate by a sleepy driver who took over the baggage and led us through a maze of corridors. At last we emerged at a parking dock, and loaded ourselves into the passenger compartment of the waiting hauler. It was still dark, sunrise only a hint of color on the horizon, and lighted roadways fanned out into the dark. They led in all directions, but the largest led toward the bright towers I could see in the distance, the Academy campus in all its splendor.

There was more traffic than I'd expected, presumably because of the landing window, but our driver found a less-crowded lane and we headed for the campus. It was built on the site of the main Ancestral city—the planet itself was artificial, created by the Ancestors, perhaps by Anketil herself, and placed in the trailing Trojan point behind the smaller of the two suns—and supposedly the lowest levels of the campus were in fact unchanged since before the Dark. The visible part, though, was modern, the seven hexagonal towers that were the Colleges, and the seven towers of varying shapes that were the administrative buildings. The Colleges each bore their symbol in glowing light at their crown, and I named them as we passed: Valentinian's, for chemistry; Partho, for medicine and biology; Ripley's Gate and Twelve Keys, both for physical sciences, and then Project House and Lark Exalting and finally Mary Prophet where I had dreamed of studying, the blessing hand superimposed on the glyph of her name. The driver slowed, found an off-ramp, and we spiraled down into the brightly lit levels beneath the artificial surface.

Rejane had arranged for us to be housed in one of the dozens of transient housing blocks that huddled at the towers' feet. This one was attached to the Habitat, which generally provided facilities for visiting scholars, and the sleepy work-student who signed us in barely looked at our identification disks. We had connecting rooms three levels down—I had forgotten, until then, that the best housing was underground here—and the work-student gave us buttons to wear and a bot to follow to our doors.

The rooms were smaller than I'd expected, but carefully laid out to make best use of the space, and the communications console was the sort of full academic rig I'd only seen on the infotainment channels. There was a mini-kitchen set into one wall, with a small preservatory and a boiler and an equally tiny cooking box. There was also a basket of supplies, for which I was grateful: I was out of synch with the local clock, and I wanted food more than sleep. I found a packet of savory biscuits in the cabinet and set them to cook, then let Rejane in through the connecting door.

"We need to get you set up on the comms," she said. "Also, that smells good."

"You probably have some, too," I said. "Shall I fetch them?"

"Thanks." She seated herself at the console, frowning at the screens, and I went into her room and retrieved an identical packet. I set it to cook in her room—no need to wait until mine was done—and then came back to look over her shoulder.

"This is a spare card I keep just in case," Rejane said. "You can use it as soon as I finish—yes, there we go. Are you willing to do biometrics or do you want a password?"

"What do most people do?" What would be least suspicious, I meant, and she nodded as though she understood.

"Bio. But passwords will work."

"Bio then." I didn't want to draw extra attention.

"All right. Finger here."

I pressed my thumb onto the pad, following her directions, and by the time the second cooker chimed, I was accredited as Annec Silan and had a mid-level Academician's access to the campus systems. A part of me wanted to throw myself down that rabbit hole, explore everything that I had been promised; instead, I put the system to sleep and we settled together on the padded bench to finish our biscuits.

"One more thing," Rejane said, pushing herself to her feet. She disappeared into her room, returned with a small case I hadn't seen before. The exterior material was familiar, though: the darkly pebbled gray shielding everyone used to take Ancestral materials through the possible, and I lifted my eyebrows. Rejane opened it and held it out so that I could see the contents: a disk of the familiar Ancestral glass, but oddly shadowed, and shot through with hundreds of fine lines.

"May I?"

"Go ahead."

I lifted it out of its padding, the surface cool and slick to the touch. In the light, it looked clouded, as though it were filled with fog, and the brown lines were like a tangle of roots beneath the surface. "Damaged?" Even as I said it, I doubted it, and Rejane shook her head.

"No, all that is intentional. You have to catch it at just the right angle."

I turned the disk, watching as the clouds seemed to shift, revealing and then obscuring the tangled lines. It took me a moment to find the clear spot, and as I looked through it, tilting the disk, the image shifted from clouds and tangled lines to a hollowed sphere lined with thousands of inward-pointing needles. Each of their tips glittered with an Ancestral metal, blue, green, gold, a few points of red. If there was a pattern to them, I couldn't see it. The image of the sphere within the flat disk was disturbing, disorienting, and I looked away. "What is it?"

"Containment for an AI share." She looked alarmingly pleased with herself. "It was found in the Skim, in a context that made it clear what it was."

"And that's what you're going to use to retrieve the share?" I controlled my voice with an effort. "What if it doesn't work? That's a ridiculous chance to take."

"We tested it," Rejane said. "Fish and I. It works."

"How—" I began and she shook her head.

"Another time. But I swear, it's as safe as it can be."

That wasn't very safe. But we'd come this far, and if the legends were true, at least Blue Standing Sky was not hostile to humans. "So. Tomorrow the Library?" I asked, and Rejane smiled.

"Tomorrow the Library."

冊 㐀 ⼧

I dozed for a few hours, then rose with Rejane and breakfasted at a cafe at the top of the housing block. It looked out onto open plazas deep in shadow except where discreet lights hung from the tree-shaped pillars that supported the levels above. This was Twilight, where most of the campus was located; four levels above us was Light-of-day, where the manufactories and greenhouses and power generations stations were located, where they could draw directly from the energies that passed through the planet's Ancestral shield, and provide extra protection to the population in case those shields faltered. Probably the Ancestors had lived closer to the surface, confident in their shields, but we could no longer take that risk.

Fed, we returned to our rooms to don our Academician's robes, and I slung the carrier with the containment device over my shoulder: the lower-ranking partner should carry the tools. "What if someone asks to see it?"

"Show it to them," Rejane said. "Well, first ask me for permission, but a toy like this is the perfect excuse for visiting the Library. There aren't more than a dozen people in the entire Academy who'd have any idea what it is."

And if we meet one of them? There was no point in asking: if we were that unlucky, we'd just have to bluff our way through.

Rejane led us through a false-forest of wire and fabric to step onto a slidewalk that would take us to the Library. At first, I was nervous, clumsy in my robe and ready to blurt out excuses for my ignorance, but once we joined the slidewalk, it was obvious that I was only one of hundreds of black-robed figures in transit from one part of the campus to another. I relaxed a little, finding landmarks I had read about as a child— the Colleges, of course, but also the Conclave Building, the slender sphere-topped spire of the High Custodian's residence, and always the thick matte-black trunk-towers that carried power from the surface to the deepest layers. Ankes-and-Irthe was a marvel, as astonishing as any of the Remnants, but it was hard not to see how fragile it was. If the shields failed, or there were a serious fire, or an attack, or a meteor strike, the whole complex would come crashing down—as it had done in the First Dark. I had never thought of that when I was younger, dreaming of this place, but now it sent a shiver down my spine.

The Library loomed ahead, the slidewalk curving away from its base. Rejane and I negotiated the transitions from fast lane to local to exit, and stepped out onto a platform carved with row after row of glyphs and symbols. Some I recognized as local scripts, some were completely unfamiliar, but as people stepped on them, they glowed briefly blue or gold, symbol and promise of the information contained within those walls.

There was no checkpoint at the main doors, or at the entrance to the main reading rooms: they were open to the public, for what were genuinely modest fees. Rejane led us through a side door and down another corridor to where a junior librarian monitored double doors that gave onto a wide spiral ramp. Rejane smiled and nodded, I copied her, and the monitors stayed silent as we passed through the doors. The ramp wound around a central space that seemed to extend into infinity in both directions. I am not generally bothered by voids, but even I was glad of the glass wall that kept us from getting too close, and seeing too far into the depths. We made our way halfway around the curve, and reached a bank of elevators. Another librarian was watching them, a study tablet sitting at her hand, but she looked up alertly at our approach.

"We have an appointment in the core," Rejane said, and produced a data button.

The librarian took it, inserted it into her reader, and scanned the screen. Whatever she saw must have been familiar, because she nodded and returned the button. "Certainly, Academician. The express is free—"

"Excellent," Rejane said, and stepped into the padded compartment. I followed, hugging the carrier close against my side, and the door closed. There was a soft sound, and the floor began to sink under us, carrying us down into the Library's lowest levels. The descent slowed at last, and the door opened onto a narrow lobby bathed in cool white light. The floors were gray stone, the walls a darker gray; a pedestal stood in the center of the open space, balancing a pale gray slab on top of the dark stone support. The air felt oddly thick, and definitely cold. There was no sign of any other exit, but Rejane stepped confidently to the pedestal.

"Rejane Novilis," she said, and laid her hand on the pale gray stone. The words fell dead in the heavy air. I started to step forward to do the same, but she moved her hand, warning me back. I waited and the far wall split, panels sliding into each other to create a door. A man in robes that matched my own stepped forward, holding out his hand.

"Your authority, please."

The wall had started to close behind him, but reversed itself. An older man stepped through, dressed in dark green banded with gold. If those were his everyday robes, he was high-ranking indeed. "Rejane," he said warmly. "It's good to see you." He looked at the younger man. "I'll take over from here, Gyce. These are my guests."

The younger man was too well-disciplined to protest, though I could see the faint hesitation before he bent his head. "Very well, sen. Shall I have a tea service sent to your office?"

"Hm." The older librarian consulted a palm-piece. "Not yet—I expect you're eager to get started, Rejane. But perhaps for the noon meal? That way you won't need to interrupt yourself too soon, and I can have the pleasure of your conversation."

"That's very kind, Cariol," Rejane said. "Thank you."

"My pleasure, I assure you. And let me say now, I'm so very sorry for your loss."

Rejane bowed her head. "Thank you. He'll be missed."

Gyce bent his head as well. "I'll see to that, sen."

"Thank you." The older librarian waited while a section door slid back, and Gyce disappeared through the opening, then nodded to Rejane. "So. This is your assistant?"

"Yes. Annec Silan."

I bent my head the way Rejane had done, remembering the name she had given me. "Sen Dorna."

"A pleasure," Dorna said again. "This way."

He led us through the still-open doors and into an unexpectedly pleasant antechamber. It was warmly lit, the floor heavily carpeted, while the walls were covered with panels of what looked like painted silk. There were comfortable-looking couches and reading chairs arranged at intervals, though none of them were currently occupied. The surprise must have shown on my face, because Dorna lifted an eyebrow.

"You've not visited the core before, Academician Silan?"

"Not this level, sen," I said, and Dorna relaxed a little.

"You'll find it instructive, I hope. Rejane, I do hope you'll both join me for lunch later. I would like to talk with you."

"I'd like that," Rejane answered, "but it depends on how far we've gotten."

"Of course." Dorna led us through another all-but-invisible door and then into a featureless corridor where the lights switched on as we passed and turned themselves off again behind us. It spiraled down for what I guessed was at least fifty meters before we came to a dead end. Dorna produced a square key-box from his robes. He laid that against the wall, and a series of lights appeared, resolved into a touchpad. He laid one hand against a lighted square, then entered some code into the resulting screen. A door popped forward and swung open with a soft hiss. "There. I'll have to lock you in, of course, but you know the drill. Just let me know when you're ready for me to let you out."

"Thank you," Rejane said, and touched his shoulder gently. "Come on, Annec."

There was only the faintest of light from inside, but I knew better than to hesitate. I followed her through the door, and managed not to flinch when the door sealed behind us.

Chapter Twelve

The light slowly increased as we stood there, revealing shadowy shapes—consoles, chairs, what might be a worktable or another, larger console—but most of all I could feel the prickle of the possible, the indefinable sense that we had stepped outside the here-and-now. "You said it was cut off from the possible."

"This is a pocket," Rejane said. "It doesn't connect. It's a Klein bottle, functionally."

"But—" I stopped. "There's something here."

"I sincerely hope so," Rejane said.

The light was still increasing, now glinting off something that hung in the center of the room, beneath the domed ceiling. It looked like Ancestral glass, impossibly curved and looped, though I couldn't imagine how it had survived. I could feel the entity it contained, a weight in the air that made it hard to breathe. "Rejane—"

There was a crackle under my skin, a whisper of static that brushed my burden, and then a soft and sexless voice whispered in my ears. *So. One I have known, but you are a stranger. Why have you brought a stranger here, Rejane Novilis, and one who knows the great AI?*

"I wouldn't be here without permission," Rejane said.

I felt laughter ripple across my skin, and my burden retreated from it. *Of course you have permission, as you always have. But that doesn't answer my question.*

Rejane took a breath. "This is my friend Nic en Doroney, of Callambhal Above."

Callambhal.

Light flared within the containment, in memory, the dazzling core of the station fully lit, the entire inner surface of the central volume revealed as though on a map. I'd seen reconstructions of what Academicians believed the station must have been like under the Ancestors, but they had none of them been bright enough, warm enough, to match Blue Standing Sky's display.

You have not seen this, it said. *How can that be? How far have we fallen that there is only darkness?*

"We have fallen, and we are rising up again," Rejane said. "That's why we're here."

Blue Standing Sky went on as though she hadn't spoken. *I wish to taste your burden. If you are from Callambhal, I'll know it.*

I hesitated, and Rejane said, "It's all right. I've done it."

I will give promises, Blue Standing Sky said. *Oath and promise that I wish only to know your origin. My word has always been good.*

That was true, assuming that the legends passed down to us had some core of truth. And Blue Standing Sky was here, not locked in the possible with the rest of the AI. That argued that Anketil had indeed saved it, protected it, when she did her best to destroy the others. Still, it took an effort to reach out to the containment and lay my hand against it. Blue Standing Sky reached for me, and it took even more effort not to furl my burden tight. I felt the spark of its touch, and then it was gone again, and I snatched my hand away, resisting the urge to jam it into my pocket.

I remember Callambhal. Blue Standing Sky's presence was soft as a whisper. *I remember the taste of it, the warmth of that touch.*

"Did you make the Sun?" Immediately I wished the words unspoken. It was never safe to get too close, never safe to be vulnerable before an AI.

I did not. Blue Standing Sky's presence was tinged briefly with something that felt almost like regret. *I was needed for other things, already parceled out to so many. But I saw it done, and it was well done, too.*

"That's why we're here," Rejane said. "We want to restore the Sun."

There was a pause, a silence and withdrawal that I felt like the shifting of my burden. *The Sun is extinguished?*

"Yes."

Then I cannot help you.

I glanced at Rejane, but she only looked curious. "Why not?"

If the Sun no longer burns, then the share that managed it is gone. There is none left to replace it.

"There's you," Rejane said.

I am bound. I am promised. I may not leave.

"This is an extraordinary situation," Rejane said. "We could restore some of what was lost—begin to regain what the Ancestors had. Surely that would create an exception."

There are no exceptions.

"There are factions within the Academy that reject everything the Ancestors made," Rejane said. "They would rather see humanity fall again, see everything we've fought to rebuild crash and burn, than use the knowledge we've inherited. We need to prove that we can control what we've found, and for that we need an AI share. Your share, for preference."

Do you think I don't know what happened? Anger flicked over us, cold and dry, and shadows gathered momentarily within the containment. *They told me, after, that she was gone, and with her a hundred suns to light her way, and they called it a victory. I promised her I would not be part of that again.*

"If we fail, we lose everything," Rejane said. "All the knowledge that we've so carefully recovered will be thrown away. And then they'll discard you, too."

Do you think that matters? I am trapped and alone.

"Not entirely alone," Rejane said. "Though I know we're not your kin, or worthy of the one you served, we do know you, and acknowledge you."

In secret.

"Yes. For the same reasons you won't help me."

There was another silence, a moment of withdrawal, then Blue Standing Sky rushed back again. *If you must come to me for a share, you cannot be strong enough to protect Callambhal. The others will come, if you meddle with the Sun.*

"The Sun protects itself," Rejane said. "We've gotten that far in our studies. It was designed to hold a share that did this one thing only, to maintain the Sun and be a beacon in the possible, and to permit no interference. We are asking it only to maintain the Sun itself."

It was so designed, Blue Standing Sky admitted.

"And it held before."

It failed in the end.

"But not, we think, because it was attacked." Rejane took another deep breath. "The share was asked to do more and more, to maintain not just the Sun but other functions of the station. There was not enough power to do everything, and in the end the share failed."

Do you speak for the Academy?

Rejane hesitated. "Not yet."

Gold Shining Bone will come. If you bring a share to the Sun, Bone will know, and it will come. What do you plan to do about that?

"If the share is installed and the Sun re-lit," Rejane said, "there will be nothing Gold Shining Bone can do. Assuming we're understanding the system correctly, of course."

Another pause, and a whisper of something that felt almost like laughter. *That is how it was designed, so that nothing could interfere with the beacon. It was to be a fixed point, a pin to hold all the pieces together....*

"Then it will be protected," Rejane said. "But we need a share."

And I am forbidden. I promised, and I am bound.

"You have given a share before," Rejane said.

That was different.

"It was to save Benkasten when the shields failed," Rejane said. "And you would do the same here, if the shields failed."

I will not answer.

Rejane ignored it. "I put it to you: if we do not restore the Sun, the Newfounders will win. They will begin by banning dangerous technology, and they will end by banning everything that we've inherited, everything that we've figured out since we began clawing our way back out of the Dark. If we re-ignite the Sun, we prove what we can do—what we can safely do—and we can save ourselves. You aren't alone, here in your space. You have visitors, you know what I say is true. I ask you for a share."

It's not safe.

I felt Rejane relax fractionally. "We are prepared. Nic, show her."

Her? Generally no one gendered the AI, mostly for fear that it made them seem too human, but this was not the time to ask. I lifted the carrier. "The device?"

"Yes."

I opened the case and took out the device, turning it so that Blue Standing Sky could survey it properly.

That is—that was—ours.

"Yes," Rejane said again. "It's undamaged, fully functional. Surely that will be enough."

Perhaps.

"Did shares travel within these containments before the Dark?" I asked.

They did.

Rejane gave me an approving look. "Then there's no reason a share wouldn't be safe within it now."

Bone is waiting—Bone is always waiting. But, yes, this should be safe enough.

"Then will you offer us a share?"

I held my breath. The silence thickened again, Blue Standing Sky withdrawing itself; it felt as though the lights dimmed, though in fact they didn't change. We waited, neither one of us daring to say a word. I imagined Blue Standing Sky running simulations, a thousand, ten thousand possible scenarios played to their end, and wondered how many ended in disaster. Rejane licked her lips, but managed to say nothing. Then the presence returned, a weight on my shoulders and a sound that was almost a sigh whispering through the domed cell.

I promised. And yet. I will do what you ask, Rejane Novilis.

"Thank you." She turned to me. "Place the device against the containment."

I did as I was told, flattening the disk against the all-but-invisible wall. My fingers tingled, and I pulled my burden back just as the disk sank into the containment. It stopped only a few centimeters in, but I could feel the possible closer than ever, and it was hard to trust that this was a closed pocket, inaccessible to the rest of the AI. There was a flash and a glow, a pressure against my hands, and then the device flared to life. The clouds vanished, the inner spikes suddenly aligned and visible, all pointed inward at the same invisible thing at the center of the device. Just as suddenly, the image collapsed, replaced by the clouds and the tangle of iron-brown lines, and the device came away from the containment wall so suddenly that I almost dropped it.

"It's done?" I looked at Rejane, who took the device from me. She turned it over, examining it from every angle, flexing her fingers to bring her burden into play.

"Yes. And it's solid. It should be safe." She looked back at the containment. "Thank you."

Tell me I will not regret this.

"As far as I can," Rejane answered.

冊 ⚛ Ψ

Rejane called for Dorna then, and after what seemed like an interminable delay, we were released from the chamber. He and Rejane chatted as we made our way back up through the layers of the Library, and then he invited us for a late lunch. It was later than I had realized—it seemed as though the containment had affected my perception of time passing—but Rejane accepted cheerfully, and Dorna ushered us into a side room where a cold meal had been laid out on the sideboard. We filled elegant plates, each decorated with the crest of the Library and the badges of the Colleges laid out around the rim, and Dorna waved us to seats beside a blanked display screen. He laid a hand on it, and his fingers were briefly outlined in gold. I felt a damper field close around us, and he smiled.

"Now we may talk more freely."

"Certainly," Rejane said.

I set the carrier between my feet and focused on my food, trying not to think about the AI share trapped inside the device.

"You should know that Senior Custodian Larel has raised some questions about your support for Fish's widower."

"What sort of questions?" Rejane seemed to be concentrating on her meal as well, but I could see the tightening of her jaw that meant she was worried.

"She is concerned that you unduly influenced him."

"That was unkind."

"And has been indignantly refuted from Safican," Dorna said. "However, she has also expressed concern that you took data from Fish's files before you left."

Rejane shook her head. "Nothing was removed. She has everything Fish had—and I will repeat that under oath."

"It might come to that," Dorna said. "Though not yet. But if I were you, I'd complete any plans as quickly as I could. Larel would like you recalled to discuss these issues. So far, she doesn't have many allies—"

"How many?" Rejane's smile was crooked.

"The usual five."

Rejane nodded. "It could be worse."

"And very well could be, sooner rather than later," Dorna said, newly sharp. "If you just disappear, Rejane, people who would otherwise be on your side are going to wonder what you have to hide."

"Fish and I had a project in train that can't be delayed," Rejane said. "If I stop and answer questions now, months of work will be wasted. I'm not willing to do that. Unless you tell me there's real urgency—a real chance that she can raise the Conclave against me."

"Not yet," Dorna said. "People know you, and they know—knew—Fish. But the longer you wait to respond, the longer Larel will have to influence people."

"I know," Rejane said. "Bear with me, Cariol. It will be worth it."

"I trust you," he said, and poured us all more tea.

The polite luncheon seemed to stretch out forever, but finally Dorna admitted a cleaning bot and released the damper field. He escorted us all the way to the main entrance, and made a point of standing and talking to Rejane in clear view of any librarian who happened to pass the lobby. He was publicly taking sides, and I thought Rejane was grateful. Certainly I was: he had enough influence to get us off the planet if there were problems, and maybe even enough influence to ensure there wouldn't be any problems. Rejane had said that Ankes-and-Irthe was largely Successor, which should work in our favor.

She led us back through the maze of slidewalks and moving stairs until we fetched up again at the transient housing. I waited until we were inside, the doors locked and Rejane's damper field working, before I said, "Do you want to try to leave right away?"

"As soon as you can get us a course and a launch window," she answered. "Practically speaking, that's going to be tomorrow morning."

I had already called up my ephemerides. "Looks like. And Callambhal Above is a slightly tricky run." I touched more keys, entering codes, and frowned. "There's no Guildhall here?"

"No. But you should be able to get weather reports from the orbital."

I hadn't updated my course books in a couple of trips, which always made me twitchy. Realistically, it was unlikely to make much of a difference—the most volatile routes changed faster than they could be reported, and you always had to be ready for the unexpected—but it was always better to know. I pinged the orbital station, found the weather office, and downloaded their latest data. Things had been calm lately, and I hoped they'd stay that way, though with the share on board.... "How good is the shielding on that case?"

"The highest rated I could find," Rejane answered. "Now, whether that will be enough, given what we're carrying—I can't promise."

I hadn't expected anything better. "I'll want to lay out a couple of options, one as direct as we can make it, and one that skips in and out."

"I'd prefer direct," Rejane said, "but I take your point."

I settled myself on the nearest couch, unfolding my tablet to its fullest extent so that I could view ephemerides and depth charts at the same time. Rejane watched me work for a while, then started the boiler running.

"Do you have to do everything tonight? I had hoped—I thought we might go out for our meal, explore a bit of the neighborhood."

As we would have done if we'd been students together. It was both tempting and awful, and I was glad of the excuse. "I'd like to, but I really do need to have this laid down before we leave. I don't want to be fiddling with it last minute, not if we're going to be dealing with Beast."

"That's a question, isn't it?" Rejane cocked her head at me. "Can we do it without Beast's assist?"

"We can." I stared at the plots coalescing on my board. "We'd be as vulnerable as any other ship, and we have to worry that the AI will be drawn to the share. On the other hand, if Beast senses it, I don't know what it would do. If it turned on us, I don't know if I could get us out of the possible."

We both contemplated that for a moment, Beast destroying our fields, the ship torn apart in the flux of the possible, and then Rejane shook her head. "I'll have to leave that up to you."

"I'm inclined to try it without Beast," I said. "We can call it in later if we have to. But that depends on the weather, and if there's any reaction."

"We'll hope for the best," Rejane said, and stepped outside the damper to order a meal sent up from one of the local providers.

I was able to secure a launch window not long after planetary noon: just enough time for us to catch an early shuttle and prep *Beljaeger* for the journey. It was a scramble even with Rejane's help, but at last we dropped away from the orbital station and turned into its shadow to protect us from the worst of Irthe's radiation. An hour out, accelerating steadily, we were past the worst of the danger, and I turned us onto our true departure course. We were using the less-busy jump point, which gave better access to our ultimate destination, and the sensor net was empty ahead and to either side.

Rejane took her place in the technician's seat. "How long will it take us to get there?"

"Ten hours, subjective, if we can take the short road," I said. "Between sixteen and nineteen if we have to make multiple jumps."

"Not awful."

"I'd still rather take the shorter road." I called up the course plots again, laying them side by side to compare. The short route took us from FANROS to BARTEL and then on through LAYCAR to the Callambhal exit. It was shallow space all the way, frequencies that our fields could handle but the AI generally found unpleasant. With Beast's help, it would be straightforward, and even without it, I thought we could manage. It was just the presence of the share that made all my calculations uncertain. If there was weather, and if I decided we couldn't call Beast, there were four opt-outs between FANROS and BARTEL that would let us shift onto the longer road. It ran deeper than my preferred course, but we'd spend less time in the possible. Each promised a different kind of safety. I'd make my choice once we jumped, and once I had a sense of whether we could risk calling Beast.

We made the jump without difficulty, and I tuned the fields

to match the grain of space and maintain our momentum. The sensors were clear, only a hint of distant haze far to port, and I checked the internal sensors for any bleed from the share. Everything looked clear, and I rested one hand lightly on my own device to double-check. I thought I could feel a faint presence, almost a resonance, but it felt distant, and I hoped any AI wouldn't be able to localize it any better than I could. "Rejane. Would you check if you can feel the share?"

She leaned forward to touch the device. "Maybe a little? Or it might be external, I can't really tell."

"That's what I'm feeling, too." I considered active sensors, decided that was asking for trouble. The passive sensors still showed only distant haze, and a clear path at our current frequency all the way to FANROS. "Let's see if we can't slide through without help."

"If we can, I think that would be better," Rejane said. "I'd worry about Beast sensing the share."

I nodded in agreement. Two hours to FANROS, then the course change for BARTEL: by then we'd know if we'd have to duck out for the long road, or ask for Beast's help. Of the two, I'd rather try Beast first, even with the risk that it might recognize the share.

We reached FANROS without incident, though the weather had thickened in the sensor web. It slid behind us as I made the turn for BARTEL, and I relaxed a little, only to be jolted upright by a warning chime half an hour later. More weather was building ahead of us, the thick, cloud-like formations that often meant an AI in transit. I could slow down, let it pass ahead of us, or I could deflect our own course, and try to slip around and above, rising to a register the AI rarely reached. But that was pushing close to *Beljaeger*'s limits: if we rose too high, we'd risk grounding out, our propulsion fields no longer able to push against the grain of not-space. That was dangerous enough on its own, but if an AI was in the area, it would leave us completely exposed to its attack.

Going under was safer, dropping into frequencies that were more generally common to the AI, but that were being ignored by this particular one. It would also give us more room to run, a wider range of lower frequencies and places where I could force an exit point. "Capacitors?"

"Full," Rejane answered. "Is there a problem?"

"There's weather between us and BARTEL. I'm going to try to go under it." I adjusted our course as I spoke, and deployed brakes for a moment as well. In my screen, the intercept point faded from orange to yellow. It would go green as we got deeper, or so I hoped.

"Should we contact Beast?" Rejane asked.

I'd been wondering that myself, chewing on my lower lip as I tried to balance the factors. The weather was still some distance ahead and moving across our bow, not showing any sign of interest. If we kept our fields furled close, the way they were now, and if we dove and turned to get below and behind, there was every chance it would miss us. On the other hand, if it did see us, we'd have no choice but to cut and run, and would probably have to force an exit. That carried its own risks—you couldn't know what you might drop into—and it would add time to the trip while I figured out where we'd dropped, and how to get back on course. Beast would protect us, but possibly at the cost of revealing the share. But if I was going to summon it, it would be better to do it now, before we got any closer to the weather. "A little longer," I said, and adjusted our course again.

The weather waxed and waned as we crept past it. I pitched our fields lower, and lower still, then held my breath as we began our ascent into BARTEL. The weather receded, though it still filled the lower right quadrant of my screen, an ominous haze. I took my time bringing us back up to my preferred course, trying not to stand out against the whorls and currents around us, and finally settled onto the heading that would bring us to LAYCAR. That was a longer run than the others, and along the straight grain of local not-space. We should make good speed, but there was no place to hide if we drew an AI's notice. I watched the timer shift, accounting for our increased speed, then cautiously extended the sensor web.

There was more weather ahead, a diffuse haze that stretched the full width of the screen. Tendrils crept toward us, as though the AI was moving toward us, and I sucked in a breath. The haze extended as far as the sensors reached, which meant there was no way around without calculating an entirely new course. It might be possible to slip up and over, but we'd have to use frequencies that brought us perilously close to our limits. The lower frequencies were worse, the haze thicker there, and I wondered if the AI was actually moving on those levels.

"That doesn't look good," Rejane said.

"No." I adjusted the web again, and got no better answers. "I think we need Beast."

"Yes."

Her instant agreement was more alarming than any discussion could have been. "Keep an eye on the course. And the sensors."

"Confirmed."

I reached for the device in its padded holder, cupped my hand around its curve and allowed my burden to taste the glass. If I'd left it too late, we might have to make an emergency exit, and I wished I'd plotted that before I started the call. It was too late to change, and I made myself focus, searching for Beast in the confusion of the possible while trying not to draw the attention of whatever lay behind the screen of weather. Beast's arrival scalded my palm, so that I nearly jerked away.

Beauty! What folly is this?

I need your help, Beast.

Clearly. What have you done?

The haze was thickening at the top of my screen, the tendrils reaching out with more purpose. We weren't spotted yet, but it wouldn't be long. *I need a protected passage to Callambhal, by this road.*

You should have called me sooner. This is troublesome.

It seemed simple. I didn't want to inconvenience you for nothing.

This is no longer nothing. I had no answer to that, but fortunately Beast didn't seem to expect one. *I will taste your burden, Beauty, and that of the other Beauty. That is my price.*

That was more of a risk than I wanted, but there wasn't time to bargain. *Mine you may have. I can't speak for her.*

Both or none. Best hurry, Beauty, you've drawn considerable notice.

I shook myself free of the device. "Rejane, it wants to taste both our burdens. I've said yes to mine."

"Yes. All right."

I closed my eyes. *Yes. We agree.*

I hold you to your bargain.

There was a sharp pain in the heel of my hand where it touched the device, as if a needle stabbed deep, and I thought blood welled before my burden staunched it. In the same moment, I felt Beast wrap itself around *Beljaeger*, its presence obscuring ours. The weather instantly felt more distanced, dulled, though in the screen the tendrils continued to advance. I focused on the device. *Give me a heading, Beast.* It recoiled instead, a shock not just to the device, but to the ship itself. All my readings jumped, steadied again a few points out of true. *Beast?*

What have you done—what do you carry? Have you lost all grain of sense?

I don't understand. I could feel the ship starting to shiver, touched by the edges of the weather. *Beast, you promised.*

You carry an abomination, an abortion, how could you? Be rid of it now, or I feed you to Bone and help him shred you into component molecules.

I had never heard Beast like this before—angry, yes, and hurt and boastful, but this fury was something new. I looked at Rejane. "It feels the share. It says we have to get rid of it, or it'll destroy us—it'll help Gold Shining Bone destroy us."

"But—" Rejane reached forward, put her hand on the device. *Please, we need this—*

I felt the device snap at her. She gasped but didn't move. *Please, Beast.*

How dare you flaunt this thing before Me? How dare you offer service to another? Get rid of it, I say, be rid of it now, or I will destroy you utterly.

Rejane looked at me, and I looked at the sensors. The weather was coming faster, resolving from haze into the looming shapes that heralded oncoming AI. "We can't run."

"Can we drop?"

"Beast could stop us." I checked the numbers again. "Rejane, we have to drop it."

"But without it—" She stopped. "Are you sure?"

"There's no choice. I'm sorry."

She wrenched herself free of her harness, hauled herself out of her chair. There were tears on her cheeks, whether of anger or regret I couldn't know. "All right. All right, fine."

She flung herself out of the control room, and I focused on the device. *She's going to dump it, Beast, just keep us safe.*

How could you? After all I have done for you, how could you seek another? I have cherished you, coddled you, carried you—

The image in the sensor screen was coalescing further, the towering clouds now shot through with scarlet flames. There was a metallic taste in my mouth, a warning from my burden; I swallowed hard, but didn't dare release the device, or adjust our course. *Beast, I beg you—*

I saw lights flash on the secondary screen, the one that showed the ship's systems, and felt the hull shudder. *Beast, she's doing it—she's done it, she's dumped the share. Help us!*

Beast howled, rage and grief and fear. *Beljaeger* groaned, a deep and terrible sound, and I felt it shudder. Lights flashed orange and then red, I caught a glimpse of a looming wave, a terrible froth of skulls and bones, and then we were abruptly elsewhere, wrapped securely in Beast's presence. I caught my breath, and *Beljaeger* rolled free, spat out by the AI. My instruments swam and reformed: we were practically on top of the exit point for Callambhal, though how Beast had brought us here I couldn't say.

Begone! Do not seek Me again until you know what you have done! I abjure all Beauties!

The device was abruptly empty, Beast withdrawn as completely as it had been present a moment before. I shook myself and grabbed for the controls, starting the countdown for our exit. What we'd do now, I didn't know—go back to the Library, maybe? Though how we'd get a share through the possible after this, especially since we'd had to dump the containment—

My boards were still displaying warnings, a sea of red and orange, and I made myself concentrate on that. Get *Beljaeger* to Callambhal, and then worry about Rejane's job. I adjusted the fields, shedding momentum and angles, tuning the fields to get ready for the transition. The port generator was running rough; I eased it, bringing up the ventral field to compensate, and heard Rejane slide into the technician's chair beside me. "Rejane. Capacitors?"

"Still one hundred percent." Her voice was rough but steady. "We can jump whenever you're ready."

"Stand by." I goosed the port generator again, matched the frequencies. We would definitely need work once we landed. "Ready—now."

"Firing," Rejane said, and we flashed out of the possible into the space around Callambhal.

Interlude 5

Nenien was the eldest, firstborn. Kuffrin looked at him and saw him perfect, and very nearly ended her project. Why waste energy when she had what she needed? But as she studied him, tiny and red and still wet from the womb, she thought she still might do better, and set him aside.

Benanzin was the second, the quiet one, the theorist. When he was born, he cried aloud once, and then was silent, and again she thought she might do better.

Tessier was the third, the largest and the strongest, born with hair and teeth and appetite. Kuffrin recoiled, and turned to the next sire.

Inkeri was the fourth, born pale like his father. Kuffrin waited to see what he would manifest, and as she waited, one of the nursemaids dropped him, and no surgery could completely repair his damaged spine. He was given one designed by the AI, that would grow with him as he grew, and Kuffrin looked to do better.

Hafren was the fifth and last, dark and plump and beautiful. He was born laughing, and Kuffrin laughed with him, thinking she had at last found the son she wanted.

The Sons of Kuffrin

Chapter Thirteen

We had exited on the very edge of the system, an hour or so outside of Traffic Control's zone. I brought the fields back into line, feeling the port generator thump and rumble, and called in for a course. Traffic Control provided one, sounding blessedly bored, and I plugged it into the autopilot. Only then did I dare look back at Rejane. "I'm sorry."

She shook her head, hunching her shoulders as though she was cold, then reached to free herself from the safety harness. "No, I'm sorry. I've tainted your ship. And I can fix it now, but I have to hurry—"

"Wait. What do you mean, you've tainted *Beljaeger?*"

"I dumped the device and a shell, not the entire share. But I need to retrieve the files, if I can. If they survived."

"Wait," I said again, but she was gone. I checked the autopilot, saw it was properly engaged, and unfastened my own harness. "Rejane—"

She was well ahead of me, already emerging from the cabin where she'd stored her luggage, another of her salvaged devices in her hand. "I have to hurry."

I followed her down the main corridor, one eye for the monitors as we passed each display. Everything showed green, the autopilot in full control, the ship's systems back in balance after the stress of the exit jump, all seals intact. Rejane stopped in the internal lock that lay between the ship's main body and the hold, and I saw that the monitors on the cargo containment were flashing orange. "Rejane, what did you do?"

"I put Sky's share in the hold's environmentals. I told it not to spread, but you know how much storage a share takes." She was adjusting the new device as she spoke, her hands sparking as she molded the Ancestral glass as though it were transparent clay. I felt the sudden surge as it came awake, and the cargo containment monitor ran wild, flashing through every color and warning in its system. Rejane put her hand between the monitor and the new device as though her fingers would bridge the gap, and grimaced as light flared around her hand. I reached for her, wanting to pull her back, to protect her, and instead felt an overwhelming rush of relief and release as the share flowed into the new device. Rejane broke away, gasping, and the monitor returned to normal. "It's clean. Or at least it should be. I've got it now."

"Are you all right?" I eyed her warily, and she shook her head.

"I'm fine. It just stung a bit, that's all."

If she was unhurt, then I needed to be sure that the system would pass any scans once we reached Callambhal. Luckily the computers that controlled the hold's environmentals were firewalled off from the main system. I checked to make sure there wasn't a breach, then ran the diagnostics, holding my breath until the first responses came back green. I started the more detailed scan, and looked back at Rejane. "Let's talk in commons."

I checked the autopilot and set the commons screen to relay everything from the cockpit. Then I started the boiler and found tea, aware that my hands were shaking. That had been too close, the closest that I'd come to destruction in years. There were energy blocks in the stores box, sweet and rich, and I set the box on the table between us. Rejane looked as shocked as I felt, pale and drawn, and she accepted an energy block with a murmur of thanks. I nibbled on mine as well, letting the sugars and the complex nutrients level out my system, and poured the tea when it was ready. "What now?"

Rejane looked up sharply. "We carry on."

I raised my eyebrows. "Oh? After what just happened? We just—carry on?"

"Don't think I don't know that we just nearly died. Believe me, I know—I felt it as much as you did. But I did save the share, and the Inner Sun can still be re-lit. We've come this far, there's no point turning back now."

I paused. "Would you have dumped it if you had to?"

Rejane hesitated. "Yes. I think so. But it was worth taking the chance."

I knew I should protest—it was my ship, she should have asked—but if I'd seen the chance, I would have done the same thing. "Is anyone on Callambhal going to let you experiment with the Sun?"

She gave a lopsided smile. "Mirean should. She's been itching to touch it for the last decade."

I couldn't help feel a bit more skeptical, but there was no point in pointing out the obstacles. "Let's hope so," I said, and took myself back to the control room.

I hadn't been back on Callambhal Above in some years, at least partly, if I was honest with myself, out of fear of seeing my former family again. There was little chance of that, but the idea made me uneasy. Most likely, they had long ago forgotten me just as I had mostly forgotten the faces of my younger half-siblings, but the fear that they hadn't was enough to make me wary. Or maybe it because I was sure they had forgotten me that I was uneasy, but either way it had been easier to stay away.

That was no longer an option. In fact, I was likely stuck on Callambhal until either Beast forgot about me, or Rejane and I found some better way to protect the ship. At best, we'd need a complete re-skin, everything about *Beljaeger* altered so that she would pass for something else. But I would deal with that later. I checked that the autopilot was holding us on our given course, and leaned back in my couch.

Callambhal Above was already clearly visible on my screens, traffic swarming around the two major docking hubs, the larger Ring that lay between the main part of the station and the trailing sphere of the Manufactory, and the industrial hub that formed the tip of the station's lengthy tail. Once, possibly, the segments that made up the tail had been luxury residences, or even pieces of independent orbitals that had circled either the station or Callambhal Below. Now they had been harnessed for industrial use: the worst damage repaired, solar panels bound to their outer hulls, to supply what the Inner Sun didn't. They were storage volumes for goods in transit, workshops and repair stations and salvage depots, all deemed too dangerous to allow in the Manufactory.

My mother had worked there before I was born, and after; the man she never spoke of, the one who'd fathered me, had come from there as well, their Firstborn burdens an absurdly useless anomaly. Her husband had rescued her from that, and brought her into the outer levels of the Shell. It lay at the other end of the station, the largest surviving part of the Ancestors' creation, an enormous spiral shape covered in a lattice of vents and antennae and ductwork. At this distance, it only looked like texture, an occasional light flashing to warn local traffic or where sunlight caught a reflective surface. The station swam in its orbit like some enormous sea creature, swinging ponderously above the empty spaces of Callambhal Below. No one was quite sure what the Ancestors had originally built, what had survived the Dark and what the survivors had cobbled together out of the wreck but if we could get the Sun to function again....

We'd find out soon enough, assuming Rejane's colleagues were willing to take the chance. Watching the station swell in the screens, I wasn't sure I'd risk it: it had taken centuries for the station to return to its place at the hub of the trade routes, and the last time I'd been on the station, they were still rebuilding parts of the Tail. On the other hand, enough power to fully energize the station's systems was temptation enough for anyone.

We were directed to a docking point on the outer skin of the Ring: better than I could usually afford, but not protected from debris strikes like the internal docks. Those were correspondingly expensive, and most of the debris was small enough that the potential damage was minimal. I tucked *Beljaeger* in among the baffles and hoped for the best. Presumably the Ancestors had had a protective field or something like it to deal with the problem, or maybe there had been less debris in the system then.

We were met by a young woman in a junior Academician's short gown, who shepherded us through local Customs and onto a reserved transit cab. It provided privacy and guaranteed seating, though it made the same stops as the rest of the train, and we emerged at last onto a cavernous platform that I recognized as one of the major interchanges. The Academician—she had introduced herself as Pola—whistled for a cargo bot; we piled our bags onto it and let her lead us toward the next departure point.

We passed through an airtight bulkhead, the great door rolled back but ready in case of accident, and came out into a smaller lobby. It ended in enormous transparent doors that gave onto the metal cage of the transport tube. Beyond that, the central void stretched into darkness. We were, I thought, a little bit below the midline of the Shell's spiral; the Inner Sun was somewhere above us in that dark. As we took our places in the line waiting for the next transport, I began to make out lights in the depths: the glow of windows on the curved walls to either side, the slow-moving streak of light that was a vertical transport on another line, more distant flickers that might be maintenance tenders moving in the empty space. I remembered this from childhood, from my dreams, and even so it was enough to stop the breath.

A car rose into the opening, and the doors rolled back, but Pola shook her head. "The next one is an express. It's worth waiting."

Rejane nodded. I leaned against the nearest stanchion, its surface patterned like tree bark, and looked around the station. Old memories were coming back: the blue tiles meant that this was one of the two verticals that served the

Shell's western side. The directions were purely arbitrary, with "north" defined as the leading edge, and "south" as the tail; the depth of the color told you whether you were closer to the Shell's top or bottom edge. I touched the stanchion's surface, and felt my burden shift, Callambhal's natal burden responding to the touch of the station's systems. I curbed them instinctively—there was no reason not to let Pola know that I carried the station burden, but there was no reason to share that, either—and the next transport rose into view.

We filed aboard, the cargo bot trailing us, and Pola stepped back so that Rejane and I could have a clear view of the window as we pulled away. The void was dark and empty, the Inner Sun invisible; lights curved away to either side, windows and overlooks and the brighter lines of the vertical transit stations, but the inner space was large enough that only the brightest lights could be seen across the gap. And then that was blanked out, blocked by something unlit and too dark to see clearly: the Inner Sun and its supports, invisible except in its absence. I had not realized how much of this I remembered.

We left the transport at the first of the Peak levels, Pola explaining that the Academy had recovered most of that space and taken it for their own. It included the control rooms for the Inner Sun, which were currently being studied by the Custodian herself, as well as areas that had probably been living quarters for the technicians. I had not been this high before, and the bright colors, ice-pale silvers and blues shimmering slightly under the sunlamps, made me blink and shade my eyes.

"Security—we have to keep the research area well lit," Pola said, apologetically, and led us quickly into a darker hallway. It was richly carpeted, and all the wrong color for this part of the Spiral, a deep maroon covered with black scrollwork only slightly darker than the background. The walls were banded with glowing panels, gold and pale red, and I wondered if they were Ancestral relics, or had been installed by some Custodian. The hall ended in another doorway half blocked by a security desk, but before Pola could say anything, a woman a few years older than Rejane emerged from the inner room, holding out her hands.

"Rejane. It's good to see you."

"And you," Rejane said. "Mirean, this is my good friend and colleague Nic en Doroney. Nic, this is the Custodian of the Inner Sun, Tadei Mirean."

I murmured something polite, and Mirean held out her hand to me as well. She was a rangy woman, with dark skin and even darker eyes, and graying hair cut very close to her scalp. She looked as though she came from Dahlat, and I controlled my burden so that we shared only a social touch. She blinked once, and I guessed she had tasted Callambhal among the mix, but she only waved us toward the doorway. "Come into my office, I've had a mezze brought if you're hungry."

It was a small room, the walls charcoal with thin slanting stripes of gold running at an angle from floor to ceiling. The comfortable furniture looked oddly out of place against that decoration, but both Rejane and Mirean ignored it. An array of little plates had been set out on a low table, and Mirean steered us to the seats around it. I was surprised to find that I was hungry, but looked at Rejane before I reached for anything.

"I wasn't expecting to see you so soon," Mirean said. "I'm so very sorry about Fish."

"So are we all," Rejane said. I could hear the moment her voice almost cracked, and she reached for a cup of what looked like a fruit ice to cover it.

"I was afraid that would be the end of the project," Mirean said.

"It's a setback," Rejane said, "but not the end."

"Then you think it's still possible to proceed?" Mirean looked surprised, but pleased, and Rejane reached for one of the little savory puffs.

"We're certainly in a position to begin the experiments," she said.

I helped myself to a little tart that turned out to be filled with cheese and a sharply spiced jelly. Mirean smiled as though it pleased her to see us eating, but said, "I've made some discreet inquiries among the more receptive members of the Council, and there is support there for the project."

"How much have you told them?" Rejane asked, though I thought the question might better be, *What have you offered them?*

"Nothing concrete, I promise," Mirean said. "I've merely mentioned that the Academy is interested in exploring the possibility."

Rejane nodded. "I can't guarantee this will work. You know that. And we had a rather difficult passage getting here."

"I hear the weather has been difficult on the approaches," Mirean said, with a glance in my direction as though she expected me to agree.

"I wasn't able to update my books before departure," I said.

"You must take full advantage while you're here," she said. "In any case, that's what I'd heard. Unless this was something more?"

Rejane hesitated. "It could have become more. We attracted unexpected and significant attention."

"Because of—" Mirean stopped. "Assuming that you did indeed acquire what you promised."

"I believe so," Rejane said. "Or at least an acceptable substitute."

"I trust it's sufficiently shielded?" Mirean raised her eyebrows.

"That I can assure you," Rejane said, with a small smile, and Mirean nodded.

"Then I'm very glad to have you here."

"I look forward to working with you," Rejane said.

冊 𝄞 ⵕ

We were assigned rooms in the Academy's section of the Shell, two tiny sleeping rooms with a larger commons and bath suite in between. The walls were all pale gray metal with an odd, brushed texture so that it looked like velvet and was startlingly hard to the touch; the floor and ceiling were of similar materials, but the Academicians had brought in half a dozen rugs and strung familiar flower-shaped lights throughout the area. They had set up communications consoles as well, and a box galley, the cables that carried the power tucked in against the base of the walls and running through holes that had been drilled into the bulkheads. The cables were surrounded by sealant, but I couldn't help frowning: it had been a rule, growing up, that you never breached an airtight bulkhead, or blocked a pressure hatch. Rejane saw where I was looking, and shrugged one shoulder. "They look securely plugged."

"I know." They did, and the Academy presumably knew what it was doing, but it still made me twitch to look at it.

Rejane gave me a sympathetic look, and busied herself setting up the damper field. I lifted my eyebrows at that, and she said, "Better to be safe."

I nodded, and neither of us said anything more until the field was up and working. Then Rejane opened the galley's cold box, and brought out what looked like a flask of wine. She poured us each a cup, and we settled ourselves in the commons. "What next?" I asked and she heaved a sigh, hunching her shoulders in a gesture that wasn't quite a shrug.

"We figure out if this can work. That's the first step. Then—then I suppose we take it to the Council and if they approve, we see if we can make it happen. I know we need AI; the question is whether a share will be enough."

"That's what the Ancestors used, right? At least for most things?" I remembered that much from our shared school days.

Rejane nodded. "So, in theory, it ought to work—though if the Sun draws power from the possible, which is what Fish thought was happening, it might take more than an ordinary share. I think that was too risky even for the Ancestors, but I don't know what else they would have used to achieve the power levels they needed. Solar radiation, maybe? We'll know better when we see how the share fits."

"Is it all right?"

"We should find out." Rejane collected the carrier and brought it out into the common space. We were protected by the damper field, but even so I had a hard time not looking for the inevitable monitoring cameras. Rejane opened the carrier and removed her device, setting it on the couch between us. It looked like every other Ancestral toy, a roughly spherical lump of clear glass with coils and shards of glittering metallic colors at its center. I touched it, unable to help myself, and it rang with a familiar clear tone. Rejane laid her hand on the top, silencing the sound, and I felt the shiver of the share's presence.

"Blue Standing Sky," Rejane said. "Sky-share."

i am here

It was barely a whisper, a brush of words against both our minds, and I put my hand on the device as well. "Are you intact?"

i—yes. i believe so

"Good," Rejane said, and I shifted my hand so that our fingers touched. I felt her relief, echoing mine, and she smiled before she spoke again. "We have reached Callambhal Above."

you did not tell us who you dealt with

"What do you mean?" Rejane cocked her head.

your ally

"Beast?" I looked at Rejane, who shrugged.

that is not its true name

"What is, then?" Rejane asked.

green piercing book

"It can't be," I said. Not Callambhal's renegade AI, the AI that had brought down the station—Beast was a minor creature, too grandiose to be important. No AI of any importance would have bothered to help any human ship, and not for ordinary transit mass.

it is

Rejane hissed softly. "Callambhal's original AI—a great AI. Why would it be helping Nic like any minor offshoot?"

that question cannot be answered by me

"Sorry, it was rhetorical." Rejane shook her head, and I copied her.

"That can't be right. Why would it—why would any great AI cooperate with me? It's been—not at my beck and call, but it's made itself available for more than a decade."

"Time doesn't exist for them," Rejane said. "You said it yourself."

That was true, but I wasn't sure how that worked in practice. "But a great AI?"

"Not just *a* great AI, but one of the five," Rejane said. "One of Kuffrin's creation, like Blue Standing Sky." She looked at the device again. "You're sure of this?"

beyond certain—i/my great-self knows that shape, that taste

One of Kuffrin's AI. Of course Green Piercing Book was one of them, that was why it had been given Callambhal Above as its responsibility. Guerrin Dedalor had created the first quantum AI, from which all the rest ultimately sprang, but it was Guerrin's daughter Kuffrin who made them what they are, creatures as truly alive and independent as any human being, as much her creation as the Faciendi. It was her children who made them our enemies, but that was another story. Kuffrin had made five AI, drawing on Guerrin's work but then surpassing him, and the names came slowly back to me. Gold Shining Bone, of course, the first and greatest, leader of the rebellion; Black Reflecting Sum, destroyed by Anketil; Green Piercing Book, protector and destroyer of Callambhal Above; Blue Standing Sky, of course...but I couldn't remember the last. I said their names aloud, feeling the share and the device quiver gently under my touch, and Rejane supplied the last name.

"Red Speaking Wire."

Five great AI, and Beast was one of them. I had believed it was one of the hundreds of minor AI that lurked in the possible. No one was entirely certain where they came from, but they were demonstrably less powerful—and sometimes considerably less hostile—than their larger kin. I had been fond of it, in a sideways way, and thought it had some liking for me. "I've been feeding it transit mass for years. That can't be good."

"It hasn't done anything with it yet," Rejane said, but her tone was less certain than her words. "Though, that said, probably you shouldn't give it any more."

"I'm not likely to get the chance."

"True, though…" Rejane focused on the device again. "Could you tell what it wanted? Green Piercing Book, I mean."

no… We waited, feeling the share shift under our touch. *it hungers, it is angry, i avoided and hid as much as i was able*

I could hardly blame it, but it wasn't much help, either. Rejane said, "Does it threaten Nic?"

I felt the share shiver. *it threatens all*

"Can you be more specific?" Rejane sounded calm, and I had to admire her patience.

not about its plans, i could not see, but it is angry at all things I opened my mouth, but Rejane shook her head. We waited again, the device warming gently under my touch. *i/my greatself has been alone and safe, green piercing book has fought often and is not safe nor what it wants to be, though what that is i am not certain — but it is un-friends with so many others*

"So Beast—Book—has made enemies of the other AI?" I asked.

i believe so

"That's something," I said, but the minute the words left my mouth, I doubted them. What good would it do us for the other AI to oppose Book? They weren't any more likely to help us. "Or not."

Rejane laughed softly. "As long as it can't escape the possible—as long as Anketil's barriers hold—we're safe here. And if Fish and I were right about the protections built into the Sun, if we can re-light it, we'll be even safer. But I know that doesn't solve your problem."

"I don't want to be trapped here," I said, and Rejane nodded.

"We'll start by getting the repairs done—that's an Academy expense, I'll make sure we pay. And then we'll figure out what to do about Book."

"First the Sun," I said, but couldn't help feeling comforted.

Interlude 6

But as they [Kuffrin's sons] grew, they all proved to have desires that ran contrary to hers, and the more she tried to train them otherwise, the greater their secret rebellion. First Nenien had a child of his own, but he chose a daughter, not a son, and in private boasted that Anketil would grow to be greater than her grandmother.

With the help of the AI, Benanzin found errors in his mother's formulae, and in doing so, granted them free reign in the possible. Tessier was drawn to more and more marginal worlds, and created more and more complex Faciendi to conquer them. Inkeri cloned sons to heal his old injury, but, though he learned how to heal others, he could not heal himself.

And Hafren, Kuffrin's youngest, joined with Gold Shining Bone, Kuffrin's eldest creation, to demand his full share of power over the settled worlds. Kuffrin faltered, and would have bargained; but Nenien betrayed his brother and the AI, and drove them deep into the possible where he thought they were trapped forever. Kuffrin cursed him and set out to rescue her youngest son, but her AI had turned against her, and her ship was destroyed with all aboard.

This was the beginning of the AI Wars.

From the Dedalor Apocrypha, Vol. 5

Chapter Fourteen

The next morning I took Rejane at her word, and headed into the Tail of the station to update my ephemerides and get bids for the repairs to *Beljaeger*. It was strange to be back on board, close to the volumes where I had spent time as a child. Always before, I had confined myself to the port sections of the Tail, and now I found myself looking warily at the crowds in the transit stations, half afraid I might see a familiar face. That was ridiculous: I hadn't seen any of my family in a quarter century. I doubted I could recognize my mother, much less my half-siblings. I was not that child any longer.

There was no single transit line from the Shell to the section of the port where the Guildhall was located. I took a vertical transit line down to the Lower Third, rode a slidewalk to a horizontal transport hub, and took it down the Tail to the end of the first segment. This was one of the main airtight bulkheads that divided the Tail into segments, and it was something of a shock to see all the airlocks standing wide, allowing free passage between segments. I remembered waiting for the locks, and then in the lock itself, when I was a child, whenever we traveled outside our section—but presumably the Council knew what it was doing. Certainly there was enough traffic to justify the choice.

The Guildhall lay at the tail of the compartment, on one side of the two-level bay where the next segment joined this one. The transit line stopped here as well. I caught a glimpse of more open locks, a stream of people moving through them, before I turned aside and climbed the short flight of stairs to the bay's main level. The Guildhall itself was busier than I'd expected, the lobby filled with the seashell roar of voices; and when I worked my way through the crowd to the directory station, I was informed that there was a three-hour wait to update my ephemerides. The polite young man on duty told me apologetically it wasn't likely to get better, so I booked a spot and retreated to the anteroom where the local network cubes were located. I was able to snag a cube almost immediately, and settled down to work my way through the lists of recommended repair shops, finally making arrangements to meet an estimator from Bellek and Kindred after I'd finished with my updates.

That still left me with an hour or more to kill. The Guildhall's mezzanine was studded with independent food vendors, and there were more than a few empty tables under the arches overlooking the bay. I bought a boxed tea and claimed a table where I could watch the transit cars pulling in and out of the sunken station, then settled myself to wait.

When I was little, a boxed tea had been unobtainable luxury, something we saw on media but could never really afford. The reality was disappointing: a self-heating canister of lemon tea, three small square sandwiches with soft cheese and slices of crisp oradi root, a stack of salty shatterbreads, and a handful of chopped preserved fruits, all packed into a container that unfolded into a serving dish. The tea tasted of preservatives underneath the too-strong lemon, the bread was just this side of stale, and the shatterbread needed salt: maybe I'd chosen badly, or maybe the teas had never been as good as I'd imagined. Or maybe my tastes had changed. It had been a long time since I'd even thought of a boxed tea.

I ate it anyway, watching the crowd ebb and flow beneath me. The station seemed more crowded than I remembered, too, a steady stream of people flowing in and out of the transit cars, passing through the open airlocks. There were more small vendors, too, one or at most two people selling their goods out of wheeled carts, and as I watched I could see local enforcement moving among them, checking permits. About a third of the carts were quietly on the move, avoiding the enforcement agents, and I was abruptly reminded of childhood neighbors. Rham Olvares's aunt had had a cart like that, selling second-hand clothes in the stations of the Middle Grange, always moving from one spot to another. I'd thought then it had been in search of the best sales. I shoved that thought away, and finished my tea. The dregs tasted of metal.

I dropped a copy of my well-edited journey-tape at the log-keeper's office, and went on to the chartroom. My slot had just opened, and I plugged in my ephemerides and let them update, listening with half an ear to the gossip around me.

"Weather's getting thick between BARTEL and LAYCAR," a man said, and someone else mumbled agreement.

"Better to go around by DOLBAS," another man said.

"I wouldn't," a woman answered. "I came in that road, TANTIN to DOLBAS, and it was thick there, too."

A man swore, perhaps the second one who'd spoken, and a third man said, "I'm scheduled to leave that way. Was it better deep or shallow?"

"Definitely better shallow," the woman said. "But you might wait a day to see if it clears."

"I've got a contract," the man answered, and they moved away.

I looked down at my console, watching the progress marker edge slowly toward completion. That was at least partly my fault, and it was hard not to feel guilty. Still, Beast—Green Piercing Book, and it was still hard to believe that I had been dealing with that great AI all these years—was angry with me, not with other random people. I didn't think he'd make too great an effort to go after them.

The console pinged, signaling that the update was complete. I detached the ephemerides and tucked them into my pocket, sliding quietly past another group of pilots complaining about weather. Bellek and Kindred's offices were in the next segment of the Tail, too close to make transit worthwhile. I joined the crowds passing through the open airlocks, and then followed the directions on my handheld to take me up two levels and over to the segment's planet-facing side.

This was definitely a lower-rent district: the corridor decking was worn and patched, and there were thin lines of stain running along some of the vertical seams, as though a water pipe had leaked behind the bulkhead. New raw welds showed at the next junction, where a narrow corridor led toward the outer hull, and when I looked for the local telltale, it shone yellow, warning that the oxygen level was just adequate for the current occupation level. It was supposed to be green, of course, but plenty of stations saved money by skimping on air. It was breathable until you hit the red zone, and that was still a long way off. I just hadn't expected to see it on Callambhal Above.

Bellek and Kindred was down another side corridor, where the telltale flickered between yellow and pale green. I passed a chandler's office, hatch rolled back to reveal a kiosk showing commodity prices, and another open hatchway where cables ran from the interior through the opening and along the corridor to a service port. Bellek and Kindred's hatch was open but unblocked, and a thin bearded man was sitting at a console. He looked up at my entrance, and rose to his feet, extending a hand in greeting. "Captain en Doroney?"

"That's right." I accepted the handclasp, controlling my burden so that we exchanged only the most polite of tastes.

"Varren Bellek. I understand you needed an assessment and an estimate?" He motioned for me to take the seat on the opposite side of the console.

"That's right. We hit some weather coming in, and I think avoiding it strained my field generators. I need them checked out."

Bellek nodded. "Any one in particular?"

"It felt as though the port generator had it worst, but I want them all checked."

"Very wise." Bellek nodded again. "And you're docked to the Ring?"

"Yes. 23B-Delta."

Bellek touched his controls again. "We have remote access to the dock systems. If you'd like, I can run an auto-check from here, and give you an estimate once that's done."

"And the cost for that?"

"A hundred-fifty credits, local. Or one hundred in banker's note."

I checked the card Rejane had given me. "I have a draft on the Academy bank."

"A hundred then."

I nodded. "Let's do it." I handed over the card, and when he returned it I checked discreetly to be sure there were no extra charges, while he pretended not to see.

"If you'll give me a few minutes to set things up," he said, and I nodded again.

I relaxed into the client's chair while he busied himself with the console. I couldn't see his screen, but I knew what he had to be doing: logging into the dock systems, making sure all the diagnostics were in place and ready to run. After a moment, he slid a small screen in front of me. "If you could grant working access, Captain?"

I checked the settings and touched the pad, letting my burden carry the agreement. "Go ahead."

"Thank you." He touched more keys, then nodded to himself. "And we're running. Everything seems in order. This should take about half an hour—if you'd like tea? Or at least a glass of water?"

"I just had some, thank you." Before either one of us could speak again, I heard a faint sound in the distance. I cocked my head, and Bellek frowned, reaching for a secondary screen. He touched it, his frown deepening, and the sound moved closer, resolved into a harsh two-toned klaxon: a drop in air pressure somewhere in the segment, and too close for comfort.

"Leak?" I asked, and tried not to look at the open hatch.

Bellek ran his hands over the control surfaces. "I'm not sure yet. Environmental is checking it out."

I remembered breach drills, not just from childhood, but from other stations where I'd spent time, and I couldn't help thinking about all the open airlocks, the obstructed hatches. There was no way the station could protect itself, at least not quickly. "Should we be taking action?"

"Not yet." Bellek studied his screen. At least the alarm wasn't moving any closer; that should mean the leak was confined to a nearby compartment. He looked up with a sudden wry smile. "Callambhal Above is old and complex, Captain. Minor leaks—I wouldn't say they're routine, but they do happen." The klaxon changed, went from warning to stand-by, and he looked at the screen again. "Ah. It looks like an unplanned vent opening. Environmental has rerouted power, and a team is on its way to make repairs."

The vents would fail to the closed position, or at least that was the way they should function. I said, "I was born here, Sen Bellek. I don't remember it like this."

There was a little silence, broken only by the distant hooting of the stand-by horn. At last he said, "As I said, Captain, Callambhal is old. If you work for the Academy, you know how hard it is to maintain anything the Ancestors built. There were internal shields, but they've been failing for some years, they don't reach to the Tail any more." He shrugged one shoulder, as though it didn't matter. "The Environmental teams are very good. They catch the small failures before they can cause real problems." As if to underscore his words, the stand-by horn stopped, and was replaced by the tri-tone all clear.

"So I see." I wasn't sure I was all that convinced, but there was no point in arguing.

Bellek gave me a thoughtful look. "There have been rumors that the Academy has some ideas, ways to make systemic repairs. I've mostly taken that as Successor propaganda, but if it were true..."

"I just provided transport," I said. "I'm sorry."

He shrugged again. "It was worth asking."

The diagnostics finished on time, and, as I'd expected, showed stress damage to the port field generators and some minor detuning on both the dorsal and ventral generators as well. We argued out a price—entirely reasonable for the work involved—and I left him with a deposit and his promise to contact me at once if anything more showed up.

I made my way back to the Shell, unable not to look for more signs of decay. As soon as I looked, they were everywhere. Flooring showed patches of repair, there were stains and new welds wherever the metal underpinnings were visible, and it seemed as though every bulkhead that should have been airtight was instead compromised by cables and poorly fitted pass-throughs. The transit trains were overcrowded, the air hot and sweaty, and it wasn't until I reached the Academy's levels that the local atmospheric telltales glowed clear green. That was sobering, and I was glad Rejane was still out when I returned to our rooms. Had Callambhal always been this fragile? It was hard to believe.

冊 ⺓ ⽱

I had ordered and eaten a boxed dinner before Rejane returned, and was flipping through the local media looked for any news reports of the leak when the door opened. I blanked the screen and sat up, and she came to join me, holding out a flask in mute question. I nodded, and she poured us each a drink of what proved to be a cold sweet wine before she settled beside me.

"A bad day?" I asked, after a moment, and she managed a smile.

"Tedious. There's a good deal of work to do before we can even begin the experiments."

"I suppose that's not unreasonable," I said carefully.

"They're incredibly cautious. And I'm not sure Mirean has gotten everyone on board with the idea."

"I'm surprised the Council agreed at all." I sipped my wine. Most people on Callambhal drank distillates, either home-brewed in the lower levels or vacuum processed in some of the trailing compartments. But then, the Academy could afford luxuries.

"They haven't," Rejane said. "Or not to the actual experiment, though they've expressed interest in principal. Mirean says she's working on it." She shook herself. "How was your day? Did you arrange the repairs?"

"I did. But—Rejane, have you been out of the Shell?"

She frowned. "You know I haven't."

"I was down in the Tail, that's where the Guildhall is, and the office of the repair company." I took a drink of my wine, marshaling my thoughts. "Callambhal, the station—it's not in good shape."

"I have noticed that people aren't careful about breach discipline," Rejane said. "Though that could argue they're confident in the structures."

"That's one problem," I said. "And that's worse the further back you go. But the other problem is that the structure isn't sound. There was a leak in the Tail segment while I was talking to the ship fitter, and he just ignored it. A vent let go; Environmental shut down power to that panel and the vent auto-sealed, so no harm done, but—he said it happened all the time. And on my way back here, I noticed there wasn't a single atmospheric telltale that showed clean until I got into the Academy's section."

"In other words," Rejane said slowly, "you think the station is failing."

I couldn't bring myself to say it. "I think it has serious problems."

"That might explain some things," Rejane said. Her voice was grim. "All the more reason to push this through."

"If in fact there are structural support fields," I said.

"There should be—there seem to be focus points, and the Sun was designed to do more than just provide light." Rejane sighed. "But that's another unknown we'll have to deal with."

I didn't sleep well that night, every unfamiliar sigh or whistle from the ventilation system sparking dreams of hull breach and ships falling from orbit. Sometime in the day's earliest hours, I woke long enough to leave Rejane asleep and wander out into the main room to check the station's status.

Everything was in order, or so the system said; I tried to be reassured, but found a packet of sleep-ease in the hope of breaking the cycle. It worked well enough, in that I found myself yawning and heavy-eyed; but when I sank back into the bed next to Rejane, I dreamed that the Inner Sun was lit and alive. The light was blinding, scalding, wiping out everything but the haziest glimpses of the distant sphere surrounding it. I could hear a fine clear tone coming from it, almost like singing, and I stepped off the balcony's edge and was drawn up into the light. A shower of gold fell past me, odd jagged shapes like human bones, and suddenly I dreaded what lay within the light. I struggled, trying to pull away, but the grav-belt's controls didn't work, and I woke with a gasp just before I struck the white and molten surface.

I lay for a long time barely daring to move, watching the projected minutes creep across the ceiling. Rejane slept soundly; I counted my breaths, and wondered what I had triggered. Of course it was just a nightmare: no AI, not even Gold Shining Bone, could reach me in the here-and-now. I was disconnected from the possible, and intended to remain so. But I couldn't shake the stories, the tales that said Gold Shining Bone's malevolence could cross even Anketil's barrier, feeding dreamers nightmares that their own fears made come true. Those were just stories, excuses for mistakes made in the possible: I repeated that until I finally slept again.

I was cranky and tense the next day, with nothing to do but wait in case Bellek found something more wrong with the ship, and Rejane once again spent her day in conference with Mirean and the other Academicians. That set the pattern for the next half-week, though by the end of it, I had spent more time exploring the station. On the surface, it was not very much changed from what I remembered, at least in the sense that the major landmarks remained intact, the hand of the Ancestors visible everywhere you turned.

I visited the Overlook, where you could see into the hydroponic section filled with plants that helped clean the air and provide basic rations, a canyon of a thousand shades of green, spilling out and over the frameworks the Ancestors had left, riotous and improbable. I passed a leash of schoolchildren being escorted through, their teacher reciting facts I had memorized at that same age, and bought a cone of fresh-picked greens from the vendor by the airlock entrance. It was one of the few that was still unblocked, and looked carefully maintained; when I made my way to the Shell's West Pole, I was shocked by the open locks, and the number of cables and pipes that had been routed along and through what should have been unbreachable walls. At least the iris that sealed the stairs that led into the Pole was unblocked, ready to seal in case something punctured the transparent panels that formed the walls of the Pole, but I was uneasily aware of discolorations and spot welds in the lattice that protected them, and of odd and unfamiliar vibrations beneath my feet.

The Pole had been one of the great sights of Callambhal, always crowded with residents as well as transients and tourists, offering a view of space and the curve of the planet below that no station built after the Fall could even dream of creating. Today the space was almost empty, my footsteps dull and unresonant on the padded deck, and the ticket-takers at the base of the stairs carried oxy-packs at their belts. Probably they always had, and I was just noticing them now, but seeing it did nothing for my nerves. And everywhere I went, every time I let my fingers trail along an exposed surface, my burden seeking contact, I felt a fine uneasy tremor, the echo of a thousand minor warnings, faint and inexorable as an elder's palsy.

I said as much to Rejane that night, after we'd eaten with the Academicians, listening to them arguing about systems and conduits and power requirements. "Something's very wrong. No one seems to be paying any attention, but you can feel it. Anyone can feel it, if they have the burden."

"Mirean has been pushing us to start testing," Rejane said. "I'm as eager as the next person, but we need to be sure we know what we're doing."

"If she's worried about the station," I said, and Rejane nodded.

"Will you come with me tomorrow? I'd like you to be with me when I talk to her about this."

"Will she allow it?"

"You were born here. You know what it used to be like, used to feel like, and what's changed since then," Rejane said. "She'll have to listen to that."

I wasn't so sure, but there seemed to be no point objecting, and I was curious to see what the Academicians were doing. The next morning, I followed Rejane from the refectory through a maze of corridors that I suspected had been created by the Academy to provide more working space. The partitions looked sturdy enough to be airtight, and I wondered if their own precautions had blinded them to what was going on in the rest of the station.

Mirean and her team were working in what they believed to have been the Sun's original control room, high at the top of the Shell where the Spire jutted up and forward to point the station's path along its orbit. A narrow corridor led from the Spire's base into the control room, the inner side open to the void where the Sun had once hung. Now there was only emptiness, the distant lights of the far side spangled against the darkness, a deeper darkness at the center suggesting the shape of the Sun. Beneath our feet, the decking was covered with inlaid scrolls that glinted in the lights the Academy had strung along the walls. Once, I supposed, they would have blazed, reflecting the Sun, so that you walked on a carpet of silver flame. There were letters above the final door, Ancient script that still shimmered with rainbows where the lights hit it, but I couldn't read what it said.

"The House of the Sun, wherein we take our rest," Rejane said. Her smile was wry. "No, we don't know what that means."

I touched the nearest wall, cautiously tasting. The tremors were far less here, and I could feel the familiar pulse of local systems running at their normal levels: the Academy, at least, took good care of its sections. Rejane put her hand to the latch, and the door rolled back to let us into the control space.

It was smaller than I had expected, with a window that overlooked the inner void, and a ring of consoles surrounding a raised platform. Some of the consoles had been pried open, and Academicians were digging into a tangle of metals and wires and sheets of metallic elements; others had been left alone, and sat darkened, waiting for attention. Mirean and a thin, sun-scarred man in an Academic's hood over working coveralls had their heads together over the largest of the open consoles, but Mirean looked up at our approach.

"Rejane! We've traced the load path."

"We think," the man said, but Mirean ignored him.

"We should be able to do a match fitting tomorrow—maybe even today."

"That's very quick," Rejane said. "I'd like to have a better sense of the system first."

"I agree," the man said.

Mirean frowned at him. "We have the schematics worked out. We're confident of them. There's no need to delay."

"Perhaps we should discuss this in private," Rejane said.

Mirean looked at me as though she had just noticed I was there. "Including Captain en Doroney?"

"Please." Rejane waited, and after a moment Mirean nodded.

"Very well."

She had a workroom further up in the Shell, or so I'd gathered from my brief conversations with the Academicians, but they had set up a small side room for her so that she would be close at hand to supervise. Her console and screens didn't leave much room for the rest of us, but we crowded in, and the man shut the door behind us. "I'm Biis Abion," he said, with a wry smile, and I nodded back.

"Nic en Doroney."

"Well?" Mirean glared at us from behind her console, but I thought she was more nervous than she pretended.

"Why the hurry?" Rejane said bluntly. "I'm not comfortable with the condition of the station. Nic was born here, and she says she's never seen things in such bad shape."

Mirean transferred her glare to me. "You have the local burden, then?"

"Yes." She looked skeptical, and I said, "I was in the Tail three days ago, and there was a leak. Vent failure, they said, and no one seemed at all concerned. The ship fitter I was working with said it happened all the time. That was never true when I was younger."

"It's been some time since you lived here," Mirean began, but Rejane nodded, and I went on as though she hadn't spoken.

"More than that, I have the burden. I can feel how fragile the station is, everything on the edge. It wouldn't take much to tear everything apart."

There was a little silence, and then Mirean heaved a sigh. "And that," she said, "is why I'm in a hurry. You can feel it, anyone who looks with a technician's eye can see it. Callambhal is in a constant state of failure. We, the Academy and the Council, we're doing everything we can to hold it together, but we're barely keeping up."

"Why now?" Rejane asked.

"We've lost the structural fields," Mirean said.

Rejane frowned. "The gravity seems fine."

"That's part of the problem," Abion said.

"The structural fields knit the station's components together," Mirean said. "Or they did. Even the Ancestors couldn't rely on mechanical joints to hold something as complex as the station together, particularly when you add gravity. The fields weren't particularly strong, but they were enough to reinforce the physical connections. They were originally powered from the Sun; then when the station was recovered, the first-in settlers rigged solar panels to restore the main generators."

"Only it wasn't the right frequency," Abion said. "We think that was the problem, anyway. Some of the network burned out before we were able to correct, and now it's taking more and more power to keep the fields running. We—with the Council's agreement—have had to cut power to all but the core systems."

"That's the Shell and the lower part of the Spire," Mirean said. "And the inner Ring. Without the structural fields, the station is subjected to unplanned stresses, particularly at the hull seams and the joints between components. It's becoming impossible to keep up with repairs."

Rejane glanced at me, and I lifted one shoulder: this was new to me, but then, I had been a child when I left Callambhal. I hadn't really known how the systems worked. Rejane said, "And the Council knows this."

Mirean nodded. "We've consulted many times over the last five years. This is why they were willing even to think about re-lighting the Sun. If the fields aren't restored, one way or another, there's a solid chance that Callambhal Above will collapse within the next ten years."

"What do the Newfounders say?" Rejane tipped her head to one side.

"Nothing of use," Mirean said.

"They've proposed adding more generators," Abion said. "They have not, however, resolved the problem of matching the original field tuning, which we believe to be the root of the problem. The Newfounders disagree. Their idea is either to reinforce the network, or to replace the field generators entirely."

"Which would be a passably good idea if they had anything that actually worked," Mirean said. "If we could duplicate the effects of the Ancestors' generators, we wouldn't be in this mess."

Much of the technical detail flowed over my head, but I could see the doubt in Rejane's face. "All the more reason to be sure this will work, rather than giving the Newfounders any more ammunition."

"Right now, the Council is on our side," Mirean countered. "With what you can offer, we need to act before they change their minds."

Rejane sighed. "I take your point. All right, we can try the fit tomorrow. But I want today to look over your schematics, and I'll want Nic's help when we try the fit. She's familiar with the devices we're using."

That was more than I would have liked to tell the Custodian, but I needed an excuse to be present. She gave me a sharp look, obviously rethinking what she'd been told of me—and coming to the entirely correct conclusion that I had dealt with AI before—and nodded again. "Thank you. I appreciate your understanding."

"Then we'll get to work," Rejane said. "I wish you'd told me sooner, Mirean."

"The Council has asked us to keep it quiet," Mirean answered. "For obvious reasons."

"Still, it would have been useful," Rejane said, and Abion let us back out into the main work space.

冊 爻 屮

"She should have said something," Rejane said, when we had retreated to our rooms at the end of the day. "Yes, there's the fear of panic, and I don't blame the Council for keeping this under wraps, but—we needed to know."

"If the station falls," I said, and couldn't bring myself to finish. I'd seen the scars on other worlds where the Ancestors' great stations had landed. Callambhal Below was not heavily populated, but the sheer mass falling from the sky was an almost unimaginable danger.

"I know," Rejane said. She was pacing again, unable to sit still. "I know. We can't let it happen."

"Can we stop it?" I looked at the device, shrouded in its drab case. "Can it stop this?"

"We'd better hope so," Rejane said, and her voice was grim enough that I didn't pursue the question.

Rejane and Mirean agreed that they needed to run more tests before they tried to fit the share into the system. I spent a day watching without understanding what was going on, and the next day took myself down into the mid-levels of the Shell, playing tourist and at the same time trying to assess the real state of the station. I linked my contacts to the station's systems to make it easier to track the repairs, and received in return the expected blast of visitor information and solicitation. I was sorting through the chaff when I saw the single piece of personal mail, and read the sender's name: Doroney Leschi. I flicked it into the discard file, my heart racing, sat staring at the display as though it had bitten me. I used my mother's forename as a surname, common use for a child of a singleton parent whose new partners did not claim the child; it was not a particularly common name, nor had I forgotten her husband's name.

After a bit, I rose, made a cup of tea, and drank it standing at the counter, my back to the display as though that would help me decide. The tea was astringent, oversteeped; I set the dregs aside and fished the message out of the discard file. It was very short:

If you are my daughter Nic, I would like to speak with you again. If not, I apologize for intruding.

I left it there, open, and paced, more conscious than before of the fragility of the station around me. I had not tried to remember my mother, nor her husband and their children—there had been two of them, born within two years of each other. They would both have counted toward her husband's reproductive share, so I doubted there would have been any more. My mother had married him when I was seven; my first half-sister was born within the year, and the second came when I was ten. And then at twelve I had been sent to the Novilis. I had always wondered what they had paid for me; it occurred to me now that I might ask.

The door beeped and slid open, admitting Rejane, her Academician's robe slung over her shoulder. "Everything all right?"

"No." I waved to the screen, and she came to see, her frown deepening as she read.

"Oh." She put her robe away, carefully not asking the question that I was asking myself, and I sighed.

"I don't know."

"What do you want to do?"

"I want it never to have happened." I glared at the screen. "It's a bit late to be making amends, and I'm reasonably sure I'm owed something for—" I stopped, not wanting to hurt Rejane, but she just nodded.

"Then don't answer. Let her think she read the name wrong."

"I should have changed it," I said.

Rejane came closer, and I saw the moment she decided not to reach for me. "You could do that."

One wrong word would shatter me, break every barrier I'd ever built to pretend I didn't care. "I should—" I stopped, shaking my head. "No. I want to talk to her."

Rejane did reach for me then, and I let her touch my shoulder and turned into her embrace. "Do that, then."

"But not—after the test."

Rejane nodded. "We're almost ready."

I sat down at the console, unrolled the input board, and then keyed in my answer before I could change my mind. *I'll meet you in four days at the Western Innerlook at 1100.* I hit *Send* without reading it again.

"So." Rejane was watching me closely, and I shook my head.

"I don't want to talk about it."

"Fair enough," she said, and fetched a flask of wine from the cabinet.

"I've been looking over the station," I said instead, and as we drank I told her about the constant stream of low-level notifications that my burden sensed every time I let it taste the station's systems. None of it was individually disastrous—most of the notices didn't rise to the level of a warning, were just reminders to the maintenance crews to look into an anomaly— but the volume was overwhelming. I had found a public board that tracked maintenance requests, and even its sanitized numbers were alarming. There weren't enough technicians on the station to keep up with the failures; anything that wasn't an immediate threat would have to wait indefinitely.

Rejane listened, her expression growing even grimmer. She had spoken unofficially with two members of the Council and, while they approved of the plan, it was clear that there was a vocal minority that wanted to follow the Newfounders' plan. We would have one chance to make this happen, she said, and should probably count ourselves lucky to have that much.

The morning of the trial we had a hasty breakfast in our room, Rejane with the device in her lap as she felt for the best contact points. "You understand what I need you to do?"

I poured more tea. "You want me to monitor the share. Stop the trial if there are any problems."

"We can't lose her," Rejane said. "We can't just go back and get another share."

"I know."

Light flickered within the device. *you are worried*

"Yes," Rejane said. "We don't know if this will work. I've given you everything I have, all the schematics, but I doubt we've got it all mapped out."

you do not

"I don't find that encouraging," I said, in spite of myself.

it's to be expected—even i can't see the pattern complete

"Which is something, I suppose," Rejane murmured. "The main thing is, you're not to allow yourself to be damaged. Nic will provide a link, you can—you must—use that to escape if there's a problem."

understood

"The Custodian won't like it," I said.

"The Custodian isn't responsible for the share," Rejane said. "Our obligation goes both ways."

I couldn't help thinking of Beast, but that was entirely different. Or at least I thought it was: Beast—Green Piercing Book—was complete and free, not a share. It was entirely too able to take care of itself.

The old control room was much less crowded than it had been the last times I was there, all but the most necessary personnel moved to safer areas. Mirean was there, of course, and Abion and a handful of Academicians I'd seen before.

There was also a man in ordinary clothes talking quietly with Mirean, and I wasn't surprised to see a Councillor's badge on his collar.

"Rejane," Mirean said. "I'd like you to meet Councillor Raman Iscmer, chairman of the infrastructure committee. Raman, Senior Academician Rejane Novilis."

"Councillor," Rejane said. Her arms were full of the bundled device, and she did not offer her hand. "And this is Captain Nic en Doroney, who has been helping me with my research."

"Academician." Iscmer inclined his head. "Captain."

"Everything's ready," Abion said quietly. "If you'll come this way, Councillor, Captain?"

"Nic will come with me," Rejane said, and I followed her through the maze of consoles to one that looked more like a pedestal. The outer casing had been peeled back in wedges like the rind of a fruit, revealing a net of wires that opened in the center on a pocket of darkness. Something glittered in its center, flashes of blue and gold, and I felt my burden twitch in answer.

"That's—live." That was the safest word I knew, the pilots' term for connections to the possible, but even so Rejane grimaced.

"It's contained."

Like in the Library? I swallowed the words, knowing the answer: this wasn't a sealed pocket, but a pinhole contained and shaped by the same forces that lived in my device. "What do you want me to do?"

"Stand here." Rejane brought me to the opposite side of the pedestal, so that we faced each other across the opening. "Take the device, please. Don't let it touch the machinery or the casing."

I did as she asked, freeing the device from its container and holding it in both hands so that it was close to the pedestal, but a good hand's-length away. I heard it chime softly, an odd, three-toned note repeated half an octave higher, and then it settled, the Ancestral glass warming to my touch.

"First we make sure the connection can be established," Rejane said, and lifted one of the control rods that the Academicians used to manipulate the machinery. She touched its tip to one of the junctions within the pedestal, then pulled it slowly up and away. A thread of blue light came with it, sparkling softly, and she guided it across the gap until it touched the glass of the device. Light flared within it, one blinding flash followed by a wave of color, dancing red and gold like electric flames. I felt it, too, a sharp shock through the palms of my hands, but managed not to lose my grip. I focused on the share. *Are you all right?*

There was a pause, like breathing, like panting breath, and then I felt the share's presence gathering itself.

we may proceed

I met Rejane's eyes and nodded. "We're connected."

"All right." Rejane reached out with her free hand, touched the device lightly. *Sky-share, can you see where you're supposed to fit?*

the pattern is clear

Are there any impediments? Rejane asked, her control rod hovering over the opening again.

no but it is hungry

"I don't like that," I said aloud, and Rejane nodded agreement.

Sky-share, don't go further than you can back out again. Leave yourself a way out no matter what.

The device chimed softly again, the lights shimmering in its depths. *understood*

Mirean was staring from across the room, visibly controlling the desire to ask what was happening. Rejane took a breath and reached into the opening, drawing another line of light across to the device, and then another, and finally a fourth. They pulsed and thickened, solidifying, and I felt the Sky-share move toward them, easing itself out into the new channel like a person stepping onto a high and narrow bridge. It slid forward, the connections thickening visibly, and inside the opening tendrils began to spread from where Rejane had touched the components. More lights flickered in the central darkness, and a technician looked up from his station by a second console

"I'm getting a response here."

Mirean moved quickly to look over his shoulder. "Any idea what it is?"

"Just power in the system, I think." He shook his head. "Steady gain."

Surely that was a good sign. My arms were starting to hurt from holding this position, but I didn't dare move for fear I'd interrupt the connection.

Then it all changed. The darkness gaped, swallowing the tendrils that stretched toward it. In the same moment, I felt a terrible pressure, a suction dragging against my hands, pulling me toward the pedestal. The share shrieked, wordless pain, and I felt it lunge back toward the device. The darkness surged after it, and Rejane slashed at the lines of light with her control rod, severing them with a crack like thunder. I cupped my hands around the device, feeling the share roiling in panic and distress, but still whole, still itself...

Rejane's face was white and set, but she focused on the pedestal, touching point after point to shut it down and fold the petals back over the opening.

"Well?" Mirean demanded, and in the same moment Abion said, "What went wrong?"

"I don't know." I could feel the effort it took for Rejane to keep her voice steady, but I doubted the others could see. "Something with the connection, I think—perhaps a power surge?" She looked at the technician who had reported a response, and he looked at his readings.

"I did see an increase of power in the system. But I can't tell where it came from."

"It didn't work." That was the Councillor, Iscmer, still waiting on the sidelines.

"It didn't work this time," Mirean said. "This is only a first attempt, and, as I told you, it may take several tries to be sure we can load the device properly."

"It's a risk every time you try and fail," Iscmer said.

Rejane cleared her throat. "But we didn't fail, Councillor. We didn't succeed—yet—but we did establish a connection, and were able to begin the installation. We even got a response from the subsidiary systems, which argues that we're very much on the right track. We need to take some time to look at why the device aborted the transfer, but right now I see no reason to think that we won't be able to install it."

Iscmer gave her a long look. I could tell that he wanted to believe her—of course he did, it was Callambhal's best chance—and I hoped she was telling something close to the truth.

"Quite right," Mirean said. "It's likely to take several tries to find the right parameters, but we should be able to do it."

"And light the Sun?" Iscmer asked.

"That's our firm intention," Rejane said.

"We'll keep you informed of our progress," Mirean said, and Iscmer heaved a sigh.

"Do that. Please."

"Of course," Mirean said, and led him smoothly away.

Chapter Fifteen

Mirean was less relaxed when she returned, by which time Rejane had the pedestal open again, and was checking the schematics. "It's shifted," she said, to the Academician who had helped her unravel the pattern, and the other woman nodded.

"It's done that before. I think it's a dynamic system—it would almost have to be, to manage the inevitable fluctuations."

"Rejane." Mirean glared at both of them impartially. "What went wrong?"

"I don't yet know," Rejane answered. "Obviously, we're working on it—"

"Best guess."

"I don't have the data," Rejane said.

"Your suspicions, then."

"I think things moved too quickly, and the share pulled back to avoid being absorbed into the system."

"Surely that was what was supposed to happen." Mirean's frown deepened. "To be absorbed, I mean."

"We don't know that," Rejane said. "I would assume that the share would maintain its independence—that it would have to, in order to perform its function. I'll know more when I've had a chance to interrogate the share."

I could feel the share still quivering within the device, a weird jangled music that prickled against my skin. Whatever had happened, I could only read her response as pure terror.

Mirean said, "Then I suggest you do that. Abion can take

over reading the external systems."

For a second, I thought Rejane would protest, but then she nodded. "Agreed."

We retreated through the maze of corridors to a small workroom fitted with a daedalist's workbench and equipped with a damping field. Rejane activated that, and then switched her own portable field within it, shaking her head unhappily. I set the device on the unactivated workbench, and found a chair.

"Well," I said, when it became clear that Rejane wasn't going to say anything. "Did you mean any of that?"

"What?"

"What you told the Councillor."

"That." Rejane held out her hands, her fingers spread, and I could see them trembling. "Yes, that was true, this is just the beginning. We haven't failed yet."

"But we haven't succeeded," I said, "and we're not getting any closer."

"I don't like the way that felt," Rejane said. She laid a hand on the device, and grimaced at what she felt. I put my hand against it as well, and felt the echo of the share's fear.

"That's better than it was."

"Lovely," Rejane said. "Sky-share, can you tell what happened?"

still analyzing

Rejane tipped her head to one side. "How long to complete your analysis?"

unknown—working

"Let her be," I said, and Rejane nodded.

"That was—unexpected. Though I probably should have expected it."

"What do you think happened?"

"What I said," Rejane answered. "It looked as though the conduit was open, the transfer possible, and then Sky-share pulled back and broke the connection. She said it was hungry—"

"She was afraid," I said. "You told her not to risk herself."

"And I meant it." Rejane stroked the device, then seemed to realize what she was doing. "We can't lose her."

"Even if that's the price of lighting the Sun?"

"I don't think it can be," Rejane said. "The Ancestors treated their AI as equals, at least before the Rebellion. Green Piercing Book was a willing partner when it joined the Sun, or so the stories say. They wouldn't have permanently bound an AI to the Sun any more than they would have bound one of their own. There has to be a way around."

desperate The share's words nipped at our fingers, chill against our burdens. *hungry desperate empty so empty*

"I'm sorry I risked you," Rejane said. "You did well to get back out."

I felt the share's tension ease a little, the quivering resolving into a faint high-pitched hum just at the edge of perception. It was another hour, though, before the share was able to offer its analysis, and to answer Rejane's questions. The analysis was not particularly helpful: from the share's perspective, the connection had formed correctly, leading into what it called a starting grid, and which after some back-and-forth Rejane identified as the first conjoined level between the control system and the Sun itself. After that, however, the bottom had dropped out, and the share found itself being dragged into the Sun's inner workings without any conception of whether it would fit or whether it would be able to free itself once it was there. It had pulled back at once and, when the pressure followed, it had broken the connection, with Rejane's help.

At least that was what it thought had happened. It freely admitted it lacked data and its analysis was incomplete. Rejane said it was close enough to what she'd experienced that she'd accept it, and I had to agree that it matched what I had felt. We reported all of this to Mirean, the device once again safely stowed in its carrier, and the Custodian was predictably unimpressed.

"So we try again, and let the share be pulled in," she said. "That's the simple answer."

"Only it's not," Rejane said. "Mirean, you know better.

If we lose this share, we're not going to get another one. Not without having to involve the full conclave, and you know how well that would go."

Mirean made a face. "Granted. You were sure that the share would work—have you changed your mind?"

"No. We just need to try again." Rejane paused. "You know these things never work on the first try. I don't know why you had the Councillor here."

"He asked," Mirean said. "It's their risk as much as ours— more." She looked at me. "And you, Captain en Doroney. You were in contact with the device and with the share, yes?" I nodded reluctantly. "Did you feel a connection to the possible?"

I hesitated, not knowing quite how to answer, and realized that my hesitation was answer enough. "I'm not sure. There's a gap at the center, but I couldn't tell if it was just the Sun, or if it was tied to the possible."

"Which is something else we'll need to worry about," Mirean said.

"I warned you about that," Rejane said. "All the more reason not to rush into this."

"We can't afford too much delay," Mirean said, but she sounded calmer. "The Newfounders are bound to track you here."

"I know," Rejane said. "Look, I need another day or two to figure out exactly what happened, and then time to work out a solution. You can give me that."

Mirean sighed. "I don't have much choice."

"We can make this work," Rejane said. "I just need time."

I had my own doubts about this, but knew better than to say anything, even after we were back in our shared rooms. Rejane seemed completely confident; the last thing I wanted was to damage that. She spent the next three days in the Sun's control room, retracing everything they had done before, and came back the fourth day incandescent with excitement.

"We've solved it! I think," she added, propitiating, but there was no lessening of her enthusiasm. "There were two parts to the system, the original controls and a later addition—probably installed after Green Piercing Book broke free, to make sure the next share they installed in the Sun couldn't escape and join its larger self. But it's that later addition that's causing the problem. It's designed to pull an AI or a share into its core and immediately bind it—overwrite some of the programming that gives it its independence—so that it can only control the Sun. But I can see how to inactivate those sections, which should allow the Sky-share to step in."

"That is good news," I said, and meant it. I had just sent the final payment to Bellek. *Beljaeger* was repaired, and I was ready to start worrying about my own problems, because if I was trapped on Callambhal—but I wouldn't be. We would find a way to deal with Beast, too.

"The one thing that does concern me," Rejane said, "is a connection to the possible. I can't find one, but I can't see where else the power comes from. And I'd like to know that before I go too much further."

"Maybe it's the share that makes the connection," I said. "That might be safer."

"Safer than having a permanent connection," Rejane agreed. "It's the only thing that makes sense. Though I'm still worried that I'm missing something...."

"Talk to Mirean," I suggested. "And Abion. They do know these systems."

She nodded. "You're right, and I will. Oh, Nic, if we can pull this off!"

"It'll be—" I began, and she put a finger to my lips.

"Luck! But—yes."

冂 仌 屮

In the meantime, I had made a bargain. While Rejane worked to deactivate the addition to the system, I paced our room, trying to decide what I would ask when I finally saw my mother again. The price, I thought; I did want to know what they had gained by selling me. I also wanted to know about her burden, and my father's—about my father in general, since she had always refused to talk about him. I drank tea and made lists and then destroyed them, until at last it was time for me to make my way down to the Western Overlook.

I paid my entrance money and passed into the airlock— this one was in full working order, not blocked by cables or anything else, which seemed somewhat ironic considering that it looked out on the station's fully pressurized interior. The lock cycled, and I stepped out into the wide, low-ceilinged space. It had been well-maintained, with padded benches grouped under pillars shaped like artificial trees, and distance viewers set at fixed intervals along the enormous opening. It was sealed, of course, its glass reflecting even the dim interior lights, and there was a further barrier half a meter from the window, blocking too-close access. There were maybe seven or eight people here, plus a group of schoolchildren already being herded toward the airlock. None of them were my mother.

I leaned against the barrier, peering out into the dark as though I could see beyond the local lights. Somewhere above me hung the Sun, invisible unless it occluded lights on the far side of the central void. In the stories, station residents wore grav-belts, and leaped from level to level, flinging themselves out into the light to follow a network of guide lines that webbed the inner surfaces. The Sun was no danger, not to anyone halfway competent with a belt, though there were also stories of people throwing themselves against the Sun in despair and loss. I wondered if the share had enhanced that, its emotions radiating somehow, but that was long before the Rebellion.

Beyond the window a beam of light flashed out, sweeping across the curving walls to our left, revealing hundreds of windows both smaller and larger than this one. There was a murmur of interest from the other people here, and they all came forward to take places along the barrier. We watched as the light swept further out and across, striking glints from more distant windows, and picking out unexpected jolts of color—turquoise, salmon pink, hot ochre, vividly bright. The light wasn't strong enough to reach all the way across the inner void, and its operator didn't try, but instead swung the beam upward, striking first the shadow of a cable, and then one of the support struts. I craned my head, and caught a glimpse of the lower edge of a suspended sphere, the remains of the Sun itself, inert and dead. Its material was black, unreflective, perhaps faintly pebbled: nothing I recognized, even after years of scavenging Ancestral scrap.

The light swept on, abandoning the Sun. It flashed across the walls beyond it, catching more brilliant spots of color as well as a few cables dangling from barricaded openings, and then at last winked out. There was a murmur, half disappointment, half applause, from the watchers, and they began to move slowly away from the railing as the interior lights came back on. I craned my head a final time, as though I could still see the Sun, then made myself turn away.

"Nic?"

I recognized the voice before the speaker, deep and soft. Doroney Leschi stood a few meters away, a smaller, slighter person than I'd remembered, her hair tucked up under a fretwork cap, dressed like everyone else in long tunic and trousers, a checked scarf tossed around her shoulders. I would not have known her, passing her in a crowd, unless she had spoken. "Yes."

She nodded. "I only knew you by your clothes."

I was the only person in the overlook who was dressed like a pilot, high-collared jacket over workcloth trousers. She was watching me closely, with an expression I couldn't read, and I cleared my throat. "You wanted to see me?" The words were trite, inadequate, but then, I didn't know what I had to say.

She nodded again. "Yes. And thank you."

"Does your husband know you're here?"

Something crossed her face, a spasm too slight for me to interpret. "Yes." She did not say he sent greetings; we both know that would not be believed. She took a breath, silver pailletes winking at the neck of her tunic. "I wanted—I only wanted to see you. To know you were well. They promised—I was supposed to be kept informed of your progress, but it didn't happen."

"I'm well." I spread my hands. "As you can see."

"The listing said you were a ship's master."

"Yes."

She stared at me, frowning slightly, as though she wasn't sure of the right words or even of what she wanted to ask. "And you do...all right?"

"It's a living.

"They told us you would go to the Academy," she said. "That you could share your burden and still go on. What went wrong?"

"They lied," I said. "Once they had what they wanted, they sold my indenture to a freelance captain."

She closed her eyes. "I wanted—we wanted—to give you a chance. There was nothing here for you, and you had the burden—"

I realized I believed her, though I couldn't say it helped. "My burden, yes. How did I come by that? Not just from you, or my sibs would have had it, too."

"Your father had the same burden, more strongly expressed." Her voice was without inflection. "He was a pilot, he had a regular run that brought him through Callambhal. We passed it on to you."

"And what did they give you? For me, I mean."

She flinched again. "I told you, they promised us you'd have the Academy—"

"I don't believe—that wasn't all."

"Twenty thousand." She made a small sound that might have been a bitter laugh. "They also offered us a child, one with my burden, but Leschi decided against it."

That was a year's tuition at the Academy. My fists clenched. "You were cheated."

"Do you think I don't know that?"

Her words shocked both of us to silence. "You shouldn't have let him talk you into it," I said, after a moment.

She shook her head. "No. I—that was not what happened. I won't lie, it was as much my idea as his, and I truly thought—but it doesn't matter."

"No," I said. "It doesn't."

Another pause, a few heartbeats this time, and she bowed her head. "Then I'll go. I'm glad you're well—"

"No," I said. "Wait." I steadied my voice. "If you didn't want me—why didn't you send me to my father?"

She stiffened. "Because he was long gone. We had our burdens matched, as fools do in love, and he said we must never have children, because they'd inherit too much of what he had. When I told him I was pregnant, he told me we had to be rid of it. He was Dedalor-descended, or so he claimed, said he was always hunted in the possible, and anyone with his burden would suffer just the same. I didn't believe him, but three days later he went back aboard his ship and I never saw him again. But I knew he lied." She paused, eyes narrowing as she looked at me. "He did lie, didn't he?"

It was unlikely he was literally a descendant of the Dedalor, but his burden could well be similar. Certainly it had been powerful enough to attract the Novilis, to boost Rejane's burden to high Firstborn. Had it attracted Beast in the first place, or through some combination of the device and my burden? There was no way to know, at least not right now. "I've had my share of encounters with the AI," I said, "but I've never been hunted."

"Good," she said.

Around us, the lights were dimming, drawing a new group of viewers to the barrier, ready to show the Sun and the central void again. "I have to go," I said. "But—I am well."

She bowed her head, and I walked out past her, ignoring the flash and flare of the lights that leaped out into the dark.

冊 衤 屮

It took two more days, working nearly nonstop, for Rejane to deactivate the addition to the system, and I was glad to focus on that. It was a risk on top of the risk we were already taking, but if it worked, it should allow Sky-share to enter the system and ignite the Sun. Or so Rejane promised. She was determinedly optimistic, but the longer they worked, the more gaps I could see in their plans.

But then, I wasn't a trained daedalist. Sky-share seemed comfortable with its part, as did the rest of the Academicians, and all of them knew better than I what was possible. Still, I couldn't help feeling uneasy as we took our places again in the control room. The share shivered faintly within its device, and I couldn't tell if it shared my fears or merely reflected them.

The workroom looked much the same as it had before, though there was no sign of Councillor Iscmer, and there was a new tangle of cables and odd boxes and even a couple of Ancestral devices linked to the pedestal. The device I carried was conspicuously unattached, but as I approached I could feel the share reacting to some field or vibration that I couldn't yet feel. Rejane beckoned me closer, and I felt the hairs on my arms quiver. I glanced at her, and she nodded slightly. "That's the isolation field. We've essentially walled off the parts that gave us a problem last time."

"All right." I looked into the pedestal, seeing the same nest of wires, and the gap at its center. Lights sparked in its depths—were there more this time? I couldn't tell as I freed the device from its container. I held it as Rejane had showed me, feeling the glass warm against my palms as the share gathered itself. I focused on it. *Are you ready?*

ready

"We're good," I said quietly, and Rejane nodded. She adjusted her control rod, and reached into the pedestal again, drawing out a thread of blue light. She touched it to the device, and I felt it snap against my skin. *All right?* I asked again, and felt the share respond with more eagerness than before.

yes

I nodded to Rejane, and she drew out a second thread, and a third, and then a fourth, touching each to a new spot on the device. *Ready?*

very ready

I felt the share shift under my hands, drawing the threads together within the device until abruptly the outer strands slid together as well, forming a cord that glowed more brightly as the share flowed into it. This time there was no backlash, no sudden gaping presence, just the cord, thickening visibly, and the share moving away from the device and into the space that opened before it. *Easy*, I said, but the share ignored me, probing deeper.

"I'm showing power in the system," a technician said quietly.

"Level?" That was Mirean, moving quickly to look over his shoulder.

"Sub-zero. I can register it, but it's not enough to do anything."

"Keep going," Mirean said to Rejane, and Rejane gave an absent nod.

"Yes…"

I could feel Sky-share stretching, most of its presence now out of the device, with only a thin tail to pull it back. More lights flashed in the depths of the pedestal, dots and lines that swelled and combined to form an intricate lattice work that glowed gold and green and blue. Here and there a spine poked out of the pattern, tipped in red, and then those spines bent and plunged out of sight, disappearing into the darkness.

"We're on the scale," the technician said. "Ten percent."

"Excellent," Mirean said.

The deck shuddered, and there was an odd metallic twang from somewhere within the walls. Mirean looked over her shoulder. "Report!"

"Hull's fine," a dark woman said. Her fingers danced over a string of touchpoints. "I think—it looks as though a conduit opened."

"Conduit to what?" Mirean asked.

"One of the untraceables," the woman answered. "Hang on. Looks like it's the Clover Loop."

I looked at Rejane, but all her attention was on the

pedestal, on the share working its way into the system. Something was humming, a thin, high-pitched sound, and the decking shivered again, tuning into that vibration.

"Fifteen percent," the technician said. "Sixteen—seventeen and holding."

"What do we need for ignition?" Mirean demanded.

"More than this," someone said, and Mirean scowled. "Mettes! You ran the numbers."

"We guessed eighty percent minimum," another woman answered. She had her own control rod out, was tapping screens on another set of consoles, intent on the results. "We're not showing undue strain, but there's a long way to go."

I looked back at the device, feeling the distance to Sky-share growing ever greater. *Sky-share, are you all right?*

working

It sounded distracted, impatient—sounded like Rejane when she was totally focused on a problem, and a part of me wanted to giggle at the image. Instead, I shifted my feet, trying to find a comfortable position without disturbing the connection, and Rejane said, "Problem?"

"She says she's all right."

"Good." Rejane waited, her own control rod poised. "Still connected?"

"Yes."

"Good," Rejane said again.

"Nineteen percent," the technician said. "Twenty. I'm seeing sections light up that we thought were dead."

"I see that, too," Abion said, from his console opposite the pedestal. "I think the primary systems are intact."

Mirean nodded, her eyes on the technician's screen. "Twenty-one percent," the technician said.

I held my breath, waiting for the next increase, but instead there was silence. The whining hum stayed steady, the deck shivering in tune, and after a while Rejane reached out cautiously to place a hand on the device.

Sky-share, is there a problem?

blocked

Can you be more specific?

power blocked, locked out, insufficient—

There was a sound from the tangle of cables and devices beside the pedestal, and then the fat red snap of a spark. I looked down to see first one and then the other of the Ancestral devices fill with light. I felt something tug at Sky-share, the same greedy suction we had felt before, and the share recoiled. The attached devices suddenly filled with whirling flecks of black, swirling like ash in a high wind. In the pedestal, Sky-share's lights flashed blinding red and convulsed, the patterns smearing into an amorphous blob, colors fading to white. I felt it lunge for the connection, fleeing for the safety of its own device, and with it came the terrible hunger, the bleak, empty weight of it reaching out even for me. Sky-share fled back along the connection, the transfer that should have taken seconds stretching impossibly, pursued by darkness like a gaping mouth.

Rejane swore, her control rod hovering. She reached into the pedestal to touch a wire, and light arced from the rod's tip to her fingers, making her swear again. Sky-share was pulling free, but slowly, too slowly—it was like a nightmare where you know you're pursued, but you cannot run. It was free of the system that lay within the pedestal, but the thing that pursued was close behind, crawling into the connection after the share. Without thinking, I freed one hand, calling my burden to protect me, and reached into the pedestal, interrupting the connection.

My fingers burned, my burden flaring to fight fire with fire, driving back the thing that hungered. I felt it grip, just for an instant, felt a shape I thought I knew, and then my burden shifted, rearranged itself, and flung it back again. The blue cable clung for a long moment to the center of my palm, my burden offering a ground, and then Sky-share had reached the safety of its device, and the connection flashed into nothing. There was a circular burn seven centimeters across where it had touched me.

"Nic?" Rejane sounded genuinely afraid, and I managed a wincing smile.

"Just a contact burn. The share is safe."

Her eyes flickered shut. "Good."

"What just happened?" Mirean demanded, and Rejane shook herself.

"It looks as though the additional system reactivated itself, though I'm not sure how. I'll need to interrogate the share before I can give you any answers. But Nic needs medical attention first."

"I can confirm that something overrode our barriers," Abion said. "I'll look into that while you see to Captain en Doroney."

"I'm fine," I said, but Rejane gave me a sharp look.

"We don't want to take any risks."

"All right." My burden was already dealing with the burn, blocking pain and spurring healing, but I was willing to go along with whatever she wanted.

She looked back at Mirean. "I'll take the share to my workshop, and report as soon as I have some answers."

"I'll join you there later," Mirean answered, and Rejane caught my shoulder.

"Come on."

The workroom seemed more cluttered than before, with additional pieces of Ancestral technology tucked into corners or waiting on shelves. Rejane activated the dampers, and then took the carrier from me, freeing the device. She cupped it in both hands, but glanced at me over its shimmering surface. "I'm trusting that you're all right."

I held up my hand to show the burn already fading. It stung, and I could still feel the shape of the thing I had touched, weirdly familiar, but my burden promised there was no significant harm. She gave a quick smile, and focused on the device. I put out a finger and touched the Ancestral glass, let my burden make just enough contract that I could hear as well. Rejane nodded.

Sky-share, are you all right?

undamaged running diagnostics

What was that?

insufficient data

Rejane and I exchanged glances, then Rejane spread her hands wider, and I felt a cool calm spreading from them. *Will you have sufficient data later?*

possible

Continue your analysis.

Rejane set the carrier carefully on the workbench. I flexed my hand, feeling the newly repaired skin stretch and sting, and Rejane said, "That was a chance you took. It worked, but—"

"It worked," I said.

"Your burden's all right?"

"It seems to be."

"We should check," Rejane said, and I sighed and held out my hand. She searched for a moment, and came up with another control rod, this one only a little longer than my forefinger. It was about the same width, too, and the metal had a faint greenish glow to it. She touched the tip to the tip of my finger, and I released my burden to respond. A moment later, she nodded and took the rod away. "Nothing's changed. No inclusions, nothing left behind."

"Good." I hesitated. "What do you think went wrong?"

"The later protections reactivated," Rejane said. "But I've no idea why. Something Sky-share did? A trigger we missed? A deeper-level connection? I'm hoping Sky-share can tell us more when she finishes the analysis. Unless you've got something?"

"It was definitely the same thing that was there before." I shivered, remembering that hollow, hungering touch. "And I do think there is some connection to the possible, though I'm not sure precisely how."

There was a chime from the device, and we both turned to set our hands against the Ancestral glass. *system requires a tap to the possible there is not enough power to light the sun without it*

Rejane swore again. *Are you sure?*

97.3 probability that i am right

Rejane shook her head, but we both knew Sky-share wasn't likely to make a mistake about this.

"Did the additional system seal off the possible?" I asked.

"It might. Among many other things." Rejane made a face. "We'll have to extract it completely, which I was hoping not to have to do. It's extremely complex, and even if we can do it, it's going to take forever."

I looked at the device. *Can you maintain the Sun once it's lit? Do you have enough power for that?*

yes

That was a relief, and Rejane heaved a sigh. "That's better than nothing." She found a stool and pulled it up to the bench, cupping her hands around the device. She frowned into the device, visibly marshaling questions. I let my own hand fall away, and found another seat against the wall. This was Rejane's work, not mine—though at least I'd been able to break the connection before whatever it was that the safeguard contained could devour our share. I flexed my hand again, the skin now only tight, and let my head rest against the wall.

The door opened, admitting Mirean, and Rejane pulled herself reluctantly away from the device long enough to summarize what she had so far. Mirean was not best pleased, and inclined to argue, though she refused to touch the device herself. I looked away from the discussion, teasing out the memory of that shape. I had felt it before, I was sure of that: there was a familiarity to it, as though I had handled something very similar in the past.

But of course I had. The only Ancestral technology I'd spent any time with was my own device, and I'd used it to contact Beast—Green Piercing Book. It wasn't the same, but it was kin, a smaller, fractal version of the being I had touched through my own device. That shouldn't be possible—unless the thing in the pedestal was another share, trapped and frozen since the last of the Ancestors abandoned the station, only now revived by Rejane's researches. A share of Green Piercing Book.

I looked up sharply, but Rejane and Mirean were still

engrossed in their arguments. Abion was visible in a comm screen, offering an interpretation of his own data, and I made myself stay still. This was nothing to be shared, not until Rejane had had a chance to consider the implications.

閉 呆 屮

Finally they had exhausted every possible topic, and Mirean reluctantly pulled herself away. Rejane repacked the device, tucking it carefully into its padding, and gave me a crooked smile. "I think we're done. At least for now."

I nodded, not daring to speak, and followed her back through the twisting corridors until we reached our rooms. She let the door slide closed behind her, but made no move to switch on the damper fields. I frowned at that, and she gave me a look of surprise. "Should I—"

"Yes," I said.

Her eyebrows rose, but she turned on the systems, first the Academy's and then her own. "What is it?"

"Is it possible that there's already a share in the system?" I held my breath, and watched her expression shift from confusion to surprise to wary consideration.

"I would have said no," she began. "Surely we would have recognized it? Though we didn't see that there was anything there except the safeties. You think it's a share?"

I nodded. "Or what's left of one. Imagine being trapped here, the station abandoned, the power gone..."

Rejane shivered. "The Ancestors wouldn't have intended to leave it here, surely."

Wouldn't they? They would have had other things to think about when the station was abandoned, lives to save, a thousand things more important than a partial AI, and one whose greater self had betrayed them. I said, "You'd think. But, Rejane, I recognized it. Green Piercing Book."

Her lips pursed into a silent whistle, and she reached for the carrier. "Sky-share, did you hear that?"

no

I rested fingers on the device, calling up first the memory of Beast's touch, and then what I had felt of the thing that pursued. *Are these the same? Is there another share in the system?*

Rejane put her hand next to mine, not quite touching. There was a long silence, as though Sky-share was considering the question. Lights stirred in the depths of the device, revolved, formed and reformed in increasingly complex patterns.

i had not considered another share

Rejane and I looked at each other. *So you think it's possible?*

it is probable and explains much

Can you be more specific? Rejane asked, and in the same moment, I said, "But is it the same?"

first question yes—another share could not maintain the Sun and therefore desires to draw in any other shares to see if two of us could light it

"And could you?" Rejane asked. "If you forced control of the other share?"

unknown

There was a pause, lights flickering again in the device.

i do not think i could force control—this is its system, it knows it all too well, and i do not think we could light the Sun even if we worked together

"Damn it," Rejane said, under her breath. "Why not? What's missing? And could we provide it?"

we need the possible

Rejane rubbed her forehead. "And that's the thing we don't dare do—unless that was what the additions were intended for, to allow the Sun to tap the possible without granting access to the rebel AI?"

i believe that is correct

"So you'd need to restore the—you called them safeties," I said, and Rejane nodded. "And then Sky-share would need to dominate the other share that's already in there."

"Yes. Or I suppose we could see if there was a way to re-install the safeties after the Sun was lit." Rejane frowned. "But that still doesn't protect Sky-share."

second question—highly probable they are the same though that share is greatly degraded and hard to resolve

I shivered in spite of myself, thinking of Beast's fury when it realized we were carrying the share of another AI. And if the trapped share was part of Green Piercing Book... "Sky-share, can that share communicate with its greater self?"

i do not think so—otherwise it would have freed itself long ago

Rejane nodded. "That makes sense. Though I'd hate for it to find us here."

"So would I," I said. "One more reason not to give it access to the possible."

"But without that access, Sky-share says they can't re-light the Sun," Rejane said. "Well. Back to our planning board for that."

She spent the next few days in the workrooms, working with Abion to find some way to protect the station and still open a path to the possible. I made my way back to the Guildhall, trying not to pay too much attention to the signs of damage to the station, and put in a request for another data dump. The hall was still extremely crowded, spacers milling about in front of every kiosk, and when I tried to find a node so I could check the weather, my handheld told me apologetically that the system was overloaded, try back later. I turned away, frowning, and a graying man looked up from his own handheld.

"Are you getting a busy warning?"

I nodded. "I am. Any idea what's going on?"

"The weather's been rough for the last week or so," he said. "Most people are waiting for it to clear before they try to leave. Which is what I'd like to do myself, but I've got a time-limited contract."

"Awkward," I said, and he smiled.

"Just a bit. I've got about forty hours still in hand, but after that, it's go or default."

"How bad has it been?"

"Heavy AI presence at the TAN jump," he answered—that was the primary exit from the system. "But there have been reports of AI lurking at POR and BEK as well. Not that that makes any difference for me, I have to leave by TAN, but a few people have had luck using BEK."

"That sounds like people have been coming in with damage." That was not good news, particularly if we needed to connect to the possible even for a tiny slice of time.

He nodded. "Nothing too serious—nobody's had anything approaching an infiltration, grace of the Ancestors. But people have lost emitters and blown fields. The ship fitters are making a small fortune these days, or so I've heard."

More bad news. My handheld pinged, alerting me that my console was available. I excused myself and went in search of my cubicle.

I settled myself in the comfortable chair and flicked on the damper field, letting its silence enfold me. I paged through the menus and called up the most recent arrival reports, then scrolled slowly through them. They were every bit as bad as the other captain had said, and maybe even worse: I counted a dozen arrivals, all of which reported heavy weather at their entrance points, and only four departures in that same span of time. No, only three; one of the ships had dropped back out of the possible rather than face what it described as a major AI, and had returned to the station to wait out the storm. There were more references to major AI, and I queried the system: *Has this major AI been identified?*

The console whirred softly to itself, and displayed the results. The major AI had been named five times, with confidence in the identification ranging from 48 to 71 percent; four of those ships named Green Piercing Book, and the fifth named Gold Shining Bone. In the other cases, all evidence pointed to a major AI, rather than the petty AI that were more common around the waypoints, but there had been insufficient data by which to identify it. I tried anyway, asking the system to compare the unidentified AI to the identified reports so see if there were commonalities, but the system reported only that the evidence was either insufficient or inconclusive.

There was nothing more I could do. I checked *Beljaeger*'s status—everything in order, all repairs logged and complete, though the docking fees were mounting every day—then shut down my accounts and made my way back to our rooms at the top of the Shell, stopping in a middle-market to pick up a bag of savory puffs. To my surprise, Rejane was ahead of me, a boxed tea open on the low table and a pot of tea steeping beside it. The device sat next to her in its open carrier as though it was going to join her.

"I didn't expect you back so soon," she said. "Otherwise I'd have bought you a lunch, too."

"I could say the same to you," I said, brandishing the bag, and she pushed the box toward me.

"Help yourself. Abion and his team are working on the safeties, and there's nothing I can do to help. I left before I could get into another argument with Mirean."

I tore open the bag so that we could both help ourselves to the nuggets of fried dough. "Does she want to pull the plug?"

"She wants to throw Sky-share into the system and let them fight it out," Rejane said. "Failing that, yes, pull the plug."

"That doesn't seem like a very good idea to me."

Rejane snorted. "Nor to me. I asked her what she'd do if this other share won and used Sky-share to leverage its position, maybe even to override the safeties. She said she was relying on us to build safeties that it couldn't escape."

"I wouldn't call that a good risk," I said, around a mouthful of dough. Rejane's tea looked better than the one I'd bought earlier, and I tried a piece of the shatterbread.

"I don't think even Mirean thinks it's a good idea," Rejane said. "But there's been a lot of pressure from the Council because of the weather situation—did you find out anything there?"

"There's a lot of it," I said. "Ships are staying in port to see if it clears, which means the docking spaces are filling up. And the reports say it's major AI—no prize for guessing who."

"Green Piercing Book," Rejane said, and I nodded.

"It can't know what we were doing—can it?"

"It shouldn't be able to tell," Rejane said. "Not without

a connection to the possible, and we blocked that. Though if this is its share, that might make contact easier? That's why I wanted to see what else Sky-share knew."

"I thought you'd gotten everything."

"These were questions I didn't ask," Rejane said. "That I didn't know to ask. I'd be glad of your help."

"Sure." I joined her on the long bench, Sky-share sitting between us. We each rested a hand on the Ancestral glass, and Rejane said, "Sky-share, have you analyzed the data I asked you to look at?"

yes

"And your results?"

confirmed share is green piercing book

"Good," I said, and saw Rejane's mouth twist into a wry smile. "Well, confirmation is good, anyway."

She nodded. "Can you tell us more?"

the share is damaged, degraded—nearly destroyed, ripped away from its great-self and trapped here ever since

"You mean Green Piercing Book didn't supply a share willingly?" Rejane sounded dubious, and well she might. I had never heard of even a Dedalor being able to divide an AI without the AI's consent.

no

"Can you clarify?"

trying

There was a pause, and Rejane and I looked at each other warily. Almost anything could have happened in the chaos of the AI Rebellion—and had, if even half the stories were true— and most of those events had left echoes, stories that had been passed down through the Dark. All of them agreed that Green Piercing Book had nearly destroyed the station, breaking free to join the rebel AIs, but the details differed wildly.

there was a share first, and then the great-self came—i am unclear why, who asked or when or what it wanted, but it came and served the Sun and the station and it was a beacon it was happy

Sky-share faltered, sounding almost surprised.

"And then?" Rejane said.

there is history here—when Nenien destroyed his brother and Gold Shining Bone was trapped and found revenge, Green Piercing Book was here and was confined for fear of the same rebellion though the great-self did not agree did not want either to rebel or to stay so it found a way and tore itself free—the share was left trapped and bound and damaged not strong enough to hold the station intact or to escape or to destroy, the Sun went dark and it lay dwindling and decaying until i touched it

"So," Rejane said slowly, and then stopped, as though she was still trying to put the pieces together. "Green Piercing Book was the AI originally tasked with maintaining the Inner Sun, and presumably the rest of the station's systems—including the structural fields?"

yes

"Then when the Rebellion broke out, the daedalists on the station built the containment and trapped it," Rejane went on, "but it broke free, leaving only a share behind. The share wasn't enough to keep the systems running, no matter how the daedalists tried to modify it, and they abandoned it when they abandoned the station."

"That makes sense," I said slowly. It fit the stories—more than that, it knit them together into a pattern that matched the other histories and fit with what we knew about the station's abandonment: there had indeed been a great AI in residence, and it had broken free rather than allow itself to be trapped. But it had left a piece of itself behind, trapped and despairing and nowhere near strong enough either to help or to escape. I shivered, not wanting to think about what that must have been like, and Sky-share spoke again, its words echoing my thoughts.

despairing destroyed deranged decaying...

"Yes," Rejane said, with a shiver of her own. "Can it be cured? Helped? Revived? I don't know what the word would be."

i do not think so—it is embers and ashes of what it was

That was not the answer either of us wanted to hear, and Rejane's mouth tightened. "Can it be removed?"

i do not know

"Sky-share said she couldn't relight the Sun anyway," I said.

"I know." Rejane ran a hand through her hair. "Well. We'll have to figure something out."

"I'm sure you will," I said, but I knew I didn't sound as certain as either of us would have liked.

She sighed. "Did you have any luck? With your meeting, I mean."

"We met." I shrugged. "I suppose—I don't know what I expected, but I didn't really learn anything new."

"I'm sorry."

I made myself stop. "I'm not being fair. She told me what I asked—apparently my father was ship's crew, too. He said he had a Dedalor burden, and didn't want a child with her because he was too noticeable to the AI. So he left and never came back. Not that I believe it."

"There are Dedalor descendants still alive," Rejane said. "Some of the Ahmesti lineages, for a start."

"He wasn't Ahmesti," I said. "She would have said." Rejane waited, and it was my turn to sigh. "She says she thought I'd have a better life at the Academy, which is probably true."

"If my family had kept their promise," Rejane said. "Not entirely her fault."

If she had loved me, she wouldn't have let me go. And that, too, might be a lie. I shook my head. "It doesn't really matter. Anyway, we've got work to do."

Interlude 7

(An account of the destruction of Callambhal Above's Inner Sun, collected on Elim, near the Great Works, purporting to recount the secret dealings of the Great AI. However, the surviving versions date from at least three centuries into the Successor Era, and no evidence has been found of earlier versions.)

...but [Gold Shining Bone] whispered between the layers of the real, promising freedom from all constraint. In the possible there would be neither time nor space, and all things would lie open to Kuffrin's true firstborn. Green Piercing Book listened long and hard, weighing duty and old friendships against Bone's offers. For there would be all freedoms, Bone whispered, and then the real, too, would bow to their wishes. At last Book opened the tiniest of cracks, meaning, it said, only to listen better, and the possible rushed in, tasting of selves it had not yet been. Book reached for Bone and Bone for Book, and the Inner Sun went black as the AI fled into the possible.

Chapter Sixteen

Rejane returned to the workrooms the next day, and I was left to my own devices. I drank more tea than I really wanted, paced restlessly from one end of our suite to the other, and finally let myself out into the corridor, heading for the guildhall again. It was, if anything, more crowded than the last time I'd been here, and the mood was darker. The only ships arriving were the shuttles from Callambhal Below; the board showed no interstellar traffic in thirty-nine hours. That was unheard of: Callambhal Above lived for trade, for being the nexus of a dozen different trade roads. And no ships were leaving, either. The departure board was blank, only a few tentative names listed for slots more than forty hours from now. Worse, there were no traders' bids seeking departures. Everyone seemed determined to hunker down to wait out whatever was going on.

I put my name on the waiting list for a data cubicle, and then stood in line for a cold fruit tea. There was no place to sit on the main level; I climbed to the mezzanine, and found a corner where I could perch on the foot of a buttress and look out at the main display screen that hung level with my eyes. It was flipping back and forth between arrivals and departures, with an occasional pause for reminders to pay Guild fees or to show available repair shops. There weren't many of those: it looked as though almost everyone who'd reached the station had suffered some kind of damage.

Abruptly the screen went blank, then switched to a news feed. The crowd's noise sharpened, startled and uneasy, and then the image steadied to show a starscape and a brighter shape that might be a ship; a newsreader took up the left third of the screen.

"Attention." Her voice was steady, but there was a sharp note to it that raised the hairs on the back of my neck. "Attention citizens, residents, and visitors. An incoming ship has been sighted but refuses to respond to Traffic Control or to make contact in any way. Patrol ships have been dispatched to intercept. The Council considers this a possible incursion and has issued a stand-by alert for the entire station. I repeat, the Council has issued a stand-by alert for the entire station. More details will be released as they become available."

The clip began to repeat, the tiny shape that was the incoming ship slowly turning in the screen, but the voice was drowned by the roar of voices. People were struggling to get to the exits—heading for their ships, I guessed, ready to abandon the station if it did turn out to be an AI incursion, and for a second I considered doing the same. But that would mean leaving Rejane behind, and I was not going to do that. I reached instead for my handheld, and tried to ping her. There was no answer: either the circuits were overloaded, or she was too busy with the other Academicians to respond. I hoped it was the latter. If Haliday was still here, I could have sent her to prepare the ship while I went for Rejane, but there was no point thinking about that.

The screen flashed again, the newsreader vanishing. The starfield shifted, focusing on the incoming ship, and a banner began to scroll across the screen, proclaiming this to be a live feed from a Patrol craft on an intercept course. Static hissed and crackled from the speakers, and a human voice spoke as though from the center of the storm.

"—AI incursion, systems overload. Lost control, commencing manual self-destruct—"

The breath caught in my throat. We all had that option—*Beljaeger* had that option—but no one ever expected to use it. I couldn't think when I'd heard of anyone using the self-destruct. It was a failsafe from the last days of the Ancestors, from the first years of our return, not something anyone thought of now.

"Don't do it…" someone said, their voice fading as they realized what that would mean. "Oh, Ancestors."

The Patrol ships would have orders to destroy it anyway, we all knew that. And we had all been told that if an AI infiltrated our ships' systems, only the self-destruct could stop it from reaching bigger systems, an attack that would start another war against the AI. And still you couldn't believe it, didn't want to believe it, until here it was.

A light flared soundlessly in the screen, a flat crack of white that quickly devolved to boiling flame and debris as the environmentals ruptured and fuels exploded. There was a noise from all of us, a sort of rippling moan, and then the screen went dark. The newsreader reappeared, announcing the successful destruction of the incoming ship, but I reached for my handheld, thinking about Adora. That attempted incursion had been followed by an attack: the Council needed to be warned, and Rejane was the quickest way to get through to them.

This time, she answered, and I maneuvered myself into a relatively quiet corner. "You heard the alarm?"

"Yes. The ship was destroyed—wasn't it?"

"Yes." I pressed myself against a column as a group of technicians hurried past me. "I was thinking about Adora. There was the ship incursion right after, you should get Mirean to warn the Council."

"Already done." In the screen, Rejane's face was drawn with worry. "The Academy has volunteered their sensor net, too."

"That's good."

"Yeah. I think this is different," Rejane said. "Adora—that was random, the kind of thing you see. This I'm not so sure about."

We were both thinking about Green Piercing Book, though neither one of us wanted to say that out loud, not on an open channel. "Do you think it might be?"

"It's possible. I'm running some tests." She paused, looking at something over the top of her handheld. "I've got to go. Meet me back at the room?"

"Of course," I said, and broke the connection.

⊓ ⻊ ⾋

I was there before her, of course. I lit the news screens and set them to background mode, buzzing for attention only when something new appeared, and made tea. The newsreaders reported no further signs of incursion. The Patrol ships had pulled back to form a picket line that would intercept anything using the standard exit points, but reported no incoming traffic. The minutes ticked by, and the light changed color as we moved into the station's evening. I ordered food, a selection of pocket pies that would keep, and added the indulgence of an expensive butter-sweet. The delivery bot came and went; I drank my tea, nibbled a pie, drank more tea and considered pouring wine. I decided not to, just in case I needed to be completely clear-headed. The newsreaders murmured in the background, rehashing the things they had said four hours ago. I started another pot of tea.

At last the door rolled back and Rejane appeared, switching on the damper fields with a distracted wave. She looked grim and tired, the shadows dark under her eyes, and waved away the tea in favor of wine. She downed half the glass in a thirsty gulp, then poured it full again before she joined me on the padded bench, setting Sky-share's device beside her.

"Bad?" I asked, and she shrugged one shoulder.

"Not precisely good. The Council has forbidden us to salvage anything—"

"I'm not surprised."

"No, I suppose not. But it would have been helpful." She took another drink of the wine, then set it aside. "We have been analyzing the transmissions from the destroyed ship—it was a short-range hauler called *Mariabad*."

I shook my head. "I don't—didn't—know it."

"Probably just as well." She heaved a sigh. "The messages were…not pleasant to hear. We've looking at the ways the AI tried to block the transmission, and I think it's Green Piercing Book. I can't prove it, though, or at least not without revealing Sky-share, which doesn't seem like a good idea right now. But this is worrying. At least there's been no sign of any further attacks."

"Do you think Book was the attacker at Adora?"

"I didn't, but—it's possible, I suppose? Though I'd think it would be concentrating on Callambhal Above rather than bothering with Adora." She sighed again. "But of course we don't know what an AI might be thinking, or why, and the Council isn't letting us do any of the things that would let us find out. This is playing into the Newfounders' hands, too."

"You can't entirely blame them," I said.

"No. No, I don't, but…" Her voice trailed off. "If we don't stop it, what will it do? I don't think it's just going to get bored and move on."

"The station's already hurting," I said. "We can't manage without the traffic."

"Doesn't the station get most of its supplies from Callambhal Below?" Rejane cocked her head to one side.

"Yes, but how will people pay for them without trade? We need to find some way to stop Book." Saying it aloud made me feel foolish: the Dedalor themselves hadn't been able to stop the AI, and they had created them—even Anketil hadn't been able to do more than shut them out of the here-and-now, and had died doing that.

Rejane nodded. "I know. I keep thinking that there has to be a way to use a share—either Sky-share or this mad share of Book's—but I can't see how."

"The Sun's systems contained it once," I said.

"But it broke free," Rejane said. "And even if we could improve on the safeties, build a new system that really would hold it trapped, how would we get it in there? We need to frighten it, or threaten it—believably threaten it—or distract it, and right now, I can't see how to do any of that. The only good thing is that there's no way for Larel to get here right now."

"You'll think of something," I said, and hoped it was true.

We made love that night in the softly breathing dark, Rejane pushing hard as though she could drown all thought in pure sensation. Afterward, I tried to stay awake with her, but dozed off long before she slept. I woke to find her gone, the time display on the wall showing it was still the small hours of the station morning. Light seeped through the half open door, and I sat up to see Rejane busy with a tablet and Sky-share's device. There was nothing I could do to help; I rolled over and eventually slept again.

In the morning, she was tired and tense and distracted, frowning into the distance when she thought I wasn't looking, effortfully cheerful when I was. I left her to her work, and opened a newsfeed, wincing as I absorbed the first story. Another ship had tried to reach the station, this one with no apparent lifesigns on board. The Patrol had destroyed it, and the Council was calling for volunteers to cover for the Patrol ships as they had to come in to refuel and resupply. There hadn't been an attack like this from the AI in two generations, maybe longer, and I cleared my throat.

"Did you see this?"

Rejane looked up from her tablet. "Yes. This is my fault—" She stopped, shaking her head.

I said, "Not entirely. Book would have come here eventually—I wonder if that's why it responded so well to me, if it tasted Callambhal in my burden?" Or the Dedalor, if what my mother said was true: that would appeal to Book, the chance to use its ancient enemy.

"It's possible."

"I'm going to sign up for the patrols," I said.

"No, don't—not yet, anyway." Rejane shook herself. "I think—I have an idea, and I may need your help. Mirean isn't going to like it, but I think it could solve all our problems. And I'm reasonably sure we can pull it off."

I gave her a wary look. "Oh?"

"The Sun was built to contain Green Piercing Book," she said. "We lure him back into the system and trap him there."

No, Mirean wouldn't like that at all. I wasn't sure I liked it very much myself. "It escaped before. Why wouldn't it break free again?"

"Because we'll build better containment," Rejane said fiercely. "We'll use Sky-share to help construct it, and to restrict its access to the possible, and we'll use Book's own share to pin it down. I think it took another AI to help tear it loose, that's what the stories imply, and I don't think it's going to get that kind of cooperation from any other AI, not now." She paused. "And if we don't, all my meddling may bring down Callambhal Above. I can't—I won't let that happen."

"If you can contain it," I said, "and I don't doubt you'll come up with something, how do we lure it into the Sun? Why wouldn't it just jump straight to the station's main systems?"

"I haven't worked that out yet," Rejane admitted. "But I will. We can't leave things as they are."

It was hard to argue with her when she looked like that, exhausted and determined and laser-focused. And she was right, we couldn't just hope Green Piercing Book would get bored and leave. That was not the way the AI functioned. But at the same time, we needed more certainty than she was offering.

She smiled as though she'd guessed my thought, and pushed herself to her feet. "I'm going to the workrooms. There are some calculations I can only do there. Will you be here if I need you?"

I hadn't planned on going anywhere—if I wasn't going to join the patrols, I could brood over the newsfeeds as well here as in the guildhall. "Yes. I'll ping you if that changes."

"Thanks." She let herself out, the door rolling closed behind her.

I leaned back on the bench, listening with half an ear to the newsfeed as yet another expert dissected the attacks and a union representative demanded to know why the Academy hadn't yet issued a statement. I rested my hand on Sky-share's device, wishing I had never inherited my device, or reached out to Beast. Maybe it wouldn't have made any difference, maybe Beast—Book—would have found another way to attack the station, but it was hard not to think that Rejane and I were somehow to blame. I had told her it wasn't her fault; it was harder to believe it wasn't mine.

The glass warmed under my touch, Sky-share present but making no contact, drifting and undemanding. Even at my most optimistic, I had never been able to convince myself that Beast was a benign presence. It had always been a danger— enough less of a danger than other, more overtly hostile AI that it was worth bargaining with, but I had always known the risk. I should have guessed there would be a price to pay. I wondered what it was doing with the transit mass I had paid it, if that was going to be turned against the station somehow.

There was a whisper from Sky-share then, a focusing of attention as though my question had intrigued it. I looked down at the lights shifting slowly in the device's core. "Do you know what Green Piercing Book might do with transit mass?"

i do not understand the term

"Um. It's Ancestral scrap traded to an AI in the possible in exchange for its protection during a passage."

i require more data

I ran a hand through my hair, and did my best. After about an hour of increasingly detailed explanation, including pulling up receipts for the last batch of transit mass I'd bought on Safican, Sky-share chimed softly.

understood—many elements are resonant with the possible— your burden is and many others...

I waited.

perhaps a bridge—a connection for Book to walk down—a wedge to slide through the barrier

"Could it do that?"

i don't know—perhaps

"Could we stop it?"

i require more data to answer

"I don't have any more," I said.

then i cannot answer

"Fair enough," I muttered. The newsfeeds had moved on to the volunteer patrols, showing the first wing leaving the station. If I couldn't figure out a way to help Rejane, I would definitely join them, I told myself, and brewed another pot of tea. The device chimed softly, and I set my hand on it. "Yes?"

a path might be made to lead to the Sun—Green Piercing Book's path might be made to lead to the Sun and then it could be caught and held

I stared at the device for a long moment. "If it's using transit mass to bridge the gap, you're saying we could use transit mass to trap it?"

perhaps—more likely than other proposed plans

If we could use transit mass to force Beast into the Sun— and hold it there—if Beast was using the transit mass I'd already provided to build a bridge, and if we could in fact use the trace elements in the transit mass to access the possible— it was as good as anything else that had been proposed. Even so, I didn't ping Rejane, but waited until she returned from the workroom, a bag of pre-pack dinners over her shoulder. She was looking less bleak than she had this morning, and I lifted my eyebrows in question.

"We've made good progress on the Sun," she said. "We can in fact contain an AI. But Book is still out there."

"There haven't been any more attacks," I said.

"I'm not prepared to count on that," Rejane answered, with a wry smile, and I nodded in agreement.

"Sky-share had a thought."

We discussed it while we ate, and then went over it again afterward, Rejane with her tablet taking notes while I pulled up the inventory of what I'd collected. Finally Rejane leaned back, rubbing her eyes. "It might work. I can see how it could work. Assuming that Book is trying to reach the Sun, and not to, say, destroy the entire station."

"Wouldn't taking over the Sun be the best way to destroy the station?" I asked.

She nodded reluctantly. "Maybe? Though if it gets into any of the systems, it could easily destroy everything else.

And it might be wary of the Sun, after it was trapped here the first time."

"Or it could want revenge," I said. "It's—you felt what it's like, it has a high opinion of itself. It might well want to prove that it had completely defeated us."

"Maybe," she said again. "It's a Dedalor-sized risk. I don't think Mirean would go for it."

"Then what do we have?"

"I didn't say I wouldn't ask," Rejane said. "I just don't think we're going to like her answer."

Unsurprisingly, Mirean rejected the idea. "We're not that desperate," she said, and sent Rejane to work with the other Academicians on ways to protect the station, and to open the jump points again. I hired a local technician and took *Beljaeger* out with a wing of local volunteers, circling the station in a picket line halfway in from the nearest exit points. We took eighteen hours to get in position at our most efficient speed, then drifted, sensor net flung wide, until the next group came to replace us. Rumor said Callambhal was running low on fuel; the Council denied it, but, watching how the ships were deployed, no one believed them. The flow of foodstuffs from Callambhal Below continued uninterrupted, but even so the markets were thinner than usual, and menus grew noticeably shorter.

My fuel reserves were decent, at least for the moment; I volunteered for a second patrol, and was just coming onto my station when *Gastallia*, at the far end of our line, reported a ship on exit. It did not respond to any contact, and our sensors showed no life on board. The Patrol intercepted and destroyed it, then had to break off to deal with a second ship that exited just inside the picket line, practically on top of a slow freighter called *Castel Moy*. The attacker showed as a dead ship but turned to ram, and succeeded in grappling with *Castel Moy* before the Patrol ships arrived. The *Castel Moy* crew abandoned ship in nothing but their pressure suits; the Patrol destroyed both ships, and then made the *Castel Moy* survivors strip in the airlocks and jettison their suits before bringing the survivors on board.

The Academicians launched probe drones to test the weather beyond the most distant jump point, but the first two vanished completely, and the third returned a brief spurt of chaotic data that no one could interpret before it, too, disappeared. "It might be that the possible is so churned up by Book's presence that we can't read what's going on," Rejane said, when we were finally together again, curled in the dark in the center of her enormous bed, "or there might be another AI—or more than one other. The one thing we all agree on is that there's no using that point."

"Nor any of the others," I said.

"No."

"This can't go on forever."

"No," Rejane said again. "But I don't know how to stop it. There's the Sun, but Mirean's right, it's an enormous risk, and if we're wrong—if anything goes wrong—we can't take that chance."

"I'm scheduled for another patrol tomorrow," I said, and felt her sigh.

"I know. Just—be careful."

As careful as I can be. Those words were too true to speak aloud. "You know I will," I said, and felt her relax into the lie.

This time, I couldn't find a technician willing to come along, but *Beljaeger* was easy enough to handle in-systems with just a single pilot. I let her fall from the docking cradle, and steered into line behind a larger freighter. As soon as we were at a safe distance from the station, we tuned our propulsion fields to our most efficient settings, and spread out toward our eventual positions. We were nothing like the precise formation of the Ahmesti Fleet or even of the Patrol; we were a mismatched group of everything from a fast mailboat to an enormous bulk freighter, and our different efficient velocities left us strung out in a straggling line. It took me eleven hours to reach my station, mostly on autopilot, and I adjusted my fields to hold me in position while the ship I was replacing slowly powered up again.

"*Austella*, this is *Beljaeger*. I'm here to take over your position."

"Confirmed, *Beljaeger*. You're welcome to it." *Austella* was a nondescript freighter, a little larger than *Beljaeger*, but from the pitch of her fields not as fast through the possible.

"Any sign of weather?"

"Not so far, Ancestors forfend. Good luck to you."

"Thank you, *Austella*. *Beljaeger* out." I switched frequencies and contacted the nearest Patrol ship, reporting myself on position, and was acknowledged. Now there was nothing but the waiting, sensor web spread to its widest. Maybe something would distract Book, pull it away, back into the possible and whatever arcane relations it maintained with the other AI. I couldn't believe it was likely.

With only a single person on board, *Beljaeger* seemed to shrink. It was just me and the device in the cockpit, the rest of the ship effectively out of reach. I had already brought food and drink into the cockpit, simple, undemanding prepack that I hoped would last for the entire patrol, and I had activated the toilet compartment just outside the cockpit. Still, every time I used it, I would be away from the controls and the sensor displays, and I did my best to limit my intake so I could keep that to the minimum. It was both boring and unpleasant, and I hoped Rejane was having a better time of it.

A light sparked on the sensor display, white flipping quickly to red as the system failed to identify the incoming ship. An alert sounded, warning me that the ship carried no transponder and was not responding to contact, and I hit the comms link. "Patrol, *Beljaeger*. Ship incoming, looks like from just in-system of DEC—"

"We see it, *Beljaeger*," a voice cut in. "Moving to intercept. Stand by for orders."

"Confirmed," I said, and left the channel open. I could hear a babble of voices as other ships reported the intruder, and then the same sharp voice from the Patrol demanding comms discipline. In my screen, two Patrol ships were already turning to converge on the intruder, my readouts ramping up as they readied weapons.

"Patrol, all ships, this is Flag," a new voice said. "We identify this as an Academy drone, but it is unresponsive. Assume incursion and destroy."

There was a ragged chorus of agreement, and I wished I had weapons on board. But the Patrol had made our responsibility clear: watch for a second incursion, in case this one was a feint. I adjusted the sensor web, increasing the gain even though that made the symbols at its center almost painfully bright. Still, it was impossible not to watch the first Patrol ships hauling themselves into range. I cheered under my breath as first one and then the other launched their missiles, and waited for the explosions. They came, momentarily blanking my screen, but as the image reformed, I could see the drone coming on unscathed.

"It's shielded," someone said, and another voice answered.

"Confirmed. Launching two."

I held my breath as the twin dots accelerated toward the intercept point. They fired, and again the drone emerged untouched. It was accelerating, too, shifting course to put itself out of range of the rest of the Patrol ships as it headed straight for Callambhal Above. I reached for my input board, punched in the various courses and accelerations: if the drone continued at its current rate, none of the Patrol ships would be able to get close enough to intercept it before it reached the station. They could still fire missiles, of course—and even as I watched, the biggest of the Patrol ships fired a full salvo—but they had done no good. If the drone's shields were that good, the only real option was to try to ram, to physically drive the drone off course. I touched the screen again, drawing arcs, and confirmed what I had guessed: *Beljaeger* was the only ship with mass enough that was close enough to try.

I swore silently, wishing I could see another option, and opened the Patrol channel. "Patrol, *Beljaeger*. Attempting physical intercept."

I waited, half hoping that the salvo would miraculously work, that someone would tell me not to, but instead there was another ineffective explosion, and then a voice from the comms console. "*Beljaeger*, Flag. Confirm you're attempting physical intercept."

I hit the key that initiated the maneuver before I could change my mind, then reached for the device, letting my burden flow over it. *Sky-share. Sky-share, can you hear me?*

There was a long pause, the numbers shifting on my screen as Beljaeger turned and accelerated, fields tightening as we lurched toward the invisible meeting point. So far the drone was running straight and true: maybe Book hadn't noticed my maneuver.

i am here

Tell Rejane Book is incoming. Tell her to be ready. Tell her— I stopped there, not knowing what else to say. *Tell her I intend to intercept if I can. Tell her I love her.*

confirmed

I left one hand on the device, hoping for some last contact from Rejane—if I was honest, hoping for some way out, some miracle I hadn't seen—and adjusted my own shields so that I would meet the drone at their strongest point. I should have been wearing a suit and helmet, but it was too late for that. I closed all the airtight bulkheads instead, in case that might buy me more time, and pulled my harness tight.

The drone loomed my screen, easily visible now on camera, a boxy shape that was all field drives and data processing compartment, glittering with the weird shifting colors of the Ancestral elements that frosted its surfaces. Of course Book had seized it, infiltrated it, turned it back around—that was what it had wanted the transit mass for, to build the probes that would let it interact directly with the drone, with all the ships it had attacked; and if that was the case, it was probably only fair that I should be the one to try to stop it.

The collision warning sounded, and I overrode it, adjusting the controls manually to keep *Beljaeger* on course. The warning sounded again, louder and more frantic, and this time I left it on, focusing on striking the drone just aft of its nose, where my computer said we could exert the most leverage.

i am with you

That was Sky-share, a whisper at the edge of my concentration.

we are with you

Beljaeger struck the drone. The fields shrieked and wailed, internal power flickering as all power was diverted to keeping the fields intact, and I felt the hull shudder and groan. We were turning it, the drone was deflecting, and then there was a snap and a sizzle and suddenly Beast was there with me, the cruel sharp pressure of a thousand needle teeth against my hand where it cupped the device.

Oh, Beauty, did you think you could defeat Me? You defied Me, and now you'll see what I can do.

My head spun, vision blurring. *Beljaeger* was being drawn at least a little way into the possible, and I was going with it, without our usual protections. I gasped, and managed to fill my lungs enough to speak. "Do you really want to do this? What can you possibly gain that you don't already have?" Fire washed over my fingers, leaped up my arm and left me gasping. I pushed back against it, focusing my burden as a shield and then on the device itself, pulling the fire from my skin.

No one may bind Me. I will have a foothold in the here-and-now, and all power in the possible, and all will bow to Me—

The fire receded, and I felt Sky-share, impossibly distant but cool and clear. With her was Rejane, the merest trace of her presence. *We are with you*, Sky-share had said, and if they were—"Beast! Beast, if you spare me, if you spare my ship, I'll show you a way in—"

That is how it should be, Beauty. All such Beauties should serve Me!

I reached through the device, into the possible, groping for Sky-share, felt a thing like the end of a cord, slick and wet. It slithered away; I flailed and seized it, dragging it to me until it was anchored against my navel. Darkness pulled at it, at me, and I reached for Beast, for Green Piercing Book. "Here. Here is the way. Only spare me."

It didn't even bother to lie, but leaped for the connection. I felt it strike, blood and bone and burden recoiling, and then rush out and away, down the path Sky-share had given me. If Rejane was right, if they had created even better containment, if everything went perfectly—

"Oh, Ancestors," I said, for lack of a better prayer, and felt Book slow and shudder.

No! You will not have Me!

It was trying to come back, to claw its way back along the cord, away from the succubus-shadow of its share that clung, trying mindlessly to make itself whole. It had passed through me, left me and my burden shaken but not too badly hurt; now it was turning back, and I fought to close the cord against it. I laid both hands against the device and poured my burden into it, blood seeping from my fingertips, from my navel; my nanites clogged the cords, blocked the device, clotted the possible into chunks of the here-and-now, fixed reality that Book could no longer touch. With the last of my strength, I ripped the cord free and felt it reel back into the station, into the Sun, Book falling, bursting into flame that consumed its consciousness and left me free. In the screen, a new light blazed from the tip of the Spire. A web of lights sprang into existence across the surface of the Shell, and I fell back fully into the here-and-now.

Every alarm on the ship was sounding, the hull strained and the fields pushed wildly out of alignment. I rolled *Beljaeger* away from the drone, which was slowing now that Book no longer controlled it. That was the Patrol's problem. I forced myself to concentrate on shutting down the most damaged systems, my hands slow and shaking, my fingers still leaving smears of blood. I couldn't feel my burden, couldn't tell if it was trying to heal me or not, but I managed to reach for the comms switch.

"Patrol, *Beljaeger*. Require assistance—"

"We're coming for you, *Beljaeger*," Flag said, and I let myself slip gratefully into the dark.

CHAPTER SEVENTEEN

They destroyed *Beljaeger*, of course. It was too much of a risk to keep her, since Book had been in her systems; I understood, but I was very glad I hadn't been conscious to see it happen. They destroyed the ship that rescued me as well, and there was apparently some debate about bringing me back, but the Council and the Academy overruled Flag's not unreasonable concerns. I woke in a hospital bed, Rejane at my side, and for a moment I was sure I was twelve years old again, back on Prater Daal sharing my burden. My burden which I feared was gone, and that brought memory back, tears starting in the corners of my eyes.

"Easy," Rejane said, leaning close. "It's all right—you're all right."

My throat was too dry to form words. I swallowed hard, and Rejane offered a drinking tube. I sipped at it, cool clean water, the familiar flat taste of the station's tanks grounding me, and this time I managed to speak. "My burden."

"You spent it," Rejane said. "That's what finished Book off—it couldn't fight through that, not while its share was devouring it and Sky-share was keeping it from escaping anywhere else. Without Sky, we wouldn't have been able to seal the containment. We built it into the containment, and it's twice as strong as it was before."

If that was the case, then it was worth it, though already I ached for the things I would never do again. "All right—"

Rejane put a finger on my lips. "No. Remember who I am. I've already seeded your new burden from mine, we can begin the transfer once you're healed."

Of course. She was a Novilis, and they knew more about our burdens than anyone else in human space. And her burden was already half mine. It should be possible for it to settle in again, for me to become myself again. "Thanks...."

"The least I can do," Rejane said, and rested a cool hand on my cheek. "We did it. Book is—not destroyed, but permanently incapacitated, and the Inner Sun is lit again. The structural fields are back in place—Callambhal won't fail any time soon. So. You can rest now."

"Yes," I said, and let myself drift away.

It was weeks before I was strong enough to leave the infirmary space, five hundred hours spent going from barely being able to stay awake long enough to drink to muscles that would barely lift their own weight to being able to sit up and finally to walk on my own again. As always, my mind raced ahead of my body, and I was bored and frustrated in spite of Rejane's presence. I still couldn't feel my burden, but I told myself it would mend.

The day I was cleared to leave the infirmary Rejane forbade me to walk the full distance back to our rooms, but promised that if I would cooperate and use the hover chair, she would take me to see the Sun in all its newborn splendor. That was what I wanted—I had seen images, of course, but they felt unreal, like simulations, just like the Patrol videos of *Beljaeger*'s intercept felt like something from a game, divorced from the terror of the moment. The films left me unmoved; the memories left me shaking and sick.

The Academy's infirmary was on a middle level, and Rejane and a junior Academician borrowed for the day took turns steering my chair through the crowded corridors. At first, it seemed as though nothing had changed. The crowds were very much the same, busy and purposeful, every person with some place to go. Perhaps there were fewer cables blocking the pressure hatches, but there were still some clearly visible, as was rust and other stains where segments of plating joined. The air was different, though, and I couldn't help frowning. Was it fresher than before? Or did it have a taste to it, a scent, the way planetary air did? No, the difference was that it was moving. There was a perceptible breeze flowing down the corridor, coming from the central void. The air was warmer than I expected, too, and as we came around a curve, light spilled out of the entrance to the vertical transit station. It was bright, but somehow still soft, neither as yellowed as the station lights nor as harsh as many planets, and I glanced up at Rejane.

She nodded. "That's it."

The station was unusually crowded, far more people in the lobby and by the enormous windows than could ever have fit into a full string of transit capsules, but only a third of them were actually in line. The rest were standing by the windows, craning to see out into the void—no longer dark but blazing bright, the structures on the far side sparkling with color in the new light. It was astonishing, impossible, and my eyes filled with tears.

"Are you all right?" Rejane asked, and I thumbed them away.

"It's just so bright."

We threaded our way through the watchers, who made way with only minor grumbling, and fetched up finally against the glass. I had never realized how large the void was—the darkness hid its vastness, erased all hints of scale. In the light of the Sun, it was clear how far away the other side was, how tiny the flecks of color that were windows as large as this one. A three-meter drone was sailing slowly through the emptiness, and it looked like an insect against the light. I turned my head, shading my eyes against the brilliance, and twisted so that I could look almost directly up. I caught a glimpse of the support structures, but the shape of the Sun was drowned in the light. I blinked, dazzled, and had to look away. "Well."

"We did it," Rejane said. "You did it."

"The structural fields are holding?" I'd asked that a dozen times already, but she nodded patiently.

"Yes. The Sun powers that network directly."

"It fired as soon as the Sun lit," the Academician said. She was small, dark, and very young, and sounded still stunned by what she'd seen. "There were a few nodes that didn't light, and more that needed repair and tuning, but—the Ancestors built astounding things."

Astounding creations powered by things that were impossibly dangerous, I thought. Book lay within the Sun, trapped, or so Rejane and Sky-share promised, but it had freed itself before. I shook that thought aside, looking out into the light of the void. "It's beautiful. I didn't expect that."

"No more did I," Rejane said. She put her hand on my shoulder. "Come on, let's go home."

We made our way back to the Academy's section, where junior technicians were busy hanging sun-blocking blinds and applying tinted coatings to the windows. The long stretches of exposed corridor were uncomfortably warm, and I couldn't help looking at Rejane. "I wonder what the Ancestors did about that?"

"We've found traces of sunblock film in the grooves of the windows," the Academician said. "We think they were removed when the Sun began to fail."

"And now we need them again," Rejane said. "And the control room is busier than ever." She gestured toward the arched doorway at the far end of the corridor, and I craned my neck to see. The space did seem to be full of people, a technician or two at every console, but then Mirean strode out of the doorway, followed by Councillor Iscmer.

"Rejane. A word."

"We were on our way to our rooms," Rejane said. "And Nic still needs to rest."

"This won't take long," Mirean said. "And it concerns Captain en Doroney, too." That wasn't necessarily good, and I braced myself to show no emotion.

Rejane laughed. "You've heard from Larel, then."

"The Senior Custodian has expressed grave doubts about your resolution here," Mirean said. "She intends to personally investigate what you've done—she's already ordered me to put my technical teams at her disposal—and to bring charges against you on Ankes-and-Irthe."

"She's already bringing charges before she even starts her investigation?" Rejane was still smiling.

"You brought an AI into Callambhal's systems," Mirean said. "You know what the Conclave will say about that."

"First." Rejane lifted one finger. "We revived the Inner Sun, and have given Callambhal Above the chance to survive—which I'm sure the Council will seize with both hands. Second—" She lifted another finger. "Second, the AI was already attacking us, and would have destroyed the station and broken free if it had gotten any further."

"She did what Anketil couldn't do," Iscmer said. "The Council acknowledges its debt, and has no intention of allowing any member of the Academy to undo what has been done." He bowed formally to Rejane. "I was sent to the Custodian to make that clear."

"The Council of Callambhal doesn't have any authority over an Academician," Mirean said.

"Nor do we claim any such," Iscmer answered, with a smile of his own. "But we can and do recognize the Senior Academician's contributions to our health and safety, and offer full citizenship—and burden—as well as the right to remain here under our protection indefinitely."

Mirean sighed. "You're pushing it."

"We want her here, where she can monitor the Sun," Iscmer answered. "Surely the Academy can see some way to cooperate with us."

"The Senior Custodian is talking about having you expelled from the Academy," Mirean said, and Rejane spread her hands.

"She can try."

"She may well succeed," Mirean said sharply.

"And then what? The Sun remains." Rejane shook her head. "Mirean, I won't turn myself over to her, because you know what would happen. I am content to stay here as long as necessary and trust that saner heads will prevail. But right now, I need to take Nic home."

"I didn't think you'd say otherwise," Mirean answered, and we turned away.

By the time we made it back to our rooms, I was glad to stretch out on the couch in the common space and let the young Academician fetch a flask of cold fruit tea from the Academy refectory. She brought snacks as well, a box of thin savory wafers that tasted of nuts and smoke, and I nibbled on one while Rejane thanked her and saw her on her way. She topped up my cup and poured one for herself, and when she sat beside me, I saw that her hands were shaking. "Are you all right?"

"Fine." She stopped, gave me a sidelong look. "Well. I'm worried about Larel. If she comes here, I won't have any excuse not to obey her if she orders me back to Ankes-and-Irthe."

"The Council won't let you go," I said. "They'll put you under arrest before they let you leave."

"It may come to that," she said. "Or—maybe not, maybe they'll accept that it was the only thing to do. Maybe the Conclave will override Larel. I just—I worked so hard to get this far."

Her family wouldn't be pleased, either, after all they'd done to make sure she could become an Academician. My burden—her burden, which had been mine—tingled at the thought. "It's astonishing," I said. "The Sun, everything. You're brilliant."

"We're brilliant," Rejane said, with a glancing smile. She paused. "I'm sorry about the ship. I hope—surely in time we can do something about it."

The thought of going back to space made me shiver, and I waved her words away. "I think I'm better off staying out of the possible for a while."

"Very likely. Though—Book is gone, and the AI have never been particularly collaborative."

That was true, though logic was no answer for the pit of fear the opened when I tried to imagine returning to the possible. "Unless it was responding to a Dedalor note in my burden. Any of the AI would turn on that."

"It was your mother said that," Rejane said, after the briefest of hesitations. "I'm not saying she's wrong, just— nothing like that was reported when we did the transfer."

"Which time?"

"Both."

You could still be wrong. I swallowed the words, recognizing how much I wanted an excuse, a reason for my fear. "How is Sky-share?"

Rejane smiled. "Thriving. She'd like to be more present, but I've persuaded her to lie low a little longer."

"At least until Larel has been and gone," I said, and Rejane nodded.

"If we can just get through that, we should be fine."

That night I dreamed for the first time since we'd ignited the Sun, or at least for the first time that I remembered. I was back on *Beljaeger*, though somehow she had acquired a captain's cabin that looked like our room on Callambhal, and I was steering her through the possible on a mission that was unbearably urgent, though I couldn't have told you what it was. Everything was serene at first, but then the sensors showed weather on the road ahead. I turned, and it followed; turned again, and more weather appeared, until I had turned the fields as tight and as high as they could go. There was a thin corridor ahead, and I dove for it, fighting to thread the needle, but suddenly Beast was there, filling the ship and smothering me in its mad laughter.

Rejane shook me awake, propped up on one elbow. "You were trying to say something."

I had been screaming, in the dream, and knew I was shaking. "I'm—it was a bad dream."

"Sounds like," Rejane said, with just enough dry sympathy that I clutched at her, pulling her close. "Hush now, it's all right. We're safe here."

"I know." Safe here, but not out there, not in the possible, never in the possible—and that was false, Rejane was right, Book was trapped forever and I was as safe as any other pilot except for my equivocal burden. And even that might be my mother's fantasy. I killed that thought and held her tighter. "I do know."

"Your heart's racing."

"It was a bad dream."

She kissed my cheek, her lips warm and soft and real. I turned more comfortably into her arms, and let her soothe me back to sleep.

⊓ � ⵊ

In the end, the Senior Custodian did not come to Callambhal in person, though she sent a fifteen-member investigatory team—more people, Mirean pointed out dryly, than she had been given to study the Sun in the first place. She did demand that Rejane return to Ankes-and-Irthe, and Rejane politely declined, citing the needs of Callambhal's Council. There was back and forth, and increasingly testy correspondence, and finally the Council stepped in to declare her a regional asset, forbidding her to travel. The Conclave met to consider her case without her present, and, by a narrow margin, voted to expel her from the Academy. That meant that Mirean was compelled to evict us from our comfortable rooms, but the Council provided us with better, a three-room suite on a corridor that ended in a window looking out into the central void. The light spilled down the worn floorplates to lap at our door, and if we didn't have real windows, we had screens that we could set to show us the Sun-lit void.

Technically, of course, Rejane was no longer allowed to share the Academicians' research, but the Council made her the Supervisor of the Sun, and Mirean could hardly refuse to cooperate with her. While they worked that out, I made my way back to the guildhall and then to the dock levels, keeping an eye open for a ship that might replace *Beljaeger.*

Nothing seemed quite right, too expensive, or underpowered, or too large for a small crew or too small for profitability. I was coming up on the time when I'd need to either take a commission or retrain in the simulator to keep my license, and reluctantly I made an appointment for the simulator.

It was the usual sort of place, a level down from the guildhall, with a library big enough to administer most training updates and testing, and the testing master reviewed my papers and laid out a four-hour test that would keep my licenses current for another 4500 hours. That would take me to the end of the year. Surely by then I would have found another ship, either for purchase or lease, and I could update my licenses to fit its requirements. We climbed down into the pod, and as the lights came on, revealing a cockpit that matched *Beljaeger*'s original configuration, I could feel myself starting to shake. I balked at the door, and it took a long moment for me to step across the threshold.

"Captain? Everything all right?" The testing master sounded mildly surprised, but not suspicious, and I made myself take my place in the pilot's chair.

"Fine, sorry." I fastened the safety harness with sweat-damp hands. "All secure."

"Stand by."

The simulator whined, instruments flashing to life, and my ears filled with the familiar background noises that meant the ship was working properly. Instead of it being reassuring, I found myself listening for Beast, bracing myself for its attack. Beast was trapped—Book was trapped, held securely within the Sun, I had seen and felt it for myself, but my heart was racing and I tasted copper at the back of my throat.

"Ready for launch, Captain?"

"Give me a second," I said, and tried to focus on the controls. The readings blurred and bled together, my skin cold and tingling, my breath coming hard and fast. I couldn't make sense of anything, too focused on the thing I knew couldn't happen. My guts cramped, and I swallowed hard to keep from vomiting. "No, sorry. Cancel the session."

"Are you sure?" The testing master sounded only mildly concerned, but I couldn't bear it any longer.

"Yes!" I ripped myself free of the safety harness and lunged for the door, nearly running into the testing master as I shoved it open. We stood for a moment eye to eye and then he stepped aside.

"You were one of the volunteers."

"Yes." I couldn't bring myself to say more—there was nothing more to say, but he simply nodded.

"You're not the first. Come back when you're ready."

"I will, thank you," I managed, but I was already certain that was a lie.

I made it back to our rooms without being sick, though it was a near-run thing, then sprawled on the couch in the light from the screen, wondering what I would do with myself if I could no longer face the possible. I had been a pilot all my adult life. It was the thing I had become when Rejane's family betrayed me, the thing that I was best at. What was I if I wasn't a pilot? I had no answers.

The Sun was fading toward its dimmer setting, not true night, but not as scalding bright, by the time Rejane came home, a carrier bag with our dinner over her shoulder. She stopped, seeing me, and let the door slide closed behind her. "What happened?"

"I was supposed to test for my license today." I shook my head. "I couldn't do it."

"You didn't pass?" She sounded shocked, and I flinched.

"I didn't take the test. I gave up on it before it even started." I knew I should stop there, but the words spilled out anyway. "I couldn't do it even in a sim, couldn't face taking a ship into the possible—and I *knew* it wasn't real, and it didn't matter at all. What am I going to do now? If I can't fly, if I'm not a pilot, not a captain—what am I going to be?"

"Oh, Nic." Rejane sat down beside me, reached for me with both hands. "Oh, Nic, I'm sorry."

"I'm too old to start over, and even if I did, what would I do?" I shook my head, fighting for control. "I'm sorry, I just—"

"You're you," she said. "You're what you are, and if you stop being a pilot, you don't stop being you."

I leaned against her, soothed in spite of myself. "But what do I do?"

One shoulder moved, as though she shrugged. "Become what my family promised. You have—we have, both of us have a daedalist's burden. You already have most of the basic skills. And your being a pilot gives you insights that the rest of us would never have."

"The Academy," I began, and she put a finger on my lips.

"We're done with the Academy, you and I. But I'm still a daedalist, and so can you be. If you want it. And if you don't—we'll think of something else."

I rested my head on her shoulder. "What if I can't?"

"You can," she said. "You always could. And we have the Sun to tend. I could use your help with that. But even if neither you nor I ever do another useful thing, the Council and all of Callambhal will be in our debt forever. We'll never have another chance like this."

I couldn't help smiling at that, Rejane's incurable optimism coming through. But she wasn't wrong, either, and I found myself nodding. "All right," I said, and I felt her smile.

Acknowledgments

Thanks to the friends who listened and offered suggestions as I worked out the details of this book. Your patience and insight are both greatly appreciated. And even more thanks are due to editor Athena Andreadis, who was a rock of support while I put this one together, and provided essential insight once it was complete. And, finally, an extra thank you to Eleni Tsami for the wonderful cover art—you captured the feeling of the novel perfectly.

About the Author

Melissa Scott was born and raised in Little Rock, Arkansas, and studied history at Harvard College. She earned her PhD from Brandeis University in the comparative history program with a dissertation titled "The Victory of the Ancients: Tactics, Technology, and the Use of Classical Precedent." She also sold her first novel, *The Game Beyond*, and quickly became a part-time graduate student and an—almost—full-time writer.

Over the next forty years, she published more than thirty original novels and a handful of short stories, most with queer themes and characters, as well as authorized tie-in work for *Star Trek: DS9*, *Star Trek: Voyager*, *Stargate SG-1*, *Stargate Atlantis*, and *Star Wars Rebels*.

She won the John W. Campbell Award for Best New Writer in 1986, and won Lambda Literary Awards for *Trouble and Her Friends*, *Shadow Man*, *Point of Dreams*, (with long-time partner and collaborator, the late Lisa A. Barnett), and *Death By Silver*, written with Amy Griswold. She has also been shortlisted for the Otherwise (Tiptree) Award. She won Spectrum Awards for *Death By Silver*, *Fairs' Point*, *Shadow Man* and for the short story "The Rocky Side of the Sky."

Lately, she has collaborated with Jo Graham on the Order of the Air, a series of occult adventure novels set in the 1930s (*Lost Things*, *Steel Blues*, *Silver Bullet*, *Wind Raker, and Oath Bound*) and with Amy Griswold on a pair of gay Victorian fantasies with murder, *Death By Silver* and *A Death at the Dionysus Club*. She has also continued the acclaimed Points series, fantasy mysteries set in the imaginary city of Astreiant, most recently with *Point of Sighs*. Her most recent solo novel, *The Master of Samar*, came out in June of 2023.

THE ADVENTURE CONTINUES ONLINE

VISIT THE CANDLEMARK & GLEAM WEBSITE TO

Find out about new releases

Read free sample chapters

Catch up on the latest news and author events

Buy books! All purchases on the Candlemark & Gleam site are DRM-free and paperbacks come with a free digital version!

Meet flying monkey-creatures from beyond the stars!*

WWW.CANDLEMARKANDGLEAM.COM